P.D. MARTIN

The Killing Hands

MIRA®

Recycling programs
for this product may
not exist in your area.

ISBN-13: 978-0-7783-2639-7

THE KILLING HANDS

www.MIRABooks.com

Printed in U.S.A.

To our little angel, Grace

Prologue

15 years ago
Tokyo, Japan

He took another long drag of the cigarette and flicked the butt, mesmerized by its perfect arc and fall. The red embers glowed against the white snow for a moment before the cold wetness engulfed them. The butt lay next to roughly ten others, but he wasn't really counting. He'd been freezing his ass off for an hour, catching a glimpse every now and again of a silhouette. Some of his peers would have grown impatient and charged into the small apartment, taking out both the target and his mistress. The killing of a wife would never be sanctioned, never forgiven, but a mistress…they were expendable. But why kill an innocent woman just to avoid discomfort? It was unnecessary and uncivilized; and this business could still be conducted with honor—his father had taught him that. He sighed. It wouldn't be much longer now. The mark rarely spent more than an hour with his mistress.

He returned his gaze to the window, and the entrance. Waiting. This was a big hit, and as the time dragged by he felt himself growing anxious. It was paramount that no one link the killing to him, or his boss. It had to be fast and discreet, no half-alive victim and no witnesses. He must live up to the honor bestowed upon him. To be trusted with this kill… It wasn't his first, and probably wouldn't be his last, but the high-profile nature of the target made him keen to get it over with. The warmth of his fiancée's bed also called to him. He'd had many other women, but she was different, special. She was the only one he'd wanted to marry.

His fingers slipped inside his down jacket until he felt the cold hardness of his gun. It was instinct to check it every few minutes, to make sure he could draw it fast. He looked up at the window again—movement. This time the silhouettes were moving toward the door. He slipped his hand into his inside jacket pocket again and withdrew the gun, glancing up and down the street. He could take the shot from the doorway and then slink back into the shadows, before inserting himself into the crowd that would gather around the body. The entrance light flicked on and the target came down the stairs, smiling and buttoning his full-length overcoat. A satisfied man.

He leaned back into the doorway and brought the gun up. The mark had only taken two steps onto the pavement when the bullet hit him, piercing his lung and nicking his heart. The perfect shot. He staggered backward, the smile gone from his face, and slumped against the outer glass door before sliding slowly down it. The killer watched the blood pooling and melting the snow ever so slightly, just like his cigarette butt had moments before. He smiled, happy with the visual analogy. And happy with the amount of blood. His shot had been good.

It wasn't long before the crowd gathered. He moved onto the street, toward his victim, ready to confirm the kill. Then something, a feeling of being watched, made him look up. The mistress stared directly at him from her window. They both froze, eyes locked. Then she ran, and he ran. She'd seen him. She'd recognized him.

He pushed past the dead mark and into the apartment complex, racing up the stairs. As he rounded the last step onto her floor, he saw her hurtling up the stairs and away from her apartment. She was barefoot, dressed only in a jade-colored negligee. He ran, confident he'd soon catch up.

She looked over her shoulder, panicked. "Help!" she screamed, but her plea for help was cut short as he put his hand around her mouth.

"Shh."

She struggled, kicking.

He didn't want to kill her. He'd never killed a woman before. It wasn't right. But the other option—failing his boss—was much worse.

He took a deep breath before grabbing her head in both hands and twisting. He heard the snap as her neck broke and then her body went limp in his arms. He let her fall gently to the ground, her long black hair fanning out around her milky-white skin. Her eyes were open, staring at him, judging him. She looked so helpless, so still, in her lingerie with her neck at an unnatural angle. He'd had no choice…he had to kill her. But still…

He stood motionless, trying to let his rational side catch up to his actions. He must get rid of her body. Quickly.

One

I'm sitting down, tied to a chair, when the deafening sound of a gun going off close range hits me. Searing pain follows.

I wake up to my 6:00 a.m. alarm and automatically reach for my notebook. I don't remember dreaming or waking last night, but sometimes when I dream I have no recollection the next morning, so I always check the dream diary on my bedside table. This morning I see the words *Someone shot* scrawled across the page. Someone shot…not exactly my most illuminating dream. It doesn't sound like any of my current cases—at the moment I'm profiling a series of rapes in The Valley and the homicide of a young boy who was beaten to death in a video-game arcade. No bullets, no gunshot wounds. So far the dream diary I started a month ago hasn't given me much, but I wanted to start recording as many of my dreams as possible…given some of them come true.

Half an hour later I jump on the gym scales and the digital readout levels off at 136.4. I smile, but while I am happy with my weight from an aesthetic point of view, for me it's about a lot more than getting into a size-eight dress or looking good in lingerie for my man. Besides, it's been a while since anyone's seen me in lingerie—a fact that I'm happy about most of the time. No, it's about health for me. I know firsthand that fitness can be the difference between life and death and I don't want to haul more than a hundred and forty-five pounds in a chase.

The Bureau used to test field agents every year, making sure they fell within a set weight range and that they could pass a physical, including fitness tests…until the 1990s, when a judge found in favor of a discrimination lawsuit. However, I agree with the Bureau's original stance, and so I plan to test myself every year, using the Bureau's physical requirements for its new recruits—the only time agents now need to meet the weight requirements and prove their physical fitness.

I've asked Mercedes Diaz, one of the L.A. field office's IT resources and my workout partner, to help put me through my paces. Diaz is five-six and all lean muscle, accentuated by a natural olive skin tone—no fake tan required. While her job may be tied to a computer, she makes up for her sedentary nine-to-five routine with lots of exercise. Our shared obsession has made us friends—we kept running into each other at the gym and eventually planned our workouts together. I hardly use my apartment's gym anymore, opting for the better facilities at FitnessOne, only a block away from the office. This morning it's busy as usual, but everybody starts a new fitness regime on a Monday, right?

Mercedes hovers over the mat I'm lying on. "This will be a breeze for you, Sophie."

"Hopefully," I say, even though I know I'm incredibly fit at the moment. FBI recruits need twelve points across a series of tests to pass, and members of the Bureau's elite Hostage Rescue Team (HRT) need twenty. I want to push myself and make twenty.

"Ready?"

"Yep." I lie on the mat, hands behind my head and elbows back.

Mercedes brings up her stopwatch, finger poised, and counts me in. I work on my abs a lot, with stomach exercises and pilates, but I still only have a four-pack not a six- or eight-pack. A genetic potbelly makes the lower four bumps pretty much unachievable, unless I starve myself to the verge of anorexia. Besides, I like the rounded look.

When Mercedes calls time after one minute, I've clocked up forty-eight sit-ups, equal to five points. Next I flip over for the push-ups, skipping the three-hundred meter sprint, which is too hard to do on the treadmill. Mercedes and I are meeting at Westwood Park right near my place tomorrow morning for the sprint test. I'm aiming for around fifty-six seconds, but I know that will be tough. Likewise, I'll have to push myself for the push-ups, but at least they're not timed—it's just pump out as many as you can.

I line my hands up directly below my shoulders and stretch my legs out fully. Mercedes checks my posture and pushes my bottom down slightly—no cheating, even though this isn't a real test.

"No more than an inch between your face and the mat, Sophie." Mercedes and I push each other during our workouts and today is no different.

"Give a girl a break, Mercedes."

"You don't need any breaks, Sophie," she says with a smile. "Hit it."

I lower myself all the way down and push up. Even after fifteen I'm slowing down. Fifteen is only one point on the Bureau's scale, and while that is the Bureau's minimum requirement for each activity, it's not enough for me. I keep going, pushing my muscles as each one gets harder and my arms threaten to shake.

"Keep it low," Mercedes says, both warning and encouraging me as I sink into my twentieth push-up. Twenty is two points. I decide to force myself to twenty-two and three points. The last push-up is slow and my shaking arms are on the verge of collapse, but I manage it. I flop onto my stomach, my biceps and triceps cramping.

"Excellent."

"Mmm…" It's hardly excellent, but I know my upper body is my weak point.

After a few arm stretches and a couple of minutes I move onto the treadmill for the one-and-a-half-mile run. In this one, the number of points is determined by how long it takes. I normally run fast—nine or ten miles an hour—which means the run should take me around ten minutes. And that'll give me the full ten points for the task.

The rhythm comes easily, and ten minutes and five seconds later I clock up the distance. I slow the treadmill to a steady walking pace.

"Ten, five. You'd outrun most of the guys in the office." Mercedes gives me a little wink.

That's the point—to be able to outrun most men. One man that comes to mind is AmericanPsycho, the president of an online group of serial killers that we took down eight months ago. We got three of the four members, but he managed to escape. Mercedes knows about AmericanPsycho; unfortunately most of the office docs, given he sends me a single red rose on the first of every month. But I don't point out that at some stage in my future I might have a sadistic serial killer on my tail—literally.

"You're already up to eighteen points, but if you were at the Academy you'd still need to get a point in the sprint."

I nod. One point means I have to run the three hundred meters in less than 64.9 seconds. Totally doable, given I'm aiming for fifty-six. Looks like I'll make my goal of twenty.

"What you got on today?" Mercedes jumps on the treadmill next to mine and starts walking.

"I'm working on that boy's murder, the one I was telling you about."

Mercedes nods with a little wince. In her job, she's often removed from the case details.

The murder victim's a fourteen-year-old boy who was found in the men's restroom of an arcade in South Central. I think this case bothers Mercedes because she's got a nephew that age, so she's personalized the case. Every case gets to me, one way or another, but I consciously try not to relate to the victim too much. It's hard to be objective when I'm a profiler—after all, part of my job is to get into the minds of the killer and victims—but I still need a buffer. I need to be able to come up for air and, more important, stay up.

The LAPD believes the perpetrator is a youth and that the death may be gang related, but two weeks after the murder they still had lots of suspects without any hard evidence, so they sent the case details to George Rosen, the head of the Criminal Division, and requested a profile of the perp.

"Don't worry, Soph. You'll get to it."

"I better." The case has been on the back burner for the past couple of weeks, with other cases taking precedence. I increase the treadmill's speed, moving back into a fast jog. "It's been four weeks since his murder and every time I bump the boy down the list I can't help but think about his parents."

"Can you finish it today?" Mercedes asks.

"If I get the whole day, yeah." Problem is, my caseload has been heavy and I've already been putting in thirteen-hour days, plus some time on the weekends. L.A.'s got a high murder rate—one murder every twenty-six hours according to the L.A. Sheriff's Department. And that's only in L.A. County, not the wider area that the Bureau services. It makes assigning the whole day to the boy's case difficult—who knows what will come my way?

A couple of hours later I'm sitting at my desk with the boy's file open when George Rosen pays me a visit. I immediately notice he's carrying a file, but that's not surprising given that most of my profiling work originates from his division—homicide, kidnapping, sexual assault, armed robberies and so on.

"We've got a new request from the LAPD. A homicide. We're waiting on identification of the body and the autopsy report, but the injuries are a little strange."

"How so?"

"The throat and hyoid bone have been crushed."

That doesn't sound so strange to me. "Strangulation," I say, even though to crush the hyoid bone rather than simply break it requires substantial force.

"Not exactly. Here's what I received from the LAPD."
Rosen slides the file across my desk.

When I flip it open, the photo of the victim hits me. He's
lying on top of a couple of stray bricks and wood, partially
propped up against a fence that surrounds a building site.
The front of his throat almost looks as though it's been
ripped off, like an animal grabbed him by the throat, pulled
and then let go. The front section of the vic's throat hangs
limply, and congealed blood covers the skin, exposed
muscle and the bricks on which his head rests.

"And I'm guessing there's no report of a wild dog in the
area," I say sarcastically.

Rosen raises an eyebrow. "No."

I guess the sarcasm was lost.

"This is a fresh one—it happened yesterday. Brady's
approved your involvement."

I nod. Brady's the big boss, the assistant director in
charge of the L.A. office. Brady and I didn't exactly get off
on the right foot when I started here in August, but over the
past four months I like to think I've won him over. I've also
realized that his general manner is a little distant, so he
wasn't as annoyed with me in that first week as I thought.

Rosen continues. "He said to work it in with your other
cases…sorry. And given the LAPD's called us in so early,
I'd like you to make it your priority."

I see a flash of my fourteen-year-old boy, James Santorini.

Two

I flip through the crime-scene photos. While part of me would like to leave this victim until after my profile of the arcade murder, Rosen was pretty specific. Besides, this crime scene is fresher, which means fresher leads. I can be called in at any stage of an investigation, but the more recent the crime scene, the better for me. Especially given the extra "gift" I bring to my work.

The file contains both day- and nighttime shots, indicating that the sun rose while the crime scene was being processed. The imagery's not lost on me…a new day was dawning, but not for our dead male. A quick check of the police report verifies the timing. The first photos I look at are the ones taken of the victim's full body, without much else in the frame. I can make out bricks, pieces of wood and other building debris underneath him and the mesh of the fence that partially supports him, but nothing else, no indication of the wider locale.

The victim is of Asian descent and wears jeans and a dark gray T-shirt with a black design on the front. I'm not up with the latest styles or labels, but the clothes look expensive and I make a mental note to check with someone a little more fashion-minded than I am. The clothes could even help us during the search for the victim's identity. For example, if he's wearing designer clothes we can cross-reference his photo against missing persons in the higher socioeconomic bracket. This detail may also be important for the victimology. The profile of the victim often helps us to understand how or why he or she was chosen by the killer; and ultimately that can lead us to our perp.

Next I look at close-up shots of the man's face and the throat wound. I notice a couple of thin scars on his face, one that runs halfway across his right eyebrow and a larger scar along the underside of his jaw. Childhood accidents or evidence of prior violence? Either's possible. I examine the close-ups of the throat wound carefully. There are no bite marks—ruling out any animal involvement—but also no tool marks that I can see on the skin to indicate what sort of implement caused the wound. Once the body has been washed by the coroner, the wound will be easier to examine.

The next series of photos I study are of the overall crime scene location. The building site is on the edge of a large, open-air parking lot and a quick cross-reference to the preliminary police report tells me the lot's in Little Tokyo. The body was found roughly centered between Second Street and Third Street, an area of the lot with fewer people and less light. Anyone walking along the streets on the parking lot's edge would be nearly two hundred yards away and probably oblivious to a confrontation; and the building site would have been deserted in the early hours of the morning. Despite being in the middle of downtown L.A., the crime scene was isolated. The spot for the kill was either well planned or dumb luck. Regardless, there's still a chance of a witness. Perhaps someone was walking back to their car and saw our victim prior to the murder. Or maybe they saw the killer, before or after the fact. Then there is the apartment block on Third Street that overlooks the lot, and a few businesses on Los Angeles Street opposite the crime scene. Maybe we'll find a witness there. The amount of blood at the scene certainly indicates our victim was killed where he was found. And even if time of death comes back as the early hours of the morning, that area of town would have been busy.

The next series of shots focuses on the light closest to the victim's body, a square spotlight with several globes that have all been blown out. Another photo shows shattered glass directly beneath the light. Even though the murder probably took place at night, the killer had the sense to darken the scene even further, either beforehand, during or after the kill.

I read over the initial police report, taking note of the major details. The body was discovered by two San Francisco university students, in L.A. for the weekend. They'd been sampling Little Tokyo's nightlife at one of its most popular karaoke bars and had left the bar around 4:00 a.m. After a brief McDonald's stop, they cut through the parking lot to their hotel, but one of them decided he wouldn't make it without a pit stop. So he looked for a dark nook in the parking lot; midstream he turned his head and saw the body. Bet that put a stop to the waterworks. He called 911 on his cell phone, and the LAPD was on scene at 4:30 a.m., five minutes after the witness called in. According to the crime-scene log, the detectives arrived thirty minutes later, with the crime-scene techs and the forensic pathologist hot on their heels.

The victim had no jewelry, no wallet and no ID on him, nor were any of these items found around the large area the police cordoned off for the crime-scene search. On the surface, that suggests a mugging gone wrong. In fact, if our guy was sitting in the morgue with a gunshot wound, I doubt the case would have warranted FBI attention. After I've read over the witness statements, I punch the lead LAPD detective's number into my desk phone.

"LAPD, Ramos."

"Detective Ramos, it's Special Agent Sophie Anderson calling from the FBI."

"Hey, Anderson. That was quick… You work with Rosen, right?"

"Yeah. I'm the behavioral analyst for L.A."

"Swell. You got the file?"

"Yup, it's in front of me."

"So you got questions, huh? Shoot."

"First off, any news on ID?"

"Not so far. Nothing came up on Live Scan so now I've got people going through L.A.'s Missing Persons."

Live Scan allows us to digitally scan the prints of a suspect or victim and run them against the Automated Fingerprint Identification System. No match means he's not on our radar—no criminal record and not a government or ex-government employee. Lucky for us that the body was found relatively quickly and the skin still had enough oils present for the digital system, otherwise we would have had to print the vic the old way, with ink and a card before scanning his print.

Even though we can't match his prints, maybe we can match his face—against L.A.'s Missing Persons. "You think he's an L.A. native?" I ask. "This is a big tourist destination."

"I know, it could be anyone…and Little Tokyo's popular with tourists. But Missing Persons is a start."

"It could complicate things if he's not American," I say, thinking about the repercussions of getting international consulates involved.

"Exactly."

"Tourist or resident, not many people go out without a wallet or passport." I start doodling on my notebook.

"It looks like a mugging gone wrong." Ramos voices the most obvious scenario—if it wasn't for the unusual throat wound. The lack of conviction in his voice tells me he's not sold on the mugger theory.

"Or the killer took the ID, didn't want us to discover the victim's identity, or wanted to delay that knowledge."

"But why?" Ramos is quiet, but only for a second before answering his own question. "Would buy someone time to get out of L.A., maybe even flee the country if they thought the victim's identity would make it obvious who they were."

"True. Well, let's hope the ID doesn't take too much longer." I move on to my next question. "What do you make of the two guys who discovered the body?"

"Typical college kids down for a big weekend in the City of Angels. They were a little boozed up when I interviewed them, but I can't see that they're involved in any way."

"The report didn't list any other witnesses."

"No." He pauses. "Even though the area's pretty isolated, I'm thinking someone had to have seen or heard something. But no one's come forward yet."

"You think they will?"

"Hard to know. It's probably the usual…someone saw *something* but didn't realize the significance. There aren't many Japanese residents in the area nowadays except for a few older people, but there are a few businesses nearby, and a large apartment block. I'm going back to visit them today if you want to tag along."

"Sure."

"With the light out of action, I guess it's possible it was dark enough for the killer and murder to go unnoticed."

"Maybe." I chew on my bottom lip. "And the autopsy?"

"Scheduled for this afternoon. I'll probably sit in."

"Mind if I come, too?"

"If you think it will help."

"Any firsthand contact with the victim and crime scene will help me draft an offender profile, not to mention a victimology."

"Victimology. That'd be nice."

I sympathize with Ramos. Besides a rough age range, race, height and some other vital statistics, we don't have much to work with in terms of a victim profile.

"I'll meet you at the crime scene at ten. You'll see it from Second Street…or South Los Angeles or South San Pedro for that matter."

Bright yellow crime-scene tape is hard to miss. I thank Ramos and hang up.

After spending another forty-five minutes going over the file, I come back to the victim's clothes. So who in the office would know? My first stop will be Melissa. She's always got fashion magazines poking out of her handbag. Then I might go with a cliché and try Bobby from the

Cyber Crime Division—he's gay, so he's bound to know men's fashion, right?

Melissa's typing furiously when I arrive at her desk. She glances up at me and smiles but keeps typing, showing her ability to multitask with ease. "Hey, Soph. What's up?"

"I've got a question for you."

"Fire away." She stops typing and gives me her full attention.

"You're into fashion, right?"

"'Course."

"I've got some crime-scene photos of a John Doe I'd like you to look at."

She grimaces slightly. Like Mercedes, Melissa can usually avoid photos of victims.

"Sorry," I say. "It's just that the guy looks really well dressed, and I want to confirm a level of affluence for the victimology."

She nods reluctantly. "Okay, I can do that."

I've chosen a couple of photos that show the victim's clothing fully, and in the best lighting. Moving in next to Melissa, I use the back of one photo to cover the victim's head and the neck wound. No point freaking her out more than I have to. She seems relieved when there's no visible blood or gore.

"The jeans are Ralph Lauren. And this pocket cut is new this season, so your victim's in the latest design." Her eyes move upward. "Now the T-shirt…um…oh, hang on, there's the Yves Saint Laurent symbol, just there." She points to a tiny dot on the victim's sleeve.

I bring the photo up for a closer look. "Oh, yeah, so it is." I smile at Melissa. "Thanks, that's a huge help."

"Awesome." Melissa's chuffed to have helped.

I walk back to my desk and grab my keys and bag, thinking about the case. So our victim is definitely into his appearance, taking the effort to wear the latest fashion. Maybe it is how it looks—a mugging. The guy could have been wearing a Rolex and some bling to match his designer clothes, and that's mighty attractive for someone looking for fast cash.

* * *

I pull up at the parking lot on Second Street exactly two minutes before the hour. The scene is very different to how it would have looked yesterday, but even from the street I can see the area cordoned off with police tape deep in the belly of the parking lot. Yesterday morning, people would have been overflowing from both inside and outside the tape. The cops and forensics would have been bustling inside, gathering evidence and inspecting the scene; the media and onlookers would have been pushing forward, trying to see more, find out more. Now, a lone uniformed cop keeps an eye on the area and even the tape will probably be gone by evening, certainly by this time tomorrow. Then there'll be nothing to indicate to a passerby that someone's life ended in this lot.

As I walk toward the entrance, a dark-complexioned man in his late forties to early fifties gets out of his car and makes a beeline for me. He's fit and healthy looking, with virtually no sign of middle-age spread. His black hair has a slight wave to it, and he wears it long for a man, coming down to his ears and the nape of his neck, Antonio Banderas style. Gray streaks add distinction and help give away his true age.

"Agent Anderson?" He gives me a large grin, his white teeth contrasting against dark lips.

"Yes." I take his outstretched hand. "Detective Ramos, I presume."

He nods and we both walk toward the cop and the crime-scene line.

"You're letting the parking lot carry on business as usual?"

"Yeah. Except for the area we've cordoned off."

He points to the back of the lot, and I notice the sea of cars stops well short of the fence and building site.

"It's a well-chosen location," I comment.

Ramos nods. "Little Tokyo's usually busy, but this spot's buried."

When we get to the crime-scene tape, the cop stands aside for us to enter and acknowledges Ramos by name.

"Thanks, Officer Saxon. Anything happening down here?"

"No, sir. Quiet since I took over shift at eight. Officer Graves said there wasn't much action last night, either. Just a few curious citizens coming in for a closer look."

We both nod. Same old story the world over. The thing is, one of those nosy citizens could be our killer. Killers often return to the scene of the crime. Sometimes it's just out of compulsion to see what's happening, but hardened killers will get off on it, reliving the moment of death. They see murder as the ultimate power over their victim, and they want that sense of power to run through them again and again. But that trait is more something we see in serial killers, or other types of sadistic killers. If it's a mugging gone wrong, or someone who took the victim's ID just to prolong our discovery of his identity, they'll keep a wide berth between them and the scene.

Ramos holds the tape up for me and I slip underneath it. Looks like he's old-school—I just hope he doesn't mind a woman on his homicide case. Women are still well and truly outnumbered in law enforcement and some of the older cops don't like our movement up the ranks. But so far there's nothing to indicate Ramos is one of those.

A few of the crime-scene markers are still on the asphalt, but most of the evidence has been removed and the corresponding markers with it. I recall some of the crime-scene photos and manage to fill in some of the blanks. Marker number six was a cigarette butt, and both the marker and butt are gone. Maybe the cigarette was the victim's, maybe the killer's or maybe some unrelated third party's. The butt will be swabbed for DNA and compared to the victim's. If that doesn't give us a match we can run it against CODIS, the national DNA database. Sometimes we get lucky and get a direct match on our perp.

Near the corner of the farthest parking space was marker number ten, which flagged the place where the witness urinated. It was from this point that he looked around and saw our vic.

I move back to the place where the glass from the light

fell. "Has the match been confirmed?" I ask, gazing up at the jagged edges on the light post.

"Initial visual confirmation, yes, but the lab's still going to run the glass and reconstruct the light to make sure. The light's being removed this afternoon."

I nod. "You want to take me through it?" I jerk my head to the wire fence on my left.

"Sure."

Ramos would have done an initial walk-through as soon as he arrived on site, assessing the crime scene and going through a few possible reconstructions in his head. And he's probably spent the past twenty-four hours going through it over and over again.

"How many people you got on this, by the way?"

"Me, my partner, a junior detective and I've got two uniforms at my disposal—Saxon and Graves. At the moment I've got them taking watches, but later on today I'll close up the crime scene and get them to follow up with the door-to-door canvassing."

I nod. A murder investigation goes through cycles. It often starts off with a few cops working it, but then if nothing breaks, some of those resources might have to be directed elsewhere. Conversely, if it's a time-critical or high-profile case, the resources go up as time goes by.

"Okay." He takes a breath. "I'm afraid we haven't got much at this point. Especially given we don't even know if the vic was here of his own accord or was brought here. His car might even be in the lot." Ramos motions with his hand at the now-full lot over his shoulder. "The manager's keeping an eye out for cars that have been sitting here for a while. And we're running all the plates that were here at 5:00 a.m. yesterday to interview those people, too."

"Big job."

"Uh-huh." Ramos goes back to the walk-through. "Let's start with the mugging angle. So let's say our vic is on his way back to his car, or walking along Second Street. Our attacker or attackers entice or drag him to the fence and take his wallet. Maybe our guy fights back or tells them he's seen their faces and will make sure they go to jail, and the situation escalates. No word yet on what might have caused the throat injury, but there were no obvious teeth marks and the human hand's not capable of that sort of damage, so the killer must have been holding the guy at the neck with some sort of weapon."

We really are working in the dark. At this stage we've got no ID, no witnesses to the crime itself and a highly unusual cause of death—although that will still have to be confirmed by the coroner. Our guy may have died of internal bleeding or something else and the throat wound was simply an additional injury.

"Is the area known for muggings?" I ask.

"Not really, no. But on a Friday and Saturday night there are also lots of people under the influence. Easier targets."

"And also more likely to respond violently."

"True. Again, no blood-alcohol results for our vic yet."

"Just as a matter of interest, what did our two witnesses come out at?"

"The guy who saw the vic first blew 0.12 and his friend was 0.14."

"I guess that's pretty sedate for two uni students out until 4:00 a.m."

"Yeah. They're both on track scholarships and their college coach told the team members if they get in trouble, they're out." He pauses. "I'm not convinced on the mugging theory. Seems to me maybe there'd be more of a scuffle, and more…" he searches for the word "…conventional injuries. Plus the light indicates premeditation."

If someone took out the light, they may have picked this location well before the murder actually took place. Still, we should consider all possibilities.

I play devil's advocate. "He may have shot it out seconds before the murder, realizing it was too light, or he might have done it after the deed in an effort to delay the discovery of the body."

"Also possible."

"Find any bullets or rocks?" I ask.

"No. But the parking-lot manager said the light was operational until the night before last."

"So take me through your premeditated reconstruction."

Ramos rakes his hand through his hair. "Our killer and victim arrange to meet on Second Street or even here in the lot. So they know each other. The killer came by earlier in the night to take out the light, and set up the place for maximum darkness and privacy."

"There are places a lot more private than this."

He shrugs. "Maybe our victim would have been suspicious of somewhere even more isolated. Or this could be a regular Saturday-night drug deal and the killer picked this as the best time and place to take out our vic, who might have been his client or his supplier."

"Any sign of drugs?"

"Waiting on trace evidence from his clothes and blood analysis to see if he was on anything himself."

"Maybe the client owed our vic money," I suggest. "Money's always good motivation for murder." I think about the scene, the guy's clothes. "Our vic was very well dressed. All designer stuff, apparently. So he's probably quite well-off."

"Which could tie in with drugs."

I nod. "Either he's got the money to feed his habit or he's getting money from dealing." I pause. "Let's circulate his picture to some of the cops and agents working gangs and organized crime."

"Good idea. I'll send it to the DEA, too."

I nod. Most drugs are run by gang members these days, and the DEA will have files of all known dealers in the area. Maybe our guy's picture will ring a bell.

Ramos opens his phone. "I'll get someone on it straight-away." He calls the station and requests that an e-mail with a couple of pics be circulated to all DEA, organized crime and gang law enforcement personnel in L.A. I bet that's some e-mail list.

After he hangs up he puts his hands in his pockets and surveys the scene. "What do you think, Anderson?"

"Like you said, it's early days yet. A mugging is possible—if the guy had designer clothes on, maybe he had nice jewelry, too. Or it could be a staged mugging. Our killer wants us to think the primary motivation was robbery, not murder."

Ramos nods. "The light."

"Yeah. I agree that if the light was purposely cut out of the equation, we're definitely talking about premeditation and someone who's smart enough to do everything in his power to ensure there were no witnesses to his actions."

"I'm hoping to hear back from the lab in the next day or two on the light."

I nod. "In terms of a profile, I need to find out more about the victim and his injuries before I can even start to get a picture of the person who killed him. Especially in this case, where the cause of death may be hard to pinpoint."

"Fair enough."

"You worked with a profile before?"

"Yeah, on a few cases. I know how it works."

A psychological profile gives investigators extensive information about their perpetrator, from age and sex to their educational level, likely occupation and personality traits. It doesn't give them a name, of course, but they can look at any suspects in light of the profile and use it to help zero in on the killer.

"I'm just going to take a look around." I walk away from Ramos to the fence line, hoping he'll hang back and give me some privacy. I do want to look around the crime scene some more and get a feel for the place, but I'm also hoping to induce a vision. Thankfully, he stays put.

I stand next to the fence, gazing at the building site. There's still blood on the asphalt, but the rain forecasted for this evening will soon remove that evidence. The way the vic landed, it looked like he was standing close to the fence, looking out over Los Angeles Street and the city skyline. Then he fell back and to one side, so that his right shoulder was propped up, preventing his body from falling to the full horizontal. Blood drained from his neck to the building debris and trickled down onto the ground. I kneel down to get closer to the place where he died and I'm instantly hit by dizziness.

He staggers back, blood flowing heavily from his throat. He's shocked, shocked that I've struck and shocked by the realization that the blow is fatal.

So quickly, his life is over. But I don't linger to watch his last breath. I turn back to the lot.

A sharp jab of pain hits my throat, and I have to fight the urge to double over. My face is crumpled in agony, but I manage to stay upright and resist the urge to put my hand to my throat. I look up, relieved that Ramos is talking to Officer Saxon and both have their backs to me. The pain begins to subside and is replaced by a dull ache. With no one watching me, I act on the instinct to rub my throat.

I replay the vision. From the killer's perspective I saw the victim's shock and fear, but they don't tell me much— most victims of any sort of violent crime, or even nonviolent crime, experience these emotions. The shock could also be surprise about who his killer was, but that's impossible for me to know from what I saw.

I hate experiencing a violent crime from the victim's perspective because I feel their fear and their pain. But having a vision from the killer's perspective is even more disturbing because I often feel their excitement and adrenaline—I'm happy to be murdering my prey, to be inflicting unspeakable pain. I'm the predator and I enjoy it, just like he does. After a vision from the killer's point of view, it can take a long time to orientate myself back into the real world, and to release the repulsion I feel. It also leaves me with a sense of violation.

But this time, when I switched from victim to killer, I got no sense of excitement or fear.

I take a deep breath in and clear my mind in an effort to replay the vision and any important emotional elements, or maybe even see something else. Nothing new comes to me, but I am able to visualize the last moments of the vision and experience the killer's emotions again. When he turned away from the dying man, he purposefully looked up at the light, pleased he'd dealt with it earlier. But there was no adrenaline, no happiness, no regret, no anger. His emotions feel very different from what I usually sense from a killer's perspective. It's almost…almost…

Indifference.

Three

"Hi, Agent Anderson. It's been a while." Forensic pathologist Lloyd Grove holds his hand out. I've worked with Grove on a couple of homicides since I've been at the L.A. field office.

"Yes, almost two months." Unfortunately it hasn't been two months since I worked a homicide case, just since I sat in on an autopsy conducted by Grove.

"And Detective Ramos. It hasn't been so long for you."

"No." Ramos looks at me. "Drive-by shooting last week."

I nod, remembering the news reports from last Wednesday, when a young male was caught in the crossfire between the Crips and MS-13.

"Well, let's get started." Grove flicks on some surgical gloves. "I got my assistant to take blood yesterday, so I'll get those results from my office before you go."

Grove moves toward the body and we follow. The autopsy procedure is always the same. The vic's clothes are removed, then the body is searched for any trace evidence before being washed. Finger, hand and footprints are also taken and sometimes initial blood is completed first, too, depending on when a forensic pathologist is available to do the full autopsy. While the procedure is usually conducted within twenty-four hours, law enforcement working the case can push for blood sooner, to kick things off while their vic's waiting in the autopsy queue.

In the case of our vic, his head and pubic area have also already been shaved. The hair will be examined by forensic scientists looking for foreign matter, including hairs that do not belong to the victim. It's a technique that often reaps rewards in sexual homicide cases, where the victim has usually been raped pre- or postmortem. However, we can find traces of the killer on a victim's body from almost any crime.

I lean into the throat region to take a closer look. The flap of skin and tissue has been placed back in its normal position and I can make out two indentations on either side of the wound. These are the only "tool marks" from the weapon that was used to inflict the injury.

Grove flicks on the room's recording equipment and says the time, date and case number before leaning down with me. "Yes, it is an unusual wound, Anderson. We might not be able to narrow down a murder weapon."

"I was hoping it would be more obvious once it was cleaned."

"You and me both. Can't say I've seen anything like this before."

Just what you don't want a forensic pathologist to say, especially when you've already got unknown identity in the mix.

After taking a swab for DNA from the inside of the victim's cheek, Grove methodically moves over the victim's body, looking for anything unusual. As always, he pays particular attention to the victim's hands, looking for defensive wounds.

"Anything?" Ramos peers over the body to the hand that Grove is examining.

"Slight discoloration of the knuckles, but it's an older bruise, not from the night he died."

"A punch?" I ask.

"Probably. See how it spreads down from the top knuckles onto the fingers, like the fist was clenched?" Grove clenches his own fist to demonstrate.

I lean over to get a closer look. "Uh-huh."

"So a punch seems likely. But no broken skin, and it doesn't feel like there are any broken bones, either."

"So not a hard punch?"

"It depends where the punch was delivered. If our vic punched someone in the stomach or kidneys, for example, he would have had to hit them extremely hard to produce this bruising. But if the punch was to the face, it wouldn't take much to bruise the knuckles."

Of course…striking soft tissue isn't going to cause as much damage as striking someone on the head or any other bony area.

"It's on our victim's right hand, so it seems likely he's a right-hander."

Just then Grove's assistant enters. "Here are the X-rays."

Grove takes his gloves off and inserts the X-rays into the light box. "Wow," he says.

Ramos and I move closer.

Grove keeps his eyes on the film. "We've got one fresh break, the lower left rib." He points to the floating ribs. The very bottom left rib is not just cracked, it's broken clean through.

"That's some break," I say.

"Yes, but it's one of the floating ribs, so less force required than with the upper ribs."

I nod. The bottom two ribs aren't attached to the sternum, hence the term *floating*. The upper ribs need a massive force to break clean through; even in a car accident, cracked ribs are more likely than a full break. Even so, you're still talking about significant force to break clean through a rib.

"My *wow* is about the old breaks…there's lots of them," Grove continues. "This guy saw a lot of action, or maybe he was involved in a car accident or something." He pauses. "No, the breaks aren't right. His fingers aren't broken at the moment, but they have been in the past. He's also had his nose altered—" Grove glances back at the cadaver "—and the surgery was masterfully performed. Visually, I wouldn't have guessed his nose had been altered. And he's even had hairline fractures to his lower jaw. His left little finger has also been broken, but it's the kind of break you'd see if the finger was bent back." He demonstrates on himself. "Maybe sporting, trying to catch a ball…or maybe purposefully inflicted."

"Like torture?" Ramos asks.

"Yes."

"Any other signs of his past?"

"Not in the bones, no. From the hips and cranium it looks like he's in his forties. I'd say somewhere between forty-two and forty-eight."

Again, it's nothing concrete for ID, but it gives us a better understanding of the victim.

"Obviously Asian descent, but I'll have to plug his facial dimensions into the computer to give you an exact location."

I nod, knowing that this technique is often done when a body has fully decomposed, leaving us only bones. The skull is measured and when these measurements are entered into a computer program, the software comes back with the most likely racial genotype.

"What about the scars on his face?" I ask.

Grove moves back to the body. "They're both well healed." He pulls across a magnifying glass to take a closer look at the skin. "The one along the underside of the jaw has actually been stitched—again, extremely well. The stitch marks are hardly visible to the naked eye. I don't think they're childhood scars, but they're probably about fifteen to twenty years old." He removes the magnifying glass. "See how this scar's jagged?" Both Ramos and I move in closer and nod. Grove holds a clenched fist under the victim's chin "Could be from a broken bottle held under the chin."

"That's street fighting," Ramos says. "Maybe this is gang related."

I stand upright again. "Gangs would tie in with the drugs theory, too."

"Yeah, and we have a lot of Asian gangs in L.A., plus the more organized crime structures like the many Chinese tongs and the Japanese Yakuza."

"So this guy could be Chinese or Japanese?" I ask no one in particular.

"Leave it with me," Grove answers. "But it might not be an easy question to answer. Particularly given I don't think he's full-blood anything."

"You're thinking Eurasian?"

"I'm no expert, but maybe. Or maybe mixed Asian races."

It can be hard to tell mixed racial features. Even full-blood siblings of a mixed race couple can look totally different, with one looking nearly completely Caucasian and the other completely Asian.

"You've got someone who's an expert?"

"Doctor Ramira over at California State University has been involved in a research project that looks at racial identification in melting-pot areas like L.A. You know, in two thousand years will we all look the same, as interracial marriages become the norm and our cultures blend into one?"

"Sounds interesting," Ramos says. "But I know my mother would have disowned me if I brought home a woman who didn't have Latin blood running through her veins."

Grove smiles. "Yeah, but what would *you* say to *your* children?"

"Point taken." He pauses. "Mind you, I think my wife would prefer if both our sons married Latinas."

"Your mum would have disowned you and your sons' mum would *prefer* Latino. That's a big leap in one generation. Imagine what it will be like in twenty generations' time."

Again, Grove's got a good point. It's the same story in Melbourne, my home town and one of the most multicultural cities in the world. The mix is different to L.A.— mostly Asian, Greek and Italian—and although racial boundaries still exist they're fading with each generation. I'd say it'll only be a few generations' time before most people have some Asian, Greek or Italian heritage.

I look back at the body. "But this is no smashed bottle." I point to the mushed throat.

"No. This wasn't caused by anything sharp." Grove uses his gloved finger to point to the two indentations on either side of the throat. "Whatever caused this was blunt. The skin's perforated, but it's been torn using a forward force, rather than being punctured by a point or sharp implement. But the force…"

"So the killer's strong?" Ramos jumps to the logical conclusion.

Grove nods. "Whatever was used to damage the throat like this was wielded with great force."

I instantly picture a big, thuglike attacker.

"The marks are cylindrical," he continues, "but they don't match any weapon I know of."

"Forceps?" I offer.

Grove shrugs. "It's possible, although I suspect forceps would leave a more elongated impression." Grove pulls the large chunk of skin back, exposing the throat. "The force totally crushed the hyoid bone and damaged the trachea, as you can see." He points to the windpipe and the once-horseshoe-shaped bone.

"So that's what killed him?"

"Not exactly. His airway was compromised, but he still would have been able to get some air. And if paramedics had arrived on scene within a few minutes of the attack, they could have eased his breathing further. No, blood loss is the primary cause of death. The weapon, whatever it was, ruptured the carotid artery."

"So he bled out?"

"Looks like it. Pending anything else out of the ordinary. Let me finish the external examination and then I'll open him up. That will give us a closer look at the throat."

Grove finishes the external sweep of the body, checking the victim's nose, mouth, ears and sexual organs as part of the exam. Twenty minutes later he pulls his surgical instruments toward the table and looks up at the microphone. "Okay."

Once Grove has finished with the surgical examination of the head and brain, he moves on to the chest, cutting through the skin and muscle structures. But unlike surgery, no blood seeps from the wounds—what was left of the victim's blood is drawn by gravity to his back. Once both incisions are finished, Grove peels back the whole area, revealing the organs and other internal workings of the body. The corpse is fresh, so fresh that rigor mortis is still in play, although it is beginning to wane. It begins in the eyelids a few hours after death and first spreads to the face and neck, then the limbs. After about thirty-six hours it starts to dissipate until the body is completely supple once more, about forty-eight to seventy-two hours after death. In another day our victim's body will be limp and pliable again.

Pulling the front section of skin forward doesn't shed any more light on the cause of death. We could already see the exposed windpipe and hyoid bone. However, congealed blood around the other layers of skin in the throat and neck confirm the force of the blow. If his throat hadn't been literally torn from his neck, the guy would have had a mighty bruise. But he died before the bruise could show up.

As Grove's examining the neck area, he uses one of his instruments to part the tissue around the vic's neck and points to a thin, ropelike structure. "See here…the vagus nerve is inflamed. Probably from the force applied to the throat before the weapon perforated the skin."

Again, I picture a big strong man as our attacker.

"The vagus nerve runs in between the carotid artery and the jugular." Grove uses one of his instruments to point to the carotid and jugular on either side. "And while the carotid has been totally perforated and the vagus shows signs of trauma, the jugular is intact."

The three structures—artery, nerve and vein—are all very close to one another, but the weapon has managed to only affect two of them.

We hang around while Grove checks all the organs and takes samples as necessary, before putting them back in and closing our guy up.

"Let's go check the blood work," he says, snapping off the gloves and taking off his medical gown before washing his hands and turning off the recording gear.

We follow Grove up to his office, and wait while he checks his e-mail. "Okay, here we go. Blood analysis indicated no alcohol whatsoever and no other drugs in his system, prescription, nonprescription or illegal."

"Mmm…" Ramos rests his chin on his thumb and runs his forefinger across his lips. "Doesn't rule out the drug theory. But it makes him more likely to be the seller than the buyer."

"He could have still been the buyer if the stash was empty, so empty it was out of his system," I say. "He needed supplies."

Ramos nods. "You're right, could be either if the drug theory holds." He sighs. "Or maybe we're just looking at old-fashioned premeditated murder." He slips his hands into his pockets. "With the usual motives… If it's not money, could be jealousy or revenge."

"But without an ID we don't know who'd benefit financially from his death, or who could be jealous of him, or who might have wanted revenge. Plus we've got those old injuries—a rough past like that ties in with drugs or some sort of criminal activity."

Grove nods. "And they're not injuries from boxing or anything like that. I'll send the dental records out, see if we get any takers."

"Thanks, Doc." Ramos takes his hands out of his pockets. "After you, Anderson."

I thank Grove with a handshake.

"I'll make sure I include you on my e-mail list for this case," Grove says.

"Appreciate it." I give him a nod before turning to the door.

Ramos says goodbye and is by my side within a few seconds. "Damn." He lets out a long sigh as we move down the corridor. "Let's hope we get a hit on a missing person."

The L.A. coroner's office is always busy, always full, and today is no exception, with gurneys lining the corridor—the dead waiting for their turn. I squeeze between the body bags. "Anything from Forensics yet?"

"No, not yet. But it's probably time I touched base with them."

"County lab?"

"Uh-huh." He pulls his phone out.

I go through the forensic evidence in my head. We've got the light, which is probably being meticulously examined and then glued back together as we speak, then the cigarette butt, from which DNA will be extracted. DNA will also be isolated from remnants of the witnessing student's urine and cross-referenced with the sample he gave police. I'm sure it'll be a match, but it's always good to check out the account of anyone who discovers a homicide victim. Then the fence and building debris were dusted for prints which need to be processed, and some lucky bugger's got the job of going through all the nearby building-site remnants that were removed for further examination. Leave no stone unturned.

"Did you get many prints?" I ask.

"Yeah, they lifted quite a few from the bricks and they're still looking at the fence and some wood that was lying near the vic, too. I'll check with Prints first." Ramos finds a number in his phone and dials.

I think he's dreaming—it's early days yet—but I keep my mouth shut. The crime scene would have been dusted for prints, and these would be awaiting processing at the county lab, with the head of the fingerprint area, Maggie Court. She's great—very professional and a lovely woman—but like any lab servicing such a large area, it's hard to keep up with the caseload.

I listen in to Ramos's side of the conversation and gather the current status—the fence has been examined and some prints from it are being run at the moment. That's pretty fast. Looks like we hit the lab on a slow day. Next he asks to be transferred to Sam Gould, the head of DNA at the lab. Again, I glean the gist of things—the DNA's still being processed. Finally Ramos asks to be transferred to Sally Hart and I soon realize from the conversation that she's the lab tech working on the parking-lot light. Based on my vision, I'm sure the light wasn't a coincidence. When the killer turned away from his dying victim, he looked at the light and it was already broken. There's no doubt in my mind. But I can't give Ramos or Sally Hart a heads-up. What would I say?

Ramos hangs up. "Sally Hart will have the light reconstruction finished in about two hours. She suggested we come over at five so she can take us through it in person."

"Fine by me." A visual's always good and I don't know how our killer took it out.

"I'm going back to the station for a couple of hours to check in with my people. You want to come?"

I consider it for a moment, but then decide my time is best used elsewhere. "Thanks, but I might head back to the Bureau. I'll see you at the lab."

In the coroner office's parking lot we part ways in our government cars. But instead of going back to the field office, I wait until I see Ramos drive past and give him a wave while pretending to be on the phone. Once I'm sure he's out of the parking lot I head back to our vic.

My ID is enough to get me back into the morgue and buy me some time alone with the unidentified male. My aim is to induce another vision, something more than a flash of our vic in pain and shock. I stare into the face of the man and wonder what he was like in life. What was his occupation? I look at his hands and notice they're smooth, indicating he didn't earn a living from manual labor. In fact, his hands are so well maintained they look manicured. His cuticles are neat and trimmed, his nails rounded with perhaps a millimeter of overhang between the end of the nail and the fingertip. I decide to check his toenails, too, curious as to whether his impeccable grooming extends to his feet. Sure enough, his feet are smooth and his toenails also look manicured. So we've got an expensively dressed male who has regular manicures and pedicures, someone meticulous about his appearance and who can probably afford to keep himself well-groomed—unless he was living beyond his means and was so in debt that someone took payment in the form of his life.

I shake my head, it doesn't add up...the grooming seems to be in opposition with his healed wounds. Not many highly paid professionals get into bar fights or confrontations with gangs on the weekend. But then there's the age of those injuries.

I nod my head as I come to the only logical conclusion. This man spent at least part of his life, maybe his late teens and early twenties, involved in violence but then turned his life around. It would explain the well-healed wounds and bones, and his current state of maintenance. Maybe his past came up to bite him on the ass. I'm jumping to conclusions, but all the pieces fit…extremely well.

I take a deep breath in and clear my mind of all thoughts, including my preconceptions. I need to see something about this man's life…or death. As each thought pops into my head, I force it out. I need my mind to be still. In this state of near meditation, I am the most receptive to visions. Eventually I'm rewarded.

He gets into a car and starts the engine. He's alone. His cell phone rings and he's talking. He's upset…annoyed. He raises his voice. The caller hangs up and the man's left with a dial tone. He yells into the silent phone and then throws it across the car. It ricochets off the passenger door and lands on the seat.

His anger turns to grief, and tears trickle down his face.

I open my eyes and I'm staring at the lifeless face of the victim lying on the hard metal in front of me. I replay the vision. Both his voice and the caller's were barely audible, but it sounded as if they were talking in another language. I try to replay a word or two in my head, something I could repeat or spell to try to find out the language, but it's spoken too softly and too quickly. Okay, what else was there? Whatever he and the caller were talking about, it was heated and I felt many emotions pulsing through the victim. He was initially shocked but that soon turned to concern…maybe even fear. That was quickly replaced by anger, but once he'd thrown his phone, a sense of sorrow or loss was the only remaining sensation.

I sigh, trying to piece it together. I don't think it fits with a drug deal gone wrong. So how does it fit with other motivations for premeditated murder? It could be blackmail of some sort. Shock and horror over what the caller knows or has, then anger that he's being blackmailed, and finally sadness as he realizes he has to submit to the blackmailer's demands? That would fit. What about jealousy? Could the caller have been the jealous partner of some woman, accusing our victim of impropriety? That might fit with the victim's emotions, too—he's concerned, then angry that the caller's discovered the affair, but also sad because it will have to end. I shake my head. The emotions align with many motivations behind murder, and wild speculation won't get me anywhere.

I try to induce another vision, but after twenty minutes and nothing, I sign out of the morgue and head back to my car. A glance at my watch tells me it's 4:00 p.m. Not enough time to go back to the office and work on another case. Even without factoring in the travel time, an hour's not long enough to get inside the mind of a killer or victim. You need to immerse yourself in the case, live it and breathe it. Working on something else now will be useless and it will take my mind away from our Little Tokyo victim.

I drive to the lab at California State University and spend thirty minutes in my car flicking through the case file again…live and breathe it.

Four

At 4:55 p.m. I enter the building and ask for Sally Hart, showing my ID. At the elevator doors on the third floor I'm greeted by a frizzy redhead in her mid-twenties wearing thick but stylish glasses. Her creamy skin is dotted with freckles. She wears well-cut jeans with square-toed ankle boots, a black sweater and a tailored purple jacket that emphasizes her petite waist. The smile that accompanies her outstretched hand reveals straight white teeth.

"Agent Anderson, nice to meet you."

I shake her hand. "You, too, Ms. Hart. Or is it Dr. Hart?"

She laughs. "Not yet. Another year of study, I'm afraid." She fingers her glasses. "I just got a call from Detective Ramos. He's running a few minutes late." She turns around. "Come through."

We make our way along a series of corridors and doors until we get to her lab. The light, now mostly assembled into one large piece from the million shards of glass, sits on her desk. It's a square, dark orange frame with four square panels of glass, underneath which sit the powerful bulbs. At the base of the frame is a large round hole, which marks the place where the light attaches to the post. With the reconstruction complete, four distinct bullet holes can easily be seen.

"Nice job," I say.

"Thanks. There are a few pieces missing—" she points to tiny gaps that are barely noticeable on first viewing "—but they're all insignificant…except for these ones, obviously." She bends down and points to the small holes in each panel of glass.

"Bullets."

"Uh-huh," she says. "Looks like a .45. It splintered the glass here, here, here and here." She points to the tiny cracks that radiate from each hole.

"Does Ramos know this yet?"

"Yeah, I called him once I'd finished it." She straightens up. "That's why he's late—he stopped off at the crime scene to set the techs up to take another look around, this time for some bullets."

"A bullet…gee, that'd be nice." A bullet would give us something we could match to a weapon; good for court, and sometimes good if the weapon's unique striation marks are already in the ballistics computer database.

She laughs. "That's exactly what Detective Ramos said." She takes her glasses off and gives them a polish. "I've just started the computer analysis looking at the angle of the bullets, the likely position of the shooter and the possible resting place of the bullets, but I think it'll be another hour or two before I can give the techs anything more concrete to help them pinpoint where the bullets might have landed." Hart takes me over to her computer. "I've triangulated the initial angle of the bullets, based on the way the glass shattered, and it puts the shooter somewhere between here and here, depending on his height. All four bullets were fired from the same spot and I've followed the possible trajectories through for someone five-five to six-five." She points to two dots on her computer, but so far it's just blank space, with no obvious visual relationship to the crime scene.

I look at the basic computer-generated model and try to overlay it in my mind's eye with the crime scene. "That takes him right back to the fence line, if we're talking a five-five perp."

The trajectory of the bullet tells us the angle it traveled, not its point of origin. But Hart's made a sensible call on the height range, and following the bullet's trajectory, the shorter he is the farther back he would have had to stand to produce the same angle.

"I haven't inputted everything into the model yet." She shuffles through some papers and pulls out a photocopy of the crime-scene sketch that would have been done by Ramos or one of his detectives. It shows all the key structures and points of evidence and includes exact measurements between items. Hart compares her computer breakdown with the sketch, measuring out the distances. "Yup, right on the fence, assuming the sketch is accurate."

Experienced cops know the importance of the sketch, know that it can become critical to solving the case or that it can become essential evidence in court.

"It's Ramos…it'll be spot-on," Hart continues. "So the fence line is the farthest point and if our shooter's around six-five you're looking at him standing level with the edge of this parking spot." She points to the crime-scene sketch. "I've still got to finish the model and then work out the bullet's trajectory after it hit the light."

"Could it have been a clean-through shot?" I walk back to the light to take a closer look and soon have my answer. The light has a thick metal backing, so once the bullet went through the glass, it would have hit the metal and ricocheted off somewhere.

"No, the angle's wrong," Hart confirms.

"How big are the bulbs in these things?"

She pulls an industrial-looking bulb, nearly the size of her hand, from a box on the floor. "This is the brand used in the light."

I picture the scene, picture the shot. "How high is the light?"

"Twenty-four feet."

I raise my eyebrows. "So he's a reasonable shot—to blow out all four bulbs."

She nods. "Probably. Depends on the time of day when he took the shot."

"Go on."

"Well, I'll have to do a reconstruction to be sure, but I imagine the bulbs themselves would be most visible in daylight, with the sun behind the shooter. Whereas if the sun's in his eyes it'd be harder—"

The phone on Hart's desk cuts off her sentence. "Hold on." She picks up the phone. "Hart…okay." She hangs up. "Ramos is on his way up now." She unclips her security pass from her jeans waistband. "I'll go buzz him through."

While I'm waiting, I take another look at the computer and the light. The glass that covers the bulbs is slightly frosted, so with the right lighting the bulbs would be easily visible.

A few minutes later Ramos and Hart arrive. Ramos gives me a nod and a smile and I listen in while Hart runs through her findings to date with Ramos, showing him the light itself and then the computerized trajectory.

"I've set the team up to search the whole parking lot."

She nods. "I'll keep working on the trajectory, see if I can't narrow that search area down for you."

"Before dark?" Ramos glances at his watch.

Hart shakes her head. "I doubt it. Sorry." She pauses. "I'm also going to run a reconstruction of the shooting, see if I can't give you guys a rough time of day. Or at least eliminate the possibility of a night shot."

I know the shot wasn't taken after the murder, but our killer could still have taken the light out earlier in the evening.

"That'd be great," Ramos says. "If it was a daylight shot it'll help prove premeditation." Like all good law-enforcement personnel, Ramos is already thinking about the evidence from a jury's point of view, thinking about how we can get a conviction. He pauses. "A likely time of day will also help when we're canvassing for possible witnesses. So far we've come up with a big fat zero from the area."

"I'll set it up for three tomorrow," Hart says. "You guys are welcome to sit in."

"Thanks. I'm hoping we'll have something else by then,

but—" Ramos gives her a smile "—if you're all I've got I'll be here."

"Gee, thanks." Hart smiles. "You sure know how to make a girl feel wanted."

I leave the lab at 5:45 p.m., giving myself just enough time to get home and grab a snack before my kung fu class. I've been studying kung fu for nearly eight years, and in addition to attending classes three times a week I also have one-on-one sparring training with my teacher for half an hour before the Monday-night class.

I'm only a block away from the school when my Black-Berry rings. The traffic's too heavy to glance down at the display to see who's calling, but my headset is configured to pick up after two rings.

"FBI, Anderson."

"Hey, it's Darren."

Detective Darren Carter and I met sixteen months ago, when I was new to the Bureau and working out of the Behavioral Analysis Unit in Quantico. I was investigating a serial killer who'd struck in Washington, D.C. but started off on Darren's turf—Tucson, Arizona. We hit it off immediately and have stayed in contact. And if I'm honest, Darren's a contender to maybe, just maybe, break the drought of men seeing me in lingerie. Or maybe not. Most days I don't want any contenders in that department, but sometimes…

"What's up?" I ask.

"The usual. Murder. You?" Darren works in Homicide.

"Surprise, surprise, it's murder in L.A., too."

He sighs. "Why do we do it?"

I know he's not serious, but I answer him anyway. "To get justice for the victims and hopefully save potential victims."

"That's right." The comment sounds flippant but I know it's not, not coming from Darren. Darren and I have both been touched, personally, by murder. For me it was my brother when I was eight, and for Darren it was his aunt, over ten years ago.

"What's your case about?" Darren asks.

Cases are confidential, to a point, but there's no harm in discussing the basics with a fellow law-enforcement professional.

"Little Tokyo murder. No ID and the guy's got a weird throat injury. You?"

"Nothing that interesting. Gunshot wound and we've got a jealous ex-boyfriend we like for it. We're waiting on evidence from the lab, but the ex isn't that bright. I think the forensics will nail him."

"So you've got your man."

"Looks that way."

"I'm just starting out on this one. No suspects yet." I swing into a parking space just outside the studio. "Listen, Darren, I've got to go. Kung fu class."

"Oh, yeah, Monday night. You can tell me all about the weird throat wound another time. Go kick some ass."

I laugh. "Will do."

I rush into the school right at 7:00 p.m., but still have to get changed. The place is quiet, with only three people here so far—my teacher, Sifu Lee; his assistant, Steve; and Marcus, one of the other advanced students. Lee is on the warm-up mats going through a series of blocks and strikes, and Steve and Marcus are both stretching in one corner. Lee looks up when I burst through the door.

"Sorry I'm late. I'll be out in a second."

He nods. Lee's in his forties and half-Chinese. His five-eleven frame is muscular, but not bulky, and extremely strong. He trained in China and Hong Kong in many different kung fu forms before choosing Tiger and Crane. He then trained to *sifu*—master—stage and has been teaching in L.A. for over fifteen years. And, L.A. being L.A., he's also had some involvement with the film business, training students who've gone on to become stunt doubles in movies.

In the changing room I pull on my uniform: baggy black pants, a black T-shirt with the school's logo on the front and my black sash. I also slip into my special martial arts shoes before running out to join Lee.

"I take it you're not warmed up?"

"No, sorry."

While Lee continues his own training, I do some quick stretches to warm up my legs and follow through with rotations of most of my joints. I pay particular attention to my shoulders and elbows, knowing how easy it is to jar those joints or hurt the surrounding muscles if you're not warmed up.

When I'm ready I give Lee a nod. We start with punches, which he counts out as I strike the pad he holds in front of me. Once we've done straight punches, arrow punches and leopard punches, we move on to blocks. Lee gently throws pre-arranged punches and kicks my way, which I defend.

We've been going for fifteen minutes when Lee says, "Ready to spar?"

"Sure." I'm definitely warm…and sweaty. I take a drink of water and suit up in my protective gear, putting on my shin guards, gloves and helmet. My groin guard is underneath my uniform from when I was getting changed. Lee only puts on a helmet and a groin-piece over his clothing— his hands and shins are rock hard from thirty-five years of conditioning. Once we're on the mats, Lee and I bow to each other.

"Okay, try to hit me." He gives me a teasing smile.

Our individual sparring time always starts off this way and, as usual, the invitation is enough for my competitive spirit to hit overdrive. I stand side-on to him, in horse, guard up. He mirrors this position, waiting for the first incoming strike.

I go with a left jab, followed quickly by a right, then a left, then a right. He blocks them all effortlessly and with precision, but I don't let this discourage me. A right hook punch followed by a straight kick and then a roundhouse kick still leave me no closer to hitting my target, and, in fact, I can feel a slight buzz in my shin where his forearm blocked my kick and connected with my leg. I'm wearing shin guards, but his forearms are amazingly hard. Damn, he's good. Then again, I probably shouldn't be able to connect a blow with my instructor. Not when he's been studying kung fu most of his life.

I try again, with another series of kicks and punches, including a spinning side kick, multiple jabs and even some fakes, where I start to throw a punch or kick then withdraw and go for my real move. But he's fast enough, even for these. As usual, he's left untouched and I'm left frustrated. One of these days…

He smiles. "Okay, my turn." He glances briefly at the wall clock—five minutes before class starts. Now, the stream of students coming through the doors is at its peak—allowing people just enough time to get changed. There are more sets of eyes on us, and some people have moved closer to see the action. The onlookers make me self-conscious, but they also spur me on. I may not have been able to hit Sifu Lee, but hopefully I'll be able to block most of his incoming strikes. I'm also aware that he won't be using full force or speed—that's too dangerous, especially since we're so unevenly matched. Lee's hands are lethal weapons, so he'll have to hold back.

Again we start side-on from each other, in horse stance with our guards up. Lee begins with a couple of punches delivered at low speed. After I easily block those, he starts to increase the pace. Blocking is definitely my strong point. I've always been able to pick what my sparring partner is about to do next and react accordingly. Until recently, I'd assumed it was good reflexes, but now I think maybe my psychic abilities allow me to sense what's about to come.

I adjust back and cross-block Lee's incoming roundhouse kick.

"Very good," he says, a hint of surprise in his voice. He waits only a second before sending some faster strikes my way, all aimed at my head. Again, I'm able to block these, but this time it takes complete concentration.

I move down to block a low punch—Lee changed it to catch me off guard. He keeps them coming, high, middle, low, and throws in a few kicks, but only one punch connects and even then I'd blocked almost in time, diminishing its impact.

Lee bows. "I'm impressed. Your blocks are still much better than your punches, so let's keep working on improving your strikes."

I smile and notice with some triumph that there are a few beads of sweat on Lee's upper lip. It's taken me four months of these one-on-one sessions to get him to sweat. He definitely stepped things up toward the end, too, and he may even have been close to going full speed with the last series of strikes.

We both take our helmets off and Lee gives me a small bow before turning to face the students who mill around us. "Okay everyone, line up please."

I move to the front of the class, and Marcus and the other second- and third-dan black belts join me. We always line up according to level, with the most advanced students in the front.

"You nearly had him that time, Sophie," Marcus says, before taking the spot next to me. Like Lee, Marcus is also of Asian descent, though I'd put him as only one-quarter. He's taller, at around six-two, and more overtly muscular than Lee. He wears his hair short all over, which accentuates the masculine angularity of his face—a wide square jaw, pronounced brow and high cheekbones. His skin is slightly olive, but that could be an L.A. tan rather than his racial heritage.

"One of these days I'm going to connect."

Marcus laughs, highlighting two large dimples.

"You ever tried sparring him?" I ask.

"Once. And once was enough. But I should do what you do, organize to come in early and train with him like that. It'd keep me on my toes."

Marcus is probably the best in our class. He's fast, strong and efficient—all the hallmarks of a good kung fu fighter. He doesn't really need the extra training, but at least he's modest about it.

Lee takes us through a quick warm-up before dividing

us into groups of two. The first group starts on forms with his assistant, while Lee takes the rest of us over to an area that's set up with mats and punching bags. My group works on punches, kicks, throws and techniques to break falls, before swapping with the other group to focus on our kung fu forms. With half an hour to go, we break into our levels, creating four groups—black belts, first-dan black belts, second-dan black belts and third-dan black belts. Tonight, we focus on punches, with Lee and Steve supervising and teaching us new moves as necessary.

At 8:55 p.m. Lee brings the whole group together again for a five-minute cooldown, and while my body starts to relent, my mind doesn't. When I leave just after 9:00 p.m., my adrenaline's still pumping. It's going to take me a good couple of hours before I can even think about sleep.

Five

I arrive at the office at 7:30 a.m. the next morning, after completing my three-hundred-meter sprint at Westwood Park in sixty seconds. It wasn't as fast as I was hoping, but I still got a total of twenty-one points across all the tests, enough to put me in the same league physically as the FBI's Hostage Rescue Team. Mission accomplished.

The white, twenty-story federal building looms less than a quarter mile from I-405, and the hum of the traffic is always audible from outside. The first nine floors of the building are taken up by Veterans Affairs and a few other smaller departments, with the FBI housed on floors ten to twenty. Level ten is accessible to the public and serves as our official reception point, but the rest of the FBI area is secured. Direct elevator access to floors eleven to twenty is via three clear portals in the building's belly. The portals have two security doors—you step in and the door behind you closes, trapping you in the small space, the other door only opening after you've scanned your security card and entered the five-digit pin. Great security, but a pain in the ass at peak hours when the employees are siphoned into only three units. Still, the people-jam is in step with L.A.'s traffic jams.

When I get to my desk, I notice there's already a message

on my phone, so while my computer's booting up I dial voice mail. The computerized recording tells me the call was received at 7:15 a.m., and then Ramos's voice comes on.

"Hi, Agent Anderson. It's Detective Ramos." He sounds extra cheerful, and I know instantly that he's got news of some description. Maybe a bullet was found last night. Or maybe the lab came through with a fingerprint match.

"Got a call from the DEA this morning. One of their guys recognized the picture we e-mailed out yesterday. Give me a call."

That's way better than a bullet…our victim's name. I punch Ramos's number into my phone straightaway. "Morning, it's Anderson. I just got your message. That's fantastic news!"

"Don't get too excited. It's only a visual ID. DEA's been trying to work out who this guy is for three weeks. He just suddenly showed up in their surveillance shots."

Damn. Just when I thought we had a name. "Where were the photos taken?"

"A house in Long Beach that the DEA's got under surveillance. Suspected meth lab, and it looks like the Asian Boyz are running it."

"Shit." The Bureau estimates that L.A. has over four hundred gangs, with combined numbers of around forty thousand members. The Asian Boyz is one of the biggest. "So Long Beach is their territory?"

"Yeah. Asian Boyz originated in Long Beach and nowadays Asian Boyz Eastside and Asian Boyz Northside are based there." He takes a breath. "Long Beach is also home to one of the world's biggest ports."

I follow the train of thought. "So the DEA thinks they're exporting? Using the port to ship the drugs?"

"It's one possibility. That's why they haven't moved on the house yet. They're watching for distribution."

"You know much about gangs?"

"Yes and no. I've lived in L.A. all my life, so I guess I have a good general knowledge, but I don't work gangs much. The LAPD has over three hundred cops in our Gang

Enforcement Division…it's their bag, not mine. I even had to hand over that drive-by shooting last week, once the involvement of MS-13 and the Crips was confirmed. What about you?"

"I've been reading up on them since I've been in L.A., but it's not an area of specialization for me, either." I haven't had to profile any gang-related crimes yet, although it's possible the young boy's murder in the arcade has ties to L.A.'s gang culture. Fifty-seven percent of homicides in the city are gang-related, and there are specialized cops and FBI agents who work gang-related crimes. They know gang behavior, not me. Guess it's time I learned.

"We're in dangerous territory," Ramos says. "And so was our vic. He was seen at the Long Beach house on three separate occasions. They've e-mailed me a sample of the shots and he looks pissed."

"Can you forward that e-mail?"

"Sure."

I hear typing in the background as Ramos sends the photos.

The vic being annoyed ties in with my vision from the coroner's office. I replay the images in my head and I realize…the car…it was a right-hand drive. It didn't strike me as odd at first, because right-hand drive cars still look normal to me, even though I've been in the States for over a year. It means our guy got that call when he was in a country that drives on the left-hand side of the road. So we're talking England, Australia or maybe an Asian country. The places that immediately spring to mind are Singapore, Hong Kong and Japan, but there are other Asian countries that drive on the left, too.

"Hey, Ramos. Maybe this guy is from overseas. He flies into the country to do drug business with the Asian Boyz, maybe the shipment's even bound for his home turf. And the vic being from another country would also tie in with him suddenly appearing in the DEA's surveillance shots. I bet he arrived in the States about three weeks ago.Let's check his prints with Interpol and immigration. Our guy would have been fingerprinted on the way in."

Most visitors flying into the US have their prints digitally captured and recorded. If we match this guy's prints, we'll have a name—or at least the name on his passport, if he used an alias.

"You know anyone at the State Department?" Ramos asks.

"No, but leave it with me. I'll get a name soon enough."

"Great."

"Oh, and I forgot to tell you yesterday—I went back to look at the body after you left." Given I had to sign in, at some point Ramos will find out I had another look at our vic, and I don't want him to think I was excluding him from part of the investigation. "I realized as I was sitting in my car that the victim's hands struck me as odd. It's probably insignificant, but when I went back I figured out what it was—his hands were manicured."

"Manicured, huh? So he's gay or one of those metro guys?" Ramos jokes.

I laugh. "Could be."

"Actually, male manicures in L.A. aren't that uncommon. Actors, you know?"

"I'll take your word for it." I pause. "His hands were very smooth, too. And before this news about his possible involvement with the Asian Boyz, I was thinking maybe he had a rough start but then turned himself around. That would explain the earlier injuries."

Ramos is silent for a few beats. "Or maybe he just moved up the gang hierarchy. Didn't need to be hands-on anymore."

His conclusion is more likely than mine. Here I was romanticizing the guy's past and thinking he'd grown up on the wrong side of the tracks and then straightened up, but he probably just got promoted. It certainly seems more probable now that we've got him associating with drug dealers with potential ties to the Asian Boyz.

I notice my computer has booted, so I start my e-mail program. At the top of my message list is the one from Ramos. "I've got your e-mail from the DEA." I open up the four attached images. In each one, our victim looks either stressed or very obviously angry. "He does look pissed."

"Maybe his lackeys weren't doing their jobs." He stops to consider. "If our guy is from overseas, we could have stumbled on an international drug ring."

"I guess we should meet with…" I scan down the e-mail to the bottom, and the signature. "Special Agent Joe De Luca of the DEA. See what he's got to say about our mystery guy."

"I'll set it up. You free all day?"

"Depends if we're going to sit in on Hart's experiment at three. Although obviously a meet with DEA will take priority." Watching Hart take potshots at the light might reveal some interesting facts, but our presence isn't necessary.

"I'll try to set up something with the DEA today. And I better touch base with our Gang Enforcement Division, let them know our homicide's looking like it might be their turf."

"Good idea."

"We also have an Asian Crime Unit. I'll give them a heads-up, too."

"Will the case be reassigned?" I ask.

"Maybe. Depends how it pans out. DEA might want to take the lead."

Drugs and gangs are big business, especially in L.A., and there are multiple agencies and task forces involved, with local, state and federal law-enforcement personnel. At the federal level the Bureau of Alcohol, Tobacco, Firearms and Explosives (ATF) is a player because gangs are often involved in illegal firearms, and likewise with the DEA and drugs. Then you've got the United States Custom Service, the Immigration and Naturalization Service, the US Attorney's Office, the IRS…the list goes on. And unfortunately we don't necessarily all play nice together. Lots of cops resent the FBI—see us as elitist egotists who take the credit for their hard work—and the DEA is referred to as "Don't Expect Anything" in some cop circles. We're just one big happy family.

"What about task forces?" I ask.

"Yeah, we've got a few of them to consider, especially in the wider county area."

"Let's start with the Safe Streets task force here in L.A." The Bureau runs the Safe Streets project, which has over one hundred and forty task forces around the country. Given it's Bureau-run and I know at least a couple of the FBI agents on it, it makes sense for me to take that one. "I'll contact Safe Streets here and you can follow up with LAPD."

"Okay. The ATF also runs Violent Crime Impact Teams. You wanna contact them?"

"Sure." I jot the task down. "Any other updates?"

"Not really. We've run all the license plates from the parking lot and I've got officers doing the initial interviews with owners at the moment. Nothing looks out of the ordinary…yet."

"Okay."

"Well, catch ya later." Ramos hangs up.

I figure our victim's name is the most important thing, so I get moving on the fingerprint search. My first point of contact, as always, is Brady's assistant, Melissa. She's got her finger on the pulse and seems to know a helluva lot of people in L.A. law enforcement. Maybe her knowledge extends to the State Department and, if not, I'm sure she'll be able to point me in the right direction.

Sure enough, a couple of phone calls later, I'm on the line with Lara Rodriguez from the US State Department.

"Hi, Ms Rodriguez. I'm Special Agent Sophie Anderson with the FBI."

"Hey. What can I do for you, Sophie? And please, call me Lara."

"Thanks, Lara. We've got a John Doe who we think may be a foreign national I'd like to e-mail you his prints for you to check your database."

"Sure." She spells out her e-mail address.

"I'll send the prints to you now."

"I'll give you a call the minute I get something."

"That'd be great. Thanks." I'd missed a call when I was talking to Rodriguez, so I dial up my voice mail. Ramos.

"Hi, Anderson. Joe De Luca from the DEA can't meet us until late this afternoon, so I've set up a five-thirty with him. Catch ya later."

I delete the message and add the 5:30 p.m. appointment into my calendar. Time to do some walking. My first stop is Agent Pasha Petrov, who reports to George Rosen and heads up the FBI's gang unit here in L.A. Petrov's first-generation American, and speaks fluent Russian. It makes him a major asset for dealing with organized crime run by the Russians in L.A. He consults to at least a couple of the Safe Streets task forces in L.A. Petrov also happens to share a surname with a nasty serial killer I was lucky enough to apprehend— but Petrov is a very common name in Russia and Bulgaria.

He looks up as I approach. "Agent Anderson. What brings you here?" His ice-blue eyes contrast his friendly tone, but I'm used to his eyes now and realize they're alert rather than cold. This is the first time I've come directly to Petrov, although we see each other in the weekly division-head meetings. Over the past few months I've discovered he's worked for the FBI in New York as well as L.A. and has particular experience with the Russian Mafia and to a lesser extent some of the Asian gangs and organized crime operations.

"Hey. I'm looking into a John Doe, and it seems it might be gang related."

"What you got so far?"

"Victim was found in Little Tokyo early Sunday morning. Detective Ramos from LAPD sent around an e-mail with his pic and we heard back from Agent Joe De Luca at DEA. Our John Doe was photographed coming out of a house in Long Beach."

"Yeah, I saw that e-mail from the LAPD. And I know Joe. We both consult to the Los Angeles Gang Impact Team."

"Safe Streets?" I ask, also noticing the use of Agent De Luca's first name—they must know each other well.

"That's right. The Gang Impact Team is this area's Safe Streets task force."

I nod. "Is there anyone else I should be talking to? Other task forces?"

"The e-mail should be enough for the moment. It would have gone to all the relevant people. You meeting with Joe?"

"Yeah, five-thirty this afternoon."

He nods. "De Luca is good. He knows what he's doing."

"What about the ATF?"

"I'll give the L.A. head a quick call but he would have got the e-mail with the pics, too."

"Great. That's it. See you at tomorrow's meeting."

Petrov gives me a mock salute. "See you then. And keep me in the loop on this one."

With the fingerprints moving and my ass covered in terms of who should know about our vic's possible connection with the Asian Boyz, I've got some time up my sleeve. I could continue working this case, or I could try to get a chunk done on the arcade victim, James Santorini. Realistically, things could change a lot after our 5:30 p.m. meeting, so it might be better to put this case on hold. I decide now is as good a time as any to dedicate to the fourteen-year-old boy that's been on my case list for two weeks. This job is all about juggling cases and sometimes it's hard to listen to your head and not your heart. But my head's won out for too long on this one.

To give myself the biggest chunk of time possible on Santorini's murder, I work through lunch, shoveling down a quick sandwich at my desk. Not that eating at my desk is unusual for me. At 2:30 p.m. I give Ramos a call to let him know I'm not going to make the ballistics run-through. He's busy, too, going over the initial reports on the cars at the parking lot, so we agree that Hart can call us with the findings once she's done.

It's 4:00 p.m. when Hart calls. "Hey, Anderson. I've got Ramos on the line, too."

"Hi." I get us straight down to business. "How'd you do, Hart?"

"In terms of daylight, I tried quite a few different simulations of the sun's position, and it was only in the early morning light, when the sun was shining directly in my eyes while I aimed at the light, that it was hard to see the bulbs."

"I still don't see him taking the shot in daylight," Ramos says. "It's just too risky in terms of witnesses. Even with a silencer."

"Agree," I say.

"Yes, but I needed to try all the options."

"Fair enough," Ramos says. "Go on."

"Dusk works, too. I could still see the bulbs quite clearly."

"And nighttime?" I ask.

"It was a three-quarter moon that night and clear skies, so the shooter would have had a little extra light, but even so, during the simulation I couldn't make out the bulbs. The brightness of the panels against the dark sky made it impossible. I couldn't even make out the four distinct panels."

"But broad daylight?" Ramos voices his doubts again.

"Well, I did have a thought on that. I couldn't see them, but I still managed to shoot out the bulbs." She takes a breath. "The shooter could have made the shot at night if he studied the lights during the day," she says.

"Either way, it confirms—" My train of thought is interrupted by sudden and intense nausea.

It's dark, and a few parked cars surround me. I look around, somewhat cautiously, but my heartbeat has barely risen above its resting rate of sixty-seven. Convinced I'm alone, I line up my gun's sights, breathe out and pull the trigger. The light shatters, and the edge of the parking lot is instantly darker. Flashlight in hand, I look for the bullet and pick it up. I never leave clues. Three more bullets later, my mission is accomplished.

I'm sitting down, tied to a chair, when the deafening sound of a gun going off close range hits me. Searing pain follows.

"You there, Anderson?"

It's Ramos's voice I hear first.

"Yeah, sorry."

"Are you okay?" Hart asks.

I think on my feet. "Fine. The phone went dead this end. You?" I try to bring my heart rate down with a few deep, but quiet breaths. Unlike the shooter in my vision, my heart is pounding.

"Um…I guess it did here, too," Hart replies. "You cut out just as you were saying something about 'it confirms.'"

"Oh, yeah." I bite my lip. "It confirms that the murder was planned. Premeditated." It was always more likely that the light was taken out before the murder, but until now we couldn't rule out the possibility that someone killed our vic in the heat of the moment and then shot out the light in an attempt to cover their tracks.

"I'm still surprised there aren't any witnesses," Ramos says. "Even to the sound of the shot."

"Chances are he used a silencer," says Hart, "but without a bullet it's impossible to tell."

"He's been careful, all right." I try to focus on the conversation and not the vision.

"It's good to confirm the murder was planned," Ramos says. "Thanks, Hart."

"No problem…but I still wish we had a bullet."

"Yeah, a bullet would be nice."

"So would an ID," I add, knowing we'll never find a bullet.

"Well, I'll leave the ID with you guys. I'll send you my written report in a day or two."

"Great, thanks again, Hart. Anderson, you want to stay on the line?"

"Sure." I don't really want to talk to Ramos—I want the time and space to think about the vision, but I can't tell him that.

Once Hart hangs up, Ramos says, "Just thought I'd check in. I'm still working on the cars, but nothing stands out so far. You?"

"It's a waiting game my end." I bite my lip, eager to get off the phone. "I'll call you if the State Department comes back with an ID, otherwise see you at the DEA at five-thirty?"

"Okay. Ciao."

As soon as I hang up, I replay the vision. The first part was definitely related to our Little Tokyo victim. I recognize the parking lot and the light, although realistically those types of lights are fairly common, being used in smaller playing fields and most outdoor parking lots. But the detail of shooting out that type of light is too specific to be anything but our light, our case. And the killer picking the bullets up ties in with the crime-scene team's assumption that the killer must have cleaned up after himself. Again, the darkness marries with our thoughts to date on the killer's actions. Nothing new there. But the second part of the vision doesn't make sense…not yet. I was in the role of a victim, shot. But our vic didn't get shot. And he wasn't sitting down or tied up.

I spend another fifteen minutes trying to find something useful in the vision or induce another one before moving back to the arcade case. I make good progress and by the time my phone rings again at 4:45 p.m. I've got the bare bones of the profile ready for the LAPD.

I fish my phone out of my bag and flip it open. "Agent Anderson speaking."

"Agent Anderson, it's Lara from US State."

"I was hoping it was you."

"Sorry I couldn't get back to you sooner, Sophie. One of those days."

"I hear you. Did you get a match?" I ask, flipping over my notebook to a new page.

"Sure did. His name's Jo Kume."

I scribble the name down as Rodriguez spells it out for me.

"Entered on a Japanese passport. Does the name mean anything to you?"

"No. You guys got anything on him?"

"Not much. It's his first time visiting the US. He listed a hotel in Monterey Park as a contact."

"Monterey Park…that's not too far from where his body was found. Can I have those details?"

"I'll e-mail you all the info from his entry documentation."

"Great. Thanks, Lara."

"You're welcome. Have a nice day."

"You, too," I say before hanging up and immediately punching in Ramos's number. "Ramos, it's Anderson. We've got a name."

"Hallelujah."

"Jo Kume."

"You run him yet?"

"Not yet. I'm just about to leave for our DEA meet. But State says it was the guy's first visit to the US, so I doubt we'll have anything on him."

"What time is it?" He pauses. "Darn it, I better get moving, too. I'll get someone to plug his name in, just in case."

"My contact's going to e-mail through the full details, including the hotel name he put on his form."

"It might be a false one, but can you ring those details through to me ASAP?"

"Sure. It'll come into my BlackBerry."

"See you soon."

While a bullet would have been nice, a name's mighty damn fine, too.

Six

In the car on the way to L.A.'s DEA office, I replay my vision again, trying to make sense of the second part. I was sitting down, tied up, but that doesn't gel with our vic. And why was it familiar?

The connection hits me as I'm swinging into East Temple Street, only minutes away from the DEA office. It's familiar because it's not the first time I've seen it—I dreamed it the other night. Could our killer have struck before? Shot someone else, too?

Inside the DEA office, a security guard signs me in and sends me to the sixth floor. When I step out of the elevator, a man in his early thirties greets me.

"Agent Anderson? I'm Joe De Luca."

I shake his hand. "Nice to meet you."

De Luca sports a shaved head with black stubble only on the back half of his skull. His sparkling dark brown eyes, plump lips and relatively unlined face give a better indication of his age than the receding hairline.

"Is Detective Ramos here yet?" I ask.

"He arrived a couple of minutes ago." De Luca points to the corner of the building. "I've got us set up in a meeting room."

I follow De Luca through the open-plan office to a meeting room that looks out across East Temple Street.

Ramos stands up. "Hey, Anderson. What's up?"

"Hi, Detective." I take a seat next to him, and once I'm seated he sits back down. "How'd you do with the hotel?" Before I was even out of the FBI parking lot Rodriguez's e-mail had come in, with full details on Kume, including his hotel in Monterey Park. I'd immediately called them through to Ramos.

"He was staying there all right. I've got people poring over the place as we speak."

"This is the hotel your vic was staying in, I take it?" De Luca asks.

"Yup. Lincoln Plaza." Ramos wiggles his phone. "And I just got a call—there's a laptop sitting on our vic's desk, so we're getting a computer forensics person out there, too. Now we're cooking."

I smile. "Sounds like you've got it covered."

"Uh-huh."

The FBI also has computer and forensic experts, but at this stage we're just consulting, helping out with a profile. Ramos is the man in charge.

Ramos flicks open his case file. I let him take De Luca through the bare bones of our case, including the autopsy. He finishes up with the result of his search on Jo Kume. Not surprisingly, nothing popped up under his name here in the US—no driver's license, no car registered in his name, no criminal record, no traffic offences.

"The State Department e-mailed me through his full entry details." I pull out my BlackBerry and navigate to the recent e-mail. "He's a Japanese national, but he flew in from Singapore on November 24. Singapore wasn't a connecting flight for him, it was his point of origin. We'll need to contact Singapore to get more information on him. I'm going to give Interpol a call first thing tomorrow."

De Luca nods. "It's hard to know if it's gang related when we don't know much about the vic."

Ramos leans back in his chair. "But it seems likely, given his association with the Asian Boyz, yes?"

De Luca rubs the palm of his hand over the black stubble

on his skull. "I'd say so. But I'd still like more on Kume before we jump to that conclusion. Like maybe he's got a criminal record in Singapore or Japan."

"The Japanese are part of the Visa Waiver Program, so he wouldn't have had to organize a visa in Singapore," I say.

"So no criminal check over there."

"Exactly." I scroll down Rodriguez's e-mail. "He claimed he was entering the States as a tourist, and listed his return date as January 1. He listed his occupation as 'self-employed,' he didn't declare anything coming in…no money, no food, no drugs." I manage a small laugh. "But he wasn't searched."

"He looked and acted like a well-presented businessman from Japan," Ramos says. "Probably nothing to trigger alarm bells with customs."

"Exactly." I turn to him. "I was thinking of swinging by Lincoln Plaza on the way home. Kume's hotel room might give me an insight into our victim." Victimology is one of the most important elements when constructing an offender profile. Without extensive information on the victim, it's hard to extrapolate details about the offender.

"Where do you live?" he asks me.

"Westwood."

"Way home?" He raises an eyebrow. Monterey Park is in the opposite direction to Westwood.

I shrug. "It's not very far."

"At this hour? Don't know if you're dedicated or crazy." Ramos smiles. "However, Monterey Park really is on my way home. We can sit fender to fender."

"Sounds like you guys are in for a fun night." De Luca stands up. "That's all I need for now. Keep me posted and we'll see where this thing takes us."

Ramos and I both stand and gather our things and then De Luca leads us back to the elevator.

"Nice to meet you, Agent Anderson." He shakes my hand. "And you, Detective Ramos." As the elevator arrives, De Luca disappears.

Once the elevator doors close, Ramos says, "That was quick."

"Yeah. I guess DEA isn't taking it over."

"Not yet, at least."

Ramos and I don't caravan—it would be impossible to keep him in my sights on the freeway during peak hour with cars constantly lane-hopping. When I arrive at the Lincoln Plaza Hotel, he's managed to get a spot directly opposite the main entrance and is leaning on his car. The next open space is nearly a block away.

When I get back to the hotel, Ramos is still leaning on his car. "What kept you?"

I smile. "You only got here a couple minutes before me." No way it could have been more than that.

He grins and pushes himself off the car.

The Lincoln Plaza Hotel is a cream building, and while the entrance is at the base of a single story, to the right the hotel extends upward six. The doors open automatically, but Ramos gestures "after you." Always the gentleman. The foyer has an old-world style to it, with beige marble floors, square columns and a couple of elaborate chandeliers scattered in between downlights. We cross to the reception, both reaching for our IDs.

"We're here to look at Jo Kume's room," Ramos says. "Detective Ramos, LAPD, and this is Special Agent Anderson, FBI."

"Yes, your colleagues are up there now. Room 412." She hesitates. "Do you think it'll be much longer? It's just—" she lowers her voice "—I've already had a few guests ask me about the police presence. It doesn't look good, you know?"

"I understand." Ramos nods. "We'll be as fast as we can, ma'am, but we need to look over the room thoroughly."

She nods, but also sighs. "Okay." She points to the far wall. "The elevators are over there. Take a right at the fourth floor, and room 412 is down the end."

"I wonder what made our vic choose this hotel?" I muse out loud as we wait for the lift.

"You're right. It's not exactly close to Long Beach."

Ramos pauses. "Little Tokyo's only a couple of miles away. Maybe he just wanted to feel close to home."

"Maybe. But there are hotels right in Little Tokyo if he was looking for the home-away-from-home experience."

The elevator arrives and Ramos holds his arm across the doors while I walk in. "So you're thinking something or someone drew him to Monterey Park?"

"It's one possibility."

The fourth-floor corridor is lined with patterned, dark burgundy carpet. At the end of the corridor, a man with *LAPD* in big yellow letters on his vest kneels down, dusting the last door frame for prints. Once we're closer, he looks up. "Detective Ramos. Hey." He stands up and arches his back, stretching.

"Hi, Kowoski. How's it coming along?"

"Another hour and we should be done."

Ramos nods. "Great." He looks at me. "Agent Anderson, this is Ian Kowoski. Kowoski, this is Agent Anderson from the Bureau."

Kowoski's wearing gloves, so he gives me a wave rather than shaking hands. I return the gesture and follow Ramos as he enters the hotel room.

Kume had booked himself into one of the Lincoln Plaza's suites, which includes a small living room.

"What have you got, Jackson?"

A tall African-American in his mid-twenties moves from the window toward us. After Ramos introduces Jackson as another homicide detective, Jackson flips open his notebook.

"Jo Kume checked into the hotel at 4:00 p.m. on November 24. He booked online only three days before arriving and was paid up through until January 1. He paid with a credit card, VISA, and I've organized a search on transactions. No special requests, no room service, no phone calls. I showed the desk clerk on duty Kume's picture and she recognized him. Apparently he did have an accent, but his English was perfect. I've got the names of all the other desk clerks to interview them, too, but the woman on duty said he didn't talk much." Jackson looks up at the corner desk. "Newman's looking over the computer before taking it back to the lab."

We all move toward the laptop, which should give us e-mails and Internet usage, plus whatever files might be stored on the hard drive.

Again, Ramos introduces me, before Newman gives us an update. "Everything looks in order, but I'll still copy the hard drive and run a few tests in the lab tomorrow before I boot it up, just to be on the safe side." He slips the laptop into a large plastic evidence bag and then into another padded bag.

"Nothing for us tonight?" I ask.

Newman glances at Ramos, then me.

"I told Newman not to worry about it until morning. Nothing time critical in this case."

Ramos is right. My request is based on my own desire to get the case moving, and blatant curiosity. "Sure. Sorry."

Newman swings the padded laptop back over his shoulder. "Good." He smiles. "I've got dinner plans. But first thing tomorrow…"

"Thanks."

Newman says goodbye to the other crime-scene techs before heading off.

I look around the room and cross my arms. "So we wait."

Ramos chuckles. "You're not good at waiting, are you?"

I smile. "Am I that transparent?"

"Uh-huh." He checks his watch. "It's seven-thirty, Anderson. Go home, relax. Go out."

I give him a weak smile. Truth is, my social life's pretty much nonexistent here in L.A. Apart from the occasional dinner or drinks with Melissa or Mercedes, I'm a hermit. Besides, I've got the Santorini profile to finish off tonight and that'll keep me busy for at least two hours.

"Me," Ramos says, walking toward the door, "I'm going home to my wife and kids. They may even have waited for me for dinner."

He turns to Jackson. "You okay to finish up here?"

"Sure thing."

I can tell by Jackson's age and eagerness that he's new to Homicide and keen to please the more senior detective—Ramos.

Being at crime scenes is the best way to learn.

Seven

As usual, I'm at the office before 8:00 a.m., having already done a thirty-minute jog and fifteen minutes of stretching, despite waking up exhausted. I was working on the arcade-murder profile until midnight last night, giving me less than six hours' sleep…that's going to hurt. I prefer something around the eight-hour mark, especially when my days are so busy. I could have finished the profile and been tucked up in bed much earlier, except my train of thought was interrupted by a phone call from my mum in Melbourne. She was in the mood to chat and I didn't have the heart—or courage—to tell her I was working at nine-thirty at night. I'd never hear the end of it.

First thing on my agenda this morning is Interpol. We need to gather as much information as we can on our Japanese victim, who may have been living in Singapore. It's not the first time I've had to deal with the US Bureau of Interpol—when AmericanPsycho fled the country I contacted them immediately. Unfortunately we couldn't alert the French police in time for him to be intercepted at the Paris airport, but I check in with the US Bureau and the head office in France every now and again. One time we managed to get through the many layers of high-tech security he sets up and traced one of his online flower orders to an Internet café in Paris. But he'd made sure cameras in the area were out for an hour on either side of the online order and our knowledge that he was there was useless, although it did confirm my suspicions that he was still in Paris.

My contact at the Washington, D.C. office is Latoya Burges. I look up her direct line in Outlook and punch in the number.

"Hey, Latoya. It's Agent Sophie Anderson."

"Hey, Sophie. What's up? Any more contact from our friend?"

"Just the usual." As much as I'd like to ignore the monthly red rose that he sends my way, it's impossible.

"I see."

I change the subject. "We've got ourselves a Japanese homicide vic here in L.A. I was hoping you could help."

"Sure. What you got?"

"His name, passport details and fingerprints. And we know he flew in from Singapore."

"I'll look him up. Shoot."

I read out the information.

"Hold on a sec."

I hear typing in the background.

"No criminal record coming up. Nothing on a Jo Kume in our database. But I'll place a call to our Singapore and Japanese offices later today and get a full file together for you."

"That'd be great. Thanks." I pause. "How long do you think it'll take?"

"Should only be a day or two, honey. But we've also got to factor in the time difference."

I do the calculation in my head. If memory serves me right, Singapore is three hours behind Melbourne. So given it's 8:00 a.m. here, it's midnight in Singapore. It'll be at least another eight hours before anyone even sees my request. "No worries. I'll e-mail you his prints, too. Maybe you'll come up with a hit on those, or Singapore or Japan will. Can you call me on my cell if you get something?"

"Sure thing, honey."

Next on my list is the offender profile for Santorini's murder. It feels good to finally have it done. The past few weeks it's almost felt as though I've had the boy's death hanging over my head in some way. But I know that's just me losing my sense of objectivity—a common struggle for me when it comes to victims, especially the young ones. I read over the profile and add a few finishing touches before sending it through to the requesting officer in LAPD, and CC'ing George Rosen.

I've profiled Santorini's killer as someone he knew, possibly quite well. There's something very personal about the blitz-style attack, a case of a youth who was angry with the victim and lost control. I doubt he intended to kill James Santorini, but that's meaningless. The killer will have a history of anger management issues, and is most likely someone from Santorini's school or part of a shared club or group. It's also possible the killer is a family member, although not immediate—perhaps a cousin. Despite my initial thoughts that the murder could be linked to gangs, I've now ruled that out. The attack was personal and the work of only one perpetrator. Presumably the LAPD will act on the profile, going back through all the statements they took from Santorini's school and other networks, or maybe starting in these areas again.

I'm going over Kume's crime-scene photos again when my speakers chirp with the arrival of an e-mail. It's from the forensic pathologist Lloyd Grove and the subject line reads *Racial background of Little Tokyo victim*. Even though we now know the victim is Japanese, I click on the e-mail.

After I've read it, I immediately dial Ramos's cell. "Ramos, Anderson. You seen Grove's e-mail yet?"

"No. I'm actually with Newman and our vic's laptop at the moment."

"Oh, cool," I say, excited by the prospect of getting the guy's computer history.

"What's the e-mail say?"

"That our vic is half Korean and half Japanese, with a bit of Chinese heritage thrown in, too."

"Really? So not just Japanese."

"No. I've already been on the phone to Interpol this

morning, but I'll give them a call back and ask them to expand their search to Korea and maybe even China, too, just in case."

"Great."

"It will take a couple of days, though. So what's up with Kume's computer?"

"It's looking good, Anderson. Newman said Kume hasn't even tried to hide anything on his laptop, so we've got e-mails, Internet history, favorites, everything. We're starting with financials and we've managed to trace regular transfers from a Singapore bank to a GCE account here in the States. It came out of a business account Kume had under the name Best Enterprises."

"Really? Drug payments? Blackmail?"

"All possible. Newman's not sure yet whether we'll have to get a warrant for GCE to release the account holder's details or if he'll be able to get a name from the computer records. See how we go in the next few hours."

"Things are looking up," I say. Sometimes cases crawl along, and other times the snowball effect of evidence and information can make it hard to keep up. But I always prefer the snowball cases. Makes our jobs easier and generally leads to a better outcome—the bad guy in prison sooner. Just the way I like my murder cases.

"We've come a long way from a John Doe yesterday," Ramos comments.

"We sure have."

Once I've said goodbye and hung up, I call Latoya and ask her to expand the search to Korea and China, given our vic's heritage.

"Can do on South Korea, but not with North Korea or China. They're not part of the Interpol program. The best I can do is try to contact their federal police, but I can't guarantee anything. To be honest, I doubt either country will be interested in helping us out."

"Okay." I sigh. With the world getting smaller, we need as much international cooperation as we can get. But given it can be hard enough getting all the US law-enforcement agencies working together, it's not that surprising that the world is a lot to ask. I thank her once again before hanging up and moving back to the crime-scene photos and reports.

It's still too early to draft an offender profile—I don't know enough about the vic yet—but I am starting to get a feeling for our killer. He's orderly…methodical. He picked the crime scene well, an isolated location within a busy section of a big city, cased it and eliminated the potential danger of the parking lot's lights. Then he lured Jo Kume to the parking lot and killed him using a weapon that an experienced forensic pathologist hasn't been able to trace.

By the time I've gone over the case file another two times, my sense of achievement has vanished. Despite all our inroads into the victim's identity and actions, I get the feeling this killer is going to be hard to catch. He's planned the murder exceedingly well!

I sigh, and check my watch—1:00 p.m. I've still got two hours before the division-heads meeting at 3:00 p.m. While I could continue revising the case details, I decide to concentrate on my vision of someone getting shot. If it's related to Kume's murder, maybe it means his killer has murdered before and his handiwork could be in ViCAP. The Violent Criminal Apprehension Program runs a national online database into which law-enforcement professionals from all around the US can enter details about violent crimes. Problem is, if my vision's right and a past or future victim of the killer's is shot, that'll be useless to plug into ViCAP— I'd get thousands upon thousands of shooting victims coming up. That's not going to work. I could, however, do a search on the throat wound. Maybe our killer has struck before using the same weapon…whatever it is.

I open up the ViCAP software on my computer and do a search across all US states, with the cause of death as throat wounds. With no other variables like victim race, sex, age, signature or keywords plugged into the system, I get lots of results—four hundred and twelve, to be precise. And here I was thinking I had time up my sleeve. Trying to work in my dream, I narrow the search down by adding gunshot wound to the injuries. This time, I only get thirty-five results. So there are thirty-five victims who were shot and experienced some sort of throat wound. I open up the first entry, only to find the person was shot in the throat. It could be a long two hours…

I'm still scanning through the results when my computer gives me the second meeting reminder—it's 3:00 p.m. I flip my notebook over to a fresh page and grab my BlackBerry, before scurrying to the boardroom. I walk in just as Brady kicks the meeting off.

Sitting around the boardroom table are the division heads; Brady's direct reports, like me; some of the unit heads, like Petrov; and Melissa, who takes the minutes. The L.A. field office has four main divisions. Counterterrorism led by Brad Jones, Criminal headed by George Rosen, Counterintelligence led by Sandy Peters and Cyber Crime headed by Ed Garcia. In addition, it's got programs in white-collar crime, civil rights and organized crime, including gang-related activities, and at least one person from each area is at the meeting. Except for Melissa, all the attendees are much higher up in the food chain than I am, but it's useful if I'm aware of all the cases and on hand to give my opinion from a behavioral perspective.

Brady asks for Ed Garcia's update first. Garcia has a team of computer specialists who work under him, focusing on any use of the Internet for criminal activities. It could be online credit-card scams, identity theft, money laundering or simply checking out the computer of a suspect, but most of his team is devoted to stopping the proliferation of online child pornography. With pedophiles able to download illegal photos and videos with the click of a mouse, and the World Wide Web as big as it is, it's a massive area to police.

I take notes as we move around the table, and then give everyone a very brief update of my cases, focusing on my top priority, the Little Tokyo murder.

We're almost done when my BlackBerry rings. Damn, forgot to switch it to Silent. "Sorry, I'm waiting on a few calls." I take my notebook and pencil and slip out. I answer softly, aware that I've already disrupted the meeting.

"Hey, it's Latoya. I've got something real interesting for you, honey. I got a match on those prints of yours, but not under Jo Kume. The name I got coming up is Jun Saito."

That is big news—although if our vic was a drug dealer it's not surprising he'd have fake ID, fake documents.

"Does the name ring a bell?" she asks.

"No." I bring my notebook up to the wall. "Can you spell it please, Latoya."

"Sure. *J-U-N S-A-I-T-O.*"

"Don't suppose you know if that's a Japanese name?"

"Now you're testing me, honey."

I smile. "Okay, thanks again, Latoya."

"I'll let you know when I hear something from Singapore, Japan or South Korea. I've already asked them to get back to me on both names—Jo Kume and Jun Saito."

"Thanks." Once I've hung up, I switch my BlackBerry to Silent and try to slip as quietly as possible back into the meeting. Sandy Peters, the head of Counterintelligence, is talking when I enter. I take my seat and place my notebook back on the table.

But the meeting's disrupted again when Pasha Petrov suddenly says, "Does that say Jun Saito?" He points at the large letters scrawled diagonally across my notebook.

Peters stops midsentence and everyone looks at Petrov and me.

"Um, yeah," I say hesitantly. "Turns out Interpol had a match on the fingerprints of our Little Tokyo victim, but under the name Jun Saito."

"Holy crap!"

"What's the problem, Petrov?" Brady asks.

Petrov puts his face in his hands. "Are you sure this is your Little Tokyo victim? That this guy's dead?"

"It's a computerized fingerprint match against Interpol's database verified by a specialist. It must be right."

He rubs his hands in his face. "It's going to be war."

"Spill it, Petrov," Brady demands. "And so it makes sense for the rest of us."

Petrov drops his hands on the table and looks at Brady.

"You've got to know your organized crime history." He sighs. "If this is who I think it is…" He shakes his head. "Some idiot's killed the son and only living male heir of Hisayuki Saito."

"We need a bit more enlightening, Petrov," Brady says.

"Hisayuki Saito was born in Korea in 1923, when it was occupied by the Japanese. He started off as a street hood, but he took advantage of the Japanese occupation and joined the Yakuza. Later he moved to Japan and became the first Korean Yakuza godfather. The guy only retired a few years ago, and died last year. Nowadays there's a whole Korean subculture in the Yakuza, and Saito was the founding father. So, if the Jun Saito who's lying in the morgue was the only remaining son of Hisayuki Saito, this is a big hit. Especially given Jun Saito's been missing for fifteen years, presumed dead."

"Hit?" I say. Despite the staging elements, it hadn't occurred to me that this could be a hit. I'm suddenly struck by the dispassion I felt from the killer. He got no real joy from it, it was a job. And no wonder he had the presence of mind to take out the light, and so easily. Besides, staging a crime scene to look like something it's not is characteristic behavior of a contract killer. "You're talking a professional hit man."

"Whoever did this would have wanted someone outside of their organization to execute Saito. So yeah, they would have called in a professional."

"He wasn't shot," I say, referring to the fact that most professional assassins shoot their victims, unless they're trying to make the death look like an accident. "The coroner can't work out what sort of weapon was used." I voice these details, but immediately want to race back to my desk and enter the throat wound into ViCAP, on its own this time and with a cross-reference of organized crime.

"We need to talk about the MO after this meeting. I may recognize it," Petrov says.

"Sure."

Petrov continues. "The most surprising thing about this murder is that by all accounts Jun Saito wasn't active in the

Yakuza anymore. He disappeared fifteen years ago. Some people said he rejected his family's past and went straight, starting a new life. But most felt he was at the bottom of the Sea of Japan."

Back to my romanticized version of the vic's past—he did straighten up. "Are there pictures of this guy on file? Have you seen him?"

"Only a few shots. Mostly from fifteen to twenty years ago." He shakes his head. "I guess I should have recognized him."

"People change a lot in fifteen years, Petrov," Brady says.

"Plus Grove said he'd had a nose job," I add. "That'd alter his appearance, too."

Petrov shrugs, still taking it a little personally. "So you said yesterday that he was seen entering a suspected meth lab in Long Beach, run by the Asian Boyz?"

"Uh-huh."

"What the heck's he doing there? After all this time?" Petrov rubs his face again. "What a mess. I hate to think of the repercussions."

"Payback?" Brady says.

"I'd say so." Petrov looks at me. "Saturday night wasn't it?"

"Early hours Sunday morning. The body was discovered just before five."

"And it's Wednesday afternoon now. They usually retaliate fast, which means they either don't know he's dead yet or they haven't identified who was responsible."

"By *they* you mean the Yakuza?"

"That's another problem. Who is a big question. Could be an internal hit. Someone from within the Yakuza. Or maybe the Japanese Yakuza is sending a message about Korean involvement in their organization." He pauses. "Or it could be another group entirely, one of the Yakuza's rivals, like one of the Chinese triads. Although I haven't heard of any turf problems." He shrugs. "Damn, it could even be the Russians."

"And how is the Yakuza tied to the Asian Boyz?" I ask.

"Lots of organized crime operations use gangs and gang members for some of their work. The Yakuza has ties with a few Asian gangs, so it's probably just a case of the Asian Boyz being right for the job. And they've got an arm down in Long Beach near the port."

"So the Yakuza could be the client and the Asian Boyz the freelancer."

"Exactly. And the Yakuza could be the buyer or distributor in Japan and other Asian countries if they are exporting."

After a few seconds, Brady's voice cuts through the short silence. "Right." He stands up, his voice commanding. "What do you need, Petrov? Who's going to have jurisdiction?"

Another interesting question…LAPD, the LASD, the DEA, the ATF and the FBI. Then there's the Los Angeles City Attorney's Gang Unit, which works with all agencies across the city to apprehend and prosecute gang criminals.

"I'll let L.A.'s gang law-enforcement personnel across all agencies and task forces know about this development immediately. Maybe one of our informants can point us in the right direction." He stops, obviously considering his options. "I'd like to make sure this is interagency, so we should run it out of the Safe Streets program, and specifically the Los Angeles Gang Impact Team. We'll consult with the City Attorney's Gang Unit, but I definitely want federal charges, not felony." Petrov rubs his jaw. "If we run it out of Safe Streets we'll be taking the lead, but I'll make sure all parties are in the loop."

Brady nods his approval. All the political *t*'s and *i*'s should be crossed and dotted with Petrov's approach. "Don't forget the CLEAR Program, too."

Petrov nods.

The CLEAR Program, which stands for Community Law Enforcement and Recovery, is another interagency task force in L.A., another player. The US is a big country, with a correspondingly large number of different agencies and task forces, which can make life much more complicated than law enforcement in Australia. It was overwhelming at first, but I think I'm getting the hang of it now.

Petrov looks at me. "We'll need to all work together on this."

"Sure," I reply. "What about the US Attorney's Office?" Getting a federal prosecutor involved early will help ensure the case is as watertight as possible.

"We have representatives from the US Attorney's Office and the District Attorney's Office on the Gang Impact Team."

"Great." I remember Ramos. "What about Detective Ramos? Will he still be on this?"

Petrov glances at Brady, who nods, before saying, "If his captain okays it he should stay put. Anderson, you'll work with Petrov and Ramos on this—full-time. It's a good opportunity for you to get a firsthand insight into L.A.'s gangs and organized crime."

I agree with Brady—it's a great opportunity for professional development in an area I'll clearly need in the future. Although it's certainly throwing me in the deep end. While homicide isn't that uncommon within the ranks of organized crime or gangs, targeting a high-level member, or in this case a significant figure in the history of the Yakuza, sends out warning signals to law enforcement. It's not surprising that Petrov is worried about retaliation—this could turn into a bloodbath.

Eight

Petrov and I grab a small meeting room and I take him through the case file in detail, paying particular attention to last night's developments.

"Detective Ramos organized a team to process the hotel room and so far the biggest find was a laptop. A computer tech is looking at it today, having already found records of payments to a US bank account."

Petrov raises an eyebrow. "Any name on the account?"

"Not yet. Ramos was hoping to either get a name from the computer today, or organize a warrant for the bank to release the account holder's name to us." I look at my watch. "I'm surprised I haven't heard back from him yet."

"You wanna call him now?"

"Yeah. I haven't had a chance to tell him our vic's real name yet, either." I feel bad about sitting on this knowledge for twenty minutes without updating Ramos, but since I found out, it's been a whirlwind of revelations. I dial Ramos's number on the meeting-room phone and he picks up after one ring.

"I've got news…big news," I say.

"Shoot."

"Turns out Jo Kume is an alias for Jun Saito."

Before I get to follow the ID up with the even bigger news, he says, "Alias?"

"Yup. I've got Special Agent Pasha Petrov with me and I've started taking him through the case notes in detail." I press the speakerphone button. "You're on speakerphone now. It turns out Jun Saito was high up in the Tokyo Yakuza fifteen years ago, but then disappeared."

Ramos whistles down the phone. "And I thought it was big with drugs, the DEA and the Asian Boyz involved. This is huge."

"You better believe it," Petrov says and then introduces himself.

"I was just taking Agent Petrov through what we've got so far from the hotel room. Any updates?"

"You got my message?"

"No." But a glance at my BlackBerry tells me I've had one missed call—it's still on Silent.

"We've got a name for that bank account. Monthly payments of two thousand dollars were being paid to a Mee Kim."

"Going back how far?"

"Just over a year."

"You got anything on this Mee Kim yet, Detective Ramos?" Petrov asks.

"Uh-huh. And guess where she lives, Anderson?"

"Monterey Park." I fill in the blank. That's the reason Saito chose a hotel there. "Maybe he was trying to find his blackmailer, put a stop to it."

"Perhaps he did find the blackmailer." Petrov taps his notebook with his pen.

"I gotta say, Mee Kim doesn't read like the blackmailing type," Ramos says. "Although maybe the Bureau's database will bring back more info on Mee Kim than ours."

"What have you found so far?" I flick the ring on my little finger, wondering what Saito could have been blackmailed over.

"Mee Kim is a twenty-six-year-old high-school teacher. No criminal record and a spotless driving record, too." Ramos pauses. "And she looks kinda sweet to me."

Ramos has the benefit of looking at a driver's license photo.

"We'll see what we can find on her this end, get a full file together." Petrov takes charge. "In the meantime, I think we should pay Mee Kim a visit."

"You read my mind," Ramos says.

Petrov glances at his watch. "Let's meet at her home at five-thirty. What's the address, Ramos?"

"Twenty forty-one Bleakwood Avenue, Monterey Park."

Petrov and I both write the address down. When Petrov's finished he looks up and leans toward the phone. "We'll need to present all this information to the L.A. Gang Impact Team ASAP. I'll set it up for 8:00 a.m. tomorrow and let you guys brief the team. Ramos, we'd like to keep you and Anderson on the case full-time, but we've got other specialized resources available if your captain wants to reassign you or anyone else from your team."

"I want in. But I don't know about the others. You think this could be a long-running case?"

"There are going to be lots of layers, so yeah, it's possible. Maybe even probable."

Ramos sighs. "I'll see what I can do. My boss might give me four weeks, but probably no one else. LAPD's got specialized officers for this." He seems disappointed by the prospect of having to hand the case over. "So where's this 8:00 a.m. meeting?"

"We'll hold it here, at the L.A. Gang Impact Team headquarters on level fifteen."

"You guys won't have far to walk." He gives a little chuckle.

"No." I use a small pause in the conversation to hit Ramos up. "So, you wanna do the briefing, Ramos?" Generally I brief on an offender profile, so given I don't have a profile yet, handballing the job to Ramos isn't out of order.

"Sure."

"We've still gotta figure out why Saito came to L.A.," Petrov says. "Has he been secretly involved in the Yakuza all this time and needed to come to the States to sort out his L.A. enterprise? Or was it a one-off deal? Or is blackmail the reason behind his visit? Did someone force him out of hiding?"

I flash back to my vision of Saito in his car—presumably in Singapore. Someone called him and whatever they told him made him take action, made him get on a plane to L.A. But his reactions fit both possibilities; he could have found out something was going wrong in L.A. in terms of the drug business, something he felt he had to handle personally, or he could have been told something that required him to reacquaint himself with his old life. Maybe the blackmailer was upping the ante and Saito decided he'd had enough.

"Hopefully Mee Kim can give us some answers," I say.

"Yes." Petrov changes the topic. "What airline did he come in on?"

"Singapore Airlines."

Petrov scribbles in his notebook. "Let's call the airline and see when Saito booked that flight. It might be useful down the track to know when he organized the trip."

"I'll do that." I write the task down on my new to-do list, underneath searching ViCAP for homicides with similar MOs. "I can give them a quick call before we head off to see Mee Kim. See if they'll give us flight information without a warrant. Although I also want to do a ViCAP search—maybe our hit man's struck in the US before."

"I don't recognize the MO or cause of death from any of the organized crime files, but that's not to say you won't find something in another state, or something going back before my time."

"True." This case is different from most homicides, in which most of our focus is on who committed the crime. This time we have to work out how the Yakuza and Asian Boyz are involved, to see if Saito's murder is about more than the death of one individual. The possibilities are endless.

"Okay," says Petrov, "let's get this moving. I'll come by your desk to collect you in ten minutes." He nods to me. "And we'll meet you at Mee Kim's address, Detective Ramos."

"Sure thing."

"That'll only give me time for the call to the airline or the ViCAP search." I'm not complaining, just making sure Petrov realizes the repercussions.

"I'll get one of my people to call Singapore Airlines," Ramos offers. "May as well make them work for their lousy pay grade today, given it'll probably be their last day on the case once I speak to Captain Booth."

"Great, thanks, Ramos." The day's disappearing, and fast. Any help is appreciated.

When Petrov and I pull up at 2041 Bleakwood Avenue, Ramos's car is already parked out front. One side of Bleakwood Avenue is single-fronted homes, and the other side is a baseball field, part of the East Los Angeles College.

Ramos gets out of his car and walks toward us and I notice his holster is unclipped. He's ready for anything. "Any luck with ViCAP?" he asks as I'm opening my car door.

"I need more time, but on the surface nothing like our vic's throat wound came up. I'm going to do a couple more searches tomorrow, using other variables."

"Such as?"

"Hit man, Asian victim, organized crime…" With several search terms, hopefully the results won't be too unwieldy.

Ramos nods, then looks at the house, which is a white-brick single-fronted number, with a perfectly manicured but small garden. "No movement, but I've only been here for five minutes."

The grass is cut extremely short, and a few shrubs, pruned into perfect globes or rectangles, line a garden bed that runs along the front of the house. A narrow concrete entrance path divides the lawn in two, and ends at the one small step that leads onto the house's tiny porch. A small palm plant, the only unpruned plant in sight, fans from the left-hand side of the path onto the porch.

Petrov joins me and Ramos on the curb, and takes his gun out. "It's not a known Yakuza or other organized crime residence. Or gang, for that matter."

I look at him, curious as to how he knows this.

"While you were doing your ViCAP search I was checking out this address." He nods toward the house. "I got our IT people to check it in their databases. Nothing sinister…that we know of."

Despite the lack of a known criminal element, Petrov does have his gun out. At this stage, Kim's a big unknown. She could be the mistress of a key figure in organized crime who has somehow stayed off the radar until today.

I draw my weapon, too, but both Petrov and I hold our guns loosely at our sides. Ramos leaves his gun in its holster, but rests his right hand on its butt as we climb the one step to the porch. We ring the doorbell.

Petrov whispers. "Montebello High School is her current employer. They did the standard criminal record and Live Scan check five years ago when they hired her."

In California, all public school employees have to undergo a criminal check, including a fingerprint search, as part of their job application. It's a small but essential step in protecting children. If Mee Kim is still working as a schoolteacher, there's a chance she'll be home already. But when no one answers after a few minutes and another two rings, we decide to sit in Petrov's car and wait it out.

"You updated Joe?" Petrov asks.

Ramos and I both shake our heads.

"May as well fill him in now." Petrov fishes out his cell phone and hits two buttons before putting the phone up to his ear. Obviously De Luca rates a speed dial.

The phone call is brief, with Petrov summarizing the recent developments before suggesting De Luca goes home early to see his kids. Again, even though the call is short, the reference to De Luca's home life makes me think he and Petrov are close.

Petrov flips his phone shut. "Done." He looks at his watch. "So who wants to get the coffee?"

Ramos and I both look at him uncertainly.

"I'm joking." He smiles. "We'll wait until at least six-thirty before we go for a caffeine fix."

Nine

At 6:30 p.m., just as we're about to cave and head off on a coffee run, a silver two-door pulls into the driveway. The movement triggers the outside light and from our position I can just make out that the driver is female, with long dark hair. I'll need more light and a front view before I can distinguish her exact hair color and see whether she's Asian.

Once her engine's off, she leans over the center console and straightens up with a large tote bag slung over her right shoulder. The driver door opens and she swings her legs out. She's wearing a skirt that sits just above the knees, coupled with what looks like a silk blouse from the way it moves and falls around her upper body as she gets out of the car.

"We gonna wait until she's inside?" Ramos asks.

I'm not sure who he's asking. I guess Petrov is in charge as the one who's part of the task force, albeit as a consultant, and as a senior-ranking FBI agent.

"When she's at the door."

The woman leans into the car and takes a suit jacket off the back of the driver's seat before shutting and locking the car. Moving along the path, she flicks through her keys.

As her foot hits the top of her porch step, Petrov swings open his door. "Ms. Kim?"

She turns and looks our way, as Petrov moves closer. She

seems hesitant at first, but then sees me and relaxes a little. Petrov hasn't identified himself yet, and a lone male coming toward a woman in the dark is ominous.

We walk down the pathway and now I can make out that the sporty coupe is a Hyundai Tiburon. And it looks pretty new.

"I'm Special Agent Petrov with the FBI." He moves to the porch with Ramos and I close behind. By the time we get to the step, Petrov is showing Ms. Kim his ID. "And this is Special Agent Anderson and Detective Ramos with the LAPD."

She's obviously surprised by our presence. "Yes?"

"If you've got a moment, we'd like to talk to you inside." Petrov motions to the front door.

"Um…okay," she says, but takes another, closer look at Petrov's ID before unlocking the door. Swinging it open, she invites us in before placing her bag on a peg. "Is everything okay?"

"We'd just like to ask you a few routine questions for an investigation." Petrov's eyes dart around her house, taking it in.

We're still standing in the hallway, but from here you can see an open-plan living area through into the kitchen on the left, and a more formal dining area to the right. The house has been meticulously renovated inside, with polished floorboards, plush cream rugs and modern furniture. It's also been tastefully painted and decorated, with contrasting colors on the walls. Either Ms. Kim has a very good eye for color, or she paid an interior designer to coordinate everything. From the doorway I can only just make out the kitchen, but I see lots of stainless steel, cream cupboards and a warm shade of mushroom-gray on the walls.

"Is this about one of my students?" Kim seems concerned.

"No." Petrov doesn't elaborate. After a few beats, he says, "Can we sit down?"

"Sure. Sorry." Kim leads us into the living room and we all take a seat on the black, modern couches. She springs back up within a couple of seconds. "Sorry…can I get you anything? A glass of water? Coffee?"

Ah…our coffee run.

We all say yes to coffee and she moves into the kitchen.

"Your home is beautiful, Ms. Kim. Have you always lived here?" I ask.

"Yes. My *omma,* mom, and I lived here together until a year ago." Kim looks up. "Until she died."

"Sorry for your loss." Ramos's voice holds genuine sympathy, enough that I don't see a need to echo his condolences. Instead, I stand up and start snooping. Petrov and Ramos stay seated, realizing that this is a job best left to one person. Mee Kim can see us through the kitchen bench that borders the open-plan living area and looking up to see all three of us peering at her photos and belongings might not go down so well.

The room is sparsely furnished, with only two areas of interest—a small bookshelf and a matching ornamental stand that forms gridlike shelving that can house photos, vases, statues or any other bits and pieces. The bookshelf contains mostly novels, but on the bottom shelf Mee Kim also has, to my surprise, several books on martial arts.

"You're into martial arts?" I ask her.

She leans over the kitchen bench. "Yes. I've trained in many of them, actually."

Again, interesting. Why would a schoolteacher need to be skilled in hand-to-hand combat? Then again, I know from my own kung fu class that the students come from all walks of life. Some are driven by self-defense, some use it as a more interesting form of exercise than pounding the pavement or pumping iron, while others are captivated by its Eastern origins.

"I study kung fu." I offer some personal information to help relax her and maybe make a connection with her. "Which is your favorite discipline?" I push myself off my haunches, back to standing.

She smiles. "Guess I should say kung fu, huh?"

"Not at all. Unless that is your favorite."

"Well, I'm Korean so I have focused more on tae kwon do."

I nod. Kung fu originated in China and Hong Kong, tae kwon do in Korea and karate in Japan, and within each discipline there are different styles.

"Are you taking classes at the moment?" I ask.

"Yeah, three times a week. And I practice most mornings before work."

"So you're dedicated. What level are you on?"

"Fifth dan."

"Wow. I'm studying for my third."

"What's that mean?" Ramos asks.

"There are nine levels of black belt in kung fu," I explain, "called dans."

"And it's the same in tae kwon do," Kim adds.

"Whatta ya know. I thought it was just black belt. And even that sounds pretty impressive."

"The black belts are when it really starts getting hard. Ms. Kim here is two levels above me, but that's about an extra four to six years of training."

Ramos lets out a long whistle. "I'm impressed."

Kim blushes and busies herself with the coffee. "Thanks," she manages.

I move on to the shelving area. There are a few photos of Mee Kim growing up, starting from when she was about four years old. In most of the pictures she's by herself, although there are two that show her and her mother. Looks like Mee Kim was an only child, and maybe mum was widowed, divorced or single from the outset. I also notice the absence of grandparents in Mee's life—or at least the life she likes to remember. The only photo that doesn't feature Mee is on the top left shelf. Here sits an older photo of her mother, and I can tell by the clothes and hairstyle that the picture was taken in the seventies.

"You look like your mum," I say.

"Yeah, I know." Kim pours cream into a small jug, completing the setup of a tray with four cups, a cream jug and a sugar bowl.

I can see the coffeemaker in the background, and it's half-full.

With everything ready, she moves back into the living space. "So, what's all this about?" She delivers the line politely.

I take my seat again and Kim follows suit.

Petrov fishes a head shot of Jun Saito out of his inside suit pocket. "Do you recognize this man?" The shot is cropped so it doesn't show Saito's throat wound.

Kim takes the photo and flinches at the image. "Is he…is he dead?" The closed eyes and gray undertones in Saito's skin give his fate away.

"I'm afraid so," I say gently.

She nods and takes a deep breath before looking at the photo more closely. People look different in death, but after a good ten seconds of staring at the photo, she says, "No." She looks up at us. "What happened to him?"

Petrov takes the question. "He was murdered."

"Murdered?"

"Yes."

After a considerable pause, she says, "I'm sorry I can't help you, but I don't recognize him at all. You thought I knew him?"

"Yes." Again, Petrov lets silence hang in the air before continuing. "This man transferred two thousand dollars a month to your GCE bank account, for the past year."

I watch her reaction carefully.

"What? Transferred money? To me?" She shakes her head. "I'm afraid you must be mistaken. I don't know that man." She points to the photo and her confusion seems genuine.

Ramos takes out some folded pieces of paper from his pocket. "The most recent payment was on the first of this month."

She shakes her head again. "I get two thousand dollars on the first of every month from a life-insurance policy my mum set up with a company called Best Enterprises."

We're silent once more.

"I'm sorry, Ms. Kim," I say, "but those payments aren't from an insurance company. They're from this man, Jun Saito."

Again, I watch her reaction carefully. It's the first time

we've mentioned the vic's name. Her face is impassive but she does flick her eyes down to her clasped hands. Breaking eye contact is often body language that accompanies a lie. But in this case, it could also be an expression of her confusion.

"I don't understand. What about Best Enterprises?"

"It's just a shell company Saito set up," I explain. "The payments to you are the only outgoings from that account."

"Do you think your mother knew this man?" Petrov asks.

"I don't know…she certainly never mentioned him." She looks over to the kitchen. "Oh, the coffee. Sorry."

In the kitchen she pours out four coffees, before bringing the tray over to us. We help ourselves to a cup and cream and sugar. Once she's taken her own coffee and is seated again, Petrov continues.

"He's actually of Korean descent, like you. He's half Korean, half Japanese. Are you sure the name Jun Saito doesn't ring a bell?" he presses.

Kim takes a sip of her coffee. "Saito," she repeats. "No, definitely not."

"What about Jo Kume?" I ask. "This man was also known under that alias."

She shakes her head again. "No, sorry."

"Do you have any old photo albums of your mum's? Perhaps she knew him," I suggest.

"*Omma* and her family immigrated here when she was only ten years old. I don't see how she could know this man."

"Probably not," Petrov says. "But if we could flick through any old albums, that would be most helpful to the FBI, ma'am."

She answers Petrov's not-so-subtle guilt trip with a nod. "I'll be back shortly." Putting down her coffee, she walks down the hallway and into the third room on the right. A study or bedroom perhaps. She returns five minutes later with one photo album. "This is all I can find. And I don't remember my mum ever showing me any other photos anyway."

"Only the one album?"

Mee Kim shrugs. "That's all Mum ever showed me. We've got about twenty from the time I was born, but only one from before that."

Petrov holds his hand out and takes the book. He flicks through it quickly, and then shakes his head at us once he's done. "Any other questions, Agent Anderson, Detective Ramos, before we let Ms. Kim get back to her evening?"

"Do you live alone, Ms. Kim?" I ask.

"Yes. But my boyfriend stays over occasionally."

Ramos brings his pen down to his notebook. "And his name?"

"Paul Bailey."

I wonder if the name rings any bells with Petrov. He certainly doesn't respond, keeping his face expressionless. But he's trained to do that.

Petrov stands up, and we follow his lead. He thanks Ms. Kim and gives her his business card, asking her to call him anytime if something comes to her.

I'm the last one out, and at the door I turn back to her. "Ms. Kim, do you mind if I ask about your father?"

She shrugs. "What about him?"

"Is he alive?"

She shakes her head. "He died when my mother was pregnant. Car accident."

"I'm sorry," I say, giving her a two-handed handshake and my card before walking back to the car.

Ramos instinctively climbs into Petrov's car, ready for the debrief. "What do you think?" he asks.

"Seems genuine enough," Petrov responds. "But I'm not convinced she'd never heard of Jun Saito before."

"No," I say. "She did break eye contact when I mentioned Saito's name. It's possible she was trying to hide her response, hide a recollection. And then when you pressed her on it, she took a sip of her coffee right at that moment."

"Mmm… And the flinch when she saw the photo. Could have been recognition rather than distress at seeing someone dead," Ramos offers.

"She's the right age to be Saito's daughter, you know," I say.

"I wondered about that, too." Ramos leans forward in the backseat.

"Well, if that's the case, either she doesn't realize Jun Saito is her Daddy, or she doesn't want us to know."

Petrov starts the engine.

Ten

I sink lower into horse stance, hoping better technique will help me turn the tide. I'm in a dark, secluded alleyway, fighting a man who only appears as a silhouette against the night sky. He's trained, and trained extremely well, and I have to move my arms at lightning speed to defend myself and block each incoming strike.

He lunges forward and turns his waist at the same time, using the momentum to gather extra force for a punch to my rib cage. I can't block it in time and I crumple in pain, but after another strike hits me I fight the pain and concentrate once more on blocking and protecting myself. I manage to block another onslaught of punches, followed by a flying kick, before I see a small opening. I lunge forward and deliver a punch to the man's solar plexus, momentarily winding him. But like me, he quickly resumes the fight, blocking my next strike—a side kick aimed at the ribs and meant to shatter bone. I just manage to withdraw my foot before he grabs it. I need to be faster, stronger, to beat him. I have to face it: he's better than me.

After blocking another series of punches, I process my options—fight or flight. I tried fighting; now it's time to flee. I turn and run, but I can hear him closing in behind me. I urge my legs to go faster, run harder, but they don't respond. I turn a blind corner and come to a dead end.

The man behind me laughs.

I wake up covered in sweat and look around for my attacker. Where am I? That's right…I'm in my bed, in my apartment. I instinctively reach for the gun I keep under the pillow next to me. Gun in hand, I take the safety off, but within a few seconds I shift from dream reality to actual reality. I'm in my apartment, safe. Popping the safety back on, I put the gun on my bedside table and check the time—5:55 a.m., five minutes until my alarm goes off. I flick on the light and can't resist a second look around the room to make sure I'm truly alone.

I think back to the dream and remember running down a dark alleyway with someone behind me, but I can't recall anything else. It's possible the dream is a premonition, or it could just be my subconscious—lots of people dream of being chased. Apparently it's supposed to signify anxiety in your life. Or that you're running away from something or someone. Still, this dream did have the sense of reality that my premonitions usually do…plus I'm covered in sweat, and physical symptoms are also a sign that what I've seen has already happened or will happen in the future. I write down as much of the dream as I can remember. I try to shake the fear and sense of being trapped as I get myself ready for the day and I go through my plan of attack. First off is the task-force meeting and then my ViCAP search.

I get in my twenty-minute pilates workout, some push-ups and a few stretches before eating breakfast and hitting the road. I arrive at the office at 7:40 a.m., giving me time to start my computer and check my e-mails before heading up to the briefing room.

When I arrive, Petrov is already sitting at the front of the room, flipping through his notebook. Next to him sits Agent Joe De Luca and a young Asian woman.

Petrov looks up as I enter. "Anderson."

Once I'm closer, Petrov says, "You met Special Agent De Luca yesterday, and this is Special Agent Hana Kim from the DEA."

I shake De Luca's hand and then turn to Agent Kim and shake her hand. "No relation to Mee Kim?"

"Who?"

"You'll find out all about her in the briefing, Agent Kim." Petrov turns to me. "Agent Kim is Korean, and about thirty percent of Koreans have the last name Kim."

"Oh, I see."

"Yup, there are loads of Kims." She crosses her arms. "I still can't believe that our operation was taking pictures of the son of the legendary Saito." She seems to be genuinely excited by the victim's identity. I probably don't fully appreciate the enormity of the victim's ID, because unlike Petrov, De Luca, Kim and perhaps the rest of L.A., I haven't been living and breathing organized crime and gangs for years.

"Take a seat." Petrov motions to the chair next to Agent Kim.

I put my case file and notebook on the table before sitting down. The room is large and has been set up in typical briefing style with one long table at the front and then single chairs with flip-out desks attached. This is my first time in this particular room, but I guess it's used by the Gang Impact Team and other task forces on a regular basis.

"How many coming in for the briefing?" I ask, looking at the number of seats.

"Thirty."

I nod several times. "Wow."

Petrov extends both arms out, hands up. "What can I say, L.A.'s got a lot of organized crime and gangs."

"Obviously."

"We've got twenty-four people in the L.A. Gang

Impact Team and I've also invited some of our Long Beach counterparts."

When Ramos arrives, I introduce him to Agent Kim before he takes out his flash drive and starts setting up on the laptop. By eight o'clock Ramos is ready to go and the room is full of law-enforcement personnel from FBI, LAPD, LASD, ATF, DEA, Customs, the City Attorney's Office, the D.A. and the US Attorney's Office—enough acronyms to confuse the best of us. Some are in casual clothes, and some wear uniforms or informal attire branded with their agency's logo. There are also a few men and women dressed in suits, and I peg them as the local, state and federal prosecutors. Lawyers always wear suits, right? The Gang Impact Team has been operational for several years, and the task force is well and truly commingled; no one sits in agency cliques.

Petrov kicks off the briefing. "Good morning, everyone. And thanks for your punctuality." Petrov nods at a few of the faces before continuing. "Four days ago a body was found in Little Tokyo, in the parking lot bordered by Second Street, South Los Angeles Drive and South San Pedro Drive. Yesterday, the male victim was identified as one Jun Saito, a forty-five-year-old Japanese national. Saito arrived in the States on November 24, and was caught on film by members of this task force entering what we believe is a Long Beach meth lab. The property in question has been under surveillance for several weeks now and we've made initial links to the Asian Boyz, with several of the males frequenting the house being identified as members of the Long Beach arm of the gang.

"I don't know if any of you have heard the name Saito before, but Jun Saito's death is significant to us not only because of his involvement with the Asian Boyz, but also because he's the son of key Yakuza figure Hisayuki Saito. Hisayuki Saito was the first Korean to make his mark in the Yakuza. Korea was under Japanese rule from 1910 to 1945, and while most Koreans hated their occupiers, Saito embraced the opportunities presented to him, namely becoming part of the Japanese Mafia. He moved to Tokyo and founded one of the Yakuza's most notorious gangs. From 1946 to 1958 he was arrested ten times and although he received three prison sentences, all were minor convictions and his time in prison was limited to less than two years. He was linked to murder, fraud, extortion, prostitution, illegal gambling and the booming meth trade in Tokyo in the fifties.

"Hisayuki Saito married a Japanese woman and had three sons and one daughter. His wife died while giving birth to their fourth child, and while Saito did remarry two years later, he didn't have any more children. His eldest son was killed by the police during a raid, and his second son was murdered a couple of years later.

"Jun, Hisayuki's youngest son, got into trouble early, and his first recorded offence was drug possession at the age of fourteen. For that offence he didn't get jail time but in 1984 he was charged with moving stolen goods and spent four years in prison. From 1988 to 1993 he was suspected of drug trafficking and even linked to a couple of underworld murders, but the police were unable to get any charges to stick. He was also linked to the death of his girlfriend, who was found stabbed to death in the apartment they shared in Tokyo. The last known sighting of Jun Saito was 1993, the night his girlfriend was murdered…until his body turned up in Little Tokyo four days ago."

A petite redhead wearing an FBI T-shirt raises her hand. "Do they have the equivalent of our Witness Protection Program? Is it possible he turned on the Yakuza and was relocated?"

"Japan doesn't have a formal witness protection program, but it's possible he cooperated and officials helped him disappear."

Another agent asks if Jun had any children.

"Not that we know of. However, we visited a young woman last night who Saito was making regular payments to, and she would be about the right age to be his daughter."

Saito would have been nineteen years old when Mee was born.

"Was she born here?"

"Yes," Petrov says. "I'm getting a complete dossier on her this morning, including copies of her birth certificate to see if paternity is disclosed. We're also tracing her mother. This was Jun Saito's first time in the States, so we're looking into the movements of Mee Kim's mother. Perhaps she vacationed in Japan or in a third country where they met." Petrov pauses. "Another possibility is that Mee Kim was blackmailing Saito, but we should know more when we get the full file on Ms. Kim."

Petrov looks around the room, waiting for any more questions on Mee Kim before moving on. "As Special Agent Ronaldo alluded to, it is possible Jun Saito turned informant and was given a new identity by his government. However, he would have needed to offer up some significant information for that to take place and we haven't been able to track down any references to Saito as a prosecution witness." Petrov takes a breath. "Another possibility is that Saito wanted out and went on the run from the Yakuza or that he actually managed to convince his father to let him leave the organization. It's possible, given his father's standing, that his exit was allowed."

"So what are the Japanese police saying?"

"They had two theories. One was that he murdered his girlfriend and then went on the run. The other was that he was dead. Killed by the Yakuza. If they know any different, they're not talking. At least, not to us."

When no other questions come Petrov's way, he introduces Ramos and me, explaining our roles and involvement in the case, before handing over to Ramos.

Ramos's part of the briefing takes fifteen minutes, as he takes the task force through the key elements of the case, using the projection system to show a selection of crime-scene photos and Hart's computer-generated re-creation regarding the parking-lot lights. He also shows them photos of Saito's hotel room and takes them through some of the bank statements recovered from Saito's laptop.

Once Ramos is done, it's time to assemble the Saito "mini" task force and start dishing out the leads. Obviously not everyone in the L.A. Gang Impact Team will be working on Saito's murder. In fact, Petrov will probably choose only a few. The others will continue with their current assignments, but now they'll be aware of another layer of organized crime in L.A….and what might be about to happen. Payback in crime syndicates can go on for months, bouncing back and forth between the families or organizations. Even Melbourne, which is about one-third the size of L.A. County in terms of population and with one-fifth the homicide rate, had a spate of more than ten organized crime "hits" over a six-year period. And until these gangland hits, your average Melbournian was pretty much unaware that their city had such a thriving organized crime trade. While I doubt L.A. residents will be unaware of a war on the streets if that does come to pass, let's hope that no innocent bystanders are hit in the cross fire.

Petrov singles out De Luca, Agent Kim and an ATF agent called Louis Williams before dismissing the rest of the group. The six of us make our way into a smaller meeting room to begin the real work. As we sit around the table I can't help but notice that the group represents the racial diversity of L.A. While everyone except Petrov and I was born here, we've got the Italian background in Joe De Luca, Asians represented by Agent Kim, the Latino by Ramos and Louis Williams is African-American.

"Okay," Petrov says. "I'll be officially in charge of the Saito investigation from now on. De Luca, Kim and Williams, you know where we're at from the briefing—any further questions?"

The three shake their heads.

"Agent Anderson, I presume you don't mind doing some regular investigative work on top of your behavioral analysis?"

"Not at all. I'm still gathering data for the profile anyway." Even though we now presume Saito's killer is a hit man, I'll still be able to draft an individual profile. Some elements will be characteristics of professional assassins, and some will be individual traits about our killer. The profile won't be as useful as it is in some cases, but it should still help the investigation. At least now I'll have access to enough information to complete a detailed victimology. I'd prefer not to have a fifteen-year gap in the victim's history, but it's a lot better than not even knowing his name.

"I'll get you to work on the victimology first, okay?" Petrov must be reading my mind.

"Sure. I want to complete that broader ViCAP search as a priority but after that I'll concentrate on the victimology. I'd like to look over that info on Mee Kim, too. And I might pay her another visit."

Petrov writes it down in his notebook. "I'll e-mail the file through as soon as it comes in." He looks up. "And take Agent Kim when you visit Mee. It might help to have a fellow Korean-American there."

"Great idea." I give Agent Kim a little nod and she smiles.

Petrov moves to Ramos. "Where are you at?"

"I've got Singapore Airlines calling me back today. Call's scheduled for ten-thirty."

"Anything else?"

"Lab. We should have the final fingerprints lifted from the fence, bricks, mortar and loose bits of wood that were found around the body. Hopefully we'll have some prints other than the victim's that I can follow up, maybe even an AFIS match."

"Okay." Petrov looks up at De Luca, Kim and Williams. "I want you three to spend the morning going over the case file. Then you can team up with Anderson on the victimology, Kim. And De Luca and Williams can join me." He turns to Ramos and me. "The three of us are going to concentrate on possible scenarios. We need to have a closer look at who might be behind the hit and why they targeted Saito. Then we can project the potential repercussions."

De Luca, Kim and Williams all accept their assignments with a nod.

Petrov lays his pen down. "Any questions?"

We all shake our heads.

"Okay, I'll leave you three here to work on the file." He looks at Ramos. "Detective Ramos, you okay with working from a spare desk here?"

"Sure."

"What about you, Anderson?"

"I'll head downstairs for the moment, if that's okay. I've got everything set up at my desk."

Petrov nods. "Okay, but I'll get two workstations set up here. Going forward, we should be together, and it'll be useful to be working alongside the rest of the Gang Impact Team so we can easily pass on information. Particularly if this case takes a while."

Back on the twelfth floor, I move quickly to my desk, barely stopping for a sociable nod as I pass my colleagues. Even Melissa and Mercedes only get a few seconds out of me. I want to talk to Mee at her school. Maybe interviewing her in a different environment will reap rewards. Certainly the FBI showing up at your workplace can be embarrassing, or at the very least dramatic. It might work to our advantage, with Mee wanting to give us more information just to get us out of there.

Once my computer's fired up, I open up the ViCAP database and type my first set of parameters into the search boxes. This time I leave the MO and cause of death blank, focusing on the victim characteristics.

State: All
Victim race: Asian
Victim sex: Male
Victim age: 20–60
MO: Unknown
Signature: Unknown
Timeframe: Last 10 years
Keywords: Organized crime, gangs

I keep the victim age range large, wanting to cast a wide net, but the keywords will help narrow down the search.

After about a minute, the ViCAP software comes back to me with one hundred matches. So we're probably talking every Asian male killed in the past ten years who had ties or suspected ties to organized crime or gangs. It's a large result, but not too overwhelming. I scan through the summary information for my first page of results. At page ten, I decide caffeine is in order. I don't want to take the time out for a trip to the Westwood Village Starbucks for my favored caramel macchiato, so I settle with coffee from the floor's kitchen.

I resume the search with fresh eyes and a cup of brewed coffee in hand. It's not until I hit the seventy-sixth result that I find something that intrigues me. In New York in 2004, a high-ranking gang member by the name of Li Chow was killed. His face had been badly beaten, but the cause of death was asphyxiation. Saito also showed signs of asphyxiation, even though it wasn't the cause of death. I click on the entry to see the full case details the New York cops entered into the system. They've taken the time to fill out most of the standard ViCAP questionnaire, and uploaded photos, so I'm working on a solid ViCAP entry, which is great.

When the first photo comes up, I'm shocked by his facial injuries. The man's cheekbones and eye sockets have been so badly smashed that his eyes are no longer contained by his bone structures. Rather, they hang over his face, connected only by the optic nerve. Even though the wounds are different to Saito's, the forensic pathologist was unable to determine what sort of weapon was used in the beating, just as in our case. Nor was he able to make an exact determination on what caused the asphyxiation, with no sign of strangulation. I look at the photo again, with a mixture of repulsion and curiosity. The damage to the facial bones is catastrophic. Yet the forensic pathologist noted the bruising was extremely localized as if maybe the damage was done with only one or two strikes, not repeated blows to the face.

Then it hits me—break the face, take the breath away… kung fu's Ten Killing Hands.

Oh, no.

Eleven

I sit back in my chair and shake my head, processing the validity of my hypothesis. The Ten Killing Hands are a set of strikes developed by Wong Fei Hung in China as the most effective killing strikes. It boils down to ten principles: strike the eyes; stop the breath; break the face; explode the ears; crush the groin; twist the tendons; break the fingers; dislocate the joints; break the elbow; attack the nerve points. It's nasty, but effective. And, in the hands of a trained practitioner, deadly.

One of the strikes used to break the face is the Double Back-fist targeted directly below the eyes—the aim is to blind your opponent by shattering their eye sockets so their eyeballs literally collapse over their face structure. Another option is a direct strike to the eyeballs, which usually causes permanent blindness. I look again at the photo of the New York victim, Li Chow—it fits.

And then we have the principle of taking the breath away, something that can be done in several ways. One of the Ten Killing Hands is the Dan Gwai, in which the attacker stops the blood flow to the brain by squeezing the neck and then dislocates or breaks the neck. In Jun Saito's case, there was no dislocation or break in the neck, but the killer may have used a tiger strike to literally rip his throat out, after he'd already blocked the blood flow along the carotid artery.

If I'm right, we're looking at a kung fu master, someone who's skilled enough and creative enough to adapt the Ten Killing Hands. He's deadly, and while his performance at the Little Tokyo scene tells us he's relatively skilled with a gun, he has no need for a weapon. He can kill in many different ways with his bare hands.

A small snippet of my dream from last night comes back…I was fighting someone trained in kung fu. Perhaps in the dream I was Jun Saito. Did Saito know any martial arts? He could have taken up his native tae kwon do or karate in honor of his Japanese heritage. In the dream I was punched in the ribs, and Saito's rib was broken.

I bring my focus back to the killer…someone who's trained in kung fu to an extremely high level—at least first or second dan, and probably sifu stage. Another idea pops into my head. Hollywood's just around the corner—we could be talking about someone who's a stunt double or even a choreographer on set. I punch Petrov's cell number into my landline, but then hang up before it rings. It's too early to run this by Petrov, or anyone else for that matter. I need to make sure this isn't a coincidence and the best way to do that is to search ViCAP again, this time focusing on injuries that would be present if someone was using the Ten Killing Hands. More matches would substantiate my theory enough to present it to Petrov.

I start the new search, this time searching only on cause of death and injuries. I start with the first of the Ten Killing Hands, the Side Tiger Claw. In this technique the throat is crushed and the eyes are poked simultaneously. Out of the twenty matches I get, only one looks related—the 2004 murder in Chicago of Shen Chan. After I've printed out the full details of Chan's murder, I move on to the next technique, the Double Back-fist. The technique is used to severely damage the opponent, to soften them up for the kill. It's obviously something our killer could use to his advantage whenever he wanted, but Li Chow is the only result that matches the injuries a victim would sustain from this type of strike.

Next I search for indications of the Heaven Piercing Fist. This time I get two matches, one from 1996 and New York, and one from here in L.A. in 2002. To my shock, I notice that the New York victim survived, even though he also suffered one of the other Ten Killing Hands, the Tiger Leopard Fist, which bursts an opponent's eardrums. The 2002 L.A. victim, Bao Tran, had two cracked ribs and a ruptured spleen. I print out both files and, despite my excitement about maybe finding a victim who lived to tell the tale, I put the files aside to continue with the search. I can't afford to get sidetracked, not when I've got so much to do before visiting Mee this afternoon.

The Hungry Tiger Catches the Lamb is next on my list. The injuries would vary greatly for this strike, as it can be used on the groin, the face or as a way to gouge out the victim's eyes. While ViCAP returns some results, I decide they're not in line with the Ten Killing Hands, so I move on.

The Angry Tiger Descends the Mountain targets the opponent's elbow, delivering a crushing blow to dislocate or permanently crush this vulnerable joint. Like the Heaven Piercing Fist and Double Back-fist, it's used to soften the opponent for the next set of strikes and to inflict permanent damage rather than to kill. Two of the victims I've found to date had this injury—the 2004 New York victim and the 2004 Chicago victim—and a new ViCAP search brings back one more match from 1998. I'm about to check the entry when my phone rings. I'm annoyed by the interruption, but can't let it ring out.

"Anderson."

"Hey, it's Ramos. I just heard back from Sam Gould. The DNA on the cigarette butt matched the victim's, Jun Saito."

"Damn. It would have been nice to have the perp's DNA."

"Real nice." Ramos sighs. "What you working on?"

"I'm searching ViCAP for similar attacks."

"And?"

"Not much so far." I'm still not ready to go public with the theory. I really need to do a detailed analysis of the files and autopsy results first. "I better get back to it. Speak to you later?"

"Sure."

I hang up and go back to my ViCAP screen and the Angry Tiger Descends the Mountain. The additional victim I've found is from San Francisco. However, the cause of death was cardiac arrest. I put this file with the 1996 New York victim's file for closer examination, they may not be related to our hit man.

The next technique is translated as the Squeeze and Crush; the victim's blood supply is cut off at the neck and then a twist of the hand breaks the victim's neck. One match comes back from 2000 in Chicago, and the victim was tagged as having links to the Yakuza. A grumble of my stomach breaks my concentration and a glance at my watch confirms it's well and truly past my usual lunch hour. The day's running away from me. I duck out to the Federal Café at our building's entrance and grab a tuna sandwich, which I gobble down at my desk while I keep typing. I resume the search with the seventh Killing Hand, called the Reincarnation of the Fulfilled Crane. In this strike, your hand forms a beaklike shape and you strike at your opponent's eyes. In ViCAP, I search for major eye damage, but the results are all ones that have come up previously.

The next technique is translated into Monkey Steals the Peach, and is another hard-hitting but nonlethal technique. The idea is to grab on to your opponent and twist their digits or limbs to the breaking point. Nothing in the ViCAP database looks likely.

The ninth of the Ten Killing Hands is called Double Flying Butterfly, and is used to dislocate or break the tailbone, the coccyx. I get one match, this time from 2001 in Philadelphia. The victim's name is obviously Italian and I can't help but wonder if he's a mobster. I scan through the case file and soon come across the magic word *Mafia*. I print out all his details before moving on to the final Killing Hand, the Tiger Leopard Fist. For the ViCAP search I type in burst eardrums as the injury. In Tiger Leopard Fist, you slap both hands on the opponent's ears. The hands are slightly cupped, and the striking points are the palms, a blow that bursts the eardrums and leaves your opponent disorientated and in pain. I've practiced this strike in kung fu as a defense against a front bear hug when my hands are still free. In real life, an attacker might pick me up to throw me into a car. The Tiger Leopard Fist would hurt them enough that they'd release their grip, allowing me to either escape or counterattack.

I get four hits on burst eardrums. Two of them involve only one eardrum—in both cases the forensic pathologists hypothesized that the injury occurred during a fight. But with only one, we're looking at a regular punch, not a Killing Hand. The other two look plausible—one from 2007 in San Diego and the 1996 New York victim who survived. While the 2007 San Diego file prints out, I look at the collection of cases on my desk. I think I have enough for Petrov now. I dial his cell, not bothering with his extension in case he's not at his desk.

"FBI, Petrov."

"Hey, it's Anderson. I've got something."

"Shoot."

"In kung fu there's something called the Ten Killing Hands. They're basically ten different strikes that someone skilled in kung fu can use to severely disable or kill their opponent. I think Jun Saito was killed using an adaptation of one of these strikes and I've found quite a few other victims in ViCAP that match, too."

"Go on." Petrov's all ears.

"One of the ten principles is to take your opponent's breath away. Some of the strikes simply wind the opponent, allowing you to dominate and then kill them with other strikes, but some are enough to kill."

"One strike?"

"If it's done right, yeah. Like Saito."

"Damn."

"Uh-huh."

"And Saito's throat wound? Take me through it."

"It would be easier to demonstrate in person, but I'll try to talk you through it. Hold your hand out, but bend the top half of your fingers so they're flush against the bottom part of your fingers."

"Yup."

"Now spread your hand out a little, making the gap between your thumb and index finger as wide as possible."

"Okay."

"They should almost be at right angles, forming an L-shape."

"Gotcha."

"Now imagine that hand shape strikes Saito's throat, then squeezes on either side, targeting the carotid artery to block the blood supply to his brain. The killer then retracts his hand, strikes again, but this time it's a hard and fast strike, and he grabs the skin and muscle on either side of the neck, tearing out Saito's throat."

"Ouch."

"Uh-huh."

"And the broken rib?"

"Again, that fits perfectly. The technique our killer would have used is called Piercing Heaven Fist." I use the English translation. "It's basically a strike to the floating ribs. It steals their breath away, and breaks a rib…or two."

"Okay. What else you got?" I'm not sure if Petrov isn't convinced, or if he just wants me to cut to the chase. I go with the latter and read out the victims' names and the cities in which the murders took place. When I get to the 2004 murder of Li Chow in New York, Petrov interrupts.

"Li Chow? Really?"

"You've heard of him?"

"He was the number two in New York's Hip Sing Association. It was huge news, Anderson." Petrov seems shocked that I don't know the case.

"I was in Australia in 2004. I'm afraid it didn't make the news, or the law-enforcement rounds there."

"Of course…sorry. I forget sometimes."

"Guess my accent's softening."

He gives a little laugh. "Maybe." He pauses. "Okay. Leave this with me. I need to let it sink in. Could be the hits are only related by the killer, and not the underlying employer, but I need to cover all bases."

"Is it possible our guy works in Hollywood? As a kung fu consultant, stunt man or the like."

"Possible. But my time in organized crime tells me that if they're hitting someone big, they fly in the killer."

"I see."

"Are you ready to brief the others on this?"

"Not yet." I chew on my bottom lip. "I really need to take a closer look at the autopsy reports, and I'd like to touch base with my kung fu teacher, too. Just to triple-check a few things." I want to run my hypothesis past someone who knows more about kung fu and the strikes than I do.

"Tomorrow morning?"

"That should be okay." I still want to speak to Mee Kim today, but I can call Sifu Lee tonight and go through all the files in detail then, too.

"Let's make it nine. Then you can brief everyone on the Ten Killing Hands and these ViCAP results."

"Sure. One other thing, sir."

"Yes?"

"The 1996 victim, Corey Casey…he survived."

"What?"

"I know…but I can't be sure it's related, especially given he wasn't killed."

"Well, let's make sure before we contact New York and start asking the cops there questions," Petrov says.

"Yes, sir. I'll have an answer for you tomorrow morning."

Did Corey Casey survive the Ten Killing Hands? And if he did, was he meant to for some reason?

Twelve

I swing by the fifteenth floor to pick up Agent Hana Kim.

"Sorry I had to keep pushing the time back." I rang her twice to change our meet time while I was going through the ViCAP results.

"That's okay. You're onto something?"

"Maybe." I play coy, still wanting to confirm my theory with medical backup and someone more knowledgeable about the Ten Killing Hands. In the elevator I glance at my watch. "Hopefully we'll make it before school breaks." It should take us about forty minutes to get to Montebello High School, but at this time of day an hour is more likely.

"Even if we don't, Ms. Kim and the other teachers will probably hang around for a little while."

"Did you call them?" I ask Agent Kim.

She shakes her head.

"Good." The elevator doors open and I lead the way to my car. "How long you been working with the Gang Impact Team, Agent Kim?"

"Two years now. I worked in our San Francisco office for a couple of years before I was assigned to the Safe Streets program and L.A."

I nod. "You like it?" I unlock my car and slide into the driver's seat.

Once she's in the car she replies, "Yeah. Plus my sister lives in L.A., so it's nice to be around her."

"You guys close?"

"Uh-huh. We live together and all."

"That is close." I drive out of the parking lot and head west on Wilshire Boulevard.

"Yeah." She pauses. "The people in the Gang Impact Team are real nice, too. Especially Joe. He's awesome."

"Do you work with him a lot?" I wouldn't mind finding out more about Joe De Luca, including why he and Petrov seem so chummy.

"When I first came to L.A. he was my partner. Then he got promoted and now he only consults to the task force. But I'm still one of his official reports."

"What's he like?"

"He's good at what he does, but he can have a laugh, too. You need that, especially if you're doing surveillance."

"I hear you."

Surveillance is dead boring ninety-nine percent of the time. It's all about sitting on your ass waiting for something to happen. And even if something does happen, you mostly just take a few photos, ready for analysis the next day. I know a lot of cops prefer it to canvassing an area or a building, but I figure even if you're asking the same questions over and over, at least you're out and about. Not sitting in some freezing or boiling car, hoping that if all hell breaks loose your legs aren't asleep from hours of inertia. Give me the door-knock any day. Still, surveillance can be an adrenaline-high if something goes down on your watch.

"So what did you think of the Saito file, Agent Kim?"

"Please, call me Hana. Calling everyone by last names is so macho."

I shrug. "There are more of them than us."

"Tell me about it. DEA's only got around twelve percent female agents. And you don't want to know the percentage of Asian females."

I laugh. "I can imagine. If it makes you feel better, I'm the only Australian in the Bureau."

Now she laughs. "Not quite the same, but I'll take it. Sophie, isn't it?"

"Yup." I take a right and merge onto I-405, heading south. The road is rough and in need of a major resurfacing, but how could they close even one lane of such a busy freeway? The interstate comes to a halt during peak hour as it is. "So, Saito?"

"Didn't look like a nice way to go." Hana tucks her hair behind her ears.

"No. Give me a bullet any day. Well, actually I'd prefer a heart attack at the ripe old age of ninety."

Hana laughs. "I'm with you on that one." She stares out the window and doesn't turn back to me until about five minutes later, when I'm taking the I-10 exit. "So you really aren't going to tell me what was so important you had to bump our meeting back?" She smiles.

I guess there's no harm in giving Hana a sneak peek.

"I've still got to confirm a few things, but my theory is that our hit man kills his targets using specific kung fu strikes that make up something called the Ten Killing Hands. And I found a few matches in ViCAP to back it up."

"Really? How many?"

"There are eight cases that could be related, plus Jun Saito." I pause, checking the signs. I punched our destination into my GPS before we headed off and remember most of the turns, but I glance down again now to double-check my route. For the moment its speaker is off, but I can easily flick it back on if things get hairy. "I haven't had a chance to thoroughly review each file." I keep my eyes on the road. "If they're all related, it's nine targets over the past twelve years, and for a professional hit man that figure's quite low. Not even one a year."

"That we know of."

Hana's hit the nail on the head. Our hit man may have killed dozens, maybe even hundreds of victims that we just don't know about. Some murders may not be logged in ViCAP. And who's to say he always uses the Ten Killing Hands? Plus, if we are talking about an international, freelance hit man, only some of his jobs would be US-based.

I fill Hana in. "Petrov thinks our hitter may be international. Flying in from overseas for each job."

She doesn't seem surprised. "Maybe somewhere in Asia? That'd tie in with the martial arts skill."

I shrug. "Could be. But you don't have to live in China to train in kung fu and to know the Ten Killing Hands. I mean, I know them."

"Really?"

"Yeah. I train three times a week. Going for my third-degree black belt later this year. What about you?"

She shakes her head. "I never got into it. My folks sent me for tae kwon do lessons when I was about eight, but it didn't take. I quit after a year."

"Well, you've got to enjoy it, right?"

"Yup." She looks in front again. "The ViCAP results sure sound promising."

"More victims, more crime scenes…more information on our killer."

Finally at 4:00 p.m., I swing into West Cleveland Avenue from Twenty-first Street, hitting the outskirts of Montebello High School. "That's it." I nod toward the high school and slow down to a crawl, looking for a parking space. We cruise by the main entrance, which features *Home of the Mighty Oilers* in large lettering on the wall. The homage includes the team's mascot, a man with overalls and a paintbrush in hand. I park just around the corner, on Twentieth Street.

"TV parking," Hana says.

"What?"

She laughs. "We got a parking spot right out front. And in L.A., that usually only happens on TV…TV parking."

I smile. "I like it."

We head toward the buildings, following the signs to reception.

"Do you speak Korean?"

"Yeah, but not as well as I should…according to my folks, at least."

I smile. "It's hard to maintain when you're brought up in an English-speaking country."

"Yeah. My parents always spoke Korean at home, so at least I could practice."

I pull a heavy wood-and-glass door open and we're greeted by a matronly woman on the phone. She gives us a nod and puts her forefinger up, letting us know she'll be with us soon.

Within less than a minute she's off the phone, giving us a huge but somewhat labored grin. "Good afternoon, ladies. What can I do for you?"

Hana makes a move for her ID, but I put my hand on her arm and fish out my ID. I want to confront Mee Kim into telling us as much as she knows, but a DEA badge at a school could cause her too many problems for my liking. Hana seems to jump with me on the logic, immediately retracting her hand.

I hold my ID open. "I'm Special Agent Anderson from the FBI, and this is Special Agent Kim."

The woman eyes the ID, her curiosity instantly aroused. "Yes?"

"We're here to see Ms. Mee Kim." I put my ID away.

"I'm afraid Mee's not in today. She called in sick this morning."

"Oh." That is interesting. I wonder if our visit yesterday afternoon had anything to do with her sudden illness. At least her absence will make it easier for me to speak to those around her. "How about your principal? He or she in?"

"Regarding?" Her voice has a ring of authority, one that would work on most people.

"I'm afraid I'll need to talk to your principal about that."

She nods reluctantly. "His name's Graeme Merry." She dials an extension on her phone. "Graeme, you've got two FBI agents to see you. Something about Mee… Okay, will do." The receptionist looks up. "You can go on through. Second door on your right." She points down a small corridor.

"Thank you."

I knock on the designated door, which is also marked Principal, and a deep male voice says, "Come in." Graeme Merry stands as we enter. His five-ten frame is lanky and everything about him looks weathered—his skin, his posture, his facial expression, his clothes. He looks anything but merry. He moves to us quickly, holding out his hand. I take it and introduce myself, then Hana, again leaving out which agency she works for.

"So, what can I do for you?" He moves behind his desk and motions to the two seats in front.

"We're investigating a murder that took place in Little Tokyo five nights ago and we believe Mee Kim may be able to help us with our investigation."

"Really? How?"

"We've found a connection between the victim and Ms. Kim." I decide not to give him any more details at this stage.

"Didn't Phyllis tell you? Mee's not in today."

"Yes, she did tell us," Hana says. "But we'd like to ask you a few questions, if that's okay."

He seems puzzled, but nods.

Hana kicks it off. "Have you noticed anything unusual about Mee Kim's behavior recently?"

"Um…" He considers the question. "No, can't say I have."

"She hasn't seemed happier or sadder, or preoccupied…or anything like that?" I press.

He shakes his head. "Not that I noticed. But you should talk to Doris Huntova. She and Mee are close. I'll get Phyllis to track her down." Merry picks up his phone and relays the request.

"How long has Ms. Kim worked here?" I ask, even though I know her police check was five years ago.

"Five years. Straight out of college."

"And you're happy with her? As an employee?"

Merry seems to think my question is a little strange, but he's emphatic in his response. "Absolutely. She's a very good teacher. Popular with the students and staff alike. And all her kids are doing well in math." He pauses, rubbing his fingers across his lips in contemplation. "You don't think she's involved in anything—" he searches for the word "—untoward, do you? I run a tight and clean ship. My teachers must set an example for the students."

Hana reassures him. "No, not at all. We're just hoping she can help us, that's all."

He nods, the relief evident.

There's no point sullying her name if she is an innocent bystander. If things change later and we discover she's involved in blackmail, Principal Merry would find out when we indict.

"Anything else, Agents?"

Hana and I both shake our heads.

"Doris will be here soon."

"Is there somewhere private we can talk to her?"

"There's a small meeting room opposite my office." He points to the door. "You can use that."

I nod. "One more thing, Mr. Merry. Do you know what's wrong with Mee today?"

"Phyllis took the call at around seven this morning. Apparently she sounded miserable. Nasty cold."

There's a knock on the door and a stunning woman in her late twenties comes partially into Merry's office. Huntova has long, glossy brown hair with a slight wave, with two clips keeping it out of her face and eyes. Her face is sculptured, with dark soft eyes and pouty lips. She's dressed conservatively but appropriately for such an attractive woman teaching young boys. She wears loose but well-cut navy blue woolen pants and a matching cream twin-set on top. She glances at us, then at Merry. "You wanted to see me, sir?"

"Yes. These are Agents Anderson and Kim from the FBI. They'd like to talk to you about Mee."

"Mee? Is everything okay? Is she okay?"

I keep my face expressionless, but note with interest Huntova's assumption that Mee's well-being may be in question. "Everything's fine, Ms. Huntova," I say. "We've just got a couple of questions for you."

She seems relieved, but also a little confused.

Hana and I stand and both thank Mr. Merry before ushering Huntova into what turns out to be a small meeting room with a table and six chairs crammed neatly into the space.

"So Mee's okay?" Huntova sits down, but chews on the fingernail of her middle finger. I love it when people are easy to read—it makes my job so much easier.

"Yes," Hana replies. "As far as we know. We're going to see her at her house after this, but we thought we might as well talk to you while we're here."

"Is there any particular reason why you thought something might be wrong with Mee?" I ask.

Huntova stops biting her nail and rests both hands on the table. "I rang her last night for a chat and she sounded strange. Kinda nervous. And then she started telling me what a great friend I was."

"Go on," I prompt.

"I asked her if anything was wrong, but she kept telling me she was fine."

"But you don't think she was," Hana says.

"No." She sighs. "I've known Mee for four years now, since I started working here, and we've become real close. We often talk on the phone, but last night she was definitely not herself."

Hana and I both nod.

So maybe Mee did know Saito. Maybe he is her father and she knows it.

"Any ideas what might be wrong?" Hana asks.

Huntova shrugs. "Last night all I could think of was her boyfriend, Paul. You know, maybe they'd had a fight and she was upset. But I'm sure she'd tell me about that."

"Was she usually open with you about her relationship?"

"Yes. I mean, she's not a kiss-and-tell sort of girl, but I'm sure if she and Paul had had a fight she would have confided in me. Especially given I pressed her about it a couple of times."

"Is it serious? Her relationship?" I ask.

"She hopes they'll get married."

I nod, taking notes. "Do you know Paul very well?"

"Not really. They've been together for a couple of years, but Mee and I tended to do things just the two of us. Maybe because I'm single, I don't know."

"Have you spoken to her today?" I ask.

"No, and that's when I got really worried. I called her during our first break, but the phone rang out. I've been trying her cell ever since, whenever I could."

"No answer?"

"No."

While part of me is surprised, the other part of me suspected the sick day was too coincidental. Especially given she seemed healthy less than twenty-four hours ago.

Huntova shrugs. "She gets migraines sometimes and she usually turns her phone off or to silent, so she can sleep. Maybe that's it?" She's trying to convince herself.

I change the subject. "Did Mee ever talk about her father?"

Huntova shakes her head. "It wasn't a subject she liked to discuss. She said her father died in a car accident and that she didn't remember him at all. But she also said he and her mum weren't married. And that her mum didn't like to talk about him."

That gels with what we know, and what Mee told us yesterday.

"Did she ever mention her father's name?" I ask.

Huntova pauses, thinking. "No. Don't think so." After a beat of silence, Huntova asks, "So you're going over there now?"

"That's right." I glance at my watch—4:30 p.m. "One more thing, Ms. Huntova. Have you ever heard of someone called Jun Saito?"

She gives it only a few seconds' thought. "No."

I study her reaction closely—she certainly seems to be telling the truth.

"So Mee never mentioned that name?"

She shakes her head. "No, I don't think so."

"What about Jo Kume?"

Again, she shakes her head. "Is one of those men her father?"

"We're not sure at this stage," I admit, without bothering to tell her they're one and the same person. "Anything else you think we should know?"

Huntova shakes her head and I take down her contact details before we head back to the car.

"What do you think?" Hana asks once we reach the car and some privacy.

"I think she's telling the truth."

Hana nods. "Yup. Seemed straight-up to me, too."

Fifteen minutes later we pull up outside Mee Kim's house.

"Her car's not there." I motion to the driveway. "So much for being sick."

We both get out of the car.

"Let's take a look." Hana crosses the sidewalk and heads toward the front door. She's already rung the front doorbell by the time I catch up.

We wait, but no one answers. Hana moves toward the left-hand front window, the living room, and I go to the other front window, the dining room. It looks just like it did last night. I move down the right-hand side of the house, to what must be a bedroom. The curtains are drawn, but don't quite meet in the middle. I cup my hands around my face and lean in.

"Damn!" Although I can only see a small portion of the room, the bed has several items of clothing strewn around it and the floor's the same.

"What have you got?" Hana comes up directly behind me.

"See for yourself. Clothes everywhere." I move back and Hana leans in for a look. I bite my lip. "So either Mee's made a hasty exit or someone's been in and ransacked the place."

Hana takes another look. "If she did know Saito, chances are she's been pulled into this mess, one way or another."

"Or maybe *she* pulled *him* back into the Yakuza."

Hana raises one eyebrow. "I haven't met her…did she seem like the organized-crime type?"

I shrug. "Not on the surface, no." I pause. "No, you're right. If she's involved, it's more likely Saito pulled her in."

Hana nods. "Unless it's the boyfriend. Maybe he's the one with underworld ties or ties to Saito, the Yakuza or the Asian Boyz."

"Only one way to find out…."

"You got his details?"

"Uh-huh."

Hana leans on the window ledge. "Mee could be in danger."

"Could be." I pause. "Are you thinking what I'm thinking?"

Hana nods.

If we feel Mee's in danger right now, we don't need a warrant. The fact that her car's not here makes it more probable that she's out and left of her own accord, but Hana's right…Mee could be in danger. And if our bosses or some judge gives us a slap on the hand down the track, so be it.

I suddenly remember my dream of someone being shot—could it be Mee? The situation takes a sudden turn for the worse. I draw my gun and Hana follows suit. "Both in the front?" I confirm our strategy.

"Yup, let's stick together." She flashes me a grin. "We both want to live to see ninety, remember?"

"Let's go."

I open the screen door with my left hand and lean on it, keeping it back. Hana tries the door but it's locked. No surprises there. I flash back to last night, when we were leaving, and try to recall the lock system. No use even trying to break it down if Mee uses more than one lock. She had one dead bolt, a lock on the door handle and a chain.

"She's got a dead bolt. Sorry, just remembered." I move away from the door. "Let's try out back."

We hurry down the left side of the house, looking in

windows as we go. The living room looks relatively normal, as does the kitchen, which we can see clearly from a side door. The door has glass in the top half, and from the far right angle I can see she's got a dead bolt on the back door, too.

"Looks like we're breaking some glass." I sigh.

"You go. This is a new sweater." Hana smiles and cocks her head to one side.

"Gee, thanks." I look at my suit jacket—I don't particularly want to rip it, so I use my gun's butt to smash one of the glass panels in the door. Way noisier, but we are on the right side of the law.

"Well, I could have done that," Hana jokes, but then her face becomes serious and she raises her gun. "Let's go."

Moving my arm through the broken glass, I push the handle down. The door swings open, and I lead with my gun, taking the left while Hana follows me in and takes the right-hand side of the room.

The draining board on the kitchen sink has a bowl, spoon and cup on it. "Looks like she had breakfast."

Hana's eyes dart my way for a second and she gives a nod.

My side of the kitchen's a dead end—the kitchen wall— but Hana's side is the open-plan portion that leads to the living room. A quick visual check tells us that no one's there, but we still keep our guns drawn as we move out. The living room is clear, and we move into the hallway. Again, I stay to the left, and the hall, while Hana moves toward the dining room. I leave her to that room and make my way down the hallway. The next room on the right is a bedroom, the one we could see from the outside. The room's a mess, but no Mee. I head down to the next room, a second bedroom that Mee's turned into a minimalist study. It's bare except for a bookshelf, large desk and an office-style chair. Hana meets me in the hallway and we both shake our heads. The last door at the end of the hallway is the bathroom and, like the rest of the house, it's empty.

With the house checked, we can now have a closer look, maybe get an idea of what we're dealing with. Did Mee run?

And if so, from us, the Yakuza or the Asian Boyz? Or has someone nabbed her? I need to find out if she's the subject of my dreams.

After I've pulled on some gloves, I open the medicine cabinet in the bathroom while Hana moves back into the hallway. Mee's cabinet contains standard stuff—moisturizer, toner, extra soap, tampons, deodorant, painkillers—but nothing prescription, nothing unusual. I also notice that the cabinet is neat and orderly, without any old boxes or crusty medicine.

Moving down the hallway, I pass Hana in the study. "Anything?" I ask her.

"No. But I don't want to switch the computer on."

I nod. We'll need to get a full crime-scene unit in here, and they'll deal with the computer. They certainly won't be happy if two gung-ho field agents switch it on.

"The file's only got bills." She points to a small expandable file on the desk. Again, it's neat—no bits of paper peeking out over the top. Mee certainly does work hard not to accrue excess stuff.

"Nothing unusual in the bathroom."

We move into Mee's bedroom together and the room's a stark contrast to the rest of the house. While her chest of drawers still looks orderly from the outside—the drawers are closed and photos and ornaments sit neatly on top—when you pull out the drawers the few clothes that are left inside are unfolded and jumbled, as though they've been shoved back in or rifled through.

"Someone's been through this room," Hana comments.

"Yes, but who?" I stand at the door surveying the room and chewing on my lip. "This doesn't seem like Mee, from my read on her. If she did this, it's because she felt threatened or panicked in some way."

"It does look very different to the rest of the house. If I didn't see this room, I'd say Mee was a neat freak." She shakes her head. "It's not looking good."

"No." I move us back into the living room and move around. "Two photos are missing."

"Really? What of?"

"A photo of her mum and one of the two of them together." I smile, relieved.

"That makes it look like Mee was the one who decided to clear out." Hana jumps to the same conclusion as me.

I nod. "If someone grabbed her, they might throw together some clothes for her, or look for something in her bedroom, but they're not going to take photos. Mee wanted those with her." I pause, looking around the room again. "And the dishes on the sink. She had time to clean those, she was herself at breakfast."

"So something happened after breakfast that made her run."

"Looks that way." I take out my phone. "Let's get a search warrant and some crime-scene techs down here anyway. I'll call Petrov first, let him know what's going on."

Hana nods, and takes a closer look at the photos while I catch Petrov up.

"Well?" Hana asks when I hang up.

"Petrov's on his way over. Says he'll have a search warrant and a crew together by the time he gets here."

"Great." Hana looks around again. "And we should get in contact with the boyfriend. See what he knows about all this."

"I'll call him now." Paul hadn't been a priority before Mee's disappearance, but now…

Thirteen

Paul Bailey stands out in front of the house with Agent Kim, Petrov and me, while the crime-scene techs sweep the house. We've got guys dusting for fingerprints and vacuuming for trace evidence, and a computer forensic technician is working on the computer. Bailey's Caucasian, in his thirties, and well dressed in a casual but trendy style—black jeans, print T-shirt and leather jacket. He shifts uncomfortably from side to side, hands in his pockets, looking anything but gangster hip. The guy's nervous and worried—and wearing his emotions on his sleeve. His demeanor confirms that he and Mee are probably innocent bystanders in this, but then why did Mee run?

"And you think Mee knows this dead guy?" It's the third time he's asked us the same question.

"Jun Saito. Yes. He made regular deposits into her bank account."

He shakes his head. "You're talking about her mom's life-insurance payments. Not some payments this Saito guy made."

"The payments were made by one of Saito's front companies."

"No, you got it wrong. And why would this guy pay Mee anyway?"

I shrug. "Could be he's her father?"

He shakes his head again. "No. Not possible."

"What do you know about her father?" Hana asks.

He sighs. "Not much."

We all stare at him.

"Okay, okay, nothing. She never talked about him, other than telling me that he died in a car accident before she was born."

"You didn't ask about him?" I suggest. As a relationship progresses, it's natural to ask questions. "Did you ask her his name? What he did for a living?"

"Yeah. She told me his name, but it wasn't Jun Saito. I can't even remember what it was. This is like nine months ago."

"What about Jo Kume? Does that name ring a bell?"

He shakes his head. "No, that wasn't it." He pauses. "She said he was a salesman. Does that help?"

"Salesman?" Petrov gives a snort. "Jun Saito was a member of the Yakuza." Petrov's obviously decided to drop the bomb, see what sort of a mess it makes.

"Yakuza?" Bailey puts his hands up and backs away. "No way, man. Mee's not mixed up in anything like that. The guy's not her dad."

I put my hand on his shoulder. "What if she didn't know herself?"

He considers my hypothesis. "I guess that's possible. Like her mom lied to her about her dad?"

"Maybe. We're trying to link Saito and Mee, and so far this is the most logical connection. Unless she was doing something for him here in L.A. and the bank transfers were payments, a salary, or she was blackmailing him."

"Mee wouldn't be involved in anything illegal, and no way could she blackmail someone."

That ties in with what we know about her to date, and my impression of her. Although the fact that she ran caught me by surprise.

Bailey rubs his face. "I can't believe she's missing."

"You said she called you this morning. What time?"

"It was around eight." He pulls his cell phone out of his leather jacket and flips through the call log. "To be precise, 8:02 a.m. And the phone call lasted one minute and four seconds."

"From her cell?" Hana confirms.

"Yeah."

"Did she say where she was?"

"No. But there was music in the background, like she was in the car. I already told you all this."

I nod. "And she said she was on her way to San Diego?"

"Uh-huh. Her cousin is sick and she was flying down there. She sounded upset." He wrings his hands together. "But I still can't get her on her cell."

Petrov puts his hands in his pockets. "She ever mention this cousin before?"

Bailey hesitates and looks as if he's been caught. "No." He sighs. "I asked her what was wrong with her cousin, and she said she had a lump in her breast. That they were doing tests."

"And her mum died of breast cancer?" I say.

"That's right. I think that's why Mee was flying down immediately. It would have touched a nerve, you know?"

"Or it was the easiest lie that came to hand, given she'd been through that with her mother." Petrov's not sparing Bailey's feelings.

He shakes his head. "Mee? Lie? She doesn't have it in her."

"Come on, Mr. Bailey," Petrov says. "It's obvious your girlfriend lied to you."

It's a while before he says, "Mee isn't unpredictable like this. She just isn't. If she did lie, why? You think she's gone on the run? From the Yakuza?"

"That's one possibility." Petrov keeps his voice even.

"Man." Bailey blows out a long, slow breath. "This is not good. But I still don't get why she wouldn't tell me if she was in trouble."

"Maybe she didn't want to involve you?" I suggest.

He rubs his face again. "Maybe. That's more like Mee

than just taking off for no reason. So you think she's in danger?" Bailey looks behind me and I follow his gaze. The computer guy's carrying Mee's computer out, ready to load it into his van.

Bailey pushes his hands into his pockets and hunches his shoulders. "I hope she's okay. You don't think…you don't think whoever killed this Saito guy is after Mee, do you?"

"It's too early to speculate," Petrov answers honestly. "We'll let you know as soon as any new information comes to hand. And please, if Ms. Kim contacts you, call us immediately." Petrov hands him a business card. "I can't stress the importance of this. If your girlfriend's in trouble, we can help her."

Bailey's brow is furrowed and he gives us small, multiple nods. But it's still not sinking in, not yet. "Thanks…thanks."

"I've put out an APB on both Ms. Kim and her car, so hopefully we'll get something that way." Petrov gives Bailey a nod.

We still don't know why Saito suddenly came out of hiding and why he'd been working with the Asian Boyz. And maybe if we knew the answers to those questions, we'd know what Mee's running from. It would also help us to know whether Mee and Saito were, in fact, related. We can't get DNA directly from Mee to check against Saito's, but we can swab her house and hopefully get her DNA that way to make the comparison.

Petrov, Hana and I move away from the front lawn over to Petrov's car.

"You need a hand with those ViCAP files, Anderson?"

"Nah, I'll be fine. It'll be easier if one person does the initial sort."

"I can help out if you like," Hana offers.

"Thanks, but I don't think it will take me very long."

"You sure? It's just dinner and a DVD with little sis, tonight. I don't mind."

I smile. "No, I'll be fine." The real reason I want to be by myself is to try to induce a premonition, and, as soon as everyone leaves I'll be going back into Mee's house.

Hana nods. "Okay. You going back to the office?"

"No. I'm going to take another look around inside, once the crime-scene guys are finished, and then head home to sort through the ViCAP files."

"Can I get a lift back to the office with you then, sir?" Hana asks Petrov.

"Sure. Um…guess we may as well head off now. Anderson, I've organized a few agents to keep an eye on the place for the next forty-eight hours or so. Maybe Mee, or someone else, will come back here. The agents will be here by six."

"Okay. I'll hand over to them when I leave."

Petrov gives me a nod. "See you tomorrow morning."

Two hours later, I finally get my privacy inside Mee Kim's house. The forensic computer technician left shortly after Petrov and Hana, but the others only left five minutes ago. The two FBI agents are ensconced in their lookout position a few doors down.

Ducking underneath the crime scene tape, I take in the atmosphere and layout of the house, as if it's the first time I've seen it. I can't truly bring fresh eyes to the scene, but I can try to be as objective as possible. The front door has been extensively printed, and I can clearly see about ten prints around the handle area. Of course, they could all be Mee's, or they could belong to ten different people. Most likely we'll find Mee's prints, Mr. Bailey's and maybe one or two others. The hallway is free of print dust, but Mee's bedroom is a different story. Most of the work has been concentrated on her chest of drawers, with print dust covering the top and each drawer. If someone else went through her clothes, we should find their print there, unless they wore gloves. I move into the living room, literally trying to breathe in all that is Mee Kim. I pick up one of the photos of her, focusing on her face. I picture her, in this room, talking to us, then relaxing by herself, then watching TV. Next I sit down, blank out all thoughts and focus on my breath…in and out…in and out…

Mee's dressed in jeans and a T-shirt, washing a bowl and coffee cup. The doorbell rings and she quickly rinses the dishes and puts them to drain before making her way through the small house to the front door. She leaves the chain on and opens the door a crack. Two men wait on the other side. Both wear baseball caps pulled down low over their faces, and sunglasses. Parked on the street behind them is a large black car.

"Hello?" Mee says through the crack in the door.

"Mee Kim?"

"Yes?"

"You need to come with us."

She looks down at the closest man's hands, and then runs.

The two men and Mee Kim are fighting out the back of her house. She's winning, using her skill to fight the two men.

Mee's inside, throwing things into a small overnight bag. Her heart is pounding and tears run down her face. She runs into the living room, grabs two photos, and then runs out the front door.

The vision ends abruptly, so abruptly that my body jolts. Mee did run, but she was being chased. My vision seems to tie in with our case to date, clearing Mee of any wrongdoing—unless she crossed Saito and the Yakuza in some way. But it's more likely that she found herself in this mess and did everything she could to escape—including fighting two men. But why didn't she call us for help?

I go out the kitchen door and around the corner of the house into the backyard to take a look around. Her yard is a large grassed area, with garden beds running along the three fences bordering it. On first glance it looks untouched, but then I see a few tufts of grass that have been recently upturned. I slowly move around the garden beds, and notice one camellia with a few branches snapped off, perhaps where someone fell on it. Mee did well, damn well. She fought off two attackers and gave herself enough time to throw some clothes in her bag and run. And, given the men are not still lying in her garden, she did so without killing them. I don't find any other evidence of the scuffle outside, so I go back in and sit on Mee's bed. I slow my breathing again and try to induce another vision of the confrontation, but I'm unsuccessful.

It's 8:30 p.m. by the time I turn the lights off in Mee's house and make my way back to the car. I give the agents a small nod before getting behind the wheel. On the drive home I go through the vision in my head again. At the door, Mee was focused on the man's hand. Why? I visualize that moment over and over again…the two men at the door, Mee looking down…the two men at the door, Mee looking down…the two men at the door, Mee looking down… Finally I see what she saw—part of his pinky finger was missing. He was Yakuza. A Yakuza member cuts off part of his pinky as an offering of penance to his boss, or sometimes the boss takes it as punishment. The guys were Yakuza and Mee knew it.

I decide to call Sifu Lee before making myself a quick dinner. Even though I'm starving, if I wait much later to call, it'll be downright rude. I scroll through to his cell number and hit the dial button.

It only rings three times before he answers. He seems a little surprised to hear from me at nine on a weeknight…fair enough.

"Sorry to bother you, but I'd like to ask your professional opinion on a case I'm working. I think the perpetrator might be trained in kung fu. Highly trained."

"Really?" Now he seems interested. "Go on."

Ideally I'd like to be sitting across from Lee with my eight ViCAP files and Saito's file, so we could more easily discuss the injuries and details, but a phone call will have to do for the moment—I want to speak to him before I brief the team tomorrow and make this more formal.

"There have been eight deaths and one attack over the

past twelve years that I think may be related. And I believe they all involve the Ten Killing Hands."

"What?" I have Lee's full attention. "Tell me more."

I take Lee through an overview of the cases, focusing on the victims' injuries and causes of death. For the moment, I leave off the two cases I'm not sure about—the 1996 New York victim and the guy in San Francisco whose elbow was broken but who died from a cardiac arrest.

"Was death instantaneous in these cases?"

The question seems strange, but I go with it. "As far as I know. I haven't read the full autopsy reports yet." He's silent, and then it hits me. "You're thinking *dim mak?*" I ask.

"Yes."

Dim mak is often referred to as the death touch, and is based on the premise that striking certain acupoints can cause instant or delayed death. At Lee's school it's something we study as part of our fifth dan—something I haven't done yet. But I always thought it was more legend than science.

"There are two other deaths…two cases where the victims showed signs of the Ten Killing Hands but one survived and one died of a cardiac arrest. I wasn't sure whether to include them."

"Tell me more about these two."

"There was a victim in New York in 1996 who had both eardrums burst and broken ribs."

"Tiger Leopard Fist and Heaven Piercing Fist."

"Yes, that's what I thought." I flick the ring on my little finger. "But the guy survived. It's entered into ViCAP as a violent attack, not a homicide."

"Have you checked whether he's still alive?"

"Not yet, no."

"Many of the *dim mak* strikes can cause death hours, days or even years later."

"How?"

"Take the many pressure points around the left ribs. A hard strike to this area can rupture the spleen, but the bleeding can be contained by a membranous capsule that surrounds the spleen for days. So the person can be without symptoms for days until the capsule bursts, causing death."

"There was an L.A. victim from 2002 who died of a ruptured spleen, but I assumed it was from the strike to his ribs, Heaven Piercing Fist. He was dead when he was found and the forensic pathologist noted that the injury would have killed him within an hour or two."

"In that case the direct force was probably enough to do the damage. But other strikes can cause much more of a delay between the attack and death."

I'm silent, but I wish Lloyd Grove was here to weigh in. I guess that conversation will be tomorrow.

Lee continues. "Take a strike to stomach point nine, on the carotid artery. If you strike an older person or someone else with plaque build-up in their arteries, they can have a heart attack or stroke instantly, or days later when the loosened plaque makes its way to their heart or brain. A hard strike, even on a healthy person, can cause degradation of the artery."

Again, I take mental notes to run all this by Grove.

"So it's really possible?" I try to check my disbelief. "To kill someone using acupoints?"

"Yes." Lee doesn't hesitate.

Even though some of the medical stuff Lee's run by me sounds legit, I'm having a hard time buying the concept of *dim mak*... How am I going to sell it to Petrov and the others?

"What sorts of things can I look for to verify this? To prove it?"

"Death using *dim mak* can occur in many ways—one or more of the organs fail such as the liver or kidney, internal bleeding, or cardiac arrest...like this other victim."

"He was sixty-two. The pathologist assumed the stress of the attack induced a heart arrhythmia that led to death."

"That's one possibility. The other one is that he was struck on the many pressure points that target the heart, effectively shutting it down."

"But the killer would need to be certain of death," I say.

A hit man has to make sure his mark is down, and for good. "Is *dim mak* foolproof?"

"If the killer is skilled and focuses his attack on the heart, yes."

"Oh, God," I say, suddenly realizing that if Lee's right, anyone who died of a heart attack or heart problem in the past fifteen years or so could be one of our guy's victims. "This is—"

"A nightmare."

"Uh-huh."

We're silent for a few moments before I bring us back to the effects of *dim mak*. "So cardiac arrest would be the cause of death if the heart was targeted?"

"Not necessarily. The pressure points attack the heart in one of three ways—heart attack, ventricular fibrillation or something called heart concussion."

"Heart concussion?" This time I can't hide the disbelief in my voice.

"It's real. You want the Latin name?"

"I don't think that's going to help me."

"Can we meet, Sophie? Tomorrow morning? I've got some books you should take a look at, including one written by a doctor about how the effect of striking certain pressure points can be explained medically. It talks about how the strikes affect the nervous system, blood pressure, heart…everything."

I'm silent, still trying to process it all.

"You there?" Lee's voice brings me back to the immediate.

"Can we meet tonight?" I ask, thinking of my 9:00 a.m. briefing.

"I'm sorry, Sophie, I can't tonight. But early tomorrow is fine."

"How early?"

"I could be at the studio with the books by 7:00 a.m."

"Great. Thanks, Lee. I'll see you then."

I cook dinner on remote, still thinking about *dim mak* and the victims. I shake my head. If Lee's right…I'll never be able to trace those symptoms back. Reopen every case that involved a heart attack of someone involved in gangs or organized crime? It's not going to happen. And that's assuming our hit man only targets this subset of individuals.

I'm in the middle of dinner when I stop thinking about *dim mak* and its effects on the heart long enough to remember Corey Casey. I leave my dinner on the table and go through his file in search of a phone number. I find one and dial it.

"Hello." A woman's sleepy voice.

I suddenly realize I've dialed a New York number, and they're three hours ahead of us. It's after midnight there. "Hi. I'm sorry to bother you this late at night but my name's Agent Sophie Anderson from the FBI and I'm trying to track down a Corey Casey. Have I got the right number?"

"Corey Casey was my husband. But he died four years ago."

It hits me like a slap in the face, even though Lee prepared me for the possibility of a delayed death.

"Hello?"

"Sorry," I say. "Do you mind me asking what he died of?"

"You're from the FBI?" She confirms my identity.

"That's right, ma'am. I'm sorry, I know the accent's confusing."

She gives a little snort of air. "Yes."

"I work in the L.A. field office and we're investigating a death that we think may be related to your husband's 1996 attack."

"Oh." She pauses. "My husband died of liver failure."

Fourteen

I pull into the kung fu studio's parking lot right at 7:00 a.m. I spent part of last night doing a few Internet searches on *dim mak,* but then decided to focus on the ViCAP files purely in light of the Ten Killing Hands, not pressure-point strikes, too. Besides, I want to see Lee's books firsthand. If I truly believe *dim mak* is in the equation, I'll need to go back to ViCAP anyway.

The doors are locked when I arrive, so I ring the buzzer. Within a few minutes the heavy double doors open and I'm greeted by Lee. He looks like I feel—tired.

"Hi," he says.

"Morning. Sorry to get you out here so early. I really appreciate it."

"That's okay. If your killer really is using *dim mak…*" Lee trails off, lets out a deep sigh and then leads the way into the building. Inside, he opens the door to his glass office and takes a seat.

On the desk sit four books. I glance at the titles—all of which include the word *dim mak*—while pulling out a two-page table I drafted last night. The table contains all nine victims I think may be related, arranged in date order. The last entry is Jun Saito's murder. In all, there are eight headings—*Date, Location, Name, Age, Association, Cause of death, Other injuries* and *Status*. I've blacked out the victims' names in the copy I'll go through with Lee.

"This table summarizes the victims' injuries, as well as locations and other investigative elements." I place the stapled pages in front of Lee.

He puts on small-framed glasses and taps the top book in his pile. "I'll swap you. This book goes through all the medical stuff. You might want to have a look at it, even contact the author. He's the one who talks about the heart concussion, too. The timing has to be precise—in between heartbeats—but it is possible by a skilled practitioner. I've marked some of the key pages, the key symptoms and medical explanations."

I nod. "Thanks." I flick through the book, while Lee reads through the table.

Once he's finished he looks up at me, his eyebrows furrowed. "Sophie, this is not good."

I presume he's stating the obvious—but maybe I should check. "As opposed to any other type of murder?"

"Sorry, what I mean is it's not good for you, for the FBI or anyone else trying to bring this man to justice. Your killer is extremely skilled."

"So there's no doubt in your mind that the injuries listed are most likely caused by the Ten Killing Hands?"

"No." He pauses. "Although I would like to know more about the breaks for the victims that had broken ribs and broken elbow joints…not to mention your 2001 victim with the broken coccyx. Exactly where were the breaks? What types of breaks were they?"

I've already carefully analyzed the breaks myself, but a second opinion can't hurt. I take him through each person and their injuries, describing the exact locations and angle of force determined by the forensic pathologists who worked each case. "Well?"

"Most definitely kung fu." He nods reluctantly. "Some of these patterns of injuries are quite unique."

"That's what I thought." I sigh. "But the pressure points…that's a whole new level. A new layer."

"Yes, it is. And it makes your killer all the more dangerous."

"We think the perpetrator might be from China. Flown in for these jobs. Given we're dealing with organized crime and the upper echelons of it, the person putting out the contract is more likely to bring in someone external."

Lee nods. "A Chinese national might tie in with the *dim mak,* too. Here, *dim mak* is seen as a party trick or the stuff of movies. But in China, where acupoints are ingrained in our society, it's a much more practiced and treasured form of martial arts…and healing arts."

"Healing?"

"The points are struck to cause pain and death, but they can be massaged or stimulated with acupuncture for healing purposes. They go hand in hand, for use as a weapon or as a healing tool. Yin and Yang."

I'm already screening for my briefing. I think Yin and Yang might go over as well as psychic visions with Petrov and the others. And I'm also thinking about the investigative part of this case. Latoya's already told me China's going to be a tough cookie to crumble, maybe Lee can help.

"Did you train in China? Or do you know someone over there who might be able to help?" I don't bother explaining that China's not part of Interpol, making direct contact difficult for me.

"I trained in China from the time I was five to fifteen, when we emigrated. But that's many years ago now. I'm not sure if any of the people I trained or competed against would still be active. Or that they'd be able to help us in any way."

"But they might?"

He clasps his hands together. "I'll see what I can do." He leans forward. "I also have a cousin who's a police officer in Beijing. Maybe he can help you. He could see if anyone's been killing in China using kung fu and *dim mak.* Maybe there have been similar attacks over there."

"It'd be great to have direct contact with the Chinese police, thanks. I'll put together some key elements of the type of person we're looking for, and maybe then you could contact your cousin. That will be faster and easier than using official channels."

He nods. "Yes, I'm sure it will be. China is not exactly open to sharing sensitive information." He leans back in his chair. "I'll check with Chung. He may want to keep it unofficial."

"Fine with me."

"And as for here, I can probably give you some names in the US—you know, who I think would be capable of inflicting these types of injuries. Would that be helpful?"

I think about the offer. Petrov's sure the hitter is international, but it's always good to keep our minds open. Petrov may be wrong. "Yeah, that'd be great. You think it'll be a long list?"

"Yup. And it will take me some time to compile."

I nod.

"It won't be exhaustive, but I'll give you as many names as I can." He raises his eyebrows. "Not many people are skilled enough to perform the acupoint applications, not as precisely as a professional killer. Many people may try this technique, but not many could kill efficiently with it."

Dim mak…is it really possible? I'm certainly looking forward to reading the books and talking to Grove about it. Or maybe finding evidence to support Lee's theory.

"I've been thinking about how to prove it," I say. "The only real evidence would be bruises at the acupoints, correct?"

"Yes, but that's still not going to give you proof. If we're dealing with delayed death, the bruises would be long gone. And if death was instant you wouldn't see a bruise—they take at least a few hours to show up."

Not entirely true. "We can't check with these first victims, but our Little Tokyo victim is still at the morgue. And a forensic pathologist can check under the skin, can see bruises that didn't have time to show up on the skin's surface."

"Really? Then you're right, you can confirm if his attacker used pressure points."

"If I know where to look, yes."

"Tell me everything you can about this victim, and I'll give you some likely points to check." He fingers his glasses. "Many of the points attack nerve bundles—they may show signs of trauma, too."

"The vagus nerve." I instantly visualize Grove pointing to Saito's vagus nerve and commenting on its condition.

"Yes, that is one of the pressure-point targets. Your victim showed signs of this?"

"Yes. The forensic pathologist described it as inflamed. He thought it was from the trauma to the throat in general, but maybe it was more specific than that."

Lee's nodding. "It was probably targeted by your killer. It's one of the death-touch strikes."

Fifteen

At 8:40 a.m. I owing into the FBI's lot, armed with my four *dim mak* books and an anatomy chart Lee gave me with key pressure points circled. But before I can talk to Grove, I have to brief the team. I race up to the meeting room Petrov booked on the fifteenth floor, where most of the Gang Impact Team resides. Special Agents Hana Kim and Joe De Luca are already there.

"Hi, Sophie. How'd you do last night?"

"Good, good. I'm pretty sure the two maybes are related, so that's nine in total. But there may be even more."

"More?" Hana's face crumples and De Luca looks up, also intrigued.

"Long story. I'll tell you about it in ten minutes?"

"Sure." Hana looks at De Luca. "Joe and I were just about to flip for the coffee run. Maybe now we should draw straws."

"I'm desperate for a coffee, but do you guys mind flipping for it? I need to set up in here. I'll get the next round." The Federal Café runs a coffee cart right at the front door of our building so it shouldn't take them too long.

"You're on." Hana lets the coin fly into the air.

"Heads," De Luca calls as the coin reaches its peak. It lands and spins around a couple of times, before coming to rest on tails.

"Yes." Hana pumps the air, like a tennis player who's just won a long point.

"Man, you must rig this." Despite the complaint, De Luca stands up.

"I'm just lucky."

De Luca turns to me. "That's her tenth straight win." He shakes his head. "And the killer is that the loser pays. My kids are never gonna get to college at this rate."

Hana laughs. "Sophie's getting the next one. You can put the few bucks you'll save into their education fund."

He rolls his eyes and points casually at Hana. "So, a mocha for you." He turns to me. "What about you, Agent Anderson?"

"You going downstairs?"

He nods.

"I'll have a strong latte. Soy milk."

"Done. And don't start without me." Even though I'm the one doing the briefing, he gives the warning look to Hana.

Once I've distributed the printouts around the table, I sit down. In front of each seat I've laid out ten sheets of paper. The first two pages are stapled together and feature the summary table of the nine victims I showed Lee this morning—the eight from ViCAP and Saito. In these copies, the names aren't blanked out and some columns, like the *Association* one, will be more important for us. Lee didn't need to know if the victim was Mafia, Yakuza, Russian. The other eight pages cover the previous eight attacks in more detail, one page per victim. I summarize crime-scene location, the forensic pathologists' reports, any witness statements and general comments from the law-enforcement personnel involved. It took me three hours to draft last night, but it was worth it. I feel like I have a good preliminary grasp of all the victims, and through them an insight into our killer. Maybe even enough to draft a profile. I haven't added anything into my printouts about *dim mak,* but I will cover it during the briefing.

The task force team members arrive one by one, and by 9:00 a.m. everyone's here except De Luca and the coffee.

Then again, his progress was hampered by a couple of last-minute additions to the order. Ramos arrived just as De Luca was leaving and Hana added an espresso to the list, and then decided to keep the boss happy, so she rang De Luca a minute later to request Petrov's cappuccino. His kids' college funds must really be hurting now.

It's only three minutes past the hour when De Luca walks in and distributes the coffees. "Sorry, Williams."

Williams shrugs and holds up his cup of brewed coffee from the Bureau's kitchen. "I'm covered."

We all sit down.

"Okay, people. Now that the caffeine's here, let's get started." Petrov takes the top folder from in front of him. "This is everything our IT people could find on Mee Kim and her mother, Sun-Mi Kim. We've got birth certificates, death certificates, driving records, bank accounts, immigration records…the works. The father on Mee Kim's birth certificate is listed as unknown. So it doesn't get us any closer to discovering if the connection between Saito and Mee Kim was father and daughter. However, now that Kim's gone missing, we've swabbed for DNA in her house. It'll take a few days, but we will be able to compare her DNA to Saito's and uncover any blood relationship that way."

We all nod.

Petrov continues. "We also found that when Sun-Mi Kim was alive, she received regular monthly payments, probably directly from Jun Saito."

"That sounds like maintenance," I say.

Petrov nods. "It looks likely that Saito is Mee Kim's father, but until we have the DNA there's no proof. I'm going to update you on our progress on who, or what organization, might be behind the hit, and Anderson's also got some ViCAP results she'll take us through. But first up, last night's developments." Petrov summarizes our discovery of Mee Kim's disappearance and the forensic tests currently in the lab's queue, before asking if anyone else has got any general updates.

Ramos raises his forefinger into the air. "I found out yesterday that Saito booked his flight, under the name of Jo Kume, three days prior to travel. This ties in with what we already knew from his hotel and the State Department—that he booked his hotel online three days prior to arrival and that he flew out of Singapore."

"So it wasn't a planned trip?" Williams says, writing it down.

"Probably not." Ramos looks up. "The November 24 Singapore flight was the first he could get when he called the airline on November 21…. My officers have also finished interviewing everyone whose car was in the lot at the time of Saito's murder. I've had a look through all the notes myself but nothing looks suspicious. Certainly no cars registered to people with organized-crime ties."

"Does it need any more follow-up?" Petrov's hand hovers over his notepad.

Ramos shakes his head. "We can go back to it in the future, if need be."

When we're all silent for a few seconds, Petrov says, "Anything else, people?"

The others shake their heads.

"Okay, Anderson. You're up."

I take a deep breath. "I believe that our killer, our hit man, is using the Ten Killing Hands as his primary method of attack. The Ten Killing Hands are ten strikes or series of kung fu strikes that are meant to either severely disable or kill your opponent, sometimes with one blow."

Ramos lets out a whistle. "Sounds charming."

"It is. Most of these strikes only work to their full potential if they're completed by someone extremely skilled."

"So how many people are we talking here?" De Luca takes a sip of his coffee.

"Hard to say. As an arbitrary line in the sand, I'd say black belt and above. But it's likely the person we're dealing with has trained to the highest level of kung fu, reaching master level."

Petrov rests his elbows on the table and interlaces his fingers. "I suggested to Anderson that we might be looking at someone from outside the US. Someone brought in as an external contractor to carry out the hits."

Louis Williams nods. "That'd fit with the historic MO of a hit. Particularly if some of these victims are high up in the chain of command."

"Which they are," Petrov says.

"I was going for the more interesting angle." I smile. "Hollywood kung fu expert. Until Petrov set me straight."

"Anything's possible, Anderson. It's just with organized crime, they tend to follow patterns."

I move back to the Killing Hands. "So, to give you some examples—some of the nondeadly strikes include a double strike on the opponent's ears to burst their eardrums, striking the back of a straight elbow to dislocate and damage that joint, or gouging out the eyes and breaking the floating ribs."

"All one-strike hits?" Ramos asks.

"If done correctly, yes, those ones are. Some of the other techniques can be two or three movements in combination. For instance, the Squeeze and Crush." I stand up and move to the nearest person, Hana. "In this one, you strike and grab their throat like this." I hold my hand out in a tiger shape, with Hana's throat between my thumb and forefinger. She instantly coughs. "I'm barely putting any pressure on," I explain. "It's just that the correct position blocks the windpipe instantly. Sorry, Hana."

She gives me a smile. "I'm all right. Keep going."

I nod. "Then you apply pressure until the blood supply to the brain is cut, or until the windpipe closure blocks the victim's oxygen supply, and then twist." I take my hand away from Hana's throat and twist it in thin air. "That'll dislocate or break their neck."

"But the strength required to do that, with one hand…" Williams shakes his head. "The killer must be extremely strong."

"Not necessarily." I sit back down. "Combining your own body weight with speed helps to deliver the intensity of the strike." When Lloyd Grove first talked about Jun

Saito's throat wound and the force required to produce the injury, I also pictured a heavyset and strong attacker. But now that I know kung fu's involved, it's a different story.

"What do you mean?" Williams asks.

I stand up again and move back to Hana. "Can you stand up, Hana?"

"Sure." She's a couple of inches shorter than me, and now that we're side by side, it's much more noticeable.

"Okay. So I start off in a horse stance, side-on to Hana." I position myself in front of Hana, but while she's facing me, I'm side-on to her. "Then when I strike, I twist my body around." In slow motion, I twist so I'm facing Hana but in dragon stance, with my front leg bent in a slight lunge. "The strike's strength comes more from my lower body than my upper body." I repeat the maneuver to show them again. "I use the twisting motion of my hips to propel the strike, and I hit fast, so the opponent is instantly struggling for breath."

"Okay," Williams concedes, "but our guy's still gotta be strong, right?"

"Yes and no." I scrunch up my face. "I can tell you're envisaging someone tall and bulky, but in this case it's more likely to be lean muscle than bulk."

"We're more genetically predisposed to that anyway," Hana adds. "If we're assuming the killer is Asian."

"True." I think of someone to give as an example for Williams and the others. "Agent Williams, have you ever seen any Bruce Lee movies? Or Jet Li?"

"Sure."

"If you look at them in clothes, they look slim—maybe you'd even say slight for a man. But when you see them with their shirts off, they're extremely muscular and every single muscle is defined. Yet they're not bulky like, say, Schwarzenegger."

"Okay, I see what you mean. But I still reckon Arnie would kick their asses." Williams gives a toothy grin.

I laugh. "Maybe…but I'd put a thousand bucks on a kung fu expert striking Arnie before he even got his dukes up."

Williams chuckles.

"Anyway—" I bring us back to the report "—the first two sheets of paper list all the victims, their injuries, causes of death and which of the Ten Killing Hands could have led to those injuries." I pick up the sheets of paper. "As you can see, the first match is perhaps the most interesting, because the victim wasn't killed."

"So the killer screwed up?" Ramos asks.

"Maybe. Although there is one other element…a wild card." I take a deep breath. I guess now's as good a time as any. "I met with my kung fu teacher this morning, and he brought up something called *dim mak*. The premise is that a series of strikes to pressure points can cause death, either instantly or after a period of time."

"Sounds real *Kill Bill* to me." Ramos grins.

Williams laughs. "Yeah. Maybe our guy knows Uma's Five Point Palm Exploding Heart Technique. Five blows to stop blood flow to the heart."

I know the guys are joking, but I throw in a serious comment. "You've actually hit the nail on the head. It's the same premise."

"And here was I thinking it was Hollywood hype," Ramos says.

"Well, there is some debate about whether it's reality or legend. I always thought it was more legend, but my teacher assures me it's not, and he knows his stuff. I've also got some reading material to back it up, including a book written by a doctor."

"A doctor of what?" Williams grins.

I smile. "I must admit, I wondered that at first, too. But he's an M.D., all right."

Petrov clears his throat. "So we're being serious here, Anderson?"

"Yes, sir. I need to read this book and talk to Grove at the coroner's office, but we may be able to find evidence of the use of pressure points on Jun Saito's body. The points are very specific, and if our killer is skilled in *dim mak*, Saito's body will tell us that story."

Petrov blows out a breath. "Let's wait for the medical backup before we start putting too much into this...*dim mak.*"

"Yes, sir." I pause. "But even taking *dim mak* out of the equation, the Ten Killing Hands kill without the use of pressure points."

"Okay. Let's get back to this table," Petrov says.

I look down at the pages. We're still on the first victim, Corey Casey in 1996. Time for my next bombshell. "Corey Casey died four years ago."

Blank faces stare back at me, unaware of the significance.

"And?" Petrov voices it for the team.

"He died of liver failure and that could tie in with pressure-point strikes."

"Eight years later, Anderson?" Petrov remains unconvinced.

I shrug. "According to my kung fu teacher."

"Is there any way to confirm it?" Petrov taps his pen against his notebook.

"Probably not." I think about it. "Maybe we could contact the wife again, see if he came up with bruises in some of the right areas. We could also check with his friends, family and doctor to find out the underlying cause of the liver failure."

"The guy was probably an alcoholic, is all," Williams says.

"Maybe."

There's silence until Petrov speaks. "If there was a contract on this guy, Corey Casey, our hit man would have just tried again or the person behind the hit would have hired someone else to finish the job. No one's going to wait eight years for the mark to die."

"What if the aim was to hurt the victim, to scare or warn him?" Hana suggests. "Or perhaps Mr. Casey was being used to set an example."

"But we don't know if it was organized crime or gang related." De Luca rubs his hand over his black stubble. "It says here association unknown." He taps the first entry of the table.

"Yes. It's the only match I found in which the victim

wasn't known to the police. The guy didn't have a record or any known criminal associates. If you look at the first page of victim information, you'll see he even had a legitimate job, as a stockbroker."

The others pick up the page devoted to Corey Casey and I give them a couple of minutes to read through it.

"Well, the NYPD thought he was scared of something or someone." Ramos puts the papers back on the desk.

I nod. "His attacker, or maybe the person who hired our guy."

"Okay, let's put Corey Casey up as a task." Petrov crosses to the whiteboard and writes up *Follow up Corey Casey*. "Like Anderson said, let's see if we can explain the liver failure without *dim mak*."

I continue summarizing the details. "Mr. Casey was admitted to hospital with three broken ribs, both eardrums burst and a minor concussion. That would have also been from the double strike to the ears. He claimed he didn't see his attacker, that someone jumped him from behind, but both of these techniques are performed facing the victim." I sigh, frustrated that the only person who may have seen our killer is now dead.

"So he was lying." Hana drains the last of her coffee.

"Yes, Casey saw something, or knew something, he shouldn't have." I voice the obvious. "And someone wanted to make sure he didn't talk. It's also possible that he came into contact with organized crime through his job as a stockbroker. Maybe a mob member lost some money based on some of Mr. Casey's stock recommendations."

"I guess the scare tactics worked." Hana leans her chin on her hand.

"They often do," Williams says.

I pick up the printout and move back to the ViCAP table. "So our next hit was two years later, in San Francisco. Hop Fu was a known member of the Wah Ching gang."

"Wah Ching is one of the biggest Chinese gangs in the country," Petrov says. "And staunch rivals of the Asian Boyz, who are also linked to Saito's death somehow."

"You think it's significant?" I ask.

Petrov shrugs. "Hard to say at this stage."

I continue. "This is the only case where the forensic pathologist ruled that the cause of death wasn't directly caused by his injuries. The victim was sixty-two and the pathologist concluded he died of heart complications, caused by the stress of the attack. But the medical reports on the elbow injury are in line with Angry Tiger Descends the Mountain."

"Could this be related to *dim mak?*" Petrov asks.

"According to my teacher, yes. He's quite confident, but I agree we need to check Jun Saito's body again, see if pressure points were a factor in his attack. If *dim mak* was used on Saito, it's likely Hop Fu suffered the same fate." I move on. "Two years later, we've got the first direct kill with his bare hands, the Squeeze and Crush on Shiro Matsu. The victim died of asphyxiation and his neck was also broken. There were no other injuries. I'm thinking the killer caught him by complete surprise and didn't need to use any of his disabling techniques. Particularly given the victim was only thirty-one and extremely fit. The guy could have put up a fight, if he'd had half a chance. Whether *dim mak* was used as well…" I shrug my shoulders. "We'll never know, and there's probably no point trying to prove it with every victim. We've already related these nine attacks through the Ten Killing Hands, *dim mak* will give us another dimension."

"We've got the Yakuza link in this one, too. Just like Saito." De Luca scribbles in his notebook. "Only two Yakuza members in the mix, this Shiro Matsu guy in 2000 and now Saito."

"It's unlikely they're linked, but we should run it down." Petrov crosses over to the whiteboard again and writes up *Link between Matsu (2000) and Saito (2008)?*

"Like the other murders, the case remains unsolved and there were no leads, no witnesses," I say. "Law enforcement assumed Matsu was targeted by someone because of his Yakuza involvement, but they could never confirm it."

Petrov has skipped ahead to Matsu's dedicated page. "In this case, he was the regional boss for Chicago, so we're talking very high up. It's the sort of hit that could easily have been sanctioned from within the organization. Perhaps he crossed the *kumicho,* or was planning to, and the *kumicho* nipped it in the bud, or the *fuku-honbucho* may have decided it was time to move up in the world."

"Sorry, can you explain those terms?" I flick to the page on Matsu on my copy of the report, ready to write the words in.

"Sure. The *kumicho* is the name of the big boss and he may be based in Chicago or could be based in one of the Yakuza's more active areas in the US. No one's been able to ID the US *kumicho.* Matsu was the Yakuza regional boss for Chicago, which is called *wakagashira,* and his assistant is the *fuku-honbucho.*"

"The local cops also suggested it could have been the Hip Sing Association. They'd heard rumors on the street that they were fighting over territories for the distribution of heroin and crack cocaine."

"Most gang disputes are turf based." Williams jumps in. "And over their 'business' activities."

"Yup," Petrov concedes. "Either is possible."

"Next was Gino Bianco," I continue. "Forty-two-year-old from Philly, known by local cops and the Bureau to be a captain in Philly's Mafia. He died from asphyxiation and the forensic pathologist noted the cause of death was most likely inflicted by someone standing or pressing down with a boot on Bianco's throat. But his coccyx was broken, and that's consistent with the ninth Killing Hand, the Double Flying Butterfly. Our killer would have broken the coccyx, causing Bianco to collapse to the ground. Then the killer simply held Bianco down by pressing his foot against his throat, and kept exerting downward pressure until Bianco was dead."

"Pretty cold." Hana's staring out the window, into the office space beyond the project room.

All the kills are cold—like most premeditated murders—but I know what she means. When I read about Bianco's death I got the instant visual, too—our killer, standing over his prey and simply pushing down with his shoe until Bianco went limp.

It's not as fast as a bullet, or as the Squeeze and Crush. Bianco would have been in extreme pain, perhaps even partially paralyzed, as our killer looked down on him and put him out of his misery…but slowly. And the fact that he didn't bend down, didn't go down to Bianco's level physically, shows his sense of superiority. He didn't even bother finishing Bianco off with one of the Killing Hands, with his prized skill.

"In terms of a profile, hit men tend to be extremely detached from their kills. While many of them enjoy taking someone's life, enjoy the power and control, it's still a job for them. They don't get the kind of pleasure a serial killer derives from stalking and killing a victim. Remember, they don't choose the targets. The pleasure they do get from the kill tends to be more about working out the best way to make the hit—when, where, how—and the satisfaction of a mission accomplished. We're talking about a very different beast to the serial killer or an emotionally fuelled killer." I pause. "I'll be drafting a full profile in the next couple of days, but in the meantime I can e-mail through some generic psychological info on professional hit men if you like."

"That'd be great." Hana leans back in her chair and tucks her hair behind her ears. "It'd help to get a handle on what sort of person becomes a hit man."

I nod. "I'll get it to you all later today or tonight."

"But ultimately we're not just after the killer," Petrov reminds me. "We're after his employer."

It's hard to know which would be easier—to find the killer and hope he'll lead us to the source, or to work out who might have wanted Saito dead and work forward from there.

Petrov gives me a nod, urging me on.

"A year after the Philly job, our guy killed Bao Tran, a Vietnamese member of the Asian Boyz here in L.A. The cause of death was listed as a ruptured spleen, and two of his ribs were cracked. This particular strike, targeting the spleen, is considered one of the nine death touches. This could be evidence of our killer's expertise in *dim mak* or it could simply be his use of the Heaven Piercing Fist with great accuracy to fatally damage the spleen."

"That's common in car accidents, yes?" De Luca looks up.

"Yes. But most car accident victims get to a hospital pretty quickly, Bao Tran didn't. In this case the victim suffered no other injuries. The LAPD's Asian Crime Unit handled the case and while the word on the street was that it was their rivals Tiny Rascal Gang, there was no direct evidence linking them. And LAPD doesn't have anything on our killer either."

"Even a professional hit man's gotta make a mistake. Right?" De Luca holds both palms skyward. "No one's perfect."

"True. But our killer doesn't have any emotional ties to the victims or the people hiring him. Plus he has no emotional investment in the kill itself—and that means he's got the time and the detachment to plan and execute his kills. He must have removed the bullets from the parking lot on East Second Street. Shot out the lights, but took the bullets. All of the murders have been extremely well planned, and he's managed to get close enough to the targets to kill them with his bare hands, which means he's also extremely smart. Our guy was able to get close and one-on-one to commit the murders on his terms, using his methods."

"A lot of crims would like that," Williams says. "They'd want the victims to be scared, to know they're gonna die. And this guy can deliver on that for them. It's quick and a lot cleaner than torture, but it's still painful."

I nod. "Most of these victims would have been in pain before they were killed. Broken ribs, dislocated elbows, broken coccyx." After a beat of silence I move on. "In 2004 we've got another hit in New York, this time the victim's a known member of the Hip Sing Association. He'd even done ten years in prison for money laundering and low-level drug trafficking. Unusually, the victim was strangled manually—the regular way for asphyxiation. I'm not sure why the killer departed from his usual killing method, particularly when he'd used three of the other Killing Hands to severely disable his target. The victim, Li Chow, had one elbow dislocated, both eye sockets broken and both cheekbones broken. He would have been in extreme pain, and probably on the ground like the victims in San Francisco and Philadelphia, yet in this case the killer chose to go to Chow's level and strangle him with his hands." I bring my hands up in mock strangulation. "And with the regular grip." I shake my head. "It doesn't really make sense to me. If it wasn't for the fact that two other strikes from the Ten Killing Hands had been used, I may have discounted the murder."

"Could we be talking about a different killer?"

"I guess it's possible, but like I said, the other injuries are almost definitely caused by the Ten Killing Hands. It's too coincidental to have both eye sockets and both cheekbones broken. It's characteristic of the Double Back-fist." I replicate the strike in midair, clenching my fists and bringing my hands in an inward circular motion from the elbow joint, around, up and then downward onto an imaginary opponent. "And the forensic pathologist concluded that all four facial bones were broken using direct and downward force. Not like a punch that swings to one side in its arc." I shake my head again. "No, we're definitely talking kung fu."

"Maybe a different killer, but using the same techniques?" Hana suggests.

"That's possible." I say, thinking. "Unless there's some other explanation as to why he manually strangled the victim."

"Anything else come to mind, Anderson?" Petrov taps his pen against the palm of his hand.

I think about the different ways our perp could have killed the victim, and why he might not have used those methods. I come up with one hypothesis. "Manual strangulation is more personal than using kung fu. The killer would have both hands around the victim's throat and would have been close, almost intimate."

"So maybe the killer knew this victim—" Ramos glances at the table in front of him "—knew Li Chow."

I nod slowly. "I like it. From a behavioral perspective it fits."

"And it fits if the killer's Chinese." Petrov scribbles something down in his notebook as he talks. "Presumably he's more likely to know someone in one of the tongs than other racial criminal groups. Most of these groups still have strong ties to their homeland. So maybe Chow had ties with our killer." Petrov crosses to the whiteboard again, and writes *Li Chow (New York) knew the killer?*

Once Petrov's sitting down again, I continue. "The next victim, that same year, was also Chinese and from the Hip Sing Association. But it was in Chicago and it was a regular Killing Hands kill. This is the killer's youngest victim, at nineteen. Shen Chan was killed in a parking garage as he was about to get into his car. The Side Tiger Claw combines a throat grab with an eye gouge, which is why he died of asphyxiation but also had severe damage to his eyes. His left eye had been torn from its socket and was only just attached by the optic nerve. Like many of our other victims, he also had a dislocated elbow, indicating our killer used the Angry Tiger Descends the Mountain technique to soften his opponent before going for the kill strike. Unlike the previous Hip Sing murder in the same year, Okawara was very low in the organization, a mere foot soldier. Chicago police were puzzled initially, but then they discovered Okawara was the godson of someone higher up in the organization so they decided the hit was symbolic, made to anger the older man."

Again, Petrov makes some notes, perhaps wanting to confirm the why behind the hit.

"And that brings us to our last victim before Saito, one Alexander Ivanovich, San Diego, 2007."

"My comrade," Petrov says with a Russian accent.

"Yes. And the only Russian victim." I state the obvious. "A bit of a departure from MO again here in terms of cause of death, but we've still got definite links to the Killing Hands, with both of Ivanovich's eardrums burst. He was stabbed, once, although it was more of a slice. The forensic pathologist even thought the blade was big enough to be some sort of sword."

"I know the Japanese use samurai swords, what do you use in kung fu?" Ramos asks.

"Kung fu uses the butterfly swords, which would fit with the one-and-a-half-inch wound to the chest. The killer did severely damage the heart, and the ultimate cause of death was blood loss. The heart was pierced and pumping blood out of the wound."

"So why the sword?" Ramos asks me.

"I'm not sure." I stop to consider. "Petrov, any reason why this method of killing could be requested for a Russian victim?"

Petrov runs his right fingertips across his lips. "Nothing racial or cultural that I can think of. But maybe personal?" Petrov strides to the whiteboard and writes it up as *Sword for Russian victim in San Diego?* He stays standing and looks at me. "Anything else?"

"Well, I would like to spend more time on the *dim mak* angle…contact the forensic pathologists in each case and get them to send their full autopsy reports and photos over. Not everything would have been logged in ViCAP."

Petrov nods. "And talk to Grove, too. The man knows his stuff. I want us to be absolutely certain that we are looking at the Ten Killing Hands and this *dim mak*. If we throw our resources at that angle and we're wrong…"

"Yes, sir." I finish off my update by telling the team about Lee's list of people in the US capable of the Ten Killing Hands, and Lee's cousin in China.

"An inside source will be invaluable," Petrov says.

I nod my agreement.

"Okay. Before we finish this list off and assign some tasks—" Petrov taps the whiteboard "—I'll take you through what we've come up with to date on who may have put the contract out on Saito's life." He turns the whiteboard around—a blank canvas. "Okay, the first option is the L.A. Yakuza themselves or someone within the Yakuza here." He writes *L.A. Yakuza* on the board and directly underneath it sticks a photo up on the whiteboard using a magnet. "This is the L.A. boss, Tomi Moto." From the photo he draws a vertical line, and then sticks up another photo directly underneath it. "And this is his second-in-charge, Takeshi Suzuki."

Both photographs are obviously surveillance shots and a little grainy, indicating they were taken from afar and blown up.

"I've put together some key information and will e-mail that through to you all after this meeting. But the basics…Tomi Moto was born here in L.A. sixty years ago. He's been the L.A. boss for ten years now, when his father handed the reins over to him. His second-in-charge, Takeshi Suzuki, immigrated here when he was thirty years old, ten years ago. He doesn't have any criminal convictions, here or in Japan, but as far as we know he started working for the Yakuza almost as soon as he arrived in the States, working his way up the ranks. He climbed the ladder quickly, and was even second-in-charge to Tomi Moto's father for a year and a half before Tomi took over. It's possible that either of these men ordered the hit on Saito." He puts little asterisks next to each of the photos. "However, our intelligence indicates that when Saito was active in the organization in Tokyo, he actually had strong ties to L.A., to Tomi Moto's father. So unless they had a falling out it's unlikely Moto ordered the hit on Saito. In fact, hitting Saito would be an extremely offensive act to Tomi Moto and an insult to his father's memory."

"His father's dead?" I ask.

"Yes. Just last year." Petrov continues, "Another possibility is that a different regional arm of the Yakuza ordered the hit. Maybe the San Francisco boss is responsible and wanted to piss off Tomi Moto here in L.A." He writes *Another regional arm of Yakuza* on the board, underneath the photos of Moto and Suzuki.

"But why would someone in San Francisco hit Saito? Wouldn't they just hit someone in the L.A. arm?" I ask.

Petrov shrugs. "It's impossible to know for sure, but like I said, Moto would take Saito's death personally." He waits a beat. "The other possibility for an internal Yakuza hit is that it's one of the Japanese members making a statement about Koreans in the organization. While Koreans have been part of the Yakuza since the 1920s, some Japanese feel that the Yakuza should be exclusively full-blood Japanese. So it's possible one of these race extremists took Saito out as the symbol of Korean Yakuza. He's not just any Korean in the Yakuza, he's the son of the first Korean to be part of the Japanese Mafia. This hit could be a racial message."

We all nod, taking in the information.

"Anything from your informants?" Williams asks. "I haven't heard anything back from mine yet."

Petrov looks at Hana, Ramos and me. "We've been trying to refine our theories a little by getting some cold, hard intelligence."

Petrov returns his gaze to Williams. "I've been squeezing everybody I know, and hard. So far no one's talking, but eventually they will."

Williams nods.

"Anything from you, De Luca?"

"No. But I only put the word out yesterday."

"Okay." Petrov writes up *Targeting Korean Yakuza—racial statement* on the whiteboard. "The next possibility is the Asian Boyz, given Saito was seen in their Long Beach meth lab. We haven't been able to confirm official Yakuza involvement in the Long Beach residence at this stage. And we still don't know what Saito was doing there, or why." Petrov writes *Asian Boyz* in a new column. "So perhaps the Yakuza was taking over their territory, and they knew of the symbolic significance of Saito's death." Petrov writes up *Territorial dispute* underneath the new column.

"Is there any other reason why the Asian Boyz would hit the Yakuza?" Williams asks.

Petrov shakes his head. "Not that we know of. But it's possible." He adds *Unknown vendetta/dispute* to the Asian Boyz column. "Okay, let's move on to other possibilities." He takes a deep breath. "There's always competition in organized crime. In some ways they operate like many normal businesses, competing for the same work, the same income sources. So, it's possible that the Yakuza has pissed off another organized crime syndicate in L.A." Petrov writes up a new column entitled *Organized crime.* "We know there are active members of the Italian mafia here in L.A., in addition to the Russian Mafia and a few of the Chinese triads and tongs." He writes each group on the board, underneath his new column. "All are possible employers of our hit man."

I look at the board. "Wow, we have a lot of options. Too many."

"Yes," Petrov concedes. "At this stage we need to come up with as many viable theories as possible and then see what fits with the evidence as it comes in."

"Evidence…that's something we don't have much of."

Unfortunately, Hana is spot-on.

"Not yet." Petrov stays positive. "But the lab's still processing the crime scene, Saito's hotel room and Mee Kim's house. Hopefully something will come through."

Williams runs his hand over his skull. "What we really need is some inside information. Any undercover operatives in the Yakuza or Asian Boyz?"

"No." Petrov flicks the whiteboard marker up and down between his fingers. "I checked the HIDTA War Room, too. Nothing."

The War Room is part of the L.A. High Intensity Drug Trafficking Areas program run out of the Office of National Drug Control Policy. It's an intelligence center that provides support and tracks all federal, state and local undercover op eratives. The aim is to stop undercover cops from shooting undercover DEA agents, and so on.

"Besides," Petrov continues, "this hit has been sanctioned pretty high up and it'd take years to get an undercover operative into that level of the Yakuza or the Asian Boyz—if ever."

"We must be able to get someone in." Williams is frustrated.

"You know how these things are, Williams." Petrov sighs. "Most of these guys grew up together, have known each other for years. And breaking into that is almost impossible."

"We could work on this homicide for twelve months and still be none the wiser." Williams's voice is softer. "We're talking about a professional hit man here. And he's good. Can we at least start the ball rolling and try to get an under-cover operative in?"

"We've got undercover agents set up as distributors and the like," Hana says.

"Yeah, but that's not going to help us with Saito's murder."

Hana is silent.

Petrov holds his hands up. "All right. I'll look into the undercover angle. But in the meantime, let's focus on what we've got and the forensics that'll be coming through. Okay?"

Williams nods.

"Great. Let's split up these tasks."

Sixteen

I look at the final whiteboard list I copied into my notebook.

Follow up Corey Casey—Kim
Link between Matsu (2000) and Saito (2008)?—De Luca
Li Chow (New York) knew the killer?—Williams
Sword for Russian victim in San Diego?—Petrov
Jun Saito victimology—Anderson & Ramos
Mee Kim follow-up—Anderson & Ramos (Kim if required)
Crime-scene prints—Lab (Ramos)
Generic info on contract killers—Anderson
Ten Killing Hands and dim mak follow-up—Anderson
End employer—Petrov, De Luca & Williams
Offender profile—Anderson

Petrov's set it up so Ramos and I are concentrating on elements of the investigation that don't need a comprehensive understanding of organized crime or gangs. And while my name's up there quite a bit, some of the tasks the others have been assigned could turn out to be more onerous.

For the moment, Ramos and I set up a project room, ready to go through the two folders on the desk—one for

Mee Kim and one for her mother, Sun-Mi Kim. But I'll be making my exit to see Lloyd Grove soon.

"I'm going to check in with the lab." Ramos pulls out his cell phone. "I'll try my charm on the phone first, see how far that gets me. Otherwise I might be making a road trip, too." He punches in the number. "Hi, Court. It's Detective Ramos…just checking on those prints from Little Tokyo… yup, I've got it here…" Ramos flips to the front of his notebook. "Case file number 543248J." The number's written in big red print across the notebook's cover. "Okay…will do. I was thinking of dropping in…right… okay. Yup. Can you transfer me to Trace, then?" He looks up. "She assures me today, and that there's no point coming in person."

I'm about to comment, when Ramos holds up his pointer finger at me, asking me to hold on. "Yup, I'm here." Ramos reads the case file number out again. "Okay… uh-huh…yep." He hangs up. "Trace is done with Saito's clothes, but they didn't find anything. No traces of hair, other fibers or drugs." He leans back. "Maybe I should drop in on Court."

I smile. "I wouldn't want you breathing down my neck, either." But even though I say it, we all know that sometimes our physical presence does get a case bumped up the list. All's fair in love and war—and homicide is war.

After a few seconds, Ramos says, "No, I'll stick with Mee, while you go see Grove."

I nod. My priority has to be Jun Saito's body. So while Ramos starts going through the files on Mee and Sun-Mi Kim, I head off to the coroner's office. Earlier, I'd quickly flicked through the four books Lee lent me and chosen one for Grove, the one written by the M.D. Grove's medical knowledge will quickly be able to back up or refute pressure points. I also take the chart Lee gave me.

It's 11:00 a.m. by the time I pull into the parking lot, and when I get to Grove's office he's sitting at his desk, Googling *dim mak*.

He looks up and smiles. "Intriguing stuff, Anderson.

Although I haven't been able to find anything concrete on the Web yet, medically speaking that is."

I pass him the book.

"Death Touch: The Science Behind the Legend of Dim Mak," he reads out.

"I need you to tell me how realistic it is. I've only had a quick look so far, but it does make for some interesting reading."

"Such as?" He flicks to the contents page.

"It actually relates the *dim mak* pressure points to the nervous system. According to this book, most of the points lie on peripheral nerves, and attacking these points can cause changes in the autonomic nervous system."

Grove nods. "Which controls blood pressure, heart rate, digestion, breathing and so on."

"So the theory is that direct strikes can fool the nervous system into doing something it wouldn't normally, like speeding up your heart rate or increasing your blood pressure."

"Sure. I can see that."

"One of the particular pressure points that my kung fu teacher mentioned was stomach 9, here." I point to the area on the side of my neck, and also show Grove one of the diagrams.

"Yes, the carotid sinus and vagus nerve. It is an extremely sensitive area. In fact, if someone's suffering from an arrhythmia, we often use what are called vagal maneuvers as a treatment."

"Vagal?"

"Along the vagus nerve. A simple massage in that area has been shown to decrease the chances of a fatal ventricular fibrillation."

"But could striking that area cause ventricular fibrillation?" I ask.

Grove's brow furrows. "What does our guy say?" He taps the book.

"It's a yes from him. I've only had a quick flick through it and there is a section on the heart. I'll leave it with you?"

"Definitely. I'll read it with great interest."

"Now, on to Jun Saito. I'd like to see if *dim mak* was used during the attack on him."

"You know the throat wound entry points are exactly on this stomach 9 point you showed me." He points to the anatomy diagram.

I nod. "And the damage to the vagus nerve is consistent, too." Some of the points are clustered very closely together, but nonetheless Saito's throat injuries are in line with stomach 9 and stomach 10 on either side of Saito's Adam's apple. "So even the way the throat was targeted could be *dim mak.*"

Grove shrugs. "Well, whether your killer was targeting the carotid artery for a bleed-out or the acupoint, death was inevitable."

"What do you think of his wound, now that we're thinking it was caused by bare hands?"

"It's still some force. And very direct. We're talking fingertips?"

I hold my hand up in a tiger shape. "The webbing between the killer's thumb and forefinger puts pressure on the trachea, and the thumb and fingertip would have struck and dug into the sides of the neck."

Grove studies my hand shape. "That's in line with the victim's body."

I change my hand shape to a horizontal open palm with the palm facing upward. "In *dim mak* that particular point, the stomach 9, can also be struck with an upward scoping method for maximum effect." I strike an imaginary target with the outside edge of my hand and keep the movement going upward. "This is the technique my teacher mentioned that could dislodge plaque and cause a stroke."

He nods. "Heart attack or stroke. Certainly if we're looking at an older individual, or anyone with narrowing arteries, a hard strike could have that impact."

I blow out a deep sigh. It might be time to go back to ViCAP, see if I can't track down some more of our hit man's victims. But only violent crimes are inputted, and if the killer only used the pressure-point techniques and not the Ten Killing Hands, chances are the victim could seem unscathed. Their death would have been ruled natural and certainly wouldn't be recorded as a violent homicide in ViCAP.

The final strike that may have been used by our killer is a knuckle strike, which I demonstrate for Grove.

"Okay. Guess it's time to pay Mr. Jun Saito another visit." Grove stands up.

"Yup."

Grove leads the way down to one of the autopsy rooms.

"The other thing my teacher said, Doc, is that for the nerve strikes, you'd be looking to stretch the nerve as much as possible or impact it against bone to compress it. Does that sound right?"

He keeps walking. "Sure. At the very least, that's going to cause extreme pain. And maybe it would have some detrimental effects on the nervous system, too." He opens the door.

Saito lies on an examination table, with a tray of surgical instruments next to him.

"I got my assistant to get him ready for us."

I nod.

"So, where am I looking?" Grove snaps on gloves.

I bring out the chart. "According to Lee, we should check a few points on the arm. The heart setups are the most commonly used death strikes. Pericardium 6 is on the inside of the arm, about two inches from the hand." I show Grove the acupoint on the anatomy chart.

"Which arm?"

"Let's check both."

Grove cuts around the area on Saito's right arm and peels back the skin. "Nothing here." He repeats the process on the left arm. "Wow, here it is. Definite trauma on this side." He points to a red and inflamed area around the pressure point.

"Bingo."

In total, Lee suggested I check ten of the more lethal *dim mak* points and we gradually make our way through each point on Saito's body. Not all of them show trauma, but four points do—stomach 9, the area around the throat wound; pericardium 6 on the arm; kidney 22 on the middle of the rib cage; and heart 3, near the elbow joint.

"What do you think?" I ask.

"These areas have definitely been struck and by a direct and forceful impact. But why would the killer use pressure points and sever the carotid artery?"

I shrug. "I guess he wanted a contingency plan. If the *dim mak* didn't get Saito, the blood loss from the throat wound would." I peer over the body. "Any sign of trauma to the heart?"

Grove shakes his head. "The heart was fine. But if these strikes really do work and it all happened fast enough, maybe he bled out before his heart could give out."

"How long would he have had once the carotid artery was severed and he started bleeding?"

"Only five to ten minutes. On the lower end of that spectrum if his heart was already pumping fast from the attack."

"That's not long."

We're both silent over the body.

After a few minutes, Grove says, "Well, I've got my weekend reading lined up… Anything else here, Anderson?"

"Not for Saito, but I do have another question."

He peels off his gloves. "Uh-huh."

"You ever heard of heart concussion?"

"Sure. *Commotio cordis.* Not a common cause of death. The reported cases usually involve sporting accidents, like trauma from a hockey puck, a baseball, a hockey stick…that sort of thing. But the timing must be extremely precise."

Lee had mentioned the timing, too.

"How precise?"

"There's a small window of time, fifteen to thirty milliseconds, when the heart is repolarizing and getting ready for the next beat. That's when it's vulnerable."

"You think it's possible with kung fu punches?"

"Maybe. Why?"

"It's one other thing my teacher mentioned. Apparently there are a few direct *dim mak* attack points in the chest wall, and that book correlates the points with heart concussion."

Grove considers it. "Again, plausible. If the force was hard enough."

"They've tested the force outputted by different martial arts punches and a boxer's punch. They're all very high."

"True. So I guess the answer's yes—a skilled martial arts practitioner could strike the chest wall hard enough to cause heart concussion."

Seventeen

When I get back to the office and join Ramos in the project room, there are papers everywhere.

"How'd you do?" Ramos asks.

"I've got proof that our killer used *dim mak* on Saito. We probably can't prove it on the other victims, unless the forensic pathologist noted underlying bruises."

Ramos nods. "You told Petrov?"

"Called him from the car with the update." I take a seat. "How's it going here?"

"Good." He takes me through the piles. "I've got financials here, birth certificate, passport and immigration records in this pile, education records here, and I've kept everything on her mother separate. I've also added in the paperwork that was in her study—bills, her tax returns, receipts and so on."

"Anything interesting yet?"

"Nope. She's the model citizen."

I spend the next hour getting into Mee's world and by the end of that time Ramos and I both know as much about her as we can without actually knowing her personally. On paper, Mee Kim looks squeaky-clean. Good student—in fact she got good enough marks to study law or medicine but decided she wanted to teach. According to her college application, she loved children and always wanted to be a teacher. She continued with the good grades in college and was actively involved in a number of campus clubs, including the tae kwon do club. In fact, she competes in tae kwon do and is considered to be one of the top females in the US. No criminal record. She photocopies her tax return before she submits it every year and keeps the photocopy, with a note of the submission date—always on time. She donates one thousand dollars every year to charity. On Saturday mornings she works in the Korean community teaching English—for free. No speeding tickets. No parking tickets. Got her license first go at age sixteen. Registered the Hyundai Tiburon last year, and before that had two cars: a Toyota Corolla from 1999–2002 and then a Hyundai Elantra. All cars were fully paid for, no finance. She's got a credit card but every month it's under a thousand dollars and is paid off in full, on time. Her bank statements don't show anything irregular, except the monthly payments from Saito. Her mother died on November 4 last year and the payments to Mee started on December 1 that year. Saito knew Sun-Mi Kim had died and that his payments had to be made directly to Mee. So Sun-Mi either contacted him toward the end, or Jun Saito had someone watching them.

"Like I said, the model citizen," Ramos says.

"Uh-huh. I keep coming back to the father–daughter angle. I just don't see this girl getting involved any other way."

"No. Unless she liked older men and Saito was her lover, not her father."

I shrug. "It's possible, I guess. But you should have seen Bailey, her boyfriend. He seemed like a nice guy and I can't imagine her going for such a bad boy when the boyfriend's more like her—squeaky-clean."

"Women go for the wrong type of man all the time."

"Ain't that the truth." Although for me at the moment it's more a case of not going for the right guy—Darren Carter. I focus on Mee again. "I don't buy it. Mee seemed so... She likes control. Everything neat and orderly. And a crime figure as a lover, that's not orderly. But if he was her father, well, as the saying goes, You can't choose your family. Plus I'm still not convinced she recognized Saito."

Ramos nods, accepting the logic before moving on. "She's only left the country once."

"The trip to Barbados in January this year. Nothing in that."

"No," Ramos agrees.

The trip was a holiday with Bailey, nothing more.

"And she's never been to Japan or Korea." Again, I think back to the vision of Saito getting the call. What if someone was threatening his daughter? My thoughts are interrupted by Ramos's phone vibrating on the table.

He flips it open. "Ramos…uh-huh…yeah, okay… thanks." He flips the phone shut and looks up at me. "That was Court. From the fence and debris at the parking lot, they got one print. It matches Saito."

"Damn." The same end result as our DNA sample from the cigarette butt—a match with the victim.

"Uh-huh." Ramos punches Petrov's extension into the conference phone. "I better tell Petrov."

Petrov picks up after two rings. "Yup."

"Prints are back from the lab."

"Anything?"

"They got one print, but it matches our victim, Jun Saito."

Petrov sighs. "Okay." He pauses. "Hey, what did you think of Mee's file?"

"She looks pretty clean to me."

"Me, too." I flick the ring on my finger, keen to get moving. "Good grades, no criminal record, perfect tax record, gives to charity every year…"

"I get the picture. What about Sun-Mi Kim?"

"The father–daughter angle is looking more likely," I say. "Immigration records place Sun-Mi Kim out of the country and in Korea for the summer in 1982."

"And nine months later…"

"Uh-huh."

"Okay. Thanks for the update. Did Ramos tell you Mee didn't ring into the school today?"

"No." I look at Ramos.

"Sorry, got caught up in this."

"I rang Montebello High, Huntova and Bailey this morning," Petrov explains. "Mee Kim didn't show up for work or call in sick and neither Huntova nor Bailey has heard from her. She's definitely on the run. You're right about the framed photos—if she'd been abducted the photos wouldn't be missing. Plus her car's missing, and it's more likely she drove off in it rather than someone abducting her in her own car. It's also possible someone came through her house after she left, but I think the rest of the house would have looked like the bedroom if it had been ransacked."

I know from my vision at Mee's house that Petrov's right—she ran. But he doesn't know that the Yakuza was on her doorstep and that there was a struggle. The crime-scene techs focused on the interior, and the backyard looked untouched anyway. I wouldn't have noticed the few small tufts of upturned grass or a couple of broken Camellia branches if I wasn't looking for evidence to support my vision. I can't tell Petrov or anyone else what I know because they'd want a source. Sometimes I can get away with passing off what I see in my visions as hunches and presenting them as possibilities, and I've also been known to flat-out lie. I guess I could make up a source—say they won't talk to anyone but me. I sigh…it's going to lead to more problems than it's worth. For the moment, I better keep my inside knowledge of the Yakuza visit to myself. Even though in some ways Mee seems so vulnerable, so clean-cut, she fought off two male attackers—she can look after herself.

"Anyway, I'll let you know if I get anything back on the APB. But so far she's lying low."

I bite my lip. "I still don't understand why she hasn't come to us. Why she hasn't called."

Ramos voices his theory. "Maybe she's hiding something…or someone."

"Anything to support that in the paperwork, Detective?"

"No."

Petrov sighs. "It sure would make me feel better if she called us."

After we hang up there's silence for a minute before Ramos says, "So where would Mee go? Presuming Huntova and Bailey are telling the truth and she hasn't contacted them, who would she contact?"

I've been trying to put myself in Mee's shoes. On the one hand, she doesn't want to drag an innocent bystander into a potentially deadly situation. But at the same time I think she'd be sensible and organized enough to know she had to think, and I mean really think. And to do that she'd need time. Staying with someone for a few days while she figured out what to do is her most likely move. And she's smart enough to stay away from the obvious choices like her boyfriend or Huntova. The Yakuza, the killer and whoever was behind the hit on Saito would know where she works and who she's sleeping with.

"She must have gone to someone she felt the Yakuza wouldn't know about. Maybe even someone she didn't think we'd find. So hotels and motels are out, because she'd probably have to use her credit card and she's smart enough to know we can track that."

Ramos puts his hands on the stack of papers. "There must be something in here."

"True."

"What about her students at Montebello High?"

I scrunch my face up. "I don't see her hitting up one of her sixteen-year-old students to crash the night. But her adult students from her Saturday-morning teaching…"

Ramos nods. "They're equals, a lot of them are probably older than her. Plus she wouldn't have to worry about parents."

"Exactly." I flick through the papers. "Okay, it's the Korean Cultural Center on Wilshire. Number 5505." I stand and scoop up all the papers, placing them into my briefcase.

Ramos nods. "I think I've seen it before. Near Dunsmuir. Should only take us about fifteen minutes." He stands up.

"I'll drive. My car's closer." I've got a spot in the Bureau's employee area, but Ramos's car is in the visitor parking lot.

* * *

Wilshire's busy, but the Korean Cultural Center is about six miles from the L.A. field office, so we make good progress.

"Take a left into Dunsmuir," Ramos directs as we come to the corner of Wilshire and Dunsmuir and a two-story building with the Korean flag flying on top.

I swing the wheel around, and from Dunsmuir we see off-street parking for the center. "How'd you know about this?"

"I worked a homicide around this area a few years back." He taps his head. "Agents aren't the only ones with good memories."

I smile and pull into one of a few empty parking spots. As we get out of the car I glance at my watch—2:20 p.m. That should give me plenty of time to interview some of Mee's adult students and still get to kung fu.

The center's quite large, and signs in the entrance advertise the center's museum, exhibition area, library and auditorium. Long posters on the wall document the more recent exhibitions, and all signs are in both English and Korean Hangeul. There are also some promotional items that appear only in Korean. "Guess we should have brought Agent Kim along for this one," I say to Ramos.

We approach the desk and a Korean woman in her thirties gives us a welcoming smile. "Good afternoon." Like Mee and Hana, she speaks with an American accent, so she obviously grew up in the States. "Welcome to the Korean Cultural Center."

"Thanks." I take my ID out of my pocket. "I'm Special Agent Anderson with the FBI and this is Detective Ramos from LAPD."

Her eyes widen slightly "Oh, what can I do for you?"

"We've got some questions about one of your employees, Mee Kim."

"Mee, yes. She's actually one of our volunteers. She teaches English every Saturday."

I nod. "Are you close to Mee?"

"Not really. I do work on Saturdays but we only talk to one another in passing—she's in classes and I'm out here."

"Have you heard from her recently?"

"No, why?"

I take a breath. "I'm afraid Mee is missing."

"Missing?" The woman seems genuinely shocked. Either Mee's not staying with her and hasn't contacted her or she's a damn good actor. "That's terrible," she says. "Do you think…do you think something's happened to her?" She shakes her head. "Of course it has if she's missing." A small tear forms at the corner of her eye. "Poor Mee."

I hold my hand up. "At this stage it looks like Mee has packed a bag and a few things from home and taken off. But we are worried about her, and want to help her. Is she close to anyone here? Maybe her students?"

"She's got lots of students. She teaches five classes on Saturdays. Her first class is teaching young children Korean, but then she teaches English to adults in the next four."

"Do you have a list of her adult pupils? It would help Mee enormously."

The woman nods her head and taps a few things into her desktop computer. "I've got names, addresses and phone numbers. Does that help?"

"Definitely."

A couple of minutes later we've got a list of twenty-eight names and addresses. A lot of them have cell numbers, which should make contact easier at this time of the day, when most people are probably at work. Hopefully we'll be able to get through a chunk of them this afternoon.

"Let's call Agent Kim," Ramos suggests. "If these students are learning English, we may have a language problem when we're interviewing them."

"Good idea." I punch in Hana's number and update her on our situation. She agrees to be our translator for the afternoon.

We sit in the car, still in the parking lot of the Korean Cultural Center. While we wait for Hana, we split the list and start phoning. We may well be able to eliminate part of our list on the phone, and certainly if we find an English-speaker at the other end of the phone we can ask about Mee Kim.

By the time Hana arrives twenty minutes later we've managed English conversations with ten people out of our twenty-eight. All of them are extremely distressed by the news that Mee Kim is missing, and they all comment on how wonderful and generous she is. Their concern is genuine, and I can tell the community relies on her. She teaches their children Korean and teaches them English.

"What's up?" Hana climbs in the backseat.

"We've managed to get ahold of ten people over the phone who had enough English to communicate with us. I don't think Mee is staying with any of them, but two of the women said that she's good friends with Sun Lee and Soon-Yi Park from her last class. Apparently it's the advanced class, and sometimes they all go out for a late lunch straight after the lesson."

Hana nods. "Let's start with those two names."

"They'll obviously speak quite good English, but there's no answer at their homes and we don't have cell or current work numbers for them."

"Okay. Well, what about her beginner students? Was there anyone you called that didn't have much English?"

"Yup. I've made notes next to each number," Ramos hands his sheet back to Hana. "*NA* means no answer and *NE* means no or not much English."

She starts dialing the first number while Ramos and I sit twiddling our thumbs. Hana speaks in Korean, leaving me and Ramos in the dark. After a couple of minutes she hangs up. "Okay, I've got another two women she's friendly with from a beginner class—Hae Koo and Mi-na Moon. Hae Koo's on this list with an *NE* next to her. Do you have Mi-na Moon?" Hana asks me.

"Yup. Only a home number listed and it rang out."

"I'll try Sun Lee and Soon-Yi Park again."

There's still no answer at Sun Lee's home, but when Hana dials Soon-Yi Park, she starts speaking in Korean.

"We're going to Sycamore Avenue. It's only a few blocks away. Mrs. Park saw Mee this morning."

"Really?"

"Yup. Let's see what she's got to say in person." She buckles up. "Get back onto Wilshire, heading east, and then take a right at South L.A. Brea Avenue."

Five minutes later Hana tells me to take a right onto Pickford Street and then a left onto Sycamore. She scans the numbers as I drive slowly down the street. "Two doors down," Hana says.

I roll the car forward two houses and pull in.

"This is it." Hana undoes her seat belt. "Let's go."

Once we're out of the car, Hana buttons up her suit jacket and runs her fingers through her hair before repositioning her hairclip. Like Mee's house, the small lawn is neat and recently trimmed, as are the two small garden beds that contain mostly succulents. Good to see the owners are embracing native plants, in line with California's dry weather.

We're not even halfway up the concrete path when the front door opens. A woman in her mid-forties stands at the door, her round face tense. Rosy cheeks contrast milky skin, dark brown eyes and shoulder-length dark brown hair. She beckons us inside, rosebud lip pursed. She says something in rapid Korean to Hana, who nods and gives a brief answer back.

"She just said how worried she is about Mee," Hana relays.

Once we're inside, Hana introduces us, talking to Mrs. Park in Korean, and to me and Ramos in English. We shake hands with her briefly and she brings out a pot of coffee—obviously made while she was waiting for us. She pours four coffees and sets them out in front of us.

"Thank you," I say.

Mrs. Park gives a small nod before launching into something in Korean.

Hana turns to us. "Mrs. Park says she knew something was wrong with Mee, but that Mee insisted she'd had a burst pipe at her house and needed to stay somewhere just for the night."

I nod. "What time did she leave this morning?"

Again, Hana talks to Mrs. Park in Korean and waits for the response before turning back to us. "About ten-fifteen. And she knew that was also strange, because Mee teaches and should have left for work much earlier. But Mee told her she was taking the day off to sort out the problems with her plumbing."

Mrs. Park says something to Hana.

"She said she knew Mee was lying. That she's a very poor liar."

I smile. "It's not a bad quality."

Hana translates for me and Mrs. Park nods her agreement. She looks at her hands, twisting in her lap, and says something else, but the sentence is forced.

"What did she say?" I don't give Hana a chance to translate before my curiosity gets the better of me.

"She asked if Mee was in a lot of trouble."

"I see." I resist the urge to nod my head, in case Mrs. Park thinks I'm saying yes. "Tell her we're concerned for Mee Kim's safety. That she's been pulled into something, but that it's not her fault."

Hana translates and once she's done I continue. "If she can help us, we can find Mee Kim and protect her. Does she have any idea, where Mee Kim was going? Where she might be now?"

Again, I wait while Hana and Mrs. Park converse in Korean.

"The only thing Mee told her was that she was going back to her house. But Mrs. Park knew that was a lie. She pushed her about it, asked if there was anything she could do, but Mee said not to worry, that everything was fine."

I sigh. I realize Mee is trying to protect Mrs. Park, but she could be risking her own life in the process. If the Yakuza catches up to her before we do…

"Ask her what she thinks of Mee," Ramos says. "You know, what's she like?"

Hana nods and repeats the question in Korean. The response is long, but Hana shortens it for us. "Mrs. Park just gave the most glowing report you could possibly imagine. Hardworking, caring, kind, beautiful, generous."

Ramos nods. "So I'm guessing Mrs. Park doesn't think Mee Kim is a blackmailer or involved in the Yakuza herself."

Hana smiles. "I'm guessing it's a no on that one." She turns to me. "I'm going to ask her about the classes. If Mee turned to Mrs. Park, maybe she'll turn to one of her other students. Someone else she's close to."

I nod and wait while Hana asks the question. After a few minutes of back and forth, Hana turns to us. "She suggests we talk to Sun Lee and Mi-na Moon."

When we're back in the car, Hana makes some more phone calls before we consider home visits for everyone.

"You're trusting everyone, I take it?" It's possible someone on the other end of the phone will lie to Hana to protect Mee.

Hana gives me a look. "You gotta be kidding me? I cross-check everyone. Remember, I'm DEA. Everybody on drugs lies to cover their habit, their tracks. Maybe these people are respectable, upstanding citizens, but I'm not letting any fast talking get by me."

I laugh. "You sound like Dr. House…you know, the show *House?* He says everybody lies."

"Yeah, I watch *House.* And I have to agree with him. Certainly most people I run in to lie."

"Maybe medicine and law enforcement have something in common—they make us jaded when it comes to human nature."

She snorts. "Maybe." She dials the next number, and I'm lost again as the Korean language flows from the backseat.

Hana makes her way through our lists quickly and twenty minutes later she's rubbing her hands together. "Okay, I reckon there are four people we should visit. The ones already earmarked—Sun Lee, Hae Koo and Mi-na Moon— plus one other, Na-yung Sung. Interestingly, Ms. Moon claimed she didn't know Mee very well at all, but we've had at least two people say Moon and Mee are close."

"Everybody lies," I quip.

"Exactly." Hana does up her seat belt. "Okay, I grew up around here and I've worked out the best order for the four visits, so we're not backtracking. Unless you want to go straight to Moon?"

Ramos and I glance at one another. "No, let's do the fastest route. I've got kung fu tonight and I'm sure you guys have got things to do, too." It's 3:30 p.m. now, and four stops could easily take us three hours, depending on how long we spend with each person.

Hana nods. "Okay. Our first stop is Sun Lee. And it'll make Ms. Moon our fourth stop."

The first three visits are strikeouts and Hae Koo managed to keep us talking for forty-five minutes before it became obvious that all she had for us was gossip. By the time we get to Mi-na Moon's home, we're restless. Unlike the first three students, Moon lives in an apartment rather than a small single-family house. The cream-colored apartment complex on South Virgil Avenue is only three stories high, made of four clusters with red pitch roofs on each building and enclosed walkways that join the four sections. There's only a small amount of greenery around the building, but despite this it doesn't look like a concrete jungle. On the contrary, there's something almost beachside and tranquil about the complex. The main entrance from Virgil Avenue is framed by a large cream archway, nearly two stories high itself. A wrought iron gate provides security, although realistically it's not tall enough to keep a determined visitor or criminal out. We buzz apartment number fourteen and wait. It takes about a minute before Moon answers.

"Yes, who is it?"

"It's Special Agent Kim from the DEA. We spoke on the phone."

"Oh. Yes. Come up." Her voice is hesitant, surprised.

"I take it you didn't tell Moon we'd be dropping by?" I whisper.

"Nope. Thought we'd make it a surprise visit."

The gate buzzes, releasing the lock, and Hana grabs it. "Let's see what she's got to say for herself."

Ramos holds the door open for Hana and me, before following us up the stairs. "My wife will be expecting me home for dinner soon."

"Dinner on the table at seven?" Hana teases.

"Pretty much. Yeah."

"Well, we better not keep your missus waiting." Hana takes the last step and knocks on the door. "I'm getting hungry, too. Maybe she could set another place at the table."

Ramos seems a little taken aback, before Hana gives him a light slap on the arm. "I'm joking. I'm going out for dinner."

"Oh." He smiles, a little awkwardly.

"She's taking her time." Hana knocks again.

It hits the three of us at once.

"Damn!" Ramos is the first to voice it.

We bolt down the flight of stairs, just as Mi-na Moon opens her front door. "You're too late. She's long gone," Moon yells down the stairs at us. But I think she's lying again…I think *long gone* is all of five minutes.

At the bottom of the stairs we split up. "I'll try out the front," I yell, running onto South Virgil Avenue.

"I'm going down." Hana dashes toward a door marked Parking.

"That leaves me around here," Ramos says.

Once I hit the pavement I quickly look up and down the street, searching for Mee, her car, or anything else unusual. Nothing. I check again, this time devoting more attention to the passing cars and every person. There's no sign of Mee Kim or her silver Hyundai. I push out a breath, hands on hips, before moving back into the apartment complex. Not surprisingly, I'm the first to arrive back. Rather than going up to question Mi-na Moon, I wait for the others, sitting on the bottom step.

Ramos comes back first, out of breath. "Nothing," he says. "Couldn't find her anywhere on the grounds." He sits on the step next to me, catching his breath.

A short while later, the door to the underground parking opens, and Hana strides out.

"Well?"

She shakes her head. "No sign of Mee, but her car's down there."

"Really? So she's on foot now." I stand up again, thinking

maybe it's worthwhile to keep searching the grounds and surrounding area.

"Unless she took Moon's car." Ramos stands, too.

"Let's check in with Moon." I lead the way back up the steps to Moon's apartment. The door is closed. "Open up, Ms. Moon. It's us." I knock loudly on it.

She opens the door and smiles. "Told you she was gone."

I shake my head. "Ms. Moon, I don't know what Mee told you, but she's in danger and we can help her."

Moon's face falls ever so slightly. "Danger?"

"Yes. Why else do you think the FBI, DEA and LAPD are chasing her?" Hana crosses her arms.

"So you really are the law?"

I show Moon my ID and Hana and Ramos follow suit.

"What did Mee tell you?" Ramos asks.

"That her ex-boyfriend and some woman were trying to get money off her, and pretending to be FBI or the cops."

"Ms. Moon, did you lend Mee your car?" Hana asks.

"Uh-huh."

"Give me the details of the car." I take out my notebook and a pen.

Moon bites her lip. "Nissan Micra 2002. Red. Plates 5FQ4500."

Hana shakes her head. "Try again, Ms. Moon."

Moon looks puzzled. "What do you mean?"

"I was just down in your basement. There's a red Nissan Micra parked in your spot."

"But I gave Mee the keys. She was using the stairs over there to get down." Moon points to a set of stairs along the corridor.

Obviously, as soon as we buzzed, Mee ran that way, avoiding the front entrance altogether. But where did she go if she didn't drive off in her car or Moon's?

Eighteen

I arrive at kung fu twenty minutes early and am happy to find Sifu Lee in his office, and alone. I knock on the glass window and he beckons me in.

"Sorry to interrupt."

"Not at all. How did it go today?"

I put my gear down on the chair opposite Lee. "Our Little Tokyo victim does have indications of *dim mak*."

"Which points?"

I tell him.

He nods. "Kidney 22 and pericardium 6 are setup points. To exacerbate the effects of stomach 9 and heart 3. Have you had a chance to read the books?"

"Not yet. I had a quick flick and I've given the one by the doctor to the forensic pathologist working the case. I think we'll both be reading about *dim mak* this weekend."

Lee nods again. "Well, if you've got any questions…."

"Thanks."

For the first hour of class we work on blocks, before Lee pairs us up for thirty minutes of partner work. Tonight, Lee puts me with Marcus, someone I don't work with very often, and I'm immediately conscious of the difference in our skills and strength. Marcus may only be one level above me, but he's also six-two and muscular. I remind myself of what

I said to Williams—bulk doesn't matter in kung fu, not if you're fast and precise.

For the first fifteen minutes we work as a group, with Lee calling out strikes for one side of the room and watching the blocks the partners come up with. The first series of strikes he calls out is left jab, right hook, followed by a double undercut. I look for Marcus's first punch, watching his shoulders to see when the movement initiates. Even though it's tempting and logical to watch the hands, it's the shoulders that give away the start of a punch. His left shoulder moves ever so slightly, and the punch comes a few milliseconds later. By the time it gets to its target, my face, I've used an upper block to defend myself, bending at the elbow so his strike lands on the bony part of my forearm. Marcus doesn't hold back, and the punch sends small aftershocks through my arm—might have a bruise there, despite my conditioning. Marcus's right hook comes extremely fast after his left jab, and I put both arms up around my head to protect myself—similar to a boxer's defensive stance. For the double undercut, which is a difficult strike to defend with a simple block, I take a step backward and bring my forearm down onto his forearms as the strike hits the place where I was standing only a second before. I keep watching Marcus, and only just manage to deflect the roundhouse kick he sends my way.

"Hey, that wasn't part of the drill!"

Marcus grins. "Just keeping you on your toes."

"Okay, swap," Lee says. "And stick with the instructions." He eyes Marcus disapprovingly. It's one thing to throw a kick when we're sparring freestyle, but to do it when I wasn't on the lookout could have been disastrous. Lee doesn't want any unnecessary injuries on his watch.

Once Marcus is in position, I move my body weight forward a couple of times as a fake, before lunging in with a jab. I follow it quickly with my right hook, and then the double uppercut. Marcus defends the strikes easily.

The next series of movements Lee calls out includes two kicks moving forward as an attack sequence and two straight punches. I attack first, sliding forward and delivering a right-side kick aimed at Marcus's chest, followed by a front kick aimed at his groin and then a right and left punch to his head.

In the next sequence, Marcus moves in for a stranglehold. I wind both arms around the outside of his, and bring them down hard on his forearms just near the elbow joints, before his hands get a grip on my throat. We switch roles again, and Marcus has no trouble keeping me at a distance.

With only twenty minutes of class to go, Lee breaks us into two groups, one he can supervise and the other is taken by Steve. Marcus and I are in Lee's group, along with another five sparring partners. He gives each couple a few minutes in the center, with one person attacking and one person defending. This final exercise is freestyle sparring, allowing us to come up with whatever combination of strikes and kicks we'd like.

"A word of warning," Lee says. "I know you've got your protective gear on, but please take it easy. I don't want anyone using full-out strength. Remember, this is a class, not the place to act like your life depended on your moves."

We all nod before he calls the first pair into the center. Most people manage to connect with their opponents, even briefly. Marcus and I are the last ones in.

"Okay, you two. We've only got a couple of minutes left, so let's see what you've got. Sophie, you can throw the first strike."

I nod and pop on my helmet, which is streaked with sweat and feels uncomfortably hot. Marcus follows suit, and we give each other a small bow. I use my footwork first, moving in fast so I'm close enough for an elbow strike to his ribs, while also making sure I keep my guard up to block any punches if he's fast enough to throw one before I get out of his immediate range. I make contact with the ribs and block his retaliatory elbow strike by pushing the palm of my hand down along my body as I move out. He moves into attack mode, sending a right hook my way. As the punch comes closer to my head, I block it with my left forearm but quickly bring my right arm under his to the outside, so his elbow joint is sandwiched between my forearms on either side. In a fight situation, I'd apply as much conflicting pressure as I could, pushing my left arm away from me while pulling my right arm toward me. The result would be a broken elbow. But in this instance I hold the position for a millisecond and apply only the slightest bit of pressure to show I've got the lock on. While I've got his right arm, I sense his left coming toward the back of my head. I move away from him and into a lower horse stance, blocking the punch with my right arm. He's closed up the space between us now, and I decide to use that to my advantage, going for another close-range strike. I move through into another horse stance, this time so I'm directly in front of him, with my back to him, and push both my elbows back into his body, before moving back to the neutral side-on standing position.

My weight's not quite balanced when Marcus tries a side kick. I only just manage to block the kick before it connects with my hip. It may be a class situation, but now my adrenaline's pumping—I almost let the kick through. Marcus follows his side kick with an immediate crescent kick and I move out of its way by sliding backward on my back foot. I team the back slide with an outside block, just in case I haven't moved far enough away from the kick. This time Marcus misses me by an inch or two.

While his leg is still in the air, I take two quick steps to get me in range of his supporting leg. I carefully target my kick to the back of his knee. In a real-life situation I'd be going for the side of the knee joint to tear his ligaments, or even for his shin. My kick connects with the back of Marcus's knee and it has the desired effect, with his supporting leg buckling momentarily. However, his left leg hits the ground a fraction of a second after I've made contact, giving him time to recover his balance. I'm now behind him, and he immediately swings his upper body downward, like a pendulum, bringing his right leg up in a tiger tail kick that's targeting my abdomen. I block and move at the same time, but if he'd put his full force into that kick he would have made contact and done some damage. Damn it. The only good thing for me is that kicks take a little longer to recover from than hand strikes, in terms of getting back into a balanced horse stance and throwing another punch or defending. So while he's still reasserting his body into position, I move in and deliver a tiger strike to his back, targeting his kidneys with the palm of my hand. I make contact, but keep the power down, so it's unlikely he'll even have a bruise there tomorrow.

"Okay, stop." Lee claps his hands together twice, just in case his voice wasn't enough to get our attention.

We both turn around to face him and receive our verdicts, taking our helmets off at the same time. Sweat drips down my neck, back and between my breasts. I've definitely got my workout tonight. And that was only a few minutes of fighting.

"Excellent," he says. "In a fight situation you both would have made contact with some good strikes."

I smile, happy that I held my own with a more experienced and much bigger opponent. Maybe my private lessons are paying off.

Two hours later I'm in bed reading and still winding down when my cell phone rings. I instinctively look at my watch—11:00 p.m.

"FBI. Anderson."

"You're looking for Mee Kim?" The voice is husky, male and softly spoken.

"Yes." I sit up.

Silence. "You left your card with my wife today." The caller speaks quickly. "You can find Mee Kim at 3560 Torrance Boulevard, in Torrance." The line goes dead.

I jot down the address while it's still in my head. Eleven o'clock…Hana's my best bet. As far as I know, she's single—at least I won't be risking waking kids if I call her now.

I dial her cell number but get voice mail. So it's Ramos or Petrov—I hardly know De Luca and Williams. I decide on Ramos, only because I don't want to get the head of the task force out of bed for a routine check, not until I know if this is a legitimate tip-off. I dial Ramos's number.

"Ramos." His voice is alert, but he also sounds a little grumpy, like maybe I interrupted something.

"Detective Ramos, it's Agent Anderson."

"Hey, Anderson. What's up?"

"I just got a tip on my cell phone. A possible address for Mee Kim tonight."

"You gonna send a patrol car?"

My natural reaction is to investigate myself, but Ramos is right—we could just ask a patrol car to do a drive-by. On second thoughts I'll stick with my original plan. "I don't want to scare off Mee with cop cars, so I'll go myself." I pause. "You wanna ride shotgun?"

"Guess you made me an offer I can't refuse."

From the tone of his voice I think he's dying to refuse, but he doesn't want to leave me without backup.

"Sorry. I did try Agent Kim first. I know I'm taking you away from your wife and kids."

"Don't sweat it, Anderson. Kids are asleep and the missus is about to hit the sack, too." He takes a breath. "One car?"

"The caller said Mee's in Torrance, Torrance Boulevard. Where do you live?"

"El Monte."

"I'm in Westwood, so let's make it two cars, but we'll meet somewhere in Torrance and then continue in one."

"Okay. How about the corner of Torrance Boulevard and South Western Avenue? You know it?"

"No, but I'll find it."

"Cool. Do any of her English students live in Torrance?"

"Don't think so. Hold on, I'll double-check." I take the list from the Korean Cultural Center out of my briefcase and scan through it. "No. The caller said his wife had my card, so I guess she's one of Mee's students, but none of them have a Torrance address."

"Maybe the center's database isn't up-to-date."

"Let's go find out," I say.

I change out of my shorts and T-shirt and into a pair of white linen pants and a dark blue singlet top. Next I slide into my shoulder holster, before putting a lightweight suit jacket over the top. The jacket only partially hides the shoulder holster and Smith & Wesson, but it'll do. Before I leave, I check my gun to make sure the ammo's full, even though I checked it this morning before leaving for work. While most people only check their guns periodically, I figure it's better to be safe than sorry. I release the magazine clip on my Smith & Wesson 910S, and check all sixteen bullets are present and lined up in the double magazine before shoving it back into the gun's butt. I also check the safety's on, and then slot the gun into my shoulder holster.

I've got a lot of questions for Mee Kim, but first off I just want to make sure she's safe and sound, with us. The fact that she's on the run can only mean one of two things: she's hiding something from us or she's running from someone else and for some reason doesn't trust us. While her story to Moon was fanciful, maybe it's based in fact—maybe she really doesn't believe we're law enforcement. Or perhaps she's worried that Ramos, Petrov or I are dirty. Either way, it's time for Mee Kim to come in before she puts herself in even more danger.

I follow my navigation system's instructions to Torrance Boulevard. I've still got a few blocks until South Western Avenue, but I scan for numbers. Sure enough, within a couple of minutes I cruise by number 3560. It's a shop front, Kyoto Deli, with what looks like a residence over the top. Maybe one of Mee's students owns the shop and is letting her hide out upstairs. I keep driving until I get to South Western. I'm surprised to find Ramos already waiting, leaning on his car under a streetlight. He's wearing jeans and a T-shirt, with his gun on his belt.

I jump out of the car and look up. "You been waiting long?"

"Nah. Couple minutes."

"You must have broken some records to get here from El Monte before me."

"Got the lights in the car."

I nod, but notice the flashing lights must be stowed away now.

Ramos motions with his head toward my car. "Take yours?"

"Let's take yours." Ramos is driving a silver SUV. "It looks less law enforcement." I lock my car and jump into the passenger seat of Ramos's Ford Territory.

He starts the engine. "I checked out the address on the computer. It's a shop."

"Yeah, I just drove by it. Kyoto Deli." I fasten my seat belt. "It's a two-story place, so maybe Mee's been given the use of upstairs for a night or two."

Ramos pulls into the trickle of traffic. "It's listed as an Asian delicatessen and the owner's one Lee Wu."

"Wu...that name's not on our list of students, either."

"Maybe the wife goes by a different name," Ramos says. "Regardless, the system didn't have anything on the shop or shop owner."

I nod, happy that Ramos got a chance to plug in the information. "At least we know Wu's clean."

"Uh-huh."

It's comforting to know we're not walking into a business with criminal ties.

Kyoto Deli is the middle shop in a small strip of stores. They're the normal mix of shops you might find in a mostly residential area—a mini grocery store, a fruit store, a post office, a couple of cafés, a dry cleaner and a newsagent. At 11:45 p.m., they're dark and quiet. We peer inside the windows of the deli, but it's difficult to make out anything but shadows and silhouettes with only a streetlight helping us out. I can see shelves, a cash register and a little more light from underneath a back door, which presumably leads upstairs or out the back. There's no movement or sound. We take a few steps back so we can see the upstairs windows, but it's the same story—not much light and no movement or sound. Next to the main door is a small buzzer, so I press it. There's no answer.

"What do you want to do?" Ramos asks after a couple of minutes. "No warrant."

I ring the buzzer again. "Maybe Mee's just asleep."

We wait another couple of minutes. "I can hear someone moving around in there." I lean in to the glass again, and jump back when I'm greeted by a face, only about a foot on the other side. But still no lights.

"I'm coming, I'm coming." As he moves closer, right up to the door, we can see the figure on the other side—an Asian man in his late twenties or early-thirties. I was expecting an older man, an established shopkeeper. He wears a dressing gown, fully closed up, and it looks like we've woken him up.

"What's up?" He doesn't make a move to open the door and I don't blame him. Even if he was the husky voice on my cell phone forty-five minutes ago, he'll want to see proof of ID first.

I hold my badge up to the glass. "FBI and LAPD." I jerk my thumb toward Ramos. "Open up, please."

He obliges, opening the door and standing aside to let us in. Great, no talk about search warrants or loitering at the door trying to get in.

Ramos lets me in first, and then follows.

"Are you Mr. Wu?" I ask, turning around as the man closes the door.

"No. I rent the upstairs from Wu." He puts his hands in his pockets and yawns. "What's all this about anyway?"

The next part happens so fast, too fast. He grabs Ramos with his left hand and brings his right out of his pocket, with a gun. He holds it to Ramos's head. The tiredness is gone, the act over.

My hand instinctively moves toward my gun, but the man shakes his head. "Don't even think about it, sweetheart." His language is condescending, and beyond his years. *Sweetheart* is old-school, more Ramos's generation than this man's.

I put my hands up. "It's okay. Take it easy." My eyes dart around the room. Ramos and I should be able to disarm one man, even with a gun to Ramos's head—at some stage we'll get the opportunity to make a move. I look at Ramos. Despite the situation he looks pretty cool. But under that blank face his heart must be pounding like mine, and his adrenaline pumping.

"You the ones been asking questions about Mee Kim?"

"Yes," I say, studying the gunman in the darkness. Half of his face is in full shadow, and half is only slightly illuminated by the nearest streetlight. He's about five-ten, a hundred and sixty pounds, and sneakers poke out from underneath the dressing gown. Why didn't we notice that sooner? The darkness certainly didn't help us.

I hear the door behind me open and I swing around. Another Asian man, also in his late twenties, steps into the main shop area. He leaves the door open, which gives us more light, and holds a gun that's pointed at me.

I take a step to one side and angle my body so I can see them both. "Take it easy."

The man pointing the gun at me closes the distance between us. "You shouldn't ask so many questions."

He's still not within physical striking distance, but even if I liked our chances with hand-to-hand—which I don't—there's no way I could disarm this guy without Ramos getting shot and probably me, too. We have to ride it out.

"Asking questions is our job, man." Ramos speaks for the first time.

"Shut up." The man at the door pushes the gun into Ramos's temple. Any sudden move and he'd squeeze that trigger, even if by accident. Like a car backfires outside, he jumps and bam, Ramos gets a bullet in the head. He's clutching tightly onto Ramos's upper arm, and the extra light from out back is enough for me to see that the very top of his pinky finger is missing. Yakuza. I take a closer look at the men, wondering if it was these two who visited Mee—but I don't recognize them from my vision.

The guy with the gun trained on me comes closer, close enough for me to make a move, but I resist the temptation. He takes my gun out of my holster.

"Nice piece," he says. "I always wanted me an FBI gun."

"It's all yours." I keep my hands up slightly, nonthreatening.

"Thanks, babe." He gives me an arrogant wink.

Babe, that's more the language I'd expect from a twenty-something.

"Knock it off." The guy at the door is annoyed. "Put the gun away and focus."

So the one with Ramos is the dominant of the two. The boss, at least in this situation.

He turns to me. "Leave Mee alone. She's gone for good."

What sort of gone? I wonder. No, she's not dead. I think I would have felt that…felt her presence or something. Perhaps I can press our attacker on the subject. Even though he's got a gun to Ramos's head he doesn't seem especially angry or jumpy at the moment. This was a planned confrontation, so he'll have some degree of self-control.

"Where's she gone?" I ask.

"Don't you worry about where she's at. You should be worried about yourself, lady, you're the one with a gun aimed at you."

He's got a point. So why aren't I worried? Both men hold their guns confidently, and while their calm attitude shows me they're not letting their emotions rule their judgment, it's also a warning sign. These guys have done this sort of thing before, perhaps routinely, and they're cool and dispassionate about it, an attitude that might extend to murder. I flash to the vision I had of Saito's attacker—he was dispassionate. Maybe one of these men is our guy. I look them over again…my one's about six foot and the other guy's around five-ten. Both are in the range Hart gave us, and both men hold their guns confidently, and could probably easily shoot out a parking-lot light. But is one of them capable of the Ten Killing Hands? Of *dim mak?* If our captors are that skilled, Ramos and I definitely won't be making a move…certainly not a successful one. A glance at Ramos tells me he's still cool as a cucumber and the tiniest shake of his head indicates we're in sync with our thoughts on taking action…wait it out.

"Come on, let's go." My guy jerks his head toward the back door, and the light. So we're going upstairs. He steps back, giving me a wide berth. As I move through the doorway I see a rickety-looking staircase that leads upward. A light at the top of the stairs allows me to see detail—the steps are painted white, but it looks like the paint's at least fifteen or twenty years old and has probably been peeling away for years. A thick layer of dust completes the puzzle—I don't think the back part has been used much and I can't imagine anyone lives up there. I mount the first step with my left foot.

The gun's muzzle pushes into my back. "Not that way. Keep going straight."

The path straight in front of me is dark, darker than the shop. I can make out the silhouettes of a couple of large industrial fridges, some boxes, and walls lined with shelves and produce. I can also see a door.

"Where are we going?" I ask, getting nervous. The situation has taken a distinct turn for the worse. Moving locations is never a good sign. In the shop—that was a threat. But being taken somewhere else....

I turn back in the hope of getting a look at Ramos's face, but my guy pushes his gun into me again.

"Move it, babe."

When we get to the back door my guy fishes something out of his pocket and gives the other guy a nod. Ramos is shoved next to me, and while the first guy keeps his gun trained on us both, mine blindfolds us. The darkness becomes complete, and with that my fear skyrockets. If I can't see, how can I defend myself? How do I know what's coming next?

"This is going to make things worse, not better," I say, falling back on what I do best—behavior.

"Speak for yourself, babe." His breath is hot and stinky on my face. And then I feel the rope slip around my wrists. If this was a stranger attack, I'd say now was my only chance of surviving, that I had to make a move before the rope was fastened and all control was taken by the perp. That's what happens in sexual homicides and serial attacks. The perp takes control of the victim, and once you've been moved away from any hope of intervention and tied up you're as good as dead. But I can't project the psychology of a serial killer or sexually motivated killer onto these two guys. They're career criminals and they've probably killed before. But they follow orders. So either they're going to take us to a boss, or they're taking us somewhere less public to kill us. Neither outcome is good because both are escalations on my original theory—that this was simply a warning.

I have to make a split-second decision. I either keep my wrists nice and still and allow myself to be almost completely incapacitated or I use what might be our last opportunity to fight. And now I don't even have the luxury of being able to look at Ramos to read his expression.

"You're making a big mistake." Ramos's voice is low and rough. "Messing with law enforcement never ends well."

"Don't worry. We'll only mess with you a bit." It's the first guy who speaks, the leader of the two.

"Why are you taking us somewhere else?"

He sighs and says calmly, "It's time for both of you to shut the fuck up."

Strong hands press tape across my mouth.

Nineteen

The car pulls to a stop, roughly fifteen minutes later. So wherever we are, at least we're not talking about some deserted country road or forest where our bodies would never be found. That makes me swing back to my warning theory. However, we can identify both men, and that's not good for our longevity.

The front doors open and I feel the weight of the car lift slightly as our abductors get out. The doors slam shut and I hear the automatic locks click.

"What do you think?" I ask, momentarily forgetting that I've got tape across my mouth. All that comes out is a series of indecipherable grunts.

Ramos responds with a grunt that rises at the end, probably a "What?" or "Huh?"

Damn.

Fifteen-minute drive. Maybe twenty. Where could we be? I visualize a map of L.A. Could be in Long Beach. At the drug lab.

A large horn sounds, like a boat's horn. We must be at the docks. I wonder... I lean forward slightly, giving my bound hands a little room behind me, and tap out *D-O-C-K-S* in Morse code against the car seat back. Does Ramos know Morse code? I've tapped it out four times and am about to give up when Ramos makes a loud grunt. I stop tapping, and Ramos starts.

He taps out *S-A-N P-E-D-R-O O-R L-O-N-G B-E-AC-H.*

Shit. So we know where we are…what good's that going to do us? We should have taken a stand at the deli. I shake my head. If we had we'd probably both be dead by now. At least this way we might get another chance, one where the odds are more in our favor. What are our fight options? Our legs are free. I wonder what Ramos's hand-to-hand combat without hands is like. Kicks could be all we have.

I tap out *F-I-G-H-T* in Morse.

At first there's no response, then Ramos taps back *H-O-W.*

He's right. My kicks are pretty good, but against a gun…or two?

With a mental block on what else to say, I tap out *S-H-I-T.*

The grunt that follows from Ramos is either a halfhearted chuckle or maybe a hysterical one.

I turn my body toward Ramos and feel along the car door for the handle. No harm in trying. But sure enough, the door's locked.

The guy who had Ramos is Yakuza, and I noticed a tat on my guy. I could only see the edge of it, but it looked like a cursive *A,* maybe for *ABZ,* which is the street name for the Asian Boyz. Is this all about the meth lab in Long Beach? Drugs and money? Probably. Although I'm still not sure how Saito and Mee Kim are involved. Man, I wish we knew what they wanted.

I roll my eyes under the blindfold. You'd think I'd have some inkling of how this was going to turn out. That something this significant would come through in a vision or dream. But as is often the case, my psychic stuff is more frustrating than useful. Then it hits me…the dream. I was shot. Shit. I assumed I was dreaming it from a victim's point of view, from a stranger's point of view, but what if it was my own?

We have to make a break. I start tapping it out for Ramos, but only get to *M-A-K-E A B-R-E-A-K W-H-E-N B-L-I-N-D-F-O-L-D-S* before the car's locking system beeps. Someone grabs the rope that ties my hands together and pulls me out of the car, hard and fast. Too fast. My foot gets caught on the door frame and I fall to the ground, landing on my right hip. The hand digs into my upper arm, bruising me as he pulls me to my feet. I can tell by the feel of the upward pull that the man who holds me now is at least six feet tall and strong—my feet are airborne before he puts me back down onto the ground. This isn't one of the guys from the deli.

"Come on." His voice sounds familiar. I try to think of all the six-plus men I know in L.A., but it's futile. I work in law enforcement, surrounded by men, and lots of them are tall.

He drags me behind him and I almost stumble again.

"Ramos?" The word comes out as a two-syllable grunt, but it's followed by a single one from Ramos. He's at least forty yards away by the sounds of it.

"Shut up, you two." The familiar voice again, this time right in my ear. I process my senses…we're in a room, a large room. There was an echo. And I don't think we went outside or through a door, so we're somewhere you can drive a car into. Like a warehouse. That ties in with the docks.

A booming voice cuts through the room, emphasized by the echo. "Teach her a lesson, Miki."

I can't see, I'm blindfolded, but I sense the fist coming my way and duck.

"What the hell?" The guy sounds pissed. "Jeez, you guys can't even put a blindfold on properly."

His hand comes down behind my head to hold me still, and he delivers the strike directly to my jaw. The punch itself is not that hard, but because he's holding my head with his other hand I can't recoil to soften the blow. I taste the slight metallic sensation of blood in my mouth.

"Now keep quiet or there's more of that to come."

The booming voice cuts through. "Give her partner a taste, too. And don't be as lenient as Miki."

Miki is in trouble for not punching me harder. A man that size could easily knock me out with one blow to the jaw.

I hear the unmistakable sounds of fists hitting flesh and bone. Ramos is fairly quiet, bar the occasional grunt or

groan in response to the force of the blows. It only lasts
about a minute, but a minute's worth of punches is a lot to
endure, especially if his attackers are the size of Miki. Once
they're finished, the only sound is Ramos trying desperately
to catch his breath, with only his nose to breathe through—
he's winded.

Miki drags me again, toward the direction of the man
with the booming voice. Could it be Tomi Moto? Or his
second in charge, Takeshi Suzuki? Whoever it is, he's
probably responsible for whatever Mee and Saito are
involved in.

"Sit her down."

Again, I flash back to the dream. I was tied to a chair
when I was shot, and now they want me to sit down.

A large hand pushes me back and down, into a chair. I
feel him hunching over me as he reaches down to my ankles.
Blindfolded and tied to a chair? When I know a bullet's
coming my way? No way.

I lean back in the chair and kick with all my might at the
man. I aim high, hoping to connect with his head or throat,
but it's impossible to target effectively when I'm blindfolded. I connect with something, but it feels more like his
chest. The force of the impact hurtles me backward and the
chair topples over. I roll with the fall, keeping my fingers
and hands closely pinned to my body to protect them. I
eventually come to rest on my back. Pulling my knees up
to my chest, I bring my hands from behind my back under
my feet and up so they're now tied in front of me. I push
myself to standing, ready.

I can feel other people around me, but I'm not sure how
many. So far, the only voices are the boss man, Miki and
our two captors. But now I hear footsteps coming closer and
they're from behind me, at least two others, maybe four.

"No! Leave her to Miki."

"Yes, leave her for me."

Miki mustn't be very bright, because he's just given away
his position. He's to my right, and close. I take a side step
to close the distance and then go for a front kick, hoping to

connect with his groin. I manage to hit him, but judging from the absence of a groan I missed my target. I follow it up with an elbow strike. With my hands tied in front like this, I can still use an elbow strike effectively and will even be able to deliver some modified punches. I throw my first punch, but it hits the hard bone of a forearm. I've been blocked—and properly. Even the contact with the forearm hurts, like a punch would. Maybe this man is our killer. Although, I wouldn't have been able to get any strikes past the man who killed Saito and the others. Before I have time to react, to try to defend myself as best I can without being able to see, a punch is delivered square into my solar plexus. I double over, gasping for breath. While I'm winded, Miki literally picks me up, slams me into the chair.

"Bitch!"

As he's tying me to the chair, I manage a swipe across his face, but it's not a well-delivered blow.

A deep chuckle erupts. It's the boss. "You drew blood, Agent Anderson. Nicely done."

Good. That means I've got his DNA under my fingernails.

"She's feisty, Miki. You didn't tell me she was this feisty."

Miki makes the final adjustments on the ropes around my ankles, and they're tight.

"Miki has been following you for the past couple of days."

"Bullshit!" I mumble through the tape on my mouth. I would notice a tail...wouldn't I?

"Remove the tape, Miki."

Miki immediately responds to the boss's order, jamming short fingernails into my cheek to peel up an edge. Once he's loosened a small corner of the tape, he rips it off in one fast movement. My lips and mouth burn and I can feel a sticky residue around my mouth.

"I would've noticed a tail," I say with more conviction than I feel.

"Our Miki is good. He knows how to be discreet. How to disappear. How to make others disappear."

"Mee," I say.

"Exactly." He's silent.

I feel Miki's hands on mine as he undoes the rope that binds my hands together. He quickly pulls my arms behind me and ties them up again. I'm panicking. I'm tied up, immobile. They have all the control. I have none.

"So you're going to make me disappear?" I force an evenness into my voice that doesn't reflect my emotions. "Like Mee?" But I still think that if Mee was dead, I would know it.

"Maybe. But let's have a chat before we make any hasty decisions, huh?" There's a hint of both humor and sarcasm in his voice and it's chilling.

I hear movement directly in front of me, and two sets of footsteps. One person trips and I make the logical leap—Ramos. Sure enough, a few seconds later I feel a whoosh of air as Ramos is shoved into a seat next to me. I hear the unmistakable sound of tape being ripped off. We can both talk, but I resist the urge to ask him if he's okay or to communicate with him in any way. Instead, I ask the boss what he wants to talk about.

"Jun Saito, Mee Kim and your investigation."

"What about it?" Ramos's voice does reveal some pain, but at least he's talking and lucid.

"Everything. Absolutely everything."

It's a puzzling question. I can only think of two reasons why they'd go to all this trouble to see where our investigation is at: (1) we're a threat somehow, getting too close; or (2) they haven't been able to track down Saito's killers themselves and they want to exact revenge. If it's the first option, then there must be something they're hiding, other than a professional hit man. So what's the big secret?

"There's not much to tell," Ramos says. "We were investigating a murder in Little Tokyo. And we found out that the victim's name was Jun Saito."

I take over, but instead of bringing in another name, Petrov's, I claim the discovery for myself. "I recognized the name, knew that he might be related to Hisayuki Saito and the Yakuza."

"How did you know the name?" The boss's voice is stern.

"In case you haven't recognized the accent, I'm Australian. We have close ties with Asia and I worked on an Asian organized-crime task force back in Oz a few years ago," I lie.

"Let me guess, some federal official gave you a 101 in the Yakuza."

I smile. "Exactly. And history was part of that briefing."

He grunts. "What about Mee? How'd you get to Mee?"

"Saito has been making payments to her for the past year. We traced it through his laptop."

"That was sloppy of him. Saito was out of practice."

"So he hasn't been working for you for the past fifteen years?"

Silence.

"Saito was out of practice," the voice repeats. "Going straight, as you'd say."

"But someone found him."

"Yes." He sighs, frustrated. "You don't know who, do you?"

"No."

Silence. He's disappointed. He was hoping we'd have more information than him, not less. The Yakuza, or at least this boss and his section of the Yakuza, were not responsible for the hit. He's fishing way too much, hoping we can give him clues. And that means option number two wins—they don't know who to hit as retaliation. At least they're not jumping to conclusions and whacking figureheads from different organizations. Our boss man is a thinker, and that's good for Ramos and me.

"Can I ask you a question?" I take my chances again.

"You can ask."

"How does Mee fit into all this? Is she Saito's daughter?"

"Yes."

"Does she know that?"

"I've been polite and answered your question, Agent Anderson. Don't push it. Now," he says. "What to do with you two."

"Assaulting or killing law-enforcement officers will bring all sorts of heat onto your organization," I say.

He laughs. "I'm untouchable, Agent Anderson. This is my town."

"What if we help you find out who killed Saito?" Ramos pipes up.

"And what would you do, Detective? Arrest him? Charge him?" Laughter again. "I have a different idea about the retribution this man will face. And law enforcement needs to learn to stay out of our turf! Tell that to your bosses." He pauses. "We'll handle this matter in-house."

I make out three sets of footsteps, moving away from us.

"Wait until we're gone." The boss is leaving and taking two others with him, probably his personal bodyguards or right-hand men.

I don't know what they're going to do to us, but he just gave us a message…to pass on to our bosses. So maybe my dream was off base. Looks like Ramos and I are going to make it out of this thing alive.

A car door opens and closes, and then another two car doors follow. I can imagine someone opening the door for the boss, and then getting into the car themselves once the boss is loaded. The engine starts and the car moves away.

"We're gonna send a strong message to law enforcement." It's a new voice and I can hear pleasure in his tone, the disturbing kind of pleasure.

I tug on my ropes, but it's futile, Miki tied me up real tight. I imagine Ramos is finding he's in the same predicament.

There's silence for what seems like an eternity, before I hear another two sets of footsteps, car doors and then a car engine starts.

Without any warning, three shots are fired. My eyes blink rapidly; I'm unable to comprehend what's just happened. What's happening.

"No!" Miki screams out. "I want to do her!" I can feel his anger boiling over. "I want to get the bitch back for scratching me. Leave!"

"Ramos?" I repeat his name several times, but there's no answer. My breathing is heavy and fast, waiting for the searing pain as the bullet enters me, just like it did in my dream.

Then the silence is broken by the other voice. "Whatever you say, Miki. Have fun." Again, there's the hint of pleasure in the voice, satisfaction. Another two sets of footsteps move away, and two car doors open and close. But the engine doesn't start. They must be waiting for Miki.

"What have you done?" I scream. "Why have you done this?"

No response.

"You don't have to do this. I haven't seen your face."

"It doesn't matter." Miki's voice is soft, almost tender.

Tears start to roll down my cheeks. Ramos is dead. Three shots. And I'm next. I take a deep breath but it's cut short by a burning pain as I fall backward.

Twenty

I force my eyes open, groggy and confused. All I can hear is beep…beep…beep. As my eyes open fully I make sense of the noise—heart monitor. I'm in hospital.

"She's awake."

I move my head to the voice. Petrov.

"Agent Petrov." My voice is raspy and dry. Weak. I suddenly recall that I was shot. "I was shot."

"Yes." He moves closer.

"Sorry about that."

I freeze. It's the voice. Miki. I instinctively reach under the pillow for my gun, but it's not there. I'm not at home now. I turn my head to the other side of the room and Marcus from my kung fu class stands next to Agent Joe De Luca. And then I realize—Marcus and Miki are one and the same person.

"He's the one who shot me." I shake my head, wondering when I'll wake up from this nightmare. Or maybe I'm dead.

"Agent Sophie Anderson, meet Special Agent Dan Young from the DEA."

"Agent? DEA?"

"Hi." He grins. "Sorry about shooting you. I went for your shoulder. It was the best I could do under the circumstances."

"DEA?" I repeat, still trying to get around the concept that Marcus from kung fu is really a DEA agent called Dan Young, who is obviously undercover in the Yakuza. Even without whatever pain meds they've got me on that'd take some processing.

He nods. "I've been undercover here for twelve months as Marcus Miki."

I look to Petrov for confirmation and he gives me a nod.

"But why didn't you say something? Why didn't you tell me?"

Petrov crosses his arms. "We've got a leak in the Gang Impact Team."

"What?" I can't contain my surprise. "Damn!"

"Tell me about it." De Luca runs his hand across his skull. "We've been trying to pinpoint who for over a year now. And that's why we got someone external, Dan, to go in. Dan's from New York and was undercover in the Yakuza over there. We needed a complete outsider and Agent Young here fit the bill, so we got him transferred."

Young takes a few steps forward. "I started doing some deals with L.A., getting to know a few people on the West Coast, and eventually someone vouched for me. I was in."

"But…" I let the sentence hang, not sure what I was about to protest. The bombshells just keep coming.

"There are only a few of us who know about it." Petrov pushes his hands into his pockets. "Me, Joe and Brady. I went to him when Joe and I first had our suspicions. Brady's in charge of our investigation into the Gang Impact Team."

No wonder Petrov seemed especially floored by Saito's death. He wasn't only thinking about the possibility of retaliation, he was also thinking about how the news would affect the task force and the leak…or whether the hit was somehow related.

"Ramos? Is he…?"

"He's in intensive care."

I breathe a sigh of relief. He's alive.

"And for the record, I didn't shoot Ramos, only you.

Moto's orders were shoot, but not to kill. But I knew straightaway that the shot to Ramos was life-threatening." Agent Young clasps his hands together. "And I didn't want them to mess up with you, too. So I stepped in. I shot you."

Even with Petrov and De Luca vouching for him, I find it hard to believe Dan/Marcus. The man shot me, for goodness' sake. I don't respond. Instead I say, "So the man in the warehouse. That was Moto?" Thinking of his voice sends a cold shiver down my spine.

"Yes. And Takeshi Suzuki was there, too."

I nod, small fast movements, but then my thoughts immediately go back to Ramos. "Ramos took three bullets." I bite my lip. Three's a lot.

"No. One bullet," Agent Young says. "The other two shots were for Jason Pham of the Asian Boyz and Ichi Noda from the Yakuza. The boss didn't want any leads from you and Ramos back to us. So he ordered them to be taken out, just in case someone saw them bring you to the warehouse. A Yakuza guy called Ken Tanabe shot them, and then turned his gun on Ramos."

I nod, relieved it was only one bullet for Ramos and feeling only fleetingly sorry for Pham and Noda.

I notice the faint scab forming across Young's cheek from my nails.

He follows my gaze and runs his finger along the one-inch wound. "You did pretty good for someone who was blindfolded."

I manage a small chuckle. "Thanks."

"Agent Young sent me a text from the car. The paramedics were there five minutes later."

I nod, still absorbing everything. "But we checked the War Room for undercover operatives. How come you're not in there?"

I ask the question of Agent Young, but it's De Luca who replies. "We've kept this operation completely off the books, because of the leak."

Young's taking risks. If I could have, I would have shot him—exactly the reason why the HIDTA War Room exists in the first place. But I understand they don't have a lot of options. "Ramos," I say. "Tell me more about Ramos."

There's silence and a few glances.

"Is he going to be okay?"

"The bullet did a lot of damage. He was in surgery for ten hours."

"And?"

"They say it's too early to be sure."

"Oh, God." I chew on my bottom lip. "His wife? Kids?"

Petrov nods. "They're here."

Young crosses his arms. "I can't work out if Ken made a mess of the shot or if it was his intention to kill you both. And if it was, was he acting alone or under someone's orders?" Young's clearly confused. "I need to talk to Moto about it…if I can."

A doctor enters the room. "Glad to see you awake, Agent Anderson."

"Anderson, this is Dr. Goldman. Your surgeon."

"Nice to meet you." I try to sit up a little and hold out my hand.

"Take it easy, Agent Anderson. You've only been out of surgery for sixteen hours."

"Sixteen hours?" Another realization hits. My parents. How am I going to tell them about this? If they find out they'll be on the first plane out here. But the Bureau probably would have already notified them. Next of kin, and all. "Do my parents know?"

Petrov nods. "They're on their way here now. Their plane lands in two hours and I've organized someone to pick them up at the airport."

I throw my head back into the pillow and sigh.

"Did I do the wrong thing?"

"My parents aren't keen on me being in law enforcement. Think it's too dangerous." I grimace.

"I see. So this will be ammunition for them…so to speak."

"Uh-huh."

The doctor moves in. "Can I have a minute please, gentlemen?"

De Luca, Young and Petrov all nod and retreat.

"How are you feeling?" Dr. Goldman asks as she shines a torch into my eyes.

For the first time I think about my body…what I'm feeling. I feel groggy and a little numb all over. "Fine. A little spacey, I guess."

She nods. "It's the pain meds. We've just moved you off morphine and onto codeine, but I'll be reducing your dose over the next few days."

"Few days?"

She laughs. "You're one of those." She finishes checking the drip and gives me a friendly but stern look. "You've been shot. You'll be in here for about a week."

"A week?"

"Yes." She leans over me. "I need to see the stitches, the wound. I'll just untie your hospital gown." As she starts undoing the ties, I realize I'm anxious to see the wound myself. It hits me again…I was shot.

At first all I can see is a white dressing that's covered in brown-colored splotches. I know it's Betadine, the disinfectant they would have smothered on the wound postsurgery, not dried blood.

She gently works on one side of the dressing and I have my chin to my chest to try to see. Once she's lifted one side of the tape, she pulls the dressing off, slowly. On my left shoulder is about a three-quarters-of-an-inch slit, with two stitches holding it together. The bullet wound would have been circular when I came in, and Dr. Goldman has sewn the skin together to form a slit. Both the wound and the stitching are small and neat. I'm lucky it wasn't a round that's designed to cause maximum damage.

"I tried to make it as neat as possible for you, but if you're concerned about the scar you can get plastic surgery to minimize it."

I shrug, not quite able to visualize it fully healed. "I don't know. Can I think about it?"

"Sure."

She moves in closer to the wound and examines it carefully, gently pressing around the area with a freshly gloved hand. "How does it feel?"

"Tender," I admit, my body stiffening with pain.

"I'll just take a look at the exit wound." She bends me forward slightly, and repeats the process on the back of my shoulder.

"Ouch!" I say as she presses the wound, but this time not so gently.

"The bullet shattered part of your shoulder blade on its way out. We got rid of all the debris from the surrounding area, but that's going to be the most painful part for a while."

"Uh-huh." My teeth are clenched, ready for another poke or prod, but nothing comes.

She puts a new dressing on both sides of the wound before checking my monitors. "Your heart rate's still elevated, but that'll come down soon, too."

"Will there be any permanent damage? To my lungs or anything?"

"No. The bullet missed your lungs…and all other vital organs. You're a very lucky young woman."

I'm silent, knowing that it was more Young's skill than my luck. Mind you, there's not really any good place to be shot. With so many vital organs to miss, plus major arteries that could have caused me to bleed out, maybe luck did play a part.

"I'm a bit of a fitness buff. I'll be able to run again?"

"Yes." She fingers the stethoscope around her neck. "But not for several weeks."

I groan, imagining how much fitness I'll lose in a couple of months. "And when can I go back to work?"

"You'll be fine for sedentary work in about two weeks, but I'd wait another six weeks before you started thinking about normal activities. You need to give your bone time to heal."

Six weeks. Man. What about the case? What about Mee Kim? If Agent Young was responsible for making her "disappear," then surely she's still alive. That's if he can be trusted. Twelve months is a long time undercover. People can easily become corrupted in that time. And I don't know how long he was undercover in New York. When you're deep within an organization it can be hard to draw the line between what's absolutely necessary for you to maintain your cover and what's not. And the line can shift. First you witness crime and can't do anything about it, then maybe you have to be more active, show everyone around you what a badass you are. Some undercover operatives get lost in the criminal world they're supposed to be undermining, even though officially an undercover agent is not supposed to engage in any illegal activities.

Once Dr. Goldman's filled out the chart at the end of my bed, she leaves and tells me she'll be back to check up on me tomorrow.

Petrov, Young and De Luca must have been waiting nearby, because within a couple of minutes they reappear.

I'm immediately all business. I still have questions. Questions I want answered. They're barely in the room when I start. "What did you do with Mee?" I ask Young.

"She's under Yakuza protection."

"Yakuza protection?"

"Yes. Moto was using *disappear* like we might for our Witness Protection Program."

"But why's he protecting her?"

"We've gradually been piecing this together, Anderson." Petrov nods at Young, giving him the go-ahead to tell the story.

"As best as we can make out, Jun Saito fled Tokyo and the Yakuza fifteen years ago. I don't know what he has been doing, if anything, since then but according to Moto he hasn't been involved in organized crime. He's been clean and lying low in Singapore. But then three weeks ago someone found him and discovered he had a daughter here in L.A., Mee Kim."

I look at Petrov and De Luca. "You knew all along that Saito was her father!"

"Kind of," Petrov says. "We didn't know names at first. Saito was using another name during his contact with the

Yakuza and the daughter's name was never mentioned. Then we discovered your victim was Jun Saito, and Young here ID'd him as Moto's recent visitor. We were still trying to get a name for the mystery daughter when the computer tech found Mee Kim's name on Saito's computer. It was only then that all the pieces fell into place for us."

I shake my head, remembering the conversations we've had wondering if Mee Kim knew Jun Saito or was even his daughter. They pretended they didn't know anything at all.

Petrov shrugs. "Our hands were tied. We couldn't reveal that we had an inside source."

"So why are you telling me about Agent Young now?"

Again, he shrugs. "We figure that given you and Ramos were both shot, neither of you is the mole."

"Gee, thanks."

"Actually, we knew it wasn't either of you because we discovered the leak fourteen months ago. But we hadn't decided whether to bring you into our confidence or not."

I turn back to Agent Young. "Go on."

"So, Saito's in hiding in Singapore when someone here in L.A. contacts him. They tell him to come to the US or they'll kill Mee Kim. But Saito and Moto are friends, so Saito confides in Moto, asking for his help to track down who is behind the threats. Moto agreed on one condition—he wanted Saito to help with a deal he'd brokered with the Asian Boyz to move a large quantity of heroin from here to Japan."

"The Long Beach meth lab," I say.

Young nods. "Moto had a falling-out with the Tokyo Yakuza over their cut on drug shipments. He was hoping to bypass the usual channels by getting Saito to call in some long-standing favors and use his father's name to get the deal done. And this shipment is going to be big…real big. Even as a one-off it would be worth it for Moto to get a cut on the usual percentage."

"And Moto told you all this?" Young must be very high up in the organization if he's got the confidence of the boss.

"No, the meetings between Moto and Saito were closed-door. But I've managed to plant bugs in two of the four offices Moto uses. We got it through the bugs."

"But Moto still has no idea who lured Saito to L.A. and who killed him?"

"No. He was hoping you and Ramos could enlighten him."

I nod, more of the conversation with Moto coming back to me. I turn to Petrov. "He asked me and Ramos to tell our bosses to stay out of it. That the Yakuza would deal with it."

Petrov shrugs. "Like that's going to happen."

"I know." I sigh.

"Moto is old-school," Young explains. "There is a family debt between him and Saito, and the thought that law enforcement would get their hands on the killer before he did…it's unacceptable." He pauses. "He's protecting Saito's daughter, Mee."

"Where is Mee?" I ask.

"I was told to pick her up Thursday morning. I sent two guys, but they came back a little worse for wear."

I think about the vision I had of her opening the door. She instantly knew that the guy's missing tip of his pinky finger meant he was Yakuza. Perhaps her mother warned her, knew about Saito's connections. Or maybe her father contacted her and confided in her before he was killed. Either way, she knew it was time to run, and when the flee option got complicated, she fought.

"Mee's highly trained in martial arts," I say, knowing for a fact how things turned out that day.

"Yes. My guys soon discovered that. She realized something was up when they came to her front door, and she ran. They figured she'd make a run for it out the back, so they ran around the house and through her side gate. They intercepted her but she fought. And won."

I smile. "She doesn't look like the sort to fight."

Young gives a chuckle. "Yeah, my boys were surprised, that's for sure…and embarrassed. But we were bringing her in to protect her. Given what had happened to Saito."

I notice the use of "my" boys and "my" guys—but he's

talking about his Yakuza associates, not law enforcement. He's entrenched, all right.

"So when did you find her?"

"She disappeared from our radar and Moto was worried Saito's killer had her, but we intercepted her yesterday as she was fleeing Mi-na Moon's house."

"How'd you know about Moon?" I ask, wondering if someone in the task force passed on the information on the Korean Cultural Center.

"Moto gave me the address. We grabbed her as she was fleeing and took her to a Yakuza hideout."

"So she's safe?"

Young nods. "I saw her myself only twelve hours ago. She's freaked out, but okay."

"Did she even know who her father was? That he was ex-Yakuza?" I ask.

"Apparently her mother said the word *Jun* on her deathbed, like a last-minute confession. But Mee had no idea what it meant until you mentioned the name to her."

"I'd like to talk to her, but I guess that's not likely."

Petrov shakes his head. "We can't blow Dan's cover. And if Ken Tanabe was given orders to kill you guys and Dan gummed up the works, he may already be in trouble."

"What will be the repercussions?"

"I don't know." Young's concerned. "And I don't know whether it'll be Ken in trouble or me."

He risked his life to save mine… "What's Moto like?"

"Moody. Punishment could be anything from a slap on the hand to…" He trails off.

"Can't we pull him out?" I look at Petrov and De Luca.

"We've spoken about this…with Brady," De Luca says. "We all agree that Dan should stay in, for the time being."

"I'm moving up in the organization. And we need someone in there, at least until we find the mole."

I nod, but still feel guilty that his actions have put him in harm's way.

"Given your wounds were less severe than Ramos's we told the press that you were able to dial 911 on your cell."

I nod, taking the detail in and convincing myself of its truth. I may have to repeat it. "So, do you guys think Moto got Mi-na Moon's address from the leak? Only a few of us knew about that."

De Luca and Petrov exchange glances. "We're not sure."

"Moto did have people looking for Mee. He told me that one of the others found out about the cultural center and her students. That the tip-off came in that way."

"But he might have been lying."

The others all nod and Petrov adds, "It's impossible to know how Moto found out about Moon. When you guys updated me, I made sure the rest of the team was in the loop."

We're silent, no one wanting to think of the possibility that Williams or Hana is the mole.

After a few seconds I change the subject. "You know about the hit man? And *dim mak?*"

"Yes. Joe has kept me up to speed. I know a little bit about *dim mak,* but I'll be reading up on it more, too."

"I've spoken to Lee about it quite extensively. It looks legit."

"Fascinating stuff." Young stares out the hospital window.

I take another look at Agent Dan Young. Was he really following me? Did I really miss a familiar face on my tail for two or more days?

"Agent Young?"

He turns from the window. "Yes?"

"Moto said you'd been following me. Is that true?"

He smiles. "Moto wanted to find out more about you, but I got most of my information from these guys." He jerks his head toward Petrov and De Luca. "Plus I already knew you studied kung fu two nights a week. Don't worry. I only tailed you for a couple of hours."

"Good to know," I say, although I'm still not happy about not noticing a tail, even for two hours. Could AmericanPsycho do the same? I push the thought away. "The doctor said it'd be another two weeks before I can go back to work, but there's no reason I can't work from here. Dial into the task force meetings, that sort of thing."

Petrov smiles. "Nice try, Anderson. But it's two weeks

and I don't think Dr. Goldman would approve of you working from here in the meantime. I don't think anyone would, me included."

"Come on." I hold my hands out. "Can I at least have my BlackBerry?"

Petrov makes his way to the door. "Let's leave Anderson to rest. She needs it, even if she doesn't think so." De Luca and Young follow Petrov's lead.

"No…guys. Come on."

They disappear.

"Guys!"

Petrov's head pokes around the door frame. "I'll send Melissa in with some magazines for you."

"FBI bulletins?"

"I don't think that'll be her choice." He disappears. "Rest up…" His voice trails off and he moves down the corridor.

Two hours later Melissa turns up, bouncing into the room as only Melissa can.

"Oh, Sophie. I'm so glad you're okay. I visited you late last night, but you were still unconscious." She shakes her head. "I couldn't believe it when Brady told me."

"Last night? But it must have been past midnight when I was shot."

"Yeah. Sorry, I mean early hours of the morning."

"And you came in?"

"Of course!"

I smile, touched by Melissa's concern. I guess I still haven't fully processed the fact that I was shot. That people would have been worried about me. I take a closer look at Melissa and notice the uncharacteristic dark circles under her eyes.

"How long were you here for?"

"A few hours. Just until you'd stabilized after the surgery. Mercedes was here, too."

"Thanks, Melissa. That's really sweet of you guys."

She dismisses it with a wave of her hand. "Don't be silly. Besides, I know you don't have family here."

"My parents are on their way here now."

"Yeah. Petrov got Agent Sandston to pick them up. He's fresh out of the academy. I just called him and they're about fifteen minutes away. Bad traffic."

I suddenly get butterflies in my stomach at the thought of my parents seeing me like this, their worst—or almost worst—fears realized.

Melissa looks around the room. "You've got a few bunches of flowers. They're beautiful."

I nod. "I haven't even got out of bed yet. Don't know who they're from."

"You should have asked the nurses to read the cards out."

I shrug. "Didn't want to bother them."

Melissa starts with the bunch near the window, red tulips. "Okay, so this one says, *Get better soon, from everyone at L.A. FBI.* That's us."

I smile. "Trust you to read out the ones you sent first."

"I didn't know what the florist sent."

"Yeah, yeah, yeah. You know I like tulips."

She shrugs. "Guilty as charged." She moves to a bunch of irises on the other side of the window. "And these are from Darren. Detective Darren Carter, I presume?"

"Yeah. I'd say so."

"I've spoken to him twice today. He heard that you'd been shot on this morning's news and rang Brady straight-away. I spoke to him, told him you'd be okay. But he wants you to call him as soon as you're up to it. He's been talking about flying up, too. He sounds nice. Real nice."

I smile. There have always been a few sparks.

"I see that smile, Sophie." Melissa gives me a wink. "And you keep telling me you're just friends."

"We are."

"Want me to read the card then?"

"Sure."

"It says, *I hear we have matching bullet holes. Thinking of you always, love Darren.* Still just friends?"

"Yes."

"I've heard that before." She looks down at the card. "Matching bullet holes? You didn't tell me he'd been shot."

. "Darren was shot in the chest. Same side, but a bit lower than mine."

"Oh. That is romantic," Melissa says sarcastically.

I laugh. "Come on, next one." I look at the only other bunch in the room, lilies.

Melissa crosses over to the vase and plucks the card out of the centre. "Okay, so this one says, *A single... Oh*, my gosh."

"What? What is it?"

Melissa's face is white. "I'm sorry, Sophie." She reads out the whole card. *"A single red rose just wasn't right this time. Get better. AP."*

I shake my head. "He won't leave me alone."

"Can't Interpol do anything about this guy?"

"They're trying, Melissa."

"I know. Sorry."

The somber mood is broken when Mum hurries into the room.

"Oh, Sophie." She runs toward my bed with such emotion and force that I have to say, "Careful, Mum," for fear she'll throw herself on my bed and rip a stitch or two in my shoulder. But instead of flinging her full body weight on top of me, she grabs my right hand in hers and uses her other hand to caress my hair as she kisses my cheek. "Thank goodness you're okay, baby."

I squeeze her hand. "I'm fine, Mum. Honest."

Dad comes to the other side of my bed.

"Hi, Dad."

"Hi, sweetie." He grabs my left hand and gives it a squeeze. "We were worried." The king of understatement...like lots of men.

"I bet Mum drove you crazy on the flight over here." I smile.

"She wasn't too bad." He gives her a strange look and she responds with a tight-lipped smile.

"What? What's up?" I ask.

"Up? Nothing?"

"Dad, you're trying to fool a behavioral analyst. Give it up."

"Sophie, I'll leave you to it." Melissa gives a little wave from the doorway.

"Sorry, Melissa. Melissa Raine, meet my parents, Jan and Bob Anderson."

She comes back to the bed and shakes their hands. "It's real nice to meet you both."

"You're the one who called us," Dad says, recognition in his voice.

"That's right. I knew you'd want to know straightaway. Before it was on the news."

I laugh. "On the news in Australia? I don't think so."

Both my parents are silent.

"Serious?"

Dad sighs. "An Australian working for the FBI got shot. Of course it made our news. We saw it at the airport."

I instantly get a flash of my parents watching the news and hearing about my gunshot wound that way. Thank goodness Melissa called. "Thanks, Melissa. I really appreciate it."

She smiles. "No worries."

"She's teaching you the Australian slang, I see," Dad says. "It took me years to pick it up."

"You don't sound very American anymore, sir."

He laughs. "The Aussies think I sound American and the Americans think I sound Australian."

Dad's been living in Australia for thirty-five years and his accent's morphed into something that sounds a little foreign in both countries.

He looks back at me. "We were so worried, Soph."

"I know, Dad. I'm sorry."

"Well, it was nice to meet you." Melissa tries her departure once more. "I've left some magazines there for you, Sophie, and I got your BlackBerry for you, too. It's been examined by forensics for the phone call you got last night."

"And?" I say, eager to find out who made the phony tip-off.

"The call was made by Jason Pham. One of the guys killed last night."

"Oh…okay." But the information is anything but illuminating. Pham's a dead end—literally.

"Wish I could bar work calls on it somehow. And e-mails."

"You know our daughter well, Melissa." My mother sits down beside my bed. "And don't let us rush you away."

"No, no, I've got to get going. I'll pop by tomorrow morning, Sophie." She smiles. "And don't forget to call Detective Carter."

"I will."

She leaves with a wave.

Mum's already shaking her head. "I'm sure the detective can wait, Sophie. You've been shot, can't they leave you alone for a couple of days?"

"It's a personal call, Mum."

"Really?" The excitement in her voice makes me regret not thinking on my feet. I would have been better copping the flack of making a work call than all the questions she's going to have for me now.

"I didn't know you had anyone special over here. Why don't you tell us these things, darling?"

"He's just a friend, Mum. We met on a case over a year ago and we've stayed in contact. That's all."

"A friend." She doesn't even try to hide her disappointment.

"Come on, Jan." Dad takes her hand. "Give it a rest."

I give Dad a grateful look, but I know this conversation is anything but over. No doubt tomorrow I'll get the biological-clock talk…again. But for the moment, Mum gives a little nod and starts to tear up.

"Sophie, I just can't tell you…can't tell you how it felt when the phone rang and Melissa said something had happened to you. I just…"

"I'm sorry, Mum. I am careful. You know that." I pause, not sure whether I should say the next bit. I bite down hard on my lip. "I don't want to put you guys through this. But I love my job. Love helping people…including kids like John."

Mum looks away, the tears overflowing, but Dad takes my hand. "We know that's why you do this, Sophie."

Silence falls. We're damaged, my family. Just like so many of the victims' families that I meet in this job. When I was eight years old my brother, John, was taken from his bedroom in the middle of the night. A year later, his body was found, but they never caught his killer. You can't have something like that happen and move on, unaffected. It chose my career for me. It changed Mum from a relatively relaxed, independent mum to a wrap-me-in-cotton-wool mum. She lost one of her babies, and she can't stand the thought that she could lose the other one.

"I'm sorry, Mum." The words aren't enough, but I still feel the need to repeat them. "I'm sorry."

But what comes out of my mother's mouth shocks me. Through her tears, she manages, "We're proud of you, darling. Proud of what you do and the families you help."

Tears flow down my cheeks and it feels as if I'll never stop crying.

Twenty-One

My hospital-room phone rings, right on time.

"Anderson," I say with as much energy as I can muster.

"I'm still not so sure about this, Anderson," Petrov says.

"Come on. I'm fine."

"You're not fine, Anderson." He pauses. "But we need to hand over some of your tasks and that's the only reason you're part of this update."

I'm tempted to argue, but I know not to look a gift horse in the mouth. "Okay."

"Hey, Sophie." It's Hana's voice. "How you feeling?"

"Much better, thanks."

"Good to hear." I recognize De Luca's voice.

"Great to hear your voice, Anderson," Williams says.

"Thanks, guys."

"Okay, let's get this moving." Petrov takes command of the meeting. "I don't want to keep Anderson too long."

Again, I resist the urge to protest and reassure everyone that I'm fine.

"So, our list from Friday. How's everybody doing with their tasks? We'll start with you, Agent Kim. How'd you go with the follow-up on Corey Casey?"

"The doctors couldn't pinpoint the cause of the liver failure. According to family and friends, Casey never took drugs and wasn't much of a drinker. There was no sign of hepatitis or any other primary cause."

"So maybe Lee's right," I say. "His death was a result of the 1996 attack."

Petrov clears his throat. "I'm going to touch base with Grove on this. You were thinking he'd be up to speed by now, Anderson?"

"Yes, sir. He was planning to read up on the *dim mak* techniques on the weekend."

In fact, Grove is probably more up to speed than me now. Lee's remaining three books sit on my bedside table, but I didn't feel up to reading on the weekend. Hopefully today my concentration will be a little better.

"Anything else, Agent Kim?"

"The wife did notice bruises after the attack, but can't remember exactly where they were."

I nod. "So they could have been targeted on pressure points or they could have been generic bruises from the attack."

"That's right."

Petrov takes over. "Okay, next on the list was looking for any link between the two Yakuza victims, Matsu in 2000 and Saito. That was yours, De Luca."

"I've pulled everything we've got on Matsu, and spoken to the cops that investigated his death. We've been going through Matsu's movements in the 1980s and 1990s, seeing if maybe he ran into Saito, visited Japan, but nothing so far."

"Okay. Keep on it." Petrov pauses, presumably looking up the next task. "Williams. Li Chow in New York. Did he know his killer?"

"I've been in contact with New York and they're sending me his file today. I'll let you know."

It is only nine o'clock Monday morning, so it's not surprising that we haven't had any major breakthroughs in the past forty-eight hours.

"Okay, next was me, looking into the Russian victim and why he may have been killed with the butterfly swords. I spoke to San Diego on Friday afternoon. Apparently the victim, Alexander Ivanovich, was known for his obsession with knives…blades. He'd been suspected in four homicides and all victims had been cut up—bad."

"So whoever ordered the hit wanted him to go the same way?" De Luca suggests.

"That's the logical conclusion," Petrov replies. "It's why our killer would have departed from his standard MO. Would that fit, Anderson? Psychologically speaking?"

"Yes. Our guy's a professional, and if a client asks for the murder to be carried out in a certain way, he'd satisfy that request. But he still marked the victim as his own by using the Tiger Leopard Fist to severely disable and disorientate him first. Plus he didn't use a regular knife, he used martial-arts weapons."

"Okay," Petrov replies. "So that anomaly makes some sense now." He pauses. "Next on our list was the Jun Saito victimology, but that was you and Ramos, Anderson."

I manage a chuckle. "Yeah, we haven't got to that yet."

"I can work on that now, sir," Hana says.

"Great. Where were you at with Interpol, Anderson?"

"Contact Latoya Burges for an update, Hana. She requested info on Saito and on his alias of Jo Kume and was hoping to get something late last week, but nothing came through."

"Okay."

"And I'll give you what I've got on his history from fifteen years ago," Petrov says. "A lot of what I told the task force at the briefing last Thursday was from memory, but I should be able to dig up some historical paperwork, too."

"Thanks, sir."

"Anderson, it was you and Ramos for the next one, too. Trying to find Mee."

"Do you want me to take that now, sir?" Williams asks.

"No, I'll look after that one," Petrov replies.

But I know he won't have to do any actual work—he knows where Mee is.

"We've also got Saito's hotel and Mee Kim's house. I'll follow up with the lab on those results." Petrov pauses, maybe writing his task down, before moving on. "The next three items were all yours, Anderson. The offender profile, giving us some generic psych material on contract killers and following up the pressure points with Grove."

"I'm afraid it'll be another few days before I'm up to the profile, but I can organize to get you that generic info. It's just a collection of documents."

"That'd be real useful." Hana's voice is light. "But only if you're up to it."

"I'll be fine." I move on. "As you know, we did find evidence that *dim mak* was used on Saito, with four pressure points showing trauma. I'll follow up Grove with a quick phone call today to see what he made of the *dim mak* book I lent him."

"I can take that, Anderson." Petrov's voice is slightly protective. "I'll ask Grove when I contact him about Casey's liver failure."

"I'm feeling okay, honestly. And I'm soooo bored!"

Petrov gives an amused sigh. "Let's do it as a conference call. I still want to hear Grove's opinion firsthand."

"Yes, sir." I try to lean forward, but find the movement painful. "There is one other thing."

"Yes?"

"I was thinking we should get a list of all Chinese nationals who entered the country within, say, a month prior to Saito's murder. If our hit man is Chinese and was flown in for the job, his name would be on that list."

"Great idea, Anderson. Who wants that one?"

"I've got a contact over at US State," I say. "It's only a phone call."

Petrov's silent, but then sighs. "Okay, Anderson. But don't even think of going through that list. Get it and pass it on to *us*."

"Yes, sir."

"Okay, that's it, people. Keep me in the loop." Petrov's wrapping up the meeting and, although I should also flag the need for some new ViCAP searches that focus on *dim mak* without the use of the Ten Killing Hands, I keep my mouth shut. Given my kung fu knowledge, I'm the best person to do those searches and I don't want Petrov hand-balling the task to someone else.

"And Anderson," Petrov says, "get some rest."

"Yes, sir."

As soon as I'm off the phone, I dial Lara Rodriguez from State. "Hey, Lara. It's Agent Sophie Anderson."

"Oh, my gosh. Are you okay? I saw it on the news…you were shot."

"Yeah, just a flesh wound." I downplay my injuries.

"Really? Are you sure?"

"I'm fine."

"You back at work already?"

"No, still in hospital, unfortunately."

"Hospital? Then what the heck are you doing ringing me?"

"I'm working on the case from here."

"Sounds crazy to me. How did it go with your vic? Did his ID help?"

"Actually, Jo Kume wasn't his real name."

"Get out of here."

"His real name was Jun Saito, and he used to be Yakuza."

"Whoa. Is that who shot you, Yakuza?"

"Uh-huh."

"You're messing with some serious people, Sophie."

"I know." I pause. "Anyway, we're looking at a professional killer and we think he may be Chinese and have flown in for the contract on Saito's life."

"Really?"

"Yup. Can you do another search for me?"

"Shoot."

"Can you e-mail me through a list of all Chinese nationals who entered the country from November 6 until December 6?" It's unlikely the killer only flew in on December 6, less than twenty-four hours before Saito's murder—it wouldn't have given him enough time to plan the hit—but I may as well keep my date range broad.

"You just want names, or full immigration details and pictures?"

"You may as well give me the works, if that's okay."

"No problem. It'll be tomorrow or Wednesday. Okay?"

"Sure." I thank Rodriguez and hang up. I'm about to call Grove when my parents walk in.

"Hi, darling. How are you feeling this morning?" Mum comes in first, and behind her is Dad, laden down with an overnight bag for me.

I push myself more upright. "Much better."

She nods but doesn't look convinced. "You look tired, darling."

"I'm fine, Mum."

"You sleep okay?"

"Yes," I lie. In fact, I tossed and turned all night, thinking about who the mole is in the Gang Impact Team. It's a large team, but it's also possible that the leak is Williams or Hana. In fact, if Tomi Moto got Moon's details from the mole, it must be one of them. I push the thought away. According to Young, Moto had lots of people looking for Mee, and Williams and Hana are only two people out of a twenty-four person task force—the statistics are in their favor.

"What you got there, Dad?"

Dad places the bag down and moves in, kissing me on the forehead. "Your mother organized a few more clothes for you. And a couple of books."

"Books...great. They'll be the only thing keeping me sane in here." Although I won't be reading any books until I finish the *dim mak* titles.

Mum unzips the bag. "I could only find two sets of pajamas, so I brought them in and picked you up a nightie at Macy's." She pulls them out of the bag. "Which do you want to wear first? The pajamas have got buttons but the nightie's low cut, so they'll have no problems checking your wound."

"Red pj's."

She nods and folds the other set of pajamas and nightie, before placing them in the top drawer of my bedside locker. "I also bought you a dressing gown and a tracksuit, for when you're up to walking."

"I can walk now. You know the doctors want me up several times a day."

"Yes, darling, but just short walks. I'm talking about down to the café or newsagent."

"Okay, but I could walk that far now and I've only got four nights left."

Mum bites her lip.

Dad puts his hand on her shoulder. "Let your mum fuss, Soph. You know it's what she does best."

"Bob," Mum says, brushing his hand off her shoulder. But she is smiling.

I stifle a laugh. "Thanks, Mum."

There's a short rap at the door. I look up to see Darren Carter's slim, five-eleven frame at the door. His black hair looks a little more tousled than usual.

"Darren, hi." I instinctively push myself up higher and wish I had a mirror to check out my hair…and face…and…

In one hand he holds a bunch of flowers, and in the other an overnight bag. "Did I come at a bad time?"

I'm speechless, focused more on his midnight-blue eyes, but Mum more than makes up for my silence. "No, not at all. I'm Sophie's mum, Jan Anderson, and this is my husband, Bob."

Darren shakes both their hands. "Nice to meet you, Mr. and Mrs. Anderson. I'm Detective Darren Carter."

"Please, call us Jan and Bob."

"Likewise, it's Darren." He smiles.

Mum turns back to me, eager. "You didn't tell us Darren was coming up."

Now that Mum's seen my reaction to Darren—and his to me—I know I'm going to have a hard time convincing her that we're just professional acquaintances. "I…I didn't know."

Darren grins. "I told you I might come up on my days off."

I vaguely remember a conversation to that effect on Saturday afternoon, but I guess I was still coming out of the general anesthetic, not to mention the pain meds, and it all seems a little hazy.

Darren's face falls. "I'm sorry. Maybe I shouldn't have come."

"Don't be silly, dear boy." Mum puts her hand on Darren's arm. "Sophie needs her friends and family around her now."

"You sure? I don't want to intrude." Darren's half talking to me, and half to Mum.

"Sorry, Darren. I do remember now. Saturday's a bit hazy, that's all."

The grin returns.

"So, where are you staying?" Mum asks.

"I've booked a hotel around the corner."

"You must come and stay at Sophie's apartment with us." Mum turns to me. "That's a sofa bed in the living room, isn't it?"

I nod, caught in the headlights of a runaway train. Darren staying with my parents…without me there…man-oh-man, this is bad.

I give Dad a look. He's usually my ally in these situations, but this time he just gives a slight smirk and even has the audacity to give me a wink. Oh, that's cruel.

"I don't know…I don't want to impose." Darren gives her a boyish shrug. "And I'm booked and all."

"No, no, no. And it's no imposition. You don't want to stay in some impersonal hotel when you could stay with us."

Darren also seems a little like a kangaroo stunned in full beams.

"Mum, some people like staying in hotels. They prefer their own space." My voice is polite, but I hope she gets the message.

But she doesn't. "Don't be silly, darling. No one would want to stay in hotel if they could stay in a home. Besides, Darren looks like he could use a few home-cooked meals."

I let my head fall back into the pillow for a second, then mouth "Sorry" to Darren.

He grins, obviously seeing the humor in the situation…or my mother. "Sounds like an offer I can't refuse."

Please tell me this isn't happening. I'm dreaming, right? Mum will have Darren and me married off by dinnertime— and I won't even be there!

Twenty-Two

"So, how are you?" Darren sits on the side of my bed. Mum and Dad left only a few moments ago with the oh-so-casual line, "We'll leave you kids alone." If there were a brick wall handy, I'd bang my head against it.

"Sorry about Mum."

Darren's dimples pucker, and I can tell he's holding back an even bigger grin.

I roll my eyes. "I know, she's a nightmare."

"She's lovely, Soph. And you're her baby girl."

I nod. "But I still don't envy you. Staying with my parents for a night or two?" I smile. "You'll never be the same again."

"Come on, it won't be that bad. And it's only a night. I'm back on duty Wednesday morning."

"You can still get out of it, you know. Save yourself now, before it's too late."

"I'm looking forward to it, actually." The cheeky grin again. "Lucky I hadn't checked in already." He looks back at his overnight bag, shoved in a corner.

"Why didn't you check in first?"

He looks down. "I needed to come straight here and see you with my own eyes." He looks up. "Make sure you really were doing okay."

"Verdict?"

"You're pale, but I think you'll pull through."

I smile. "So the doctors say."

"Did you feel like this when I was shot?" he asks.

"What do you mean?"

He shrugs. "When I first heard…" He shakes his head. "I felt so helpless. Still do."

My defensive nature when it comes to relationships kicks in. "Don't be silly. I'm fine, you were fine."

He smiles, but shifts uncomfortably on the bed. Access denied, again, and he knows it. "So, they giving you good pain meds?"

Darren's good at responding to my signals. Maybe too good. Sometimes I want him to push. But other times I'm happy he lets me keep him at a distance.

"Pretty good. It's starting to hurt a bit now, actually."

"You want me to get a nurse? Get something for you?"

"Nah. They'll come around soon. I think I'm due for a top-up."

"You sure?"

I nod.

"You look tired, Soph." He looks intently at me, his midnight-blue eyes locked with mine.

"Terrible, you mean."

He smiles. "No, just tired."

"Don't tell my folks, but I didn't sleep so well last night."

"Really? Why?"

I shrug, realizing I can't even take Darren into my confidence. Not on this one. "Just thinking about this case."

"About being shot?"

"No."

After a moment of silence, Darren says, "So tell me how you really are."

I manage a small smile. "You're persistent, as always."

"That's what friends are for, right?"

"I've been through worse than this. You know that." The case Darren and I met on got personal for both of us. "You know what, I don't even feel that affected emotionally."

"That's denial. You could have been killed, Sophie."

"I've been aware of my own mortality for a long time, Darren. I'm not dealing with that revelation, not this time."

He's silent, studying my face.

"I'm not in denial. I'm not repressing any deep, dark emotions. Being roughed up by some organized crime thugs and taking a bullet in the shoulder isn't my biggest fear."

"Don't trivialize it, Sophie. It's a big deal. You're not convincing me, you know."

"Okay, how's this?" I take a breath, ready to bare my soul to Darren. "My fear is being taken by a serial killer, of becoming a victim of sexual homicide. I've seen what guys do to those victims, what those women have to endure before they die. That's what I fear. This, I can deal with. Honestly."

He takes my hand. "I understand."

I look at his hand and manage a smile. He really does understand…Darren sees those photos, too.

He takes his hand away. "I think I better let you get some rest. You look exhausted."

"I hate to admit it, but I think I do need sleep."

He stands up. "Well, I'll leave you to it."

"My parents will be in the coffee lounge downstairs. You can get a ride with them to my apartment."

"Okay. I'll see you tonight?"

"My parents usually come in straight after dinner, but you're welcome any time. If you need to get away…"

He laughs. "I'll cope. Besides, apparently I need some home cooking." He pats his flat stomach.

I laugh. "See you tonight."

Once Darren's gone, I call Grove and dial in Petrov, too. I'm eager to hear Grove's thoughts, but I'm also exhausted so I hope the phone call is short.

"So, how'd you do with your weekend reading, Doc?"

"Well, I definitely had a better weekend than you, Anderson. Glad to hear you and Detective Ramos are okay."

"Thanks. Although Ramos is still critical."

"Yeah. I spoke to his doctor this morning. Ramos is strong, healthy. He'll be okay."

I'm not sure whether that's Grove's professional opinion or if he's providing emotional support. I imagine it's the latter, given the other doctors don't seem quite as willing to offer a definitive long-term prognosis. I need to see Ramos for myself.

"So, the reading." Grove makes a clicking sound with his tongue. "I can't advise you on whether the human hand is capable of delivering the force necessary to cause all of the devastating effects covered in the book, but the medical facts behind targeting the nervous system and other points mentioned in the book are valid. I wouldn't say unequivocally that the strikes will kill, but I can see that they could kill if they were delivered accurately and with enough force."

Petrov whistles down the phone line. "So it really is possible?"

"I can only talk to the theory and Jun Saito's body. The medical theory is sound and, while Saito died of blood loss, his body also tells us that *dim mak* strikes were used against him. Make of it what you will."

"Thanks, Doc," I say. "Can you courier the book over? I think I better add it to my reading list."

"Will do."

"We've also got another victim we'd like to talk to you about," Petrov says. "He was attacked in 1996 and died eight years later of liver failure. Apparently there was no medical or lifestyle condition that led to the organ failure. Could it have been due to the attack?"

Before Grove has time to consider it, I add, "There's a section on organ failure in the book, isn't there?"

"Yes. But the concept of delayed death…I'm really not sure about that. I can see a few hours or days if you're talking a ruptured spleen with no medical intervention, but eight years…"

"So you don't think it's likely?" Petrov asks.

"No. But officially I'm going to sit on the fence. Logically I doubt it, but the human body's a weird and wonderful organism. I guess it's also possible the attack damaged the organs and that the effects weren't obvious…until it was too late."

"The wife said he was bruised, but she can't remember exactly where," I say. "So there's no way to confirm that pressure points were targeted. Not when the attack took place so long ago."

We're silent.

Petrov clears his throat. "Guess that's everything. Thanks, Grove, and we'll call you if we've got any more questions."

"Sure thing. Take care of yourself, Anderson."

"I will." I hang up, exhausted. The ViCAP searches will definitely have to wait but I can't wait any longer to see Ramos. I flash back to the deafening discharge and echo of the three bullets, the bullets I thought had killed Ramos. No, I need to see him, and now.

I slowly maneuver myself out of bed, leaning on my right side and rolling out of bed as fluidly as I can. As my feet hit the cold hospital floor the light impact travels through my body, sending shooting pain along my shoulder blade. I wince, happy no one's here to witness my pain and tell me to get back into bed. I throw my dressing gown and slippers on and slowly make my way to intensive care.

Even though it's officially family only, I'm able to talk my way in to see Ramos thanks to a sympathetic nurse.

"He's in the corner bed," she says with a smile, pointing to the far side of the room.

I move slowly toward it. A voluptuous woman with long dark hair sits on the chair nearest the bed, her hand lying on top of Ramos's forearm. Her head is down—asleep? Once I'm a few steps away she looks up, recognition on her face.

"Agent Anderson."

"Yes." I'm surprised she knows who I am.

She stands up. "Your photos have been on the news. Yours and my Edwardo's."

I nod, realizing that until that moment I hadn't even known Ramos's first name. "How's he doing?" I look down at Ramos. His face is so pale that if you didn't know him, you probably wouldn't even guess he was Hispanic.

"He sleeps a lot." She forces a smile. "But the doctors say he's getting stronger."

I don't press her on the prognosis. In another day or two maybe the doctors will be willing to predict a full recovery, but not yet. I sigh. Could we have done anything differently that night? Anything to keep us out of this place?

"I'm sorry," I say to Mrs. Ramos. "Sorry I called him that night."

"You were doing your job. As was he. We know the risks."

At first I'm shocked by her acceptance of the night's events. If she's spent any time replaying the night in anguish she's not showing it. Or perhaps she's simply relieved she's not at home organizing a funeral.

She puts her hand on mine. "I'm glad you had each other. And so grateful to you for calling 911."

The lie…I didn't call 911, but maybe it doesn't matter.

Ramos stirs and blinks his eyes, opening them slowly. He manages a weak grin. "Hey, you. Great to see you up and about."

I smile. "Thanks. I'm looking forward to seeing you up, too."

"Soon." He takes a heavy breath. "Hopefully soon." He winces.

"You're in pain."

"A bit."

"A lot," his wife interjects before calling a nurse.

"I'll go. I just wanted to check on you, Ramos…. And say hi."

"Thanks." He grits his teeth.

"Rest up," I say and shake Mrs. Ramos's hand before shuffling away. In another minute or two Ramos will have more pain meds and be drifting back to sleep. And then hopefully in another day or two he'll be out of the woods.

Twenty-Three

On my BlackBerry, I open up the list of the three hundred and fifty-six male Chinese nationals who entered the US between November 6 and December 6 and left within a week of Saito's murder. Rodriguez sent through a list of names with their entry and exit dates in Excel, the biometric data for each person, plus JPEG images of the photos taken at their entry point—in most cases an airport.

I study the Excel list, despite Petrov's instructions to the contrary. I e-mailed it through to the team as soon as it came in yesterday, but I'm so bored in hospital…I'll go out of my mind if I don't do something. I've read all four *dim mak* books and I need something else constructive to do. The immigration info fits the bill. I know I'm still operating below par because of the pain medication, but I can't just lie here twiddling my thumbs. Today's Thursday, and I've got another two full days of hospital hell. I have to do something. But the names are merging into one big blur. I hope the others are having better luck than I am. I shake my head. What am I doing? I have another method at my disposal. I try with the names first…. I've never tried to get anything in terms of a vision or dream from someone's name alone, but I know it can be done. In fact, if you believe the rumors, the CIA used remote viewers during the Cold War—people who could give them information on a building or location just by knowing the longitude and latitude. And the US wasn't the only country that experimented in this area. While the parapsychology tests have been inconclusive, I know that some people can tune into a person from their name alone. Others need a photo, while some need to touch something personal to the subject. There's certainly no harm in me trying my usual relaxation techniques while staring at a name. I lean back in the hospital bed and consciously slow my breathing, concentrating on each breath. Then, I open my eyes and look at the first name, Chi Ho, and close my eyes. Nothing, so I move on to the next name. After the tenth name, I close the Excel document and bring up the pics. I'm about to try again to induce a vision when Mum walks in.

"Morning, sweetie."

I casually place my BlackBerry on the bedside table. "Hi, Mum." She follows my hand.

"Darling! You're supposed to be resting."

"I am, Mum."

Dad enters. "What's up?"

Mum turns around. "She was working…again."

Dad looks at us, one then the other, torn between whose side to take. His eyes settle on me. "Sophie, you're not doing yourself any favors."

I grimace. Damn. "Come on, Dad. I'm bored stupid in here."

"What about your books? TV?" Mum crosses her arms. I shrug.

"It's for your own good, Sophie. The more you rest now, the faster you'll be back on your feet…and at work."

Ouch, that's below the belt. "Nice try, Mum."

She plonks into the armchair. "Fine. I give up. Work." Silence.

"So you'll bring in my laptop then?" I've been asking for it since Tuesday—the small BlackBerry screen hasn't been helping matters. Maybe that's why I haven't been able to induce a vision.

Mum stands up. "Talk to your daughter, Bob." And she leaves.

Uh-oh.

Dad gives me a look. "Do you have any idea how worried your mum's been? How hard it is to see you like this?" He takes a breath. "To know what could have happened to you that night?"

"Umm…"

"Sophie, think. Please. If you'd seen her in Melbourne, on that airplane, you wouldn't be doing this."

I'm not used to hearing such harshness in my dad. He's usually the laid-back one. And my ally.

"But, Dad, I thought you guys understood now. You said you know why I do this. Why it's so important to me."

He sits on the edge of my bed and his tone softens. "We do, Sophie. We understand. But our natural instinct is still to protect you. And your mum is talking sense—you will get better faster if you rest."

I sigh. "I don't know, Dad."

"We don't expect you to abandon the case. But just put your health first." He places his hand on top of mine. "You've only got two more days in here, and then you're back in your apartment, with your laptop."

"And what'll Mum say when I open it up?"

Dad's silent. "Let's make a deal. You rest today and tomorrow. Then, when you're released, I'll do my best to keep your mum off your back."

I smile. "Deal."

He holds up his hand. "Hold on, you haven't heard the whole deal."

I raise my eyebrows, waiting for him to continue.

"During the week we're in your apartment, before we head back to Oz, you still have to pace yourself."

"Like?"

"Two hours a day."

"Three," I say, holding out my hand to shake on it.

Dad looks unsure. "Two and a half…but that includes phone calls." He takes my hand.

I grimace. "Okay. But I need one hour today, after you're gone, and then I'm done until Saturday."

Now his face screws up, but he shakes my hand, nonetheless.

An hour later, Mum and Dad have left me to "rest"—which I will do, but first the long-awaited ViCAP searches. The first one I look for is the heart concussion. I'm not expecting ViCAP's online system to return many hits. If our hit man used *dim mak* without any of the Ten Killing Hands, it's possible the death would be passed off as accidental, and certainly not criminal. I type in heart concussion as the cause of death and leave all the other fields blank. I get one hit, from 1999 in Washington, D.C. The victim was a politician and the case was investigated as suspicious, but the unusual cause of death complicated things. The forensic pathologist noted small, circular areas of trauma in the chest region but couldn't match it to a weapon and so the case went cold.

In the absence of a printer, I save all the details to my Black-Berry's internal memory and move on to the next search. I know there's no point looking for generic organ failure, but the strikes that target the spleen could give me matches, so I enter in ruptured spleen as the cause of death. This time I get twenty matches, but all of them bar two look like regular muggings or beatings. The two that I flag as potentially related to our killer took place in Seattle in 2003 and New Orleans in 2005.

Next is heart attack and ventricular fibrillation. I'm not expecting many results for these two either—not in ViCAP, which records violent and serial crimes—but it's worth a shot. I get three matches for heart attack as cause of death, but they're all drug-related cases in which the victim took too much cocaine or speed. All were classified as accidental deaths, but were entered into ViCAP because they were also investigated as potentially forced drug consumption. In the end, the police couldn't prove anything criminal, and whether they were murder or not, they're certainly not related to kung fu strikes.

For ventricular fibrillation as the cause of death I get five matches. Of the first four, two were induced during drowning, one occurred from extremely low levels of potassium and one from a hit and run. While all had something suspicious or criminal about them, it's only the fifth case of ventricular fibrillation that I believe is related to *dim mak,* to our killer. In this case, no specific cause for the ventricular fibrillation could be found by the forensic pathologist, but the victim was a very wealthy businessman whose new wife inherited five million dollars. The police flagged it as suspicious, but could never get anything on her or anyone else. While they had to let the case go, one of the detectives was concerned enough to lodge it in ViCAP. There could be many other cases just like this one, where the victim died of ventricular fibrillation with an unknown cause and so they were written off as accidental deaths. But I can't look up every cardiac death in the US.

Before getting some rest, I draft a quick e-mail to the team and send through my ViCAP search results. I'm not sure that the new murders I've potentially linked to our killer will do us any good in terms of the investigation, but it still had to be done. Besides, maybe the wealthy widow will somehow lead us to the hit man.

Dad holds my elbow and forearm as we walk down the corridor to my apartment door. I think it's overkill, but Mum insisted. On the outside of my apartment door Mum and Dad have put up a reindeer knocker. Christmas is in three days' time—and I couldn't feel less festive. It's come so quickly this year, and being in hospital and out of my regular routine has left me feeling decidedly un-Christmassy.

"The reindeer's cute," I say. "You just put him up?"

"It was one of the first things your mum bought." Dad keeps us moving forward.

"Oh, Bob…" Mum turns to me. "Your father's so excited about having a Christmas here in the States. He bought the reindeer, not me."

Dad shrugs. "Guilty as charged." He nods at two yellow

envelopes stuck under my apartment door. "Looks like you've had a delivery."

"I hope that's not work, Sophie Jane Anderson."

A disapproving glare *and* the use of my full name…looks like Dad didn't tell Mum about our deal. He must have decided to take each day as it comes. Brave man.

"Just a few things, Mum. Not much."

She shakes her head, and then picks up the envelopes. "Not even in the door from hospital and she's already working." Inside, Mum places the keys on the hall dresser.

"I haven't even opened the envelopes."

"No, but you will."

"Come on, Jan. She is on the mend. Maybe an hour or two each day would keep Soph sane. She's never been one to sit around."

Mum smiles. "No, she was always busy, our girl. Had to get into everything. You kept me busy as a toddler, that's for sure."

I've heard the story before, but for some reason today it makes me feel all warm and fuzzy inside.

"John was easy…you were work." She says it fondly, but mentioning my brother's name is always awkward in our family and we're all silent for a few moments.

Eventually Mum gives a tired, sad sigh. "I'd understand if this was a child-abduction case, or one of those nasty serial-killer cases you work on. Something time critical. But this is…" She shrugs and waves the envelopes in the air.

I walk down the little hallway and into the main living space. "Wow, this place looks beautiful." In the corner of the living room is a Christmas tree, decorated in purple and silver, with several presents underneath. My apartment windows have been stenciled with white Santas, reindeers and holly, and in the center of my dining-room table are two new red candle holders, with long green candles. "Thanks, Dad. It's perfect." I give him a hug. "It's good to be home."

"Your mum did help a little." He smiles but then shakes his head. "I'm just sad it won't be a white Christmas. Darn

West Coast." Dad grew up in Boston and has always been very pro-East Coast and anti-West Coast. He couldn't understand why I'd transfer from the Behavioral Analysis Unit in Quantico, Virginia, to the West Coast—and L.A. of all places.

"Mum and I will be happier without the snow."

He shrugs. "You haven't had a real Christmas until you've had a white one." Dad's accent has broadened from being back in the States for the week. It doesn't take long.

"I haven't forgotten about these, darling." Mum places the envelopes on the dining-room table. "I really don't think you're up to working. And from the little you've told us about this case, it doesn't sound like it's time critical."

"It's still murder, Mum. And a woman is missing." It's a little lie, a white lie. Mee is still officially missing, even though we know where she is through Agent Young.

She gives a stoic nod. "You're right, darling. I'm sorry."

I bite my lip, feeling guilty about my white lie already.

"We can spare Soph for a couple of hours." Again Dad steps in.

"I guess." Mum fingers the corner of one of the envelopes. "So do you know what's in these?"

"Yup. One's everything we've got on the victim, including information that's been forwarded to us from Japan and Singapore. The other one's a list of Chinese nationals who entered the country four weeks prior to the murder, with photos." It'll be nice to look at the information in hard copy instead of on my tiny BlackBerry screen. Maybe then things will make more sense.

"Looks like a lot of work, Sophie."

"Just reading, Mum."

"Mmm…" She takes my overnight bag into my room.

"Mum, you guys should stay in my room—I can use the sofa bed."

She pops her head out. "No. You're convalescing, Sophie. You need a proper bed."

"Mum, I'm fine. Really. Besides, the sofa bed is comfy."

She pauses.

"I insist. Plus there's more room in there for your suitcases." I point to my bedroom.

"Okay. If you're sure."

"I'm sure."

She nods. "I'll still leave your bag in here. I'll unpack it later."

She comes back into the living room. "I've made soup for lunch. You hungry?"

Just thinking of Mum's home cooking makes me hungry. "Sounds great."

She busies herself in the kitchen, heating up the soup and some Turkish bread, while I open the envelopes. My Dad raises his eyebrows and I mouth "Two and a half hours" at him.

"Playing with fire first thing," he says under his breath.

He's right and I would prefer to avoid my mother's wrath, but curiosity is getting the better of me. I flick through Saito's file, taking a seat at the table, while Mum's getting everything ready. A quick pass tells me that in the five years leading up to his disappearance he was suspected of drug trafficking, money laundering and even a few murders, but no charges were ever brought against him. In addition to crime-scene photos of three homicides Saito is suspected of being involved in—all male victims—there's also a photo of a beautiful Japanese woman with her throat slit. From the file, I soon gather she was his girlfriend—she was killed just before he disappeared and the police suspected him of that murder, too. In fact, his prints were all over the murder weapon. And as for his alias, Jo Kume, all Singapore had on that was a driver's license and a small apartment in his name. As Jo Kume, he stayed under the radar…unless he used other aliases in Singapore, too.

I'm still scanning documents when my mother comes over. "Sophie. We're about to eat."

"I'm sorry, Mum." I gather up the pages, glad that I'd been careful enough not to have any crime-scene photos on the top. I stack everything back into one pile and pop it on the sofa next to the other, unopened yellow envelope.

"Fifteen minutes," my Dad whispers in my ear while Mum brings another bowl of soup over.

"What, you're timing me?"

"You better believe it, sweetheart."

I sit, glaring at Dad.

"What's going on, you two?" Mum puts her bowl of soup on the table and sits down with us.

We both act innocent.

"This looks beautiful, Jan."

"Yes, it does, Mum."

She smiles. "Well, eat up."

I'm scraping the bottom of my soup bowl when my BlackBerry buzzes. "Sorry. I better get it." I fish it out of my handbag. "FBI, Sophie Anderson."

"Anderson, it's Petrov. Can you talk?"

"Sure." I move away from the table, grabbing my notebook and pen from my handbag on the way.

"First off, I've got some good news. I just got a call from the hospital. Ramos is out of intensive care."

"That's *fantastic* news." I only managed to visit Ramos a few times, and even though it was touch and go, I always believed he'd pull through. Or maybe I just couldn't bear to think about the alternative.

"Full recovery?"

"It'll take a while, but yes."

I breathe another sigh of relief.

"You get the Saito information?" Petrov asks.

"Yes, thanks. And Melissa also couriered the printouts of the State Department information, too." I'm still hoping I'll get something from the hard copy, from the photos. Despite numerous attempts to induce a vision or see something, I've had nothing for a week. Maybe now that I'm off the painkillers my head will clear enough to focus on my second sight.

I take a seat on the couch. "Any news your end?"

"No luck on a link between Saito and the other Yakuza death in 2000. De Luca has tapped all his contacts, we all have, and as far as we can make out Saito and Matsu never crossed paths. The only point of intersection is that they both knew Tomi Moto and his father. Matsu worked for Moto's father, and Saito did business with him back in the late eighties and early nineties. Although even those ties haven't been proven irrefutably. It's all based on tips from informants and undercover operations from years ago. What about you? I bet you've looked at our list of Chinese nationals, haven't you?"

"Believe it or not, no." I don't tell Petrov about my deal with Dad. All he needs to know is that I haven't found anything in the list.

"Maybe we should send it to your teacher's cousin in Beijing?"

"There are too many names on it at the moment—I don't want to burn that bridge with such a wide search."

"Fair enough. So we need to eliminate some names."

"Uh-huh."

Silence.

"Sir, what if we cross-reference our hit man's visit this time with the other ViCAP entries? Aliases or not, the guy's killed in the US at least eight times, nine if you count Corey Casey. Plus there are the other ViCAP matches I found for heart concussion, ruptured spleen and ventricular fibrillation. He can't have thirteen different aliases. And by cross-referencing Chinese nationals' details with those from around the dates of the murders, we might get a match."

"Sounds good, Anderson."

"Sorry, I should have thought about it days ago." I shake my head.

"Anderson, you're still recovering. And you're not the only one working on the case…*we* should have thought of it, too." He sighs. "Although our resource issues certainly haven't helped."

Poor Petrov. He's down two people *and* he's trying to find a mole. Plus I can't imagine it would have been easy for the rest of the team, finding out about Ramos and me and still trying to keep their heads in the game.

"I'll call Rodriguez now. Anything else?"

"Saito's hotel and Mee's apartment. All the prints in

Saito's hotel room have been eliminated, verified as either his or hotel employees'. There were two extra sets of prints, but we managed to locate the last two visitors in that room and both agreed to give us samples. They were a match."

"Trace?"

"Nothing useful. It doesn't look like Saito had any visitors in his room."

"And Mee's house?"

"All the prints on Mee's front door and her chest of drawers belonged to Mee or her boyfriend and there was nothing strange from trace."

"What about her computer?"

"Just the usual stuff—her work for school, a few personal letters and e-mails. The only big news is that the lab's come back with a paternal DNA match between our victim and samples we collected from Mee's phone. Mee's definitely Saito's daughter."

"Which isn't news to you…or me."

"No. But now it's official, on the books."

I nod—so in other words Hana and Williams know, too, as well as the wider Gang Impact Team. "About that, sir…"

"Yes?"

"I might be able to help with your search." I keep my language vague, reluctant to say straight-out "the search for the mole," especially in front of my parents.

"You sound confident."

I'm not sure whether I've offended Petrov—perhaps by suggesting that I can find the mole when no one else has been able to—or if he's relieved that fresh eyes might actually identify the culprit.

"*Confidence* is an overstatement. But I'm hoping my specific skills as a profiler and my psychology training may give us some new insights. And fresh eyes never hurt, do they?"

"I'm all for fresh eyes," Petrov responds. "Especially if you can point the finger at someone. There are a couple you might want to start with." He pauses. "Or does that defeat the purpose of fresh eyes?"

"Good question." On the one hand, there's no point in me

duplicating work that's already been done. Poring over twenty-four detailed personnel files will take time, and if Petrov, Brady and De Luca already have suspects or have some people they've eliminated... Not to mention my work quota of two and a half hours per day.

We're both silent, thinking.

In the end, I speak first. "What sort of info rang bells for you?"

"People who've worked undercover, perhaps gone bad during their time. Agents and officers who have some affiliations or informants within our target gangs. Mind you, most of the task force members have built up contacts, that's part of their job."

"Is that all in their files? Their undercover work, and so on?"

"Uh-huh."

"Okay, let's do the completely objective thing."

"Your call." Petrov shuffles papers in the background. "But you're right. It will be interesting to look at it from the psych angle. See if anyone sets off alarms from a behavioral perspective. I'll get the docs couriered over to you. Call me to confirm receipt."

Petrov is being careful.

"Will do. Can you also send me copies of the info on the Yakuza here in L.A.? I'd like to have a closer look at that."

"This is sounding like a lot of work, Anderson. You sure you're up to it?"

"Yes."

Silence, then Petrov decides, "Let's see how you go with the other one first. Then maybe next week we can talk about sending over more documents."

"But, sir—"

"Anderson, don't push your luck. I'll send the files over first thing Monday."

Monday? I keep my mouth shut and change the subject. "What about those new ViCAP matches I e-mailed through. Anything?"

"We've added them to the paperwork and we all agree

that they could be related to our killer. Williams followed up the D.C. politician, and it certainly looks suspicious. He was about to block a large development for environmental reasons and some of the building contractors have underworld links. The D.C. police were interested in our theory, but it's going to be hard, if not impossible, to prove."

"Yeah, I agree. But it's important to note that he pissed off the wrong people, the kind of people who might have ties to a hit man."

"Yes. Williams also looked into the Seattle murder and it's a similar story. It looks like it might be related, but we can't be sure." He takes a breath. "De Luca took the New Orleans vic, which turned out to be an interesting one. The police actually suspected the victim had been blackmailing someone, but could never find anything on it besides a few cash deposits that they couldn't trace."

"So maybe the person being blackmailed hired our hit man to get rid of the problem."

"It's a possibility."

"And the New York businessman?" I ask.

"I've contacted some old friends from the New York field office. They paid the widow a visit and got pushy with her. Told her they know she hired a hit man who used kung fu. According to them she did react, but again, how can we prove it? The original investigating officers already took a close look at her, tried to find evidence of a large withdrawal from her bank account before her husband's death, but they couldn't find anything. In fact, they hypothesized that maybe she paid the killer in jewelry. Apparently the woman is bling city."

I nod, knowing that in her case the best way to pay a contract killer would have been with a pricey diamond necklace or bracelet.

"They looked for evidence of someone selling a big-ticket jewelry item around the time, but didn't have any luck in that department."

"Sounds like the wife knew what she was doing."

"Uh-huh."

"So you're happy for me to add those four deaths into the US State Department search?"

"Yup… But don't work too hard, Anderson. Enjoy some time with your folks."

"Yes, sir."

"Seriously, Anderson. You've got just over a week until you're back in the office and I don't expect anything from you between now and then. If I had my way, you wouldn't be working on anything. But I've given up arguing with you…to a point."

"Yes, sir. But you will call me if you have any developments? New leads?"

He snorts. "Goodbye, Anderson."

When I look up, Dad's reading the paper and Mum's stacking the dishwasher.

"I've got one more phone call to make, and then I do need to spend an hour or so going over some of this." I hold up Saito's file.

Dad peeks over his newspaper. "Okay, darling."

When I look at Mum, she shakes her head. I don't take the bait. Instead, I dial Rodriguez, but the call goes straight to voice mail. Saturday…the weekend. I guess it'll have to wait until Monday.

"Let's go for a walk, darling," Dad suggests to Mum. I'm not sure whether he really wants a walk, or if he's clearing Mum out to guarantee I'm not interrupted for the time I've got left. Either way, it works for me.

"A walk sounds nice. And I also want to stop off and pick up a few things for dinner."

I resist the urge to look over Saito's file while they're getting ready. This way Mum will leave the apartment with the image of me lying on the sofa, rather than hard at work. And I know which imagery's better for both of us. It only takes them fifteen minutes to get organized and out the door. Then it's on to Saito.

Jun Saito was born in Tokyo, Japan in 1964. He was the youngest boy in a family of three boys and one girl. All three boys followed in their father's footsteps, joining the Yakuza as foot soldiers and working their way up. The girl married a dentist in 1990 and seems to have little or no association with her father or the Yakuza. The eldest two boys were both killed—one by a police officer in a 1981 confrontation, and one two years later. His murder remains unsolved.

Saito's first run-in with the law was in 1978, when he was arrested for marijuana possession. After that he was suspected of trafficking cocaine, heroin and running a brothel for westerners in Tokyo's Rapongi district. He was arrested four times but was eventually released, with the charges dropped each time. In 1990, at the age of twenty-six, he was linked to his first murder, that of fellow Yakuza Jiro Fuji. He was placed at the scene of the crime, but no other evidence was found against him and the Tokyo police were unable to build a case. Two years later, a leading witness in a case against one of the Yakuza bosses was killed. Again, Jun Saito was tied to the scene, this time through an informant's tip to police—but no hard evidence linked him to the death. In 1993 Tokyo's second-in-command, Hiroki Kawa, was killed and two days later Saito's girlfriend was found with her throat cut, and Saito disappears, until he's found dead here.

Looking at the crime-scene photos, I notice that all three male victims were shot, whereas Saito's girlfriend died from a knife wound. The crime scenes also look quite different, telling me that the girlfriend's death was a crime of passion, not planned. Her death was much more personal, whereas the first three kills were premeditated murder, killing for business, no doubt under orders from his father or Saito's direct boss at the time. The autopsy report also found the girlfriend was pregnant. Saito was a man brought up in a world of violence, and acted this out in his domestic life. Maybe the girlfriend just got on his nerves that day, or maybe he wasn't thrilled by the news of his impending fatherhood. Still, he did honor his commitment to Mee Kim's mother, someone we know he only met fleetingly while they were both on holidays in Korea. And he did come to L.A. to protect Mee. So there was some decency in him.

Saito would have had a lot of enemies. It's also possible his girlfriend was killed by one of them.

With my parents out and probably gone for a while, I decide to work on inducing a premonition. While I've been rationalizing my lack of waking visions or dreams as the effect of the pain meds, it's also crossed my mind that maybe my brush with death has somehow put that part of my psyche out of commission. And while a few months ago I would have loved that, I've been surprised to find myself sad and concerned by my lack of insight. I've even been more frustrated by its absence than I usually am by its presence.

I turn my phone to silent, sit on the couch and visualize Saito. I go back to the couple of visions I've had of him to date, hoping focusing on his recent movements may help me. I think about him in his car, getting the phone call. I think about his last moments before death. But instead of tuning in to Saito, I fall asleep, only to wake as my parents enter the apartment. A big fat zero, yet again.

"How are you feeling, honey?"

"Fine, Mum."

"Are you sure? You look tired."

I'd like to deny it, but it seems futile—my brain is toast, at least for today. "A little," I admit.

"Go have a lie-down, honey. Use your bedroom so we won't disturb you."

I nod, giving in to Mum's good sense. Despite my exhaustion, I can't help myself, I go through what I know of Saito in my head before falling asleep.

I look over my shoulder, scared. Someone's following me. It's time to get out. Suki and I can leave. Just disappear. Yes…we must leave. Now.

I jump in a taxi, but it seems to take forever to navigate through the busy Tokyo streets. Now that the decision's made, I'm anxious. Ready. I've got enough money, my emergency stash will see us through for at least two years. Until the baby's born and beyond.

I push the apartment door open. "Suki!" I try to keep my voice calm, but I know my tone's harsher than usual. "Suki, where are you?"

Blood...blood everywhere.

I wake to a gentle knocking on my open bedroom door. "Yes?" My voice is weak, disorientated.

"Sorry to wake you, darling, but dinner's up." Dad stands in my doorway, a silhouette against the darkened door frame. A little light streams into the room from behind him, and a heavenly scent wafts from the kitchen.

"Dinner? What time is it?"

"Six."

"Wow, I slept for over three hours."

"Guess you needed it."

"Guess so." I take another whiff. "What smells so good?"

"Your mum's made her gnocchi."

"That's enough to get me out of bed." I swing my legs onto the ground, but sit for a bit before standing up after I get a sharp, shooting pain in my left shoulder.

"Painful?"

"A little. No more painkillers now."

"I'm sure a Tylenol or two is fine."

"Yeah, it is. But I'm sick of the masks—I want to know how painful this thing really is." I point at my shoulder. Masks...I just had a dream. "I'll be out in a second, Dad."

Dad takes the hint. "Okay, honey. Take your time."

I scrummage through my bedside table until I find my dream diary. I put in today's date and write down everything I can remember about the dream: in Tokyo; being followed; goes to get girlfriend; blood—girlfriend dead. So was she already dead when he got there, or did my vision just skip the actual act of murder? No, he was going to run with his girlfriend. With Suki.

Jun Saito did not kill his girlfriend, someone else did.

Twenty-Four

First thing Monday morning I dial Rodriguez. It's possible she's on leave for Christmas, but her voice mail on Saturday was her standard message. With that, I'm just happy when I get Rodriguez live and in person.

"Hi, Lara, it's Agent Sophie Anderson from the FBI."

"Hi. How's the injury coming along?"

"Good, thanks. I'm healing well."

"That's great news. What can I do you for?"

"I've been going through the list of Chinese nationals who entered the country between November 6 and December 6, but we think the same man may have been responsible for previous killings. I'd like to give you quite a few dates to cross-reference and get any names of people who've entered the country during more than one of the date ranges."

"Sure. I'll get one of our computer guys on it. Sounds like a more complicated search."

"Yup, it is. I'll e-mail you through the details?"

"I'll look out for it."

"How long do you think it will take? Given it's Christmas Eve?"

"Good question. We're operating on a skeleton staff most of this week. I'm off tomorrow and Wednesday, but I'll have to check with our computer analysts. Maybe they're around."

"Appreciate it. Thanks."

To get the ball rolling, I write the e-mail as soon as I've hung up. I give Rodriguez a one-month date range prior to each of the ViCAP matches. We should get an extremely tight list back from this search—maybe even only a few names. The list will definitely be small enough to send through to Lee's cousin in Beijing. We're getting closer, and then hopefully we can bring Mee Kim in and get her out of this mess.

I've got lots of things on my to-do list and not much time. I'm on the clock, my dad's clock. Soon the personnel files will arrive from Petrov, but in the meantime I'm also keen to see Lee and find out how he went with his list. While I think we're on the right track by looking for someone who lives in China, rather than a Chinese American or someone else skilled in kung fu, I don't want to leave such a large investigative route unchecked. If I rely too much on Rodriguez and her list, it could blow up in my face. Better to cover as many bases as possible.

I dial Lee's cell.

He sounds relieved to hear from me. "Sophie. I'm so glad you're okay. You are okay, aren't you?"

"Yes. Back at home now."

"When I saw the news report… I rang the hospital straight away and a nurse assured me 'off-the-record' that you'd be okay."

"You know what the press is like—they always sensationalize stuff."

"Mmm…well, I'm glad you're okay." Lee seems a little uncomfortable, like it's awkward for him to tell me he's happy I'm alive. But some people aren't good with death…or near death.

"I'm pretty happy about it, too," I say, lightening the mood.

He seems relieved by the change in tone. "So, what can I do for you? You're not ready for classes yet, are you?"

"No, not yet." I even manage a small laugh. "I'm calling about those lists. The people in America you think may be capable of the Killing Hands and *dim mak* strikes. Any progress?"

"Yes, of course. I worked on the lists, even after I saw the news report, but I didn't want to bother you with them…interrupt your recuperation."

"I understand. So, can I pop in to see you?"

"Sure. Let's meet at the studio. An hour?" he suggests.

"Sounds good to me."

An hour later I'm sitting in Lee's office.

"You're not looking too bad, Sophie." Lee smiles.

"Gee, thanks." I know I'm still pale, and my step definitely doesn't have its usual spring to it. But I was shot.

Lee rustles through his desk and plucks out several handwritten pages. Guess he's not into computers. Still, Lee's Kung Fu School has its own Web site, so he can't be a total Luddite.

"Okay, so at the top of the list are the names I know offhand, or that I tracked down through my contacts. I've written as much information about each person as I knew or could find out. The first eight names are people I've trained with over the years who have reached at least fifth dan and who I think are capable of using acupoint applications to cause immediate or delayed death. The next twenty names are students of mine who expressed a keen interest in *dim mak*. I didn't show them the techniques, but they were sufficiently interested to read up on the pressure points and try to teach themselves, or they could have attended seminars or other schools. After that, I rang around all my contacts, including those in the film industry, and got as many names as I could. To be honest, it's still a bit of a work in progress and I've been adding names to the list most days. Like yesterday I got a phone call from a sifu in Miami, who'd heard through one of my old training partners that I was looking for names."

"Sounds like the network's been working overtime."

"It's even better than I'd imagined." He leans back in his chair. "I made sure not to mention specific details, but I did tell them that someone may have been using *dim mak* and the Ten Killing Hands for criminal purposes. We all subscribe to kung fu for defense, fitness and spiritual well-being. The thought that someone is attacking innocent people using these skills…"

"Well, they're not exactly innocent."

He shrugs. "Maybe. But you of all people would say it's up to the law to judge that, yes?"

"True." Although part of me can understand the underlying emotion of a vigilante. For years I was angry at the police for not apprehending John's killer. But as a law-enforcement professional, I now know that most of the time it's better handled by us, by the law. Besides, our perp's a hit man, not a vigilante. He's killing for money, not to right a wrong or balance the scales of justice.

"We don't want kung fu associated only with action movies and criminals. Traditionally, a sifu would only teach a select few students *dim mak,* for fear of this very thing."

"I understand."

"Responsible practice. That's what most of us stand for, what most of us believe in."

I nod and after a few moments of silence I tap the list. "I can't thank you enough for this."

"Yes you can. Catch him."

As soon as I walk in the door Dad says, "You done for the day?"

"Almost."

I'd like to convert Lee's handwritten list into an Excel document, but even though I touch-type it'll probably take me at least an hour to enter it all up. Instead, I'll set up the bare bones now and put in the rest tomorrow…or maybe the next day. Tomorrow is Christmas Day, after all.

"Give me fifteen minutes."

"Then we can relax and enjoy Christmas Eve as a family," Mum says firmly.

There's no point fighting a steam train...sometimes you've just got to go with it. "Why don't we go out for dinner?"

"Now that sounds like a good idea." Dad brings me in for a hug. "You know anywhere good nearby?"

"Sure. I just hope we can get a reservation." Several phone calls later, I manage to book us for an early dinner at a French restaurant about a twenty-minute walk from my apartment. The walk may stretch me, but we can always catch a taxi back.

"What's Darren doing for Christmas, darling?" Mum asks.

"I don't know."

"I hope he won't be alone. You should have invited him up here."

"Mum, his parents live in Phoenix. I'm sure he's flown out to see them."

"Well, make sure you call him tomorrow to wish him a happy Christmas."

"I will, Mum."

She gives a contented sigh. "Such a lovely, lovely young man, Sophie."

"Yes, Mum."

"Well, he is." She crosses her arms.

"I agree, Mum. And I agreed with you the first hundred times you told me how much you liked him."

She puffs air forcefully out of her lips. "A hundred times...please." She turns to Dad. "Bob, I haven't been that bad, have I?" While it's meant to be a question, there's not even the slightest hint of doubt in Mum's voice.

Dad holds both hands up in the air. "I'm not touching this one."

Mum shakes her head. "Your father and I both like him. We enjoyed spending that day and a half with him when we first got here."

I resist the urge to give her another *Yes, Mum.*

"Bob?"

Dad hesitates before saying, "He does seem like a real nice guy."

I give Dad a look, but he just shrugs.

I give in…there's no point pressing the point with Mum any more. Besides, Darren is a nice guy. I change the subject. "So fifteen minutes, then I'm all yours."

They both nod.

Before I set up my Excel template, I scan the list. There are seventy-two names in total, including Agent Dan Young, under his alias of Marcus Miki, and Mee Kim—tae kwon do may be her favorite, but Mee is obviously very skilled in kung fu, too. Even though she's in the Yakuza safe house, I'm glad she has the skills to protect herself, if necessary. Of course, a roundhouse kick can't stop a bullet, but it can give you time to run, give you a head start.

My initial columns include *Name, Sex, Age, E-mail address, Phone number, State, Kung fu level, Teacher, School* and *Point of contact,* even though I don't have these details for every person. To this skeleton I add in my own columns— *Criminal record* and *Prints on file.* I'm about to close my laptop when the apartment buzzer rings.

"I'll get it," I say.

Looking at the video screen, I'm surprised to see Agent Hana Kim standing at the front gates, fidgeting. "Hi. Come up." I buzz her in.

A few minutes later she's navigated her way through the corridors and to my front door.

"Hi, Hana. What brings you here?"

She gives me a tight smile, and her eyes flick over to my parents.

"You remember my folks from the hospital. Bob and Jan Anderson." Hana paid me a hospital visit on Thursday.

"Yes, of course." She comes in and gives them a nod. "Is there somewhere we can talk, Sophie? In private?"

"Sure."

"We'll go for a walk," Dad volunteers. "It's a nice day out anyway."

"I'm sorry, I don't mean to disturb you." Hana shifts from foot to foot.

Dad puts his hand on her shoulder. "It's fine. Just take it easy on my girl, hey?" He smiles.

"I'm so sorry… How are you feeling, Sophie?" Hana's obviously embarrassed that she hasn't asked the question sooner.

"Better, thanks."

She smiles. "Good."

My parents leave and Hana's silent for nearly a full minute. Finally, she says, "Sophie, I don't quite know how to approach this…."

"Go on."

"This is just between you and me, right?"

My curiosity is aroused. Hana is being downright cagey. "I guess so, yes. Within reason, though, Hana." If she's about to confess she's the mole, I'm hardly going to keep that to myself. "My duty's to the FBI. The law."

"What? Oh, yes, of course. It's nothing like that."

I feel my shoulders relax a little. "Shoot." I take a seat on the sofa and she follows suit.

"I don't like the way Agent Petrov is running the search for Mee. He doesn't seem to be doing anything. I feel like we've abandoned her. At least when you and Ramos were working the case, you were out there actively looking for her. We almost had her."

"The APB still stands, Hana," I try to reassure her, despite knowing exactly why Petrov isn't tying himself in knots looking for Mee. We have knowledge that Hana doesn't.

"But the APB's getting us nowhere!" She shakes her head. "It's been over a week since we visited her English students. And what's Petrov done since then?"

"I don't know, Hana. Maybe he's been calling the students, touching base with them."

She snorts. "No, I checked myself. They haven't heard from anyone except me since we contacted them the day you and Ramos were shot. Nine days and what have we done…nothing." Hana stands up and starts pacing. "Who knows what's happening to her. Where she is…if she's even still alive."

I take a deep breath, stalling. What can I say that will calm Hana down? Probably nothing. "Have you spoken to Petrov? Voiced your concerns?"

"No." Another long silence. "To be honest, Sophie, I'm not crazy about Agent Petrov. He seems so cold. Distant. I don't think he cares about Mee or this case."

"It's just his manner."

"Well, I don't care for it." She tucks her hair behind her ears, then shakes her head and flops onto the sofa.

I bite my lip. "What about Agent De Luca? You're close to him, right?"

"I thought so, but Joe's being strange. Every time I try to broach the subject with him, he closes me down. It's not like him at all. He used to be interested in my opinion, but these days…"

I wince. What can I say to her? I've only got one option—lie. "Leave it with me, Hana. I'll talk to Petrov, maybe even Brady, and make sure Mee's not forgotten in this."

She's silent for a moment, and then says, "Thanks, Sophie. I knew you'd understand."

"Sure."

"And I'm sorry to bother you at home…when you're still recovering."

"I'm fine, honestly. If it wasn't for the stupid doctors, I'd be at work now. Actually, I think it's probably my parents holding me back, not the doctors."

Hana laughs. "Your mum was funny at the hospital."

"Funny? That's one way to put it."

When Hana visited me, Mum gave us five minutes alone then suddenly reappeared in the room and as soon as the conversation turned to the case, Mum told Hana it was time for me to rest.

"You know she's right, Sophie. You do need to rest."

"If I had a dime for every time she's said, 'Mother knows best' in the last eight days I'd be a rich woman."

Hana laughs again. "Well, I hope you don't get in trouble over my visit today."

"I'll be fine."

She stands up. "Thanks, Sophie. I really appreciate what you're doing for Mee."

"It's nothing."

"Well, it's a darn sight better than Petrov."

I walk Hana to the door. "What are your Christmas plans?"

"My folks are staying with Jae and me for a couple of days. So it's Christmas in our tiny apartment."

"You doing turkey and the works?"

"Uh-huh. Plus some traditional Korean food, too."

"I bet your parents are proud of you."

She smiles. "Yeah. And looks like Jae will be following in my footsteps soon, too."

"Really?"

"Yeah, she's putting in her application for the DEA next year. As soon as she finishes college." She smiles again. "See you next week, huh?"

"Yup. Monday." I'll miss my parents when they're gone, but I am looking forward to getting back to work, full-time.

"Merry Christmas," Hana says.

"Merry Christmas."

I lean on the door once it's closed. This could get complicated. Despite my sworn solidarity to Hana, I call Petrov straightaway.

"Listen," I tell him, "I just got a visit from Agent Kim. She's concerned that we're not doing enough to find Mee."

"We know where Mee is."

"Exactly. *We* do, but she doesn't. From her point of view it looks like you've dropped the ball."

"That what she said?"

"Not in so many words."

"Mmm…I've tried to avoid this…at each update I usually include something fictitious on what we're doing to find Mee Kim. Plus I reassure Williams and Kim that if we can't find Mee, chances are no one else can, either."

"Well, I think you need to step it up." The apartment security-door phone buzzes. "Hold on, someone's at the door." A glance in the security video shows a FedEx courier.

I press the intercom and release the outer door. "Come on up."

"FedEx," I say into my BlackBerry.

"Should be the personnel files."

"Yup. I'm not expecting anything else."

"So, Hana." Petrov brings us back to our immediate problem.

"Problem is, she's also called up some of Mee's students to double-check on our efforts. She speaks Korean, and she has ties with the community. Maybe we're making her look bad." I open my front door and wait. "They're relying on her to find Mee."

"I see what you mean. But I don't want to put resources into a fictitious search. We're short enough as is."

"I hear you, Petrov." The FedEx guy comes around the corner, parcel in hand. "Hold on."

"Sophie Anderson?"

"Yup."

He gives me the envelope and holds out a digital signature pad. "Have a nice day."

I sign and give him a smile. "Thanks, you, too." I close the door and open the FedEx envelope. "I'm looking at the personnel files now," I flick open the large folder. On top is a photo of Special Agent Jeremy Acorn from the DEA. I flick through the pages on him, and quickly see that Petrov's included a photo, summary information, plus detailed information on Acorn, including employment history, finance checks, arrests, associates—the works.

"Careful with the folder, huh? It'd be a pain in the ass to have to compile that info again."

"Sure thing." I place the folder on the dining table. I know it'd be more than a pain in the ass—I don't need to be told to guard the folder with my life. Not only does it contain very personal information about each of the task force members, information I shouldn't have access to, but if someone else discovered the detailed level of the records, they'd deduce we were looking for a mole. And if the mole found the records, they'd know we were on to them.

"Anyway, you need to do something about Hana. You either trust her and tell her what's going on, or you have to pretend you're trying a little harder to find Mee."

"Okay. Leave it with me. I'll try to get creative."

Sounds like Hana won't be entering the inner circle. Not today at least.

Twenty-Five

As I'd suspected, Christmas Day was a write-off in terms of work. However, the full day off seems to have done me good because I'm feeling better. It might be time to renegotiate my two and a half hours a day with Dad. Plus, I've only got five days left before I officially start back at the office, and lots to do. I've got to work on Lee's list, chase Rodriguez for the list of Chinese nationals, take a good look through the Gang Impact Team's personnel files and draft the offender profile over the weekend, so I can brief everyone first thing Monday morning. And that's not even taking into consideration the fact that I now know Jun Saito didn't kill his girlfriend fifteen years ago. That he was on the run from someone else—not from the police and a homicide charge. But how am I going to present that possibility to the team?

"I'm feeling heaps better today," I say to Mum and Dad over breakfast.

"That's great news, honey." Mum puts her hand on top of mine. "Your color's finally returning."

I nod slowly, and then start playing with my fruit salad. "I was thinking of popping into work. Or maybe just spending a little more time on the case over the next few days."

"You'll be back Monday. That's soon enough. And it is doctor's orders."

"But, Mum, I've got so much to do."

"You've been working from home, Sophie. Isn't that enough?" She leans back in her seat and gives me a disapproving look.

"A couple of hours each day. That's nothing. And I need to draft the profile. For that, I need a solid block of time."

"We leave on Friday…can't it wait until then?"

Good question. I guess the profile could wait until the weekend—I'd have it ready for my first day back. But I still need to work on Lee's list, the info from the US State Department when it comes through and the mole. I want to get things moving faster, and increase our chances of getting Mee out from under the Yakuza's guard. They may be protecting her, and I know Agent Dan Young is keeping an eye on her, but they're still a violent organized-crime syndicate—Mee's a rabbit in a lion's den.

"We need to find the missing woman."

She sighs but her eyes soften slightly. "I don't know, honey…"

I give her my best smile, accompanied by a pleading look.

Another sigh. "I guess you *are* looking a little better."

"I feel good, Mum. Honest. Why don't you and Dad get some shopping in? You've only got a couple of days left and I know you'd love to buy some new clothes and shoes."

Dad stands up. "Don't encourage her, Soph."

Mum gives him a whack on the arm. "You stay here. You can work on Sophie's kitchen." Dad's not allowed anywhere near Mum's kitchen.

"It's a rental, guys. You can't 'work on it,'" I point out.

"I just want to put a new tea-towel rack in and fix that cupboard door. And the bathroom tap," Dad says.

"Trust me, honey, it'll keep him out from under your feet." I laugh. "Okay."

Half an hour later, Mum's gone and Dad and I are both tapping away—me on my keyboard and Dad on the kitchen cupboard's hinges. Once I've transposed everything from Lee's handwritten notes into my Excel spreadsheet, I log in to the FBI's system, jumping through the Bureau's security hoops. When I'm in, I start looking up each name to fill out my extra two columns: *Criminal record* and *Fingerprints on file.*

By 3:00 p.m. I'm just under a third of the way through the list, and I do have a few interesting names. Of the twenty-two names I've run to date, only four people have a criminal record. Two were for auto theft, one for small-time credit-card fraud and one assault charge. We have prints for these four men on file, plus prints on another ten in total—some are teachers and the others are government employees, including one ex-marine, one guy who's currently a captain in the army, two police officers and two FBI agents. I note these down with a *Yes* in the *Fingerprints on file* column. It's time to touch base with Petrov—and maybe the rest of the team.

"Hey, Petrov. It's Anderson. How about a quick update meeting?"

"Not much going on this end."

"I've got the names back from Lee. Thought maybe I should keep everyone in the loop."

"Remember, Anderson. You're not back until Monday."

"I know. It's just a list."

He sighs. "Okay. I've given everyone the day off today, but I'll organize a teleconference."

"Sounds good."

Twenty minutes later, we've all dialed in, ready to start. When the last beep announces De Luca has joined us, Petrov kicks it off,

"So, Anderson's got a quick update for us."

I thank Petrov and fill the team in on my progress with the list from Lee.

"Even though we believe the hit man is from overseas, we don't want to develop tunnel vision on this thing." Petrov's in sync with my thoughts. I always consider that we're the good guys, on the side of justice. But I know that sometimes law enforcement gets it wrong, imprisons the wrong person. There are lots of reasons this can happen, but tunnel vision from cops or other law-enforcement personnel working the case is one of the big ones. You end up convincing yourself that the evidence fits your suspect, even when it doesn't. Or the case goes unsolved because you couldn't open yourself up to other possibilities.

"It's a pity we don't have more on the guys that abducted you," Williams says. "They may have been able to lead us to the employer or the hit man."

"Dead men don't talk." Unfortunately.

"Who wants to help Anderson with the list?"

Hana volunteers.

"Okay, you two stay on line once we're done and work it out."

"Anything else? Any luck chasing down a connection between Li Chow and the killer, Williams?"

"Not so far. Although Li Chow did grow up in China—he immigrated here at age fourteen—so it's possible he met or knew our hit man in his childhood."

"Anderson, do you think that cop in Beijing could help us on this one?" Petrov asks.

"Sure," I say. "I'll see what he's got on Chow."

Petrov clears his throat. "It's probably easier to work backward…once we have a suspect we can see if they crossed paths here or in China. But let's see what Beijing can turn up." He pauses. "The only other item then is Mee. I'm putting two agents with missing-persons expertise on her search. My gut still tells me she's safe—if we can't find her no one else can—but it's also time to step up our search for her." Another pause, then Petrov asks, "Anything else?"

We all respond in the negative.

"Okay, let's enjoy the rest of the day off. Anderson, we'll see you Monday and I'll see the rest of you guys tomorrow."

"I'll stay on the line to find out about your list, Sophie."

"Sure, Hana."

We wait a couple of minutes until there's silence.

"You there?" Hana asks.

"Yup."

"Thanks, Sophie. For Mee."

"No worries."

"So, the list."

If Hana's the mole and knows who the killer is, I shouldn't let her anywhere near this list. And if I do let her follow up the names, I can't be sure the information she passes on to me will be correct. But this is the way we have to play it, at least for the moment.

"How do you want to work it?" she asks.

"Split it down the middle, I'll take the first half and you can take the second."

"Awesome."

"Don't get too excited. It's pretty boring."

"I don't mind. I'd rather be looking for Mee, but it makes sense that Petrov's assigned people with missing-persons expertise."

"Yeah." I talk Hana through my spreadsheet and the columns I've set up. "So all you need to do is look up each person, write up any criminal record they've got and put a *Yes* or *No* in the fingerprint column."

"Sounds easy."

"Yeah, just time-consuming." I flick the ring on my finger. "I'll split the spreadsheet in two and forward half on to you."

"Great. I'll get started on it today."

"Thought you guys had the day off."

"I don't mind."

"No, relax. It can wait until tomorrow. Besides, your folks are still there, right?"

"Yeah. They fly out early tomorrow morning. What about you? Are you going to follow your own advice?" Hana teases.

"I am, actually. You think my mother would let me spend any more time on this today?"

She laughs. "True."

Although I'd normally never call it a day when there's so much to do, today I find myself tired and my concentration waning. I guess this is the closest I've come to a full day's work in nearly two weeks. I'd planned to spend at least a couple of hours flicking through the personnel files, but the mole will have to wait until tomorrow.

Twenty-Six

I wake up to movement in the kitchen. Mum.

I stretch. "Good morning."

"I'm sorry, darling. I was trying to be quiet."

"That's okay." I look at my watch. "Whoa, it's eight-thirty." I sit up. "Can't believe I slept so late."

"Maybe yesterday tired you out?" She says it tentatively, trying a different approach.

Man, I hate it when she's right. "Maybe a little," I admit.

She smiles, humble but triumphant.

"But I still need to get some work done today, Mum. And I was hoping to visit Detective Ramos, too."

"How is he?"

"Getting better. I spoke to his wife yesterday, and it looks like they'll release him some time next week."

"That is good news." She brings me over a glass of orange juice. "I'm sure he won't mind if you visit him on the weekend if you're not up to it today. You need to take it easy, darling. You're expecting too much from your body."

"I'm fine, Mum. Really." I down the orange juice and stand up, giving her a hug. "I can't believe you and Dad are leaving tomorrow."

"I know." She plays with my hair. "I've really enjoyed this visit…even with everything that's happened."

I smile. "Me, too."

"I know I've nagged you a lot…about work."

"It's okay, Mum. It's probably just as well I've had someone to keep me in line."

"I'm glad you realize that, Sophie."

"I do." Despite my resistance and complaining, I know that if Mum and Dad hadn't been here I would have done more harm than good.

She brings me in for a hug. "I wish we could see you more, honey."

"What are you doing in July?" I ask.

She shrugs. "Don't know. Our usual Christmas-in-July party for your father, I guess."

"Well, after that, let's meet for a holiday in Hawaii."

She gives me another hug. "That'd be wonderful, darling."

"I'll wait a couple of weeks and then submit a request for leave."

"Oh, Soph. That sounds so good. A real family holiday." She stands up and races into my bedroom. "Bob, we're going to meet Soph in Hawaii in July."

Mum and Dad come out of the bedroom together, hand in hand.

Dad gives me a grin. "That's great news, honey." He's dressed and his hair's wet—I didn't even hear the shower this morning. I must have been in a deep sleep.

I throw a fleece on over my pajamas. "Have you guys had breakfast?"

"No, not yet."

"You wanna do brunch? Down the road?"

"Sounds good."

They're both smiling a little too much, so I decide to set them straight. "I still need to do some work today, right?"

Dad sighs. "We know."

"Give me fifteen minutes."

I jump in the shower and lean back into the water, finally able to enjoy the sensation of warm water on my left shoulder blade without pain. I am healing.

My estimate is good, and I'm showered, dressed and ready within fifteen minutes. I lead the way to a small, Italian-style café a few blocks from my apartment. It's busy for a Thursday, but we manage to get a table.

When the waiter comes to take our orders, I go for French toast and a soy latte. Mum and Dad both order bacon and eggs.

Dad raises his eyebrows. "I was sure you'd go for the fruit, yogurt and muesli."

"I normally do here, but I'm starving and the French toast is delicious." I grin. "It does come with strawberries." I've only had it a couple of times, usually going for the healthier alternative, but today I feel like treating myself.

I'm devouring my meal, eating like a woman who hasn't seen food in days, when my phone rings.

My parents both look at me, a touch-it-and-you-die look.

I hold my hands up. "I've got to at least see who it is." I grab my BlackBerry out of my bag and look at the screen. Petrov. Damn. "It's the SAC for this investigation."

"Sack?" Mum says.

"Special agent in charge," Dad whispers as I answer the phone.

"Hey, Petrov."

"Anderson. You free?"

"In about fifteen minutes."

"Good. Meet us at Joe's Diner, 10901 Lindbrook Drive, in half an hour." The phone goes dead.

Well, that was bizarre. It must be something to do with the mole.

Half an hour later I run into Petrov, just as he's arriving at the diner.

"Cloak-and-dagger?" I ask.

"Something like that." He opens the door for me and I see De Luca already sitting in the end booth. "This is our usual meeting place," Petrov explains.

"Welcome to our club," De Luca says as I take a seat.

The walk, albeit short, has left me a little breathless, a

fact that I hope I'm hiding. I'm one of the few people De Luca and Petrov can trust now, and I don't want to let them down.

"How's Agent Young doing?"

"Still alive. That is what you meant?" De Luca's words are harsher than his tone.

"Yes."

The waitress comes over and we all order coffee. When Petrov orders two, I ask him if we're expecting someone else.

"Sure are. Our boss."

On cue, I look up to see Brady opening the door. He joins us at the end table, not even glancing up until he's seated. This is obviously a regular routine for these guys.

"Gentlemen." Brady gives them a nod, and then looks at me. "Sorry to get you in when you're on leave, Anderson."

Petrov clears his throat.

Brady notices the reaction, but keeps talking. "How are you feeling?"

"Good. Much better, thanks, sir."

He nods. "So, what's the big news?"

"We've finally got confirmation from inside," De Luca says. "Young has been able to verify that the Yakuza does have someone in the L.A. Gang Impact Team, but he hasn't been able to get a name. Moto finally made a reference to an inside source, but only referred to the person as 'our insider.' Didn't even indicate whether we're talking a he or a she."

Four cups are placed in the middle of the table, and the waitress pours steaming coffee into each. "Cream and sugar on the table, folks."

Once she has gone I say, "I'm still not convinced about Hana. To say she left her BlackBerry in her car the night Ramos and I were shot…an agent is never without their phone."

"I know what you're saying, Anderson." De Luca takes a sip of his coffee. "But I'm afraid it's not the first time someone's forgotten something at an inopportune moment. It could be a genuine excuse."

I sigh. "I don't know." Even though before I got shot I was getting along well with Hana—I liked her and still do—I find myself looking suspiciously at everyone now.

"Petrov tells me you've got the personnel files."

"Yes, sir."

"I know what's going on, Anderson. That you're working from home." Brady's tone is judgmental, but I know he can't truly be upset about having another resource on the case, even part-time. He's not the caring-sharing type—he just wants the job done.

"I've been doing a little bit, yes, sir."

"You suspect Agent Kim? From her personnel file?"

"Actually, sir, I haven't had a chance to spend much time on the files. What with Christmas and all. But I was going to look at it today."

He nods. "Keep us in the loop."

"Yes, sir." I pause. "We could find out if the leak's Williams or Hana for sure. Let's feed them some information and see if it gets back to Agent Young. If it does, it's Williams or Hana. If it doesn't, we know it's someone in the wider gang team."

Brady agrees. "That's viable now that we can isolate two people."

Petrov nods. "So, what info are we going to feed them?"

"The million-dollar question." Brady shifts his cup around in his hands. "It has to be something significant enough for them to make contact with whoever's paying them for information, and something believable enough that it won't arouse suspicion. We don't want the insider to think we're on to them or the Yakuza to think their source has been compromised."

We're all silent for a minute or so. "What about something in your profile?" De Luca suggests. "You could add in something extra, something false, and see if it gets back."

"I'm hoping to draft the profile this Sunday, and brief you guys Monday. So that'd work."

"Okay, that's our first option. What else?" Brady obviously wants a few choices.

"What about your theories on the employer, Petrov?" I ask. "Maybe we can come up with a reason to point the finger in one direction. The suspected source of the hit—Asian Boyz, Yakuza, Mafia or whoever—should definitely get back to Agent Young if Hana or Williams is the leak."

"Good in theory," Petrov says, "but then someone could wind up dead. We tell them Russian Mafia hit Saito, and next thing we know Yakuza's doing a drive-by and killing Russians."

Good point.

We're all silent.

"There's one other option, but it's risky—" Brady looks at De Luca "—risky for your undercover operative."

"What is it?" De Luca asks, but his tone of voice and body language indicate he's not interested in adding to Young's risk factors.

"We could tell Williams and Hana that we have an agent inside the Yakuza and see if that gets back. We keep Young wired and pull him if there's even a hint of a threat."

De Luca doesn't even contemplate the suggestion. "No way. He risked his cover for Anderson, taking that shot. But it was a calculated risk…this plan is too dangerous."

"You know I wouldn't normally suggest anything to endanger an agent, De Luca. But Agents Kim and Williams are only two of the twenty-four-strong task force. Chances are Young will be safe, and then at least we can eliminate Williams and Kim once and for all. Bring them into the fold." Brady leans back. "Besides, you're already sure it's not Agent Kim."

This time De Luca gives the plan some thought, but eventually shakes his head. "There must be another way."

We're silent, thinking, but my thoughts stray to me and Ramos getting shot. "By the way, did Young ever question Moto? Find out if he changed the order to kill?"

"Dan was in the right, Ken in the wrong." De Luca runs his hand across his skull. "The orders were shoot to harm and Ken was heavily reprimanded. For a moment, Dan thought Moto was going to ask for Ken's little finger."

"I bet Young's happy it wasn't him in that position," I comment.

"I'll say."

We're silent again, thinking about the mole once more.

"What about the hit man's name?" I suggest. "I'm expecting to hear back from US State Department today on Chinese nationals entering the US on multiple dates that correspond to our hits. We should have a few names soon and then Williams and Kim will have those names, too. If it gets back to Young that the task force has nearly identified Saito's killer, then we know the Yakuza's source must be Williams or Kim."

My suggestion is met by initial silence, but I can tell from their faces that the silence is a good thing—they're trying to find a reason why it might not work, and there isn't one. "It's much more concrete than adding something to my profile," I add.

Brady drains the rest of his coffee and gives a small nod. "Make it happen." He stands up and leaves.

"How long till we have a name? Or a couple of names?" Petrov asks.

"I'll chase my contact now. She's been off the past couple of days, but back today. Give me a few hours and I'll let you know."

"You think you'll get one name?" De Luca seems unconvinced.

"No. I think our guy's using aliases. We'll get a few names, but they might all be the one person."

"Any point drafting a profile then? If we'll have the name of the killer soon anyway?" Petrov asks.

"A profile will help us narrow down our suspects. If we do get a few matches and they're not all different names for the one man, it should help us pinpoint the one."

De Luca leans back. "And Williams and Hana are expecting an offender profile. It'll make our planted lie more believable."

There's silence for a few moments before De Luca stands up. "Let's set it in motion."

He heads off, leaving Petrov and me to finish the dregs of our coffee. Petrov doesn't seem to be in a hurry to get back to the office…or maybe he just doesn't want to walk with De Luca.

"You normally return separately?" I ask Petrov, wondering if their paranoia extends that far.

"Yeah." He stands up. "But this time I think De Luca is just avoiding the tab." He gives me a salute and a grin. "Me, too," he says and walks out of the diner.

I can't help but chuckle. What is it with these guys and juggling the coffee tabs? I finish my coffee and pay the bill.

Walking back to my apartment slowly, I try to convince myself I'm soaking up the winter sun, but in reality this is close to my top pain-free speed at the moment, especially now that I'm not even on the garden-variety painkillers. I'm tender, no doubt because I've moved more in the past couple of days than the previous two weeks. The tenderness in my shoulder and chest makes me feel weak, vulnerable. At least it's my left side—Dan really did do me a favor. I could still draw down on a suspect, quickly, if need be. It'd just hurt.

This vulnerable sensation makes me think of American-Psycho. He stopped using his real initials with his monthly flower delivery two months ago, indicating that his old name and identity are gone forever. Now he only sees himself as AmericanPsycho, the president of The Murderers' Club. I'm sure he's in France somewhere, maybe even forming a new club. Certainly he'll be up to his old tricks. But I can't exactly hop on a plane and hang out in Paris looking for him. I could spend my whole life doing that and still not run in to him.

Twenty-Seven

As soon as I get home and get my breath back, I dial Rodriguez's direct line.

"Rodriguez." Her voice doesn't sound as refreshed as I'd expect after a couple of days off.

"Hey, it's Anderson."

"Sophie…sorry. I'll have your list in one hour."

"Sounds good. Thanks."

"You have a good Christmas?" she asks.

"Yeah. My folks are still here from Australia. What about you?"

"You know…the turkey was overdone and my uncle drank too much…the usual."

I smile, knowing that Rodriguez may well have described at least half of the population's normal Christmas Day.

"I'll e-mail it through as soon as I get it. Need me to call, too?"

"No, I'll keep my BlackBerry handy."

"Cool. Adios."

Sounds like she's having a busy day already.

"Coffee, darling?"

I look up to see Mum setting up the filtered coffee.

"That'd be great."

"How's it going?" Dad asks from behind his paper.

"Good."

They're being so well behaved that I feel guilty. They didn't even comment on how pale and tired I looked when I got back from the diner. And I know I did, because I checked myself out in the bathroom mirror. We haven't done any touristy stuff, not much together outside my apartment really.

"Do you want to go to Santa Monica Pier in a couple of hours?" I suggest.

Mum and Dad exchange a surprised glance.

"That sounds terrific, darling." Dad gives me a smile. "You up to it?"

"Sure. We'll be driving anyway."

"I thought you wanted to visit Detective Ramos," Mum says.

"You were right, Mum. Ramos can wait another day. You guys leave tomorrow."

She gives me a broad smile.

But before I do touristy stuff with Mum and Dad, I need to work on the mole for at least a bit. I take the file from my locked briefcase and go into the bedroom. I've only just laid the twenty-four files out on the bed when Mum comes in, coffee in hand.

"Here you go, darling."

I jump up from the bed, not wanting her to get any closer and see what I'm working on. "Thanks, Mum."

She glances over my shoulder briefly at the bed, but then leaves me to it.

I've got the files laid out in alphabetical order and that's how I start—with Agent Acorn. I read through the files, looking over each person's service record, family situation, psych reports, personality tests, everything. As I go, I take notes, marking down anything of interest, such as undercover work, strange cases they were involved in. I also spend a few minutes looking at each person's photo and trying to induce a vision. I get a few flashes into people's lives, but nothing particularly incriminating or interesting.

I save Williams and Hana for last and slow the process down. I want to eliminate both of them as suspects. The thought that they're somehow involved disturbs me so much that at times I have to block it out. Otherwise I don't think my acting skills would cover me.

I look at Williams's official service photo. It looks like it was taken a few years ago now; there's definitely less gray in his hair and maybe fewer lines around the eyes, too.

I fire my weapon, adrenaline pumping.

The insight into Williams's life is fleeting, but the emotional hangover is strong. Williams was frightened, and that fear and adrenaline pump through me now. I look up his file for any recorded discharge of his weapon and find one instance. It was seven years ago, armed robbery. He was off duty at the time, and during an exchange of shots, one of Williams's four bullets hit the perp. Williams escaped unscathed. The robber, an eighteen-year-old male, was shot in the stomach but the wound wasn't fatal. The perp had no ties to any gang that we know of, so it's probably not relevant to Williams's work in the L.A. Gang Impact Team. I look through the rest of Williams's file carefully, but nothing stands out.

I spend a few minutes looking at Hana's photo, waiting to see something, but when nothing comes I move on to her records. Given she's younger than Williams, her file is much thinner. Again, nothing stands out in her arrests, jobs or family. I go back to her photo. This time I'm rewarded.

A woman sits on a park bench, head down. A man sits next to her, places an envelope beside her, and then stands up.

The scene is over quickly, just as with my insight into Williams's life. I replay the images, dwelling on the obvious: What was in the envelope? It could be innocent, although the nature of the meeting suggested something more sinister. The woman's head was down and I didn't see her face, so it could also be anyone. I blow out a sigh, frustrated.

* * *

At almost exactly noon, the e-mail comes in from Lara Rodriguez. In total, there are only ten names with two or more entries that match our dates. We'd have even less if I didn't allow a full month before each attack. It's most likely he flies in two to three weeks before the kill, but I don't want to risk narrowing the dates down that much. I immediately e-mail a list to Lee's cousin in the Beijing Police, typing out the subjects' full names and passport numbers. I pick up the phone and dial Lee. Given his cousin doesn't speak English, all contact will have to be routed through him. Probably not as expedient as talking directly to him myself, but beggars can't be choosers.

Lee picks up after three rings.

"Hi, Lee, it's Sophie Anderson."

"Hey. What can I do for you?"

"I've e-mailed ten names to your cousin and I was hoping you could call him in a few hours and ask him to look them up in their system."

"It's early there… Four in the morning, actually."

"So we have to wait…four hours? Five?"

"Five will give him time to check his e-mails. Do you wanna do a three-way chat? That way I could interpret as you go."

"That'd be great." It'll also give me a chance to ask questions as we go along.

"Okay. I've got a conference facility on my office phone."

"You don't have to do that," I say. "I'll initiate the call so the Bureau picks up the tab."

"Don't forget Chung wants to keep this unofficial. Can the call be traced to the Bureau?"

"All our outgoing calls are unlisted numbers, but maybe it's better if he just gets a call from his cousin in L.A., huh?" On Lee's request, I'd already used Chung's Hotmail address rather than his work e-mail.

"Yeah, let's keep it casual."

I hang up and print out all the details for each of the ten

Chinese men who matched our criteria. We don't have much on them at this stage—just their names, dates and places of birth, passport numbers and the information from their entry cards. For the visits after 2004 we also have fingerprints, digital photos and iris scans. Although I haven't actually drafted the profile of our hit man yet, I feel as though I have a good handle on his personality. One thing that may help us narrow the list down even further is the airline. I see our guy as being a nationalist, proud of his country, and so I'm thinking he's more likely to fly Air China than any of the other carriers that fly from Beijing into the States. I use this as a point of difference, and go through the names again to see which men flew Air China. That leaves me with three names—An Kwan, Lok Ng and Quon Liao. It's possible the three people are really one using aliases.

I ring up Sifu Lee. "Sorry to bug you again, but I was hoping to run three names by you. See if you recognize them as kung fu practitioners back in China."

"Shoot."

"An Kwan, Lok Ng and Quon Liao."

"Quon Liao sounds familiar. Can you leave it with me?"

"Sure. Thanks. Bye."

We have photos of An Kwan and Lok Ng from their most recent visits, so I look at the images more closely. Certainly they look alike, maybe enough alike to be the one person using disguises. They are of similar build and while Kwan has close-cut hair almost military in style, Ng has longer hair—but nothing an expensive and well-fitted wig couldn't achieve. Kwan also has puffier eyes and a bigger, squarer jaw line. Again, someone expert in this field could easily make these adjustments to their appearance, and the two men do look different enough in the photos if you don't compare them directly. But this time I am looking at their pictures side by side. I'll need to send the digital images for a review with facial recognition software to verify my hypothesis.

In addition to their facial similarities, both men are roughly the same height according to their passports, Kwan at six feet and Ng at six-two. Quon Liao is also in the same ballpark at six-one. The fingerprints and iris scans we have for Kwan and Ng are different, and while it's extremely hard to fool these biometric scans, we are talking about a high-end professional hit man, someone with the resources for multiple identities and disguises, potentially down to finger-print pads and contact lenses to give a faulty iris scan.

Next I look more closely at the movements of my three top targets. An Kwan entered the country for the first time on March 22, 1998, flying into L.A. Hop Fu was murdered on April 4 in San Francisco, and An Kwan flew from L.A. to Beijing on April 10. I'd expect a faster exit strategy, but maybe he thought leaving too soon after the murder might look sus-picious—or maybe he just wanted to be a tourist for a few days. Four years later, in August 2002, An Kwan flew into San Francisco and fifteen days later Bao Tran was killed in L.A. And Kwan made his return trip three days after the death.

Lok Ng has also made two visits to the US. One that ties in with the 1996 New York victim who survived, and one that coincides with the 2007 murder of Russian Mafia man, Alexander Ivanovich.

Last is Quon Liao. His first visit fits for the 2000 Chicago slaying of Yakuza member Shiro Matsu, but the 2008 one doesn't line up with anything we have on the system. But given what we now know about the killer's expertise in *dim mak,* you can be sure that someone had a heart attack during Liao's visit. It's looking pretty good, but it's too early to jump to any conclusions. Let's see what Lee's cousin finds on these men, and the other seven first, see if facial recognition software identifies An Kwan and Lok Ng as the same person.

It's time to check in with Petrov, but before I do I look through the other seven names. One man is too young, so I discount him. Of the remaining six men we only have digital photos of two, but my quick visual comparison indicated they could all be the same man. I dial Petrov's number.

"Anderson, what's up? You got something?"

"Uh-huh."

"Shoot."

I tell him my findings and follow-up plans.

"Excellent. So how long until your man has something for you?"

"It's five in the morning there at the moment so I'm going to call him in a few hours."

"Okay. Let's keep it quiet for the moment."

"What if we use one of the Bureau's people for the recognition software? Someone not involved in the Gang Impact Team." Mercedes Diaz immediately comes to mind, but this isn't her area of expertise. Petrov will know someone from Ed Garcia's team.

Petrov hesitates. "Should be safe enough. E-mail me through the photos and I'll set that one up. How did you go with the personnel files?"

"Okay, but not great. I've got a list of eight people I'd put at the top of our list, including Hana."

Petrov nods. "Her name's come up a lot. She did undercover work in San Francisco for a couple of years. But Joe's sure she's clean. Who else?"

I rattle off the other seven names. I can tell by Petrov's reactions that most of them gel with his thoughts, until I get to the ATF's Rory Parsons.

"Parsons? Really?"

"So he wasn't on your list?"

"No. No undercover work that could have potentially exposed him to corruption, and all the checks on his immediate family and friends came back okay. Plus we couldn't find any skeletons in his closet worthy of blackmail. What made you add him to the list?"

"His arrest record. He was put up for a promotion eighteen months ago and I wondered why. Turns out it was because his arrests had skyrocketed."

"So you think some of the arrests were set up?"

"Could have been. Plus, fourteen months ago he arrested a guy called Aran Sarit and had previously arrested Sarit's brother-in-law, who's part of the Asian Boyz. Both of them had their charges significantly reduced and I wondered if Parsons played a hand in that."

Petrov whistles. "That does sound suspicious. I better tell the others about this. But I still think we should go ahead with our plan to test Agents Williams and Kim. When you get info from Beijing call me. But sit on it. We'll present it to the team on Monday."

"Okay. Whatever you say."

With all my phone calls out of the way we head off for Santa Monica Pier, which keeps me occupied while I wait to hear back from Lee. We're on our way back in the car when my BlackBerry vibrates, right on time at 5:00 p.m.

"Lee?"

"Yup. I'll just dial-in Chung now."

I get hold music for about a minute, before Lee's voice comes back on the line. "Okay, we're on."

"Great," I say. "First off, can you please thank him for helping us out?"

Lee talks in Mandarin to his cousin and, after a short reply, Lee tells me that Chung is happy to help.

"Thanks. Can you ask him what sort of information he'll be able to get for me, and how long it will take?"

"Sure."

I wait while Lee asks Chung and he responds. This time, the conversation is much longer. After a couple of minutes, Lee says, "He'll be able to get marital status, driver's license details if applicable, educational background and criminal offences. He said the government keeps a lot more information on its citizens, but he doesn't have the clearance to access most of it."

"That sounds great. More than we can get on this end. How long will it take?"

"Give him an hour," Lee says.

"I guess the info will be in Mandarin?" I ask Lee.

"Yes. But I'll translate it for you. Depending on how much we get, that should only take me twenty minutes or so."

"Great. Did Chung find any similar attacks or deaths in China?" I wait until Lee asks the question in Mandarin and Chung responds.

"No," Lee says. "But I've been thinking about that—in China the killer would be especially careful to make sure the death looked completely accidental, like a heart attack, because any sign of violence would alert authorities to the possible use of *dim mak*. General knowledge on the topic is quite high."

"And he'd want to avoid police attention…especially in his homeland."

"Exactly," Lee replies.

I can't think of anything else, so I thank Lee and ask him to thank his cousin.

Lee says something in Mandarin before I hear a click as Chung disconnects. "Okay. I'll call you as soon as I have the info and have it translated."

"You're a star."

"Happy to help. Speak to you later." Lee hangs up.

When my phone rings at 6:15 p.m., I snatch the handset up eagerly, hoping it's Lee on the other end with some answers. It is.

"How'd it go?" I ask.

"Good. Chung has sent through information on six of the names you e-mailed through and one has a criminal record."

"I doubt our guy has a record, but can you e-mail the info through?"

"Sure."

"And what about the other four names? Chung couldn't get anything on them?"

"No. He was a little perplexed by it, actually. There should be records of these men."

"Unless they're aliases."

"Ah, yes. Of course," He pauses. "Quon Liao. Now I remember."

"You recognize the name?"

"Yes. My father once told me a story about Quon Liao, a young warrior boy from thousands of years ago who is said to have fought one hundred soldiers—and won."

"So perhaps our killer is using the name Quon Liao as homage to this boy warrior?"

"Yes. It's when you said aliases that it made me remember. One boy I competed against in tournaments used to wear the name Quon Liao on his robe. He saw himself as the boy warrior."

"Do you remember his name?" My voice quickens.

"Park Ling."

"Would Ling have the skill for these attacks?"

"I haven't seen or heard of him for over twenty years, but if he'd continued studying kung fu, he would certainly know the Ten Killing Hands and *dim mak*."

"Really?" So, assuming Park Ling still lives in China, we have a Chinese national who has the skills for the murders and uses Quon Liao as an alias. "Thanks, Lee. Can Chung get some recent info on this Park Ling?"

"I'm sure he can. Give me five minutes and I'll call you back."

I pace on my apartment balcony, BlackBerry in hand.

After a couple of minutes Dad pops his head out. "Everything okay?"

"Yeah. Great. Just waiting on another call."

"Ah, you've got something?" Dad says.

"It looks promising, yeah."

He smiles. "I can see it in your eyes…the fire. It's kinda neat, honey. I'm glad you enjoy your job." His face crinkles. "If you can call it enjoyment."

I laugh. "I know what you mean, Dad. It's weird, but the job's horrific and rewarding all at the same time. This part—when the break's about to come—I love."

My BlackBerry rings.

"You're on," Dad says, closing the balcony door and going back inside.

"Lee?"

"Chung found him. He's forty-two, no criminal record, spent five years in the military after his compulsory two-year service and he's married with one child. He lives in Beijing now, but originally he's from the same town as Li Chow…the other name you asked about."

"Really? So they may have known each other."

"Possibly. It's quite a small town." He takes a breath. "I'll e-mail the details through now."

I'm silent, processing the information. It's not much, but it fits with my impression of the killer. It'll be good to draft the full profile and do a direct comparison between it and the six Chinese nationals we've got information on, and Park Ling.

I hang up. Park Ling…is our contract killer within our grasp?

Twenty-Eight

Mum and I are both in tears at the airport, and even Dad's looking emotional.

"Thanks for looking after me… And I'm sorry. Sorry to give you such a terrible scare."

Mum nods, but the tears fall a little faster.

"Come on, Jan. We have to go through." Dad's looking at his watch.

"Okay, Bob." She gives me one last hug, before picking up her carry-on luggage.

Dad grabs me in a tight bear hug. "Bye, sweetie."

"Bye, Dad. And thanks for everything. Including Mum."

He nods. "At least the flight back will be better than the one over here."

I grimace as Dad's grip loosens. "I'm sorry," I whisper.

His grip tightens again and he wipes a stray tear from my face before taking Mum's hand.

"We love you, honey." Mum starts walking backward toward the security checkpoint.

"I love you, too. I'll see you in July," I yell, waving.

They both smile and Dad shouts, "We can't wait, honey."

I watch as they place their personal items on the security belt and walk through the metal detector. Once they're through the security checkpoint, they turn around and wave again, before disappearing toward their gate. I wipe the last of the tears away before making my way back to my car.

When I get home at around 6:00 p.m., I heat up some leftover pasta. In another couple of days all Mum's leftovers will be gone and I'll have to start cooking for myself again…and cleaning.

I'm relaxing and trying to find something good on TV when the phone rings.

"Soph, it's Darren."

"Hi. How are you?"

He laughs. "Asks the woman who took a bullet."

I smile. "Fair call."

"So, how are you feeling?"

"Recovering well. Getting organized for work on Monday."

"Are you ready to go back?"

"Sure."

"Really?"

"You're as bad as my parents. I'm fine. I'm ready."

"Sorry. Did they make their flight okay?"

"Uh-huh. They should be somewhere over the Pacific Ocean by now."

"So how did the visit turn out in the end?"

Darren knows that I usually worry about my parents' disapproval of my profession, that it's a stumbling point for us. We didn't get much of a chance to talk about it during the forty-eight hours he spent in L.A., and my mum and dad have been within earshot during our more recent calls.

"It was good actually. Really good. I found out some stuff about them, and they found out things about me,"

"So not your regular visit?"

"No, definitely not." Normally I wouldn't reveal something as private about Mum to anyone, but Darren and I have both experienced the loss of a loved one to violent crime, so I know he'll understand. "They had to sedate my mum on the flight over here."

He makes a wincing noise.

"I know." I bite down hard on my bottom lip. "I realized

she was worried about me, but I guess I never really thought about how it must be for her…after losing John."

"People don't bounce back from that, Sophie."

"Tell me something I don't know." But despite my flippant response, he's right to emphasize the point with me. There's a difference between knowing and really knowing.

"I guess I never completely put myself in Mum's shoes. I imagined, wondered even. But I didn't think it through. Not properly."

"You were a kid, Sophie."

"When it happened, yes. But I'm not a kid now. It's taken me nearly thirty years to realize what it must have done to her. And even then I think only another mother could truly understand what it's like to lose a child."

Darren's silent. I guess there's not much to say.

"They only told me about the sedatives a couple of days ago."

"Protecting you."

"Yeah."

Silence.

"So what are you going to do?" he asks.

"What do you mean?"

"Are you staying in the Bureau? In law enforcement?"

"Of course. In fact, Mum's proud of me. Despite all the worry, all the digs, she respects what I do for other families, for other victims."

"Your mother is an amazing woman."

"I hate to think what you went through staying here with them."

He pauses. "I actually really enjoyed it, Soph. I liked getting to know your folks."

I grimace. Mum assured me she didn't question Darren about his feelings for me, or make any hints in that direction, but I don't trust her when it comes to my love life. Her desire for a wedding and a grandchild override what little tact she possesses.

"They told me how proud they are of you. They really do respect what you do, Sophie."

"Yeah, I know that now."

"You must have been tempted to tell them about your visions."

"I nearly did. But I couldn't do it in the end."

Darren is the only person who knows about my gift, and I want to keep it that way. I was extremely close to telling my parents about it last week, but each time I felt the urge, I chickened out.

"So, what's on for the rest of the night?" he asks.

"TV or reading, then bed."

"What? Not working?"

"Well, maybe…"

"Have you had many visions about the case?"

"Some. Not much this time. But I think the pain meds put my sixth sense on the fritz."

He laughs. "It makes sense. I guess they numbed everything."

"Yeah, that's what I figured."

"Well, don't work too hard."

"I won't."

"I very much doubt that." I can tell from the tone in his voice that he's smiling, dimples puckering.

"Good night, Darren."

"Good night."

It's 9:00 a.m. before I start work. I've allocated today for collating everything I need for the profile and Sunday for drafting the profile itself. Over the past few days I've added info to the other vics where possible, but I wanted to have one more look and confirm everything in my head before I put it down on paper. It's not that I need to refresh my memory of the case. Despite my convalescence and the presence of my parents, I've found it difficult to think of much else. This case almost cost me and Ramos our lives— I'm going to find that needle in the haystack somehow.

I'm finished for the day and cooking dinner when my landline rings. I pick up the phone.

"Soph, it's Mum. We're home."

"Hi, Mum." I look at my watch. Eight o'clock here, which makes it three o'clock in the afternoon in Melbourne. "How was your flight?"

"The usual. Long and boring."

"I know what you mean," I say. I haven't flown home since I've been living in the US, but I remember the feeling—even with screens in the seat in front of you and loads of movies, after about six hours, not even halfway through the seventeen-hour journey, you're over it.

"We had a nap as soon as we arrived. Decided we'd wait and call you afterward."

"No worries. I was going to call you before I went to bed tonight if I hadn't heard."

"Are you taking it easy?"

"Yes, Mum."

"That's great, honey. You need to look after yourself. And remember, the more you take it easy, the faster you'll be back to one hundred percent."

"I know." I sigh, still frustrated by my body's healing process.

"Any breaks on the case?"

"Maybe. We might have a list of suspects, but it's early days." I trust my parents with my life, with anything, but there's no need to go into any more detail. "I should know more soon."

"That sounds great, darling." She says it with genuine enthusiasm.

I'll have to get used to this "new" Mum. I'm so used to her showing little or no interest in my work that it feels weird having her suddenly so supportive. I like her change in attitude, but it's still taking me by surprise. "Is Dad around?"

"Still asleep. I couldn't wait to call you, though."

"I see." I smile. Some things about Mum will never change…and that's just the way I like it.

"And what about Darren? Spoken to him recently?"

"Mum, how many times do I have to tell you, he's just a friend."

"He flew up to see you in hospital and rang you just about every day while we were staying with you, honey. You're either lying to me or to yourself." She pauses. "Besides, I saw the way you two looked at each other."

I take a breath. "Okay, okay. You've made your point. But he's in Arizona, Mum."

"That's only a two-hour flight. He said so himself."

"Mum…" I go for a light-hearted warning.

"Yes, darling?" she responds innocently.

"You know what, Mum."

"But he's so lovely. And you're lovely…"

"So why can't we be lovely together?"

"Exactly! And you would be perfect for each other. He even understands about your job."

I sigh. "Where's Dad when I need him?"

"You can't always rely on your father. And don't think I didn't know about your little deal while we were in L.A."

"Dad told you?"

"I guessed." She pauses for a quick intake of air. "Anyway, your father knows nothing about how important it is for a woman to find a man…before she's too old."

"Mum! I'm only thirty-six."

"I was twenty-five when I married your father. By thirty-six I had two children of school age."

"Yes, Mum." I change tack, going for the "yes, Mum, whatever you say, Mum" approach.

"Don't you 'yes, Mum' me, young lady."

I hold the mouthpiece away to let out an exaggerated sigh. This could be a long phone call. "Did you get to see any good movies?" Maybe a severe topic change will do the trick.

"I watched two movies, including this heartbreaking piece about a single woman in her forties."

"Is that even true, Mum? And I'm not in my forties!"

"You will be in three and a half years."

"I think I liked you better when you were waiting on me hand and foot," I joke.

"I'm just telling it like it is."

I decide to try a few home truths myself. "Mum, I'd love to fall in love, to find a good man, but it just hasn't happened for me yet."

"And Darren isn't a contender?"

I hesitate again, unsure how to field this question. Darren has lots of qualities I admire, that I'm attracted to, but there's always been something in the way. When we first met I was seeing someone else, then I wasn't ready for a relationship. I guess I'm ready now, but it feels like he's so far away. "I'm not sure, Mum."

"How do you know if you don't give him a chance, Soph?"

I pause. "Mum, you're making way too much sense for my liking."

"Uh-huh. There is something between you, Sophie. Anyone can see that."

"Okay, Mum. You've got me. But it's not like it was when you and Dad met. You don't find someone you like and get married."

"Oh, I know that, darling. What do you take me for, an idiot? I know I may be out of touch, but a date's a start, yes?"

I sigh again. "Yes."

"It's New Year's Eve in two nights' time. Why don't you pop down to Arizona for a couple of days?"

"I can't, Mum. You know I'm officially on call except during my holidays." FBI agents are always on call, always have to be fit for duty. It's one of the drawbacks of the job. Not that it bothers me, normally.

"Then invite him up. I'm your mother and I know what's best for you." There's a hint of humor in her voice, but only a hint. "Ring him. Now!"

"Mum!"

"Seriously, I'm hanging up now, but you ring him and invite him up. And if he's not free for New Year's Eve, there's always his next days off."

"Inviting him up's pretty serious, Mum."

"You afraid of rejection?"

"No." I know what Darren's answer will be. He's made his interest quite clear in the past.

"When people are old they rarely regret the things they did, only the things they didn't do. I'm hanging up now. Call him."

"Goodbye, Mum." For a minute I think she's really hung up already. But I should have known better.

"You will call him, won't you?"

"Bye. Say hi to Dad." I blow her a kiss down the line and hang up.

Relationship advice from my mother is dubious at the best of times, but this time maybe it is good advice. I mean, Darren ticks all the right boxes for me—he's kind and caring, he's smart, he looks after himself, he's a good communicator, I find him physically attractive and he understands the demands of the job. But despite all these positive points I manage to avoid calling him—maybe tomorrow.

After a light walk in the morning, I spend Sunday drafting the profile.

Sex: Male
Age: Chronological: 30–60
  Emotional: 30–60
Race: Asian
Type of offender: Organized—well-planned murders, socially competent and controlled mood during crime. No evidence left at the crime scenes, in line with the standard MO for high-level contract killers.
Occupation/employment: Full-time professional hit man.

Probably does most of his hits for organized crime and other high-level, high-paying outfits.

May also have a cover job, something he tells his family and friends he does as a living.
Marital status: Married with children.

Although we have very few studies on professional hit men, especially the upper echelons, we do know that these individuals are capable of complete compartmentalization. They kill for business—it's their job. And so, just like any man in this age bracket, he's more likely to be married with children…successfully living a double life.

Dependents: Yes—see above.

Childhood: Any violent behavior, even that as controlled as a hit man's, is likely to be caused by exposure to violence at a young age—he accepts violence as normal. Our perp most likely experienced violence as a youth, maybe in the family or through childhood or adolescent friends who may have been involved in a violent world.

Some contract killers see themselves as doing the "work of God," stepping in where the justice system fails, so it's possible our killer was also exposed to injustice of some description early on and feels the need to act as the executioner. His targets, mostly in the world of organized crime, can all be seen as "bad" men. Our killer will rationalize this to himself, believing they simply paid the price for their chosen actions.

Personality: He will be a quiet individual, someone who others perceive as being polite, honest and hardworking. At the same time, no one really *knows* him. Those closest to him would feel this sense of distance, particularly his wife, who would feel like she doesn't know her husband.

He is also obsessively neat—most contract killers are highly methodical individuals with an overdeveloped sense of discipline. This is often partly due to a life in the military, a life where they could rationalize killing as serving their country. When they move from the military to the private world, their sense of life and death has become distorted.

Disabilities: None

Interaction with victims: While the perp "stalks" the victims, he does so purely for functional reasons, to get to know their routines and to find the best place to kill them. He has no actual interaction with his victims and feels no bonds or ties to them. Likewise, although he follows them for some time before taking action, he does not become curious about them or their lives.

Notice all victims are male. This is probably more about the type of work he's involved in (organized crime), but it's also possible he refuses any contracts on women and children, particularly given his cultural background.

Remorse: As a professional killer, our perp is unlikely to feel any remorse. He sees killing people as purely business, and doesn't derive any pleasure from the killing process— other than a sense of professional pride. No pleasure, but also no guilt.

Home life: At home, our perp would present like any normal businessman. He loves his wife and children, although he may be prone to jealousy. Given his own exposure to violence at a young age, it's likely he's trying to protect his family from this side of society —ironic given his profession. However, he's able to completely separate his work and home life.

I feel that our killer was able to channel any early anger through his kung fu, using this outlet growing up (given his current level of expertise, he would have had to start training as a youth and that would have helped him to channel and control his emotions). It's possible he has anger-impulse control issues at home, although these are not displayed in any of the murders he commits. Like other martial arts, part of kung fu also addresses a more spiritual side—being centered and grounded. It's quite possible he uses this training to curb any anger issues he may have.

Car: Given the assumption that our killer lives overseas most of the time, probably in China, and flies around the world to fulfill his contracts, we cannot draw standard conclusions about the type of car he drives. Traditionally, cars in China were too expensive for most citizens, and while use is increasing rapidly at the moment, they're still seen as status symbols.

Note: In the US, we have 8,000 cars per 10,000 people, but in mainland China it hovers around 100 cars per 10,000 people.

If he does own a car, he'd probably choose one of the most popular vehicles to blend in with his fellow citizens, despite his regular exposure to American and European cultures where cars are treated differently. The most popular makes in China are Volkswagen (Jetta, Santana and Sagitar), Buick Excelle, Toyota (Corolla and Camry) and Chery QQ (Chinese company). If our perp does own a car, it's likely he owns and drives one of these cars and given his likely nationalist leanings, the Chery QQ is the most probable.

Intelligence: Moderate to high IQ (105–120) but with highly developed analytical and organizational skills, plus extremely well-developed social skills.

Education level: High school only. This is largely culturally based, given that many Chinese people complete only the minimum of nine years of education. They generally start school around six or seven, so they leave around fifteen years of age.

China also has compulsory military service, which he would have registered for and completed. He would also have served additional time in the military and received some education and training in this setting.

Outward appearance: In keeping with our perp's attention to detail and obsessively neat nature, his preferred style of dress would be immaculate and businesslike. His normal attire would be considered very dressy for the US—mostly suits—although he would also force himself to wear more casual clothes to fit in for each job (e.g., during the evening when there aren't going to be as many people still in corporate clothing around the streets). He's a master of disguise and acting, taking on different roles for different jobs. This may mean more casual attire; however, he would do this with a considerable amount of distaste.

Criminal background: It is unlikely our perp has a criminal background—certainly nothing here in the US. He may have minor youth offences in China, but his organized and disciplined nature, coupled with his kung fu training, probably kept him out of trouble in his adolescence. Now his skills are at such a high level that he won't come to the attention of law enforcement accidentally.

Modus operandi (MO): Once the perp has accepted a contract, he will follow the victim, getting to know his routines. When he's decided on a location, he'll choose the best time and set himself up for the kill. His preference is to kill using his bare hands, combining regular kung fu strikes with *dim mak* or "death touch." However, he can change the MO in line with any requests (as per the 2007 murder of Alexander Ivanovich).

He is not aligned with any particular organization, rather he works in a freelance capacity.

Signature: He's not a signature killer in the traditional sense of the term—a serial killer who's compelled to leave a victim or crime scene in a certain manner. However, his use of kung fu's Ten Killing Hands in most of the kills is similar to a signature or a calling card.

Note: To avoid confusion with the normal use of the term *signature,* I'll refer to the Ten Killing Hands as his calling card. In addition, using kung fu's *dim mak* to injure and kill his victims is also part of his calling card. However, pressure-point bruising can only be positively verified for Jun Saito.

Postoffence behavior: The killer leaves the area quickly, perhaps double-checking briefly that the crime scene is free of any evidence that might tie him or his employer to the crime.

Staging was involved in most of the attacks, with many of them made to look like muggings, "standard" gang hits or blunt force trauma (beatings). For those made to look like muggings, part of his postoffence behavior is to take the victim's jewelry and ID.

Media tactics: Media exposure won't be helpful or detrimental in this case. The perpetrator will not be monitoring the media, and if he does happen to see a story on the murder, it's unlikely he'll pay it any more than cursory attention. He does not feel any emotion about his victims or his kills.

Once I've finalized the profile, I print out Lee's e-mail of the translated information on our six Chinese nationals and the additional information he sent through on Park Ling. However, with few details on the men, it's hard to exclude any of them except for the eighteen-year-old, who's too young. Yes, Park Ling fits the profile, but so do some of the others.

And now, there's only one thing left on my mental

"to-do" list… Darren. I take a deep breath and blow it out hard…I can't believe I'm going to do this. My stomach starts somersaulting but I pick up the phone regardless. I just faced the Yakuza and a bullet—I can face a conversation with a potential boyfriend, can't I? But the word *boyfriend* unleashes a fresh bout of nervousness.

I hang up the phone.

I roll my eyes at myself and pick it up again.

I pace.

"This is ridiculous," I say. "You're acting like a school-girl." I punch in the number but hang up before it starts to ring.

"Good God, woman. Get a grip." I hit redial.

"Sophie, hi."

I'm not surprised that Darren knows who's calling—my home and cell numbers are programmed into his phone, just like his are in mine.

"Hi, Darren."

"I was going to call you again tonight. Wish you luck for your first day back."

"Yeah, I'm looking forward to it," I say distractedly. I'm silent, suddenly unable to think of anything else to say.

"What's up? Everything okay?"

"Sure. Everything's fine."

Silence again.

If I let the silence sit for much longer, it's only going to make things worse. I dive in. "I thought it might be nice to catch up again. Have you got any plans for New Year's Eve?"

There's silence on the other end of the phone and dread envelopes me. I've assumed he's still single, assumed that he's still interested in me. But it was six months ago that he expressed his interest with a kiss and maybe he's moved on. He certainly didn't declare his undying love for me in the hospital. Sure, he called me, sent me flowers, came up to see me, but that could just be the gestures of a friend. A worried friend. Maybe Mum and I are wrong.

"I'm sorry," I blurt. "You've probably already got plans."

"No," he answers quickly. "I'd love to come up."

"Great." Another long silence. "I'll see you tomorrow then?"

"Looking forward to it."

We say a brief good night before I hang up.

My heart's racing. I'd been so worried about the phone call I hadn't thought about the reality of actually seeing him. And it won't be like other times when I could just play dumb to the attraction and avoid eye contact during any potentially intimate moments. I've invited him up. I've opened the door.

Deep breath…deep breath.

The Yakuza and a bullet are small-fry in comparison to having Darren in my apartment.

Twenty-Nine

I arrive at the office at 7:45 a.m. and it feels right...like I'm coming home. I know it's sad, but I accept that I'm a workaholic who wants my life to go back to normal—full-time work and obsessive exercising... It's not too much to ask, is it? Sadly, the exercise thing will have to wait a little longer.

De Luca stands as I approach his desk. "Anderson, welcome back."

I nod. "Thanks. It's good to be back...finally."

"Finally? I reckon you're back at work quickly...maybe too quick." De Luca is giving me his official line, even though he knows I've been working at home. But I guess full-time is different. He probably won't be the first person to comment on it today. Everyone's a doctor or a psychologist. But I know my body, I know my emotions and I know it's not too soon. Granted, I can't run a marathon, or maybe even run down a perp in the street, but I'm still valuable to this case. Most cases I worked on from the Behavioral Analysis Unit in Quantico didn't require me to go farther than the fax machine...and the coffeepot, of course.

"Seriously, I'm fine." I'm guessing I might be repeating that phrase a few times today.

"Still..." He lets the sentence hang.

I change the subject. "Do you know what meeting room we're in?"

"Number three."

I nod and make my way to the photocopier. After I've run four copies of my profile, I take a seat in the meeting room. I've just sat down when Hana walks in.

"Hi, Sophie. How are you feeling?"

"Much better, thanks."

She nods. "And Ramos? Have you seen him recently?" She rubs her right hand up and down her left arm and I can't help but interpret the body language. It's an unconscious gesture on her part, and one that could indicate discomfort, concern or maybe even guilt.

"I visited him yesterday afternoon. He's on the mend."

Agent Louis Williams interrupts. "Hey, Anderson. Good to see you."

I stand up and shake his outstretched hand.

"You did well. Making the 911 call."

I nod, familiar with the lie. "It's amazing what you can do when adrenaline and endorphins kick in."

"True. Thankfully I've never had to test that theory."

He glances around the meeting room and his eyes settle on the table. "Knock on wood." He reaches out and hits the tabletop.

I force a smile, force myself not to think about the fact that either of the two people standing in front of me could have been partially responsible for me and Ramos ending up in hospital.

Petrov and De Luca enter the room together.

"Morning." They both give us a communal nod and we all respond. Petrov sits down at the head of the table, and De Luca sits to his right. I take the seat next to De Luca, and Hana and Williams sit on the other side of the table.

"Okay." Petrov looks up. "Let's get straight down to business. The profile."

I pass the copies around the table. "Some of the profile is based on standard information we have on contract killers. However, it is an area that hasn't been studied extensively, by the Behavioral Analysis Unit or within the forensic psychology area. While it's relatively easy to get subjects from the more amateur end of contract killing, thugs who accept one thousand dollars to kill someone's wife or husband, it's much harder to track down, let alone interview and do psychological tests on, the upper echelons of this criminal subset. As a result, we don't have as much information about these types of individuals as we'd like. Certainly nothing like our knowledge of sex offenders or serial killers."

I take a breath, ready to deliver my findings. "Studies have identified three types of contract killers—amateur, semiprofessional and professional. Our guy is definitely an example of the professional subtype. Secondly, within this categorization we have professional hit men who work for one organization and those who freelance. Given the different victims and our belief that the killer's kung fu skills are more characteristic with someone trained in China, we're looking at a freelancer. And a highly paid one at that. He's called in for high-profile hits, homicides that the end employer doesn't want traced back to his or her organization."

"How much money are we talking here?" Hana looks up from the printout in front of her.

"At this level, at least fifty thousand dollars per job, maybe up to two hundred thousand dollars."

Williams lets out a whistle. "That's some dough."

"Particularly if our guy lives in China and is getting paid in US dollars," I say. "I did a quick search on it, and the average annual salary in China is around ten thousand US dollars, and the cost of living is much cheaper than here. So if he gets, say, one hundred thousand dollars per hit, that's roughly equivalent to over six hundred thousand in terms of buying power."

"Whoa…that really is a lot of dough," Williams says, shaking his head.

"At least it puts a proper value on life. Not like some of the cases we work through DEA." Hana eyes Williams.

"Three months ago some poor kid was killed for a hundred bucks' worth of cocaine."

It's impossible to put a value on anyone's life, but I understand where Hana's coming from. Somehow it makes it worse if your victim's killed for a watch or because some idiot thought it would be fun to fire his gun in a public place and see what damage could be done.

I add the hit man context, "Hits *have* been contracted for as little as a hundred dollars here in the States."

"Who are the hitters? Druggies?"

"Mostly, yes. When you're desperate for your next score, a hundred bucks can seem like a lot of money." I pause before moving back to my notes and our hit man. "Professional hit men like our perp see what they do as a job. Strictly business. There's no psychological or emotional need to kill. In their minds, it's simply a way of living." I look around the room—I have everyone's full attention.

"Any stats on the numbers of professional hit men operating?" Williams asks, glancing from Petrov to me.

Petrov takes the question. "We're unsure of the exact figure, but research indicates that in 2008 there were two hundred murders in the US that were either known or believed to be carried out for money. Of those, eighty-two were solved and fall into the amateur or semiprofessional categories that Anderson described earlier."

"So that leaves one hundred and eighteen unsolved? By how many killers?"

"That's the unknown. It could be ten professional hit men working in the States or it could be fifty. It's hard to tell."

Williams lets out another whistle.

"So, the profile," I say. "Let's start with the sex. Nearly all the professional contract killers we know about are male. It doesn't mean a contract killer can't be a woman, but it's much less likely. In our case, these stats, coupled with the skill and strength involved in some of the attacks, make me think we're looking for a man." I move on to the age. "The age range is large, I'm afraid. Again, based on the lack of

research subjects in this area. Our known cases of professional hit men have varied in age greatly, and given the first
involvement we can positively link to our killer was twelve
years ago, our killer could be anything from thirty to sixty."

I keep taking the team through the profile, and it's not
until I get to the offender's vehicle type that I get some
more specific feedback.

"Wow, those stats are incredible." Petrov voices his
surprise, which is also evident on the faces of De Luca,
Williams and Hana.

"I know. Beyond the car ownership numbers, the key difference is the attitude toward cars in China. Here, they're
seen as a necessity and almost as a home away from home.
We do everything in our cars—eat, grab that coffee, make
phone calls—whereas in China cars are a status symbol.
Again, that's changing fast, but at the moment the car you
choose, and even driving a car in itself, is a measure of your
social and economic status. So for our killer, who's used to
traveling the world, I think he probably does own a car, but
he's not going to want to stand out too much so he'll most
likely own something more common. I've listed the top-
selling cars currently in China, and given his military background, he's more likely to buy Chinese-made. However,
he's also familiar with the European and American models,
so I don't want to exclude these cars."

"That makes sense. Can we track vehicle type? Once we
have suspects?"

"I've got to check back with my contact in the Beijing
police. He's willing to help us out in any way he can." I don't
mention what he's already done for us—Petrov still wants me
to keep quiet about our list of names and Chung's research.

Hana nods. "That's great."

"Yes, it's going to help us enormously, especially when
we don't have to go through the formal, governmental
channels. No paperwork or waiting. Our only problem is the
aliases issue. He's probably used a different name for the
passport he entered the US on and the name he bought the
car with." I also don't mention the fact that I may have our

killer's real name—Park Ling. I move us back to the profile. "Intelligence."

"Surely our guy must be at the higher end of this range," De Luca says. "Organized offender, no clues left…"

"True, but it's different to serial killers who exhibit those patterns and tend to have high IQs. In the professional contract killers we've tested, and again I must stress that we're only talking about five individuals in this category of contract killer, the average IQ was one hundred and eight, only eight points higher than what's considered average. And they ranged from ninety-five to one hundred and fifteen. Interestingly, most of them functioned above their overall intelligence, due to a thorough understanding of societal principles and an ability to apply their intelligence in a practical way."

"Does that translate into street smart?" De Luca asks with a grin.

I smile at the dig. "It translates into smart in general. Common sense."

He nods, serious again.

I take them through our hit man's education, appearance, criminal background and then MO before Petrov pipes up.

"This is interesting." Petrov looks up. "Sorry, I just skipped ahead to the signature. You're right, it is like a calling card."

"Uh-huh. In layperson's terms it would be termed a *signature,* but because of the common law-enforcement interpretation of that word, I'm going with *calling card,* so we don't confuse the issue or the killer. Although he's killed many times and multiple murders over time is the definition of a serial killer, he's a different kind of beast all together."

"Understood." Petrov returns to the sheets of paper. "We can't compare a hit man to a serial killer."

I nod and point out the differences in his postoffence behavior compared to a sexual serial killer, too—a hit man doesn't need to spend time with his victims after he's killed them. "The media tactics are another point of difference," I continue. "Unlike serial killers, who often have an emotional need to follow media coverage of their kills and feed off that, a hit man won't feel the need to see his acts in print or on TV. In addition, he's probably already left the country, so any media interest generated here wouldn't reach him in China."

"What if we tried to release something to the Chinese media?" Hana asks.

"Interesting…" I think about the repercussions. "I can't imagine much would rattle our guy, but it might annoy him. He separates his personal life in China from his business life in the rest of the world, and if he suddenly reads a piece in a Chinese newspaper…" I pause, still thinking it through. "But I doubt we'd get any coverage from the Chinese media anyway."

Thirty

I've barely sat down after the meeting when Petrov's at my desk.

"Feel like a coffee, Anderson?"

I don't know whether Petrov really wants a coffee or if he needs to talk to me in private. Either way, caffeine never goes astray. My system definitely needs a shot of something, and sugar and caffeine are my drugs of choice. It helps that they're both legal. We walk across to Westwood Village and the nearest Starbucks.

"What can I get you?"

"Caramel macchiato. Soy milk."

Petrov nods and orders my macchiato and a cappuccino for himself. He looks around and comes a little closer. "Let's release the State Department information on our suspects to Williams and Kim at—" he looks at his watch "— eleven."

A little less than half an hour away.

"Sure thing. I also want to check with Lee's cousin on the car stuff. Given not many people drive in China, it might confirm one of the five men or Park Ling as our prime suspect." I'd called Petrov on Thursday night and told him everything I knew about Park Ling, including the fact that Lee knew him when he was growing up in China and that he had used the name Quon Liao as a child. Like me, Petrov thinks it's a strong lead, that Park Ling might be our hit man. No doubt he passed the information on to De Luca and Brady, but Williams and Hana are in the dark.

"Good idea. What time is it there now?"

"About two-thirty in the morning."

Petrov whistles. "It's not a showstopper. It can wait until this afternoon."

"Yes, sir."

Our orders are called out and Petrov grabs both cups, passing the caramel macchiato to me. "How do your suspects compare with the profile?"

"Chung wasn't able to give us a lot of information—date of birth, marital status, army service—so five names fit," I say, heading out the door. "Park Ling is the best fit, with extra military service coupled with Lee's knowledge of him, but the car may be the clincher. Anything from the facial recognition software?"

"You betcha. You were right, An Kwan and Lok Ng are one and the same person. And the other two photos are also very similar. Our man was positive with An Kwan and Lok Ng, but felt the matches with the other two photos were probable rather than definite."

"Wow. So four out of our original ten names could be one person anyway." That reduces our suspect pool. "Pity we don't have a pic of Quon Liao from customs." If Quon Liao is another alias, it'd reduce the suspect list even more.

"What about Park Ling? Can your Beijing contact get a photo of him?"

"I'll find out and get it e-mailed across ASAP." We're getting closer to the office and I slow down. "Have you had another look at Agent Rory Parsons?" I speak quietly, sensitive to our location—only a block away from the Bureau and the Gang Impact Team's headquarters.

"Yes." Petrov moves closer. "De Luca and I went over his file again early this morning. He's a definite contender. But let's see how our test pans out with Agents Williams and Kim. Hopefully that will cross Agent Kim's name off our list once and for all."

I nod. I can't add the extra piece of knowledge that my vision showed a woman sitting on a park bench who received something in an envelope from an apparent stranger. It may not even be related to the case or the mole.

Petrov grimaces. "If it turns out to be Agent Kim, Joe will be pissed."

I nod. "He trusts her."

"Yup."

We walk the rest of the way in silence.

Back at my desk, I e-mail Chung, via Lee for translation, asking for a photo of Park Ling and the other men from our list who entered the US before we started capturing photo images at entry points. I also attach my profile of the killer to the e-mail. We have a good suspect list, but maybe something else will ring a bell for Chung in my profile.

I'm just hitting Send on the e-mail when I sense someone hovering over me. I look up to see Hana leaning on the partition of my desk.

"Hi. How's your first day back treating you so far?"

"Good."

Her eyes narrow. "You look a little tired."

"I'm fine."

She's silent, assessing. Her concern seems genuine—and I remind myself again that before I knew we had a mole in the task force, I liked Hana.

"Really. I'm fine." It's only a half lie. For the most part I do feel okay, but I know I'm still below par physically. Normally I don't mind being a desk jockey—and lots of my work is deskbound—but now that I'm forced into it I feel like a caged animal, desperate to escape.

"Two weeks isn't much time off." Hana speaks slowly and softly. "Especially after a gunshot wound."

I can see where this conversation is going—she's offering herself as my confidant.

"If you ever want to talk…you know, about the shooting…" Her voice is still soft. "Well, you know where I am. And I know how hard it can be for a woman in this world." She gestures around at the open-plan office full of mostly male law-enforcement officers. "You feel like you have to act tough, tougher than the guys. But you don't have to do that with me."

I nod. She's making sense and my gut instinct is that Hana is one of the good guys. But even with this gift of mine, my gut can be wrong. I can't control what I see. And while I can do things to help induce a vision, it's not like I can touch Hana and instantly know her deepest and darkest secrets. It simply doesn't work like that. And as much as I might try to replay the vision of the woman on the park bench, I can't see her face. Can't be sure one way or another if it's Hana or some complete stranger.

The mole issue aside, I really don't know her well enough to open up to her, to let her know that it's not just bravado, that I really am fine. And I certainly don't want to tell her that taking a bullet in the shoulder is nothing compared to what's happened to me in the past. So instead I just say, "Thanks, Hana. I appreciate that." I keep my voice open and friendly, but the small nod and smile she gives me tell me that she knows I won't be taking her up on the offer.

"Well, you know where to find me," she says, giving it one last shot before changing the topic. "You doing anything exciting tonight?"

Tonight! It suddenly hits me—Darren. Darren will be arriving in L.A. later today. Yikes. Part of me actually considers calling up and canceling, making an excuse. But I know I'd be avoiding him because I'm just plain scared, not because I'm not ready for a relationship. And how does that saying go: Feel the fear and do it anyway. Mind you, I'd rather not feel the fear at all.

"I've got a friend coming up from Arizona. You?"

"Party. Feel free to drop in with your friend if you like." Hana writes an address down on a Post-it note.

"Your party?"

"Yeah, my and Jae's. Except I was supposed to invite people weeks ago, but I got so caught up in this case…"

"I know what you mean."

* * *

Right at 11:00 a.m., my phone rings.

"You ready?" It's Petrov.

"Yup."

"See you in meeting room two in five minutes."

I watch the others head toward the meeting room one by one, obviously as Petrov calls them. I'm the last person to arrive.

"Okay, people," Petrov starts, "Anderson's got some great news for us." Petrov's excitement is convincing. I hope mine will be, too.

"I just heard back from the US State Department and we've finally got our list of multiple entrants from China. And it's a small list, ten names, one too young to fit our profile."

"That's great!" Hana's enthusiastic.

Williams and De Luca echo her thoughts.

"It gets even better…." Petrov prompts.

"I've had a quick look at the names, and three stick out because they flew Air China, which would fit with my profile."

"Have we got anything on these three individuals?" Williams asks.

"Not yet," I lie. "But I've sent the list through to my contact in Beijing and I'm just waiting for it to hit a reasonable hour over there before I call him."

"What time is it there now?" De Luca asks.

"Three in the morning."

"Anderson also noted that some of the individuals looked similar," Petrov says.

"How similar?" Williams is keen.

"At least two of them look like they might be the same person." Again, I rewind to where we were a couple of days ago. "The different names could simply be aliases for the one person."

Williams raises his eyebrows. "How can we confirm it?"

Petrov responds, "I've suggested facial recognition software. We'll be running it soon."

"What about Mee, sir? Any news from your agents?" Hana asks Petrov.

"They're following up a reported sighting of her from two days ago. It's a little cold, but it's something."

Hana nods. "Her students are calling me. Asking for information."

"I understand, Agent Kim. I'll let you know as soon as we have something concrete."

She manages a small smile. "Thanks."

With the meeting dismissed, we all return to our desks. I'm only back at mine for a couple of minutes when I get a text message from Petrov. It simply says: *Now we wait.*

With the list through and the profile done, my only other task before speaking to Chung Lee in China is to go over the personnel files…again. Maybe I can induce a more useful vision. I send around a quick e-mail to let the others know I'll be working from home for the rest of the day and will e-mail them as soon as I've heard from my Beijing contact. I also decide to phone the homicide cop investigating Santorini's video-game-arcade murder before I head off. It's been over two weeks since I profiled the boy's killer, and hopefully by now the police have been able to use the profile to help them narrow down their suspects—or find a new one.

"It's Agent Sophie Anderson here from the FBI. Just wanted to quickly check on your progress on the Santorini file?"

"Hey, Agent Anderson. I've been meaning to give you a call."

"Yes?" Hopefully he's got good news.

"We found our guy and got a confession last week."

"That's fantastic! Who?"

"A boy from Santorini's school called Alex Tower."

The name doesn't ring a bell from the case file.

"Turns out Tower had a crush on Santorini's cousin. The feeling wasn't mutual so Santorini warned him off."

"Really? And this didn't come up before?"

"The incident happened three months ago. The family had forgotten about it, until we questioned them again asking about any boys in Santorini's life who had lost their temper in the past. Tower's name came up." He clears his throat. "Eventually Tower admitted he'd run into Santorini in the arcade and asked how his cousin was. Santorini warned him off in no uncertain terms, so our perp followed him into the bathroom."

"And released three months of pent-up anger in one short burst."

"Yup."

I thank the detective and hang up. It's nice when the requesting agency or cop passes the information on straightaway, but experience has shown me they don't always think to call the profiler. Sometimes because they don't want to give any of the credit to someone else, and sometimes it's purely an oversight due to a heavy workload. Either way, I've got the outcome I wanted—resolution and justice for the Santorini family.

I've only been home for a couple of hours when my cell rings—Darren.

"Hey. I'm in a cab on the way to your place now."

"Okay," I squeak. "See you soon." I take a deep breath. Who needs caffeine and sugar? The thought of Darren arriving on my doorstep has done the job of a triple espresso and two hundred grams of chocolate…dark chocolate.

I try to keep my mind off his imminent arrival by tidying the house. I clean the kitchen first, putting away this morning's breakfast dishes and wiping down the benches. I then have the crazy notion of vacuuming, even though Mum only vacuumed a few days ago. But within a couple of strokes I realize that's way too painful on my shoulder, even though it's the opposite arm, so I put it away and move on to the bathroom and toilet. Once they're done I get a towel and washcloth out for Darren. I'm about to get one of my spare sets of sheets out for the sofa bed when it hits me—Where will Darren be sleeping tonight?

Just as that thought makes me go into panic mode, the security buzzer sounds. Maybe I can hide? Not answer the door? Another deep breath.

I don't say anything into the intercom, frightened my voice will give away my emotional state. Instead, I just release the security door.

By the time my front doorbell rings, I'm close to hyper-ventilating. How can I answer the door like this? Pull yourself together, woman. I try to bring some of my professional calm into the equation. I can act, just like I often have to when questioning a suspect. I take a deep breath in, then out, then swing the door open.

"Hi, Darren."

"Hi." He grins.

I'm immobile.

"Can I come in?"

"Sure. Sorry." I aim for breezy, but I don't think I pull it off. I move out of the doorway, down the hall and into the kitchen. "So how was your flight?" I turn around. He's grinning way too much. He's enjoying this. Enjoying my nervousness.

"Good. The flight was good." He walks straight into the living room and puts his overnight bag on the floor next to the sofa bed. At least he didn't put it in the bedroom.

"Thirsty?" My voice cracks a little. Man, this is torture. I'm so out of practice it's not funny. Well, maybe it's funny for Darren. "Beer?"

"Sure."

I open a beer for Darren and hand it to him across the kitchen counter, trying to hide the slight shake in my hand.

"You're not having one?"

"I've got an important call coming in."

"Oh…" Disappointment. He takes a few steps back, moving across my small dining area until he's leaning on the back of the sofa. "When?"

"Five."

"So you need to work now? I can disappear for a couple of hours."

"No, it's okay. We're kinda waiting on this call…for the case. Not much more to do until it comes in." I don't tell him about the personnel files now locked away in my briefcase.

He takes a swig of beer. "I see."

Silence.

I'm still standing in the kitchen, the kitchen counter and dining room table between me and Darren. And that's just fine by me for the moment.

"So you're getting close? To finding the killer?"

"Yeah, we are actually. We've even got a couple of names. The call I'm waiting for is from China. Checking a few details."

"Sounds promising." Darren pushes himself off the sofa back and starts heading my way. I hold his gaze until he's at the kitchen bench, then I turn around to the fridge.

"Think I might have a juice."

I hear Darren's footsteps, getting closer, then a clunk as he puts his beer on the counter. He comes in behind me, close, and his hand reaches over my shoulder to close the fridge. He leans down slightly, and I can feel his breath on my neck. His arms close around my waist as he kisses the side of my neck, ever so gently. My body takes over and I instinctively lean back into him, letting the back of my head rest against his face. His kisses run the length of my shoulder, my good shoulder, before his right hand comes up to my face and he slowly spins me around. Our faces are touching and I open my eyes. It takes a moment of adjustment as my eyes focus and I see Darren up close and personal. He keeps his eyes shut, but his breathing is fast.

I run my hand along his jaw and bring him closer, shutting my eyes at the same time. My nerves are gone, replaced by desire. Our lips meet, fast, hot kisses, the sort you only get when sexual tension has been building…and building…and building.

I bring him in closer to me, my left leg encircling his waist. He moves us back until we hit the kitchen bench on my side. He lifts me up onto the bench, but it's the side with the cupboards and I forget to duck. My head hits the cupboard with a clunk.

"Ouch!" I break the silence but don't stop kissing him.

"Sorry," he mumbles into me, also unwilling to break the contact between our lips. He grabs hold of me, taking my full weight, and spins us around before backing us onto the other kitchen bench—the one that borders my kitchen and dining room.

I try to get closer to him, but our bodies are already flush against each other. I move on to his clothes, pulling his sweater up. As it comes up over his shoulders, we have to stop kissing for it to pass over his head. But as soon as it's clear, Darren brings me in close again so we can kiss. I run my hands over his chest, back, arms and stomach, reveling in the sensation of smooth, hot skin under my fingers.

He starts unbuttoning my shirt and then pushes it gently over my shoulders. His fingers run over the small plaster patch there and he stops kissing me, but keeps our foreheads pressed together.

"Oh, Soph…"

"I know." When Darren was shot I was with someone else. I was attracted to Darren and I cared about him, but we'd only known each other for a few days. Now, even before today, it would be completely different. If it had been Darren who had been shot two weeks ago I would have been going out of my mind. He tried to express it in the hospital but I brushed him aside.

I tilt my head back and bring his lips to mine again, eager to pick up where we left off. After a couple of minutes he undoes my bra and starts kissing and caressing my breasts in between kissing my lips.

As each second goes by I want him more and more, more than I've ever wanted any man before. I can feel him against me, but it's not enough. I undo his belt and jeans, pushing them over his slender hips, and then I pull him closer again. I can feel him step out of his jeans, one leg at a time. My pencil-line skirt has already ridden up my thighs and onto my hips, but I pull it up more. The sensation of his skin on mine, so close to me, makes me go even wilder.

I pull him closer and then inside me. We both let out a deep breath.

"Oh, Sophie," he says into my ear.

It's Darren who comes to his senses first. "Condom." The word rushes out of his lips on an uncontrolled exhale.

"Uh-huh," I murmur, not wanting to stop for anything.

He lifts me up and carries me to the living room, and then lowers me down onto the floor, using one hand to hunt around in his bag. Soon he comes out with a condom.

I'm usually sensible, but this time the few seconds seem unbearable. "No," I gasp as he unlinks us, tears the condom wrapper and rolls it on. He's fast, and the whole procedure takes less than ten seconds. We both let out a sigh of relief, or maybe just of lust, as we reposition ourselves. It feels different, not as good, but the seconds helped me come to my senses a little more. At least Darren was thinking.

I flip us over, my knees on either side of him, and we hold each other close as I writhe on top of him. After a while, his breathing becomes heavier, and the thought that he's about to orgasm topples me over the edge, too. His groans are followed closely by mine, before our bodies are still.

We caress each other, silent for a little while, before Darren says, "I'm sorry. I'd wanted it to be a little more romantic...tender."

I push off the ground and let my face hover above his. "Darren, that was perfect." I smile. "We can do tender later."

He laughs and I watch as his beautiful dimples form.

"Man, your dimples are sexy."

"Really? I always thought they were too boyish to be sexy."

"No." There *is* a boyishness about Darren, and I remember thinking when I first met him that he looked like a boy who'd grown too fast for his body, but now that boyishness has become sexy. I like his long limbs, and today I've unearthed good muscle tone on his naturally slender frame.

He runs his hand along my face. "You're so beautiful." He sighs. "I've wanted this from the moment I first saw you." He laughs. "You certainly put an end to my wicked ways. I haven't been able to think about another woman since I met you."

"Thanks...I think." Then I shake my head. "And you thought this would be slow and tender after fourteen months of celibacy and sexual tension?"

He laughs again. "True."

I give him a jab on the arm. "And I notice you came prepared!"

He shrugs and gives me his best boyish grin. "I was hopeful. You sounded…different on the phone."

"And you, you bastard. You were laughing at me when you got here."

"Well, come on—it was pretty funny seeing you nervous. I've never seen you nervous, Sophie. And all on my account." He pauses. "I guess it made for a nice switch-up."

"Maybe." I roll to his side and rest my head on his chest.

"How's the shoulder?" he asks.

"A little sore."

"Hope we didn't give it too much of a workout."

"I'll be fine."

"So, any plans for tonight?" He strokes my hair. "Besides the obvious?"

"We've been invited to a party. But I've also got some nice food for dinner and a bottle of champagne."

"So you were prepared, too?"

I give him a cheeky grin. "It is New Year's Eve."

We're still lounging about in each other's arms when the call comes in. I shift into professional mode quickly and easily—even though I am still half-naked.

"Hi, Lee."

"Hey, Sophie. I'll dial Chung in now."

I wait until I hear two voices speaking in rapid Chinese and then Lee says, "Okay, shoot."

"Did he get my most recent e-mail?"

After a few words in Chinese, Lee says, "I've translated it and forwarded it on, but he hasn't checked his public account yet."

"Okay. I want to find out more about Park Ling. Can you please ask Chung if he can do a search to see what type of car a person drives?"

This time during the exchange, Chung gives a short, sharp chuckle.

"My cousin wants me to explain that car use isn't like the US. Not many people own a car."

"I know, one car to every thousand people. But I think our guy, our perp does. And remember, Park Ling does have a driver's license. It would be really helpful if he can access those records. And I really need a photo of him."

Following another exchange that lasts a minute or so, Lee says, "My cousin's impressed that you know the car stats." Again, a brief exchange in Chinese. "Can you stay on the line? He can look it up for you now."

I smile. "Tell him thanks."

It's only a few minutes before the two cousins converse again.

"Okay, Park Ling drives a 2006 Chery QQ. So you think he's your guy?"

"Looks like it. But we'll have to wait until he comes to the US again before we can intercept him or maybe start the extradition process."

"You don't want Chung to pay him a visit?"

"No! Definitely not. I'm sure Chung could handle it," I say, even though I'm not sure at all, "but if Park Ling is our guy, he's extremely dangerous. You know exactly what I'm talking about."

"Yes, he is. Okay, I'll tell Chung."

"Maybe Chung can have a look at the profile I sent through and see what he thinks about Ling as a match. Or maybe there's something else in the profile he can check out."

"I'll pass it on."

"Thanks, Lee."

"You're welcome. See you back in class…soon, I hope."

"It'll probably be another three weeks."

"Okay. Take care. And Happy New Year."

We say goodbye.

"Well?" Darren says. "Good news?"

"Looks that way. I just have to send an e-mail and then I'm all yours."

"You're on."

I quickly type an e-mail telling the team about Park Ling, his use of Quon Liao as an alias, and the fact that Quon Liao's entry details into the US match some of our ViCAP dates. Once I've covered the similarities between Park Ling and our profile, including the fact that he drives a Chery QQ, I finish the e-mail off by saying: *I think we've found our contract killer.* It's true, I do think we've found the killer, but the line is direct enough that if Williams or Hana is our leak, they'll touch base with their Yakuza contact and the info will get back to Young. I send the e-mail to Petrov, De Luca, Hana and Williams.

"Done."

"Good." Darren's behind me, ready to start all over again. "I want my shot at tender now."

I laugh. "Let's try our best."

Thirty-One

I'm on a plane, reading. I glance at my watch, and then pull my personal screen out in front of me. Using the touch screen, I bring up the flight's progress. Hawaii. Eight hours to go. Enough time for a good sleep. I recline my seat fully, taking up the extra space of first class to get horizontal.

I drift to sleep, an image of my target in my mind. He's committed to memory now and I'll recognize him anywhere.

I wake up with a start. My bedside clock flashes 3:44 a.m. Still half-asleep, I reach out and pick up the notebook and pen and jot down what I can remember of the dream. The map showed the plane's progress, with the start city being Beijing and the end city being Los Angeles. That, coupled with the fact that the subject of my dream could afford first class, makes me think it's related to this case, to our hit man. The guy was also thinking about his target, but I can't bring that face into my conscious mind.

I get another start when I hear a groan, right next to me. I turn around quickly…Darren…that's right. I smile and snuggle into him. It's been a long while since I shared a bed with anyone and I'd forgotten how nice it is to roll over in the middle of the night and feel their skin against mine.

A couple of hours later I wake up feeling groggy. The radio's blasting in my ear and I hit the snooze button. Even that's not like me—normally I get up first go.

Darren rolls into me. "You really have to get up?" His voice is filled with sleep haze.

"Yeah."

"But it's New Year's Day," he mumbles.

"Oh, yeah." I'd forgotten. "You're right, we're off today." We don't always get public holidays off, but Petrov has given the team this one.

"So I've got you all to myself?"

"Uh-huh."

He rolls me into him and starts kissing my neck.

"I could get used to this," I say.

"Me, too."

We finally surface around ten, driven out of bed by hunger more than anything else. We sit across from one another at the table, eating breakfast and grinning. Soon the dream sinks into my conscious mind.

"I had a dream last night."

"What sort of dream?" Darren gives me a wink.

"Not that sort…the other sort."

"About the case you're working on?"

"Yeah. From the hit man's point of view." I have to assume it was our killer, on the way to a hit. But was it Saito, one of the other targets we've identified in the US, or a new hit, someone who may be about to lose their life? I still can't tell the timing of my visions, and because I get flashes and dreams from the past, present and future, it's impossible to know. I may be gaining some control over my skills, but I'm by no means a master. "I was on an airplane, Beijing to L.A."

"And that's consistent with your vic's murder?"

"Yes. But it could be another hit—past or future."

"Take me through it. Was there anything that would indicate a date?"

I think about the elements in the dream. "The killer was reading…"

"Can you see what?"

I focus on it, but can't get a visual image on the reading matter. "No." It could have been a newspaper with the day's date on it or it could have been a book.

"What about his surroundings? In the plane?"

"He was traveling first class. But that's in line with our conclusion that we're dealing with a high-level, freelance professional. Someone skilled, who's called in at great expense." I sigh. "Nothing new, nothing that will help me push the investigation in one direction."

"Well, it sounds like the investigation doesn't need help at the moment anyway. You've ID'd your guy, right?"

"We've got a very good suspect." But another part of the investigation could do with help—the leak. Not to mention figuring out who contracted Park Ling in the first place.

"There's something else, isn't there?" Darren studies my face. He does know me well.

"Yes. But I can't discuss it…with anyone."

He nods. "I understand." And he really does.

Darren's flight is early the next morning, but not early enough that I can drop him at the airport and still get into work at the normal time of 7:30 or 8:00 a.m.—not with the 405 between me and my desk. So we have to say our goodbyes at my apartment.

"I'll see you soon?" he says.

"That'd be good." We don't say anything, but we know it'll be hard to see much of each other around our work schedules, especially with a two-hour flight complicating things. I can't leave L.A. unless I'm on official vacation time, so we'll be relying on Darren's two days off per week and him flying up.

"We can make this work, Sophie."

I narrow my eyes. "Hey, you reading my mind or what?"

He smiles. "We can. I know we can."

He's right. Lots of people only see their partners on the weekend. If we can somehow sync our days off…

"Any chance you can change your shift work to Monday to Friday?" I ask. Homicide tends to be busiest on the weekend, so it can be hard for a homicide cop to get Saturdays and Sundays off.

"I'll give it a shot."

"That'd be great." As a more office-bound employee, my official working week is Monday to Friday, but I'm also on call 24/7.

He smiles and we lean in together for another kiss. The kiss soon turns into more, until Darren pulls away, grinning. "I'm going to miss my plane, Soph."

"Okay. Go. I'll see you soon."

We give each other one more quick kiss, and then he leaves.

I shut the door and let out a large, satisfied sigh. My best New Year's Eve ever. I quickly shower and get dressed for work—Darren's not the only one running late.

I feel weird hopping into my car and starting the drive to the office without having done any exercise. Exercising is all about setting a routine and sticking to it—I hope my six weeks off won't end with me lazing in bed hitting the snooze button when I should be at the gym or out jogging. Although, having someone lying next to you isn't exactly incentive to get out of bed. Besides, I did get exercise of a sort this morning....

I'm working on the spreadsheet of Lee's US-based kung fu practitioners when I look up to find Hana leaning on my desk.

"You coming?" she asks.

A glance at my watch confirms it's time for our 9:00 a.m. meeting. "Wow," I say. "Time flies."

"When you're having fun." She completes the cliché.

"Yeah, fun."

We're both being sarcastic, of course. The truth is, time flies when you're busy, engrossed in a case.

"You working on the spreadsheet?" Hana asks.

"Yeah." I shrug. "I know we've got a good suspect, but I decided it wouldn't hurt to finish the task off…just in case we find something to indicate our killer's not Chinese, not Park Ling."

"You think that's possible?"

I shake my head. "No. I think he's our guy. But like I said, it's good to cover all bases."

"I haven't done anything on my list since Monday afternoon, to be honest."

"It was the New Year." I stand up. "How was your party?"

"Awesome. We had a great night. Although Jae had about thirty friends there and I only had ten." She laughs.

"Sorry I didn't make it."

"That's okay. It was late notice."

Even if I'd had all the notice in the world I doubt I would have gone—Darren and I weren't interested in anyone's company but each other's.

Hana and I are the last ones to arrive in the meeting room. We don't even have our butts on the seats when Petrov starts.

"So, now that we've found a suspect, we need to look at gathering more evidence against him and confirming that he really is our guy. Let's start by focusing on who contracted him."

"Can't we just ask him?" Williams says.

"*You* want to fly over to China and interview the kung fu master?" Petrov says sarcastically.

"Point taken."

"We have to start the extradition process or wait until he tries to get into the US again. His prints, aliases and iris scans have all been flagged."

"What if he uses a new alias…new prints and contacts?" I ask.

Petrov cocks his head. "That'll make things difficult."

"Have you actually started the extradition process yet?" Williams says. "If Ling doesn't know we're on to him, there's no reason why he wouldn't go with an alias he used in the past."

"But he could have other names he uses, or he's intending to use," I say.

"We could run facial recognition software over all pics of Chinese nationals entering the US," Hana suggests. "I know there'll be a delay because the airport's not fitted with the software, but we could organize to get pics e-mailed to someone on a daily basis or after each flight's come in. And then we get someone to check the pics."

"Good work, Hana." Petrov smiles, happy to close a potential loop. "You want to make it happen?"

Hana nods and scribbles it down in her notebook. I hope Hana's not the mole—otherwise the facial recognition task might be going nowhere.

"Now, back to our contractor. The key is to find out why Jun Saito was targeted. That should lead us to the who." Petrov pauses. "Let's go back in time, see what we can dig up in his past."

"I'll look after that if you like, sir," I volunteer, knowing that I already have an insight into Saito's past and I know one thing no one else does—Saito didn't kill his pregnant girlfriend. So who did? And who was following him that night? If I can discover that, I might find our contractor. It has to be someone who lived in Japan at the time, then moved to the US. Maybe Yakuza. "I'd like to look at everything we've got on the Yakuza here in L.A., including their ties with Japan."

"Let's work on this one together, Anderson," De Luca says. "I'm up to speed on most of the players." He certainly is up to speed—he's got a direct line to Agent Dan Young and the L.A. Yakuza.

An hour later, Agent Joe De Luca and I are in a meeting room, blinds drawn and door shut. He's being careful, but I guess after over a year he just wants the leak stopped— for good.

"So, this is everything we've got, including all the information Young's fed us over the past twelve months. Anything flagged or highlighted has come directly from him and is something that only Petrov, Brady and I know about."

I nod, flicking through the papers briefly. On the top is the Yakuza organization chart, complete with digital images and the players' names. There are lots of gaps, but there are also lots of names. "When was the last time you spoke to Young?"

"Six days ago. We're scheduled for another meet tomorrow."

"It's always weekly?"

"Uh-huh. Unless he can't check in for some reason."

"He must be sick of it," I say.

"Yeah, he is. At first it was exciting, but things have got increasingly difficult as time's gone on."

I nod, well aware of the psychological impact of deep cover. He's completely alienated from his real friends and family, and may even find himself liking some of his new "friends." Plus, given his standing in the Yakuza, he's going to be witnessing crime and be powerless to do anything about it in the short term.

"We need to find the leak and get him out."

"That's the plan." De Luca leans back. "But that's been the plan for over a year now." He's disheartened.

"But you must have got some great information from him in the past twelve months? Stuff that's really made a difference."

"Some. But we can't act on much of it until he's out. Otherwise Yakuza would start looking at its people and Young would probably be the first suspect—he came from interstate and is new to the L.A. arm. Most of the other guys grew up with each other. They know each other's families, their girlfriends, who was a shit at school…everything." The disheartenment has turned to concern.

"We'll get him out soon," I say, hopeful.

De Luca nods, but without confidence.

I bring out Saito's file. "I've had a thought. On Saito."

"Yes?"

"Suppose he didn't kill his girlfriend."

"His prints were on the murder weapon, Anderson. Open and shut."

"I know. But maybe too open and shut. Like it was a setup."

De Luca's face tells me he's not going with it.

"Seriously, De Luca. Think about it…Saito had been careful the other times, careful most of his life. He only ever did time once, even though he was linked to murders. He was too careful for something like this." I point to the photos of Saito's girlfriend, covered in her own blood.

"So you're thinking someone else murdered the girlfriend?" De Luca still isn't convinced but at least he's considering it now. "But why?"

I shrug. "Don't know. I'm brainstorming here. The girlfriend's death was personal…some sort of punishment."

"By who?"

"Could be one of the bosses. Maybe Saito stepped out of line. Or it could be related to his murder vics." I take out photos of the three men Saito is suspected of killing from 1990 to 1993. "One of these guys."

"Payback." De Luca makes it a statement, not a question. I've piqued his interest.

"If that's the case we'd be looking at someone close to one of these three men. A professional acquaintance, maybe their boss or some other colleague, a family member or a friend. They suspect Saito, or maybe they know for sure he's the doer, so they take their own justice. They make him suffer…"

"They kill his girl." De Luca completes the sentence.

"Yup."

"I like it, Anderson. But I think we're talking a family member or friend, not a business acquaintance. Crime organizations like the Yakuza have unwritten codes of conduct."

"And killing someone's girlfriend is overstepping the mark?"

"Usually. Don't get me wrong, it happens in extreme circumstances. But it's more likely to be personal than business."

"Okay." I look at the L.A. Yakuza files and the Asian Boyz files. "So we need to find someone in here who knew one of Saito's Tokyo victims."

"You still got that Interpol contact?"

"Uh-huh."

"I know we've got Saito's file, but maybe it's time to get more detailed info."

I nod. "The full files on all the murder victims, info on the Yakuza in Tokyo around 1990, and anything else Interpol in Japan can dig up."

"Yup."

I make a quick call to Latoya Burges and pass on our latest request. Another waiting game. But in the meantime we've still got plenty of paperwork to keep us going.

De Luca takes a deep breath and blows it out. "Let's get to it."

Thirty-Two

At nine o'clock on Wednesday night I get a call from Petrov.

"We need to meet. At the diner. See you there in half an hour." The line goes dead.

Something's up.

I get out of my tracksuit and pull on some jeans, a black sweater, my shoulder holster and gun and my leather jacket. It'll take me only fifteen minutes to get to the diner, but I leave as soon as I'm dressed. I'd rather wait around there than here.

I'm the first to arrive and take a seat in the end booth. I order a coffee, thinking I might be in for a long night, and wait.

Five minutes later De Luca shows up. "Hi, Anderson." His face is tense, with his brow furrowed and his jaw muscles working.

"You know what this is about?" I ask.

"Uh-huh." He slides in opposite me. "Agent Young didn't report in this evening."

"He ever missed a check-in before?"

"A couple times. No point checking in if it's going to blow your cover."

"This time's different?"

He sighs. "Maybe not. It's just—" De Luca stops short and looks behind me. The waitress is within earshot. She asks De Luca what he wants and De Luca orders a coffee. Once she's out of range, De Luca leans in. "It's a combination of things this time—events that may have led to his discovery."

"Such as?"

Again, De Luca's eyes are on something behind me. I turn around to see Brady on his way down to our booth. He looks different, not himself, but then I realize it's because he's wearing jeans and a denim jacket and I've never seen him in anything but a suit.

"Anderson, De Luca." He gives us both nods.

The waitress arrives with De Luca's coffee and Brady orders one for himself plus an extra one for Petrov.

De Luca is silent so I prompt him. "Why are you worried this time?"

"First off there's still a question mark about whether Ken was supposed to harm or kill you guys. Moto confirmed the order as not to kill, but there's still doubt in Dan's mind. And now we've potentially siphoned information through to the leak. What if it came through and Dan asked one too many questions about the source? Our plan could have endangered him."

"Dan's been undercover for a while, he knows how much he can push."

Brady nods. "Anderson's right, De Luca. I'm sure he'll check in tomorrow."

"That's the protocol?" I ask.

Petrov walks in and strides down to our booth. He slides in next to me, giving us all nods and a communal "Hey."

Once the waitress has poured two more cups of coffee and departed De Luca continues. "His brief is to make contact as soon as possible after the scheduled meet. Maybe late tonight, maybe tomorrow…maybe the next day." De Luca slurps down a large mouthful of coffee.

"I'm sure he's okay, Joe." Petrov's voice is reassuring.

De Luca shakes his head. "I've got a bad feeling about this op. It's been the same ever since Saito got offed." Sometimes cops have to trust their gut instincts. De Luca knows Young, he knows the context, so if he's worried, I'm worried.

I bite my lip. "Can we extract him?"

"That's what we need to talk about."

"I understand you're worried, De Luca, but it's early days." Brady holds his hands around the warm mug of coffee. "We don't want to burn that bridge unnecessarily."

"How long then, Brady?" De Luca's voice holds unchecked aggression.

"A sensible and reasonable amount of time." Brady keeps his tone even yet forceful.

De Luca shakes his head. "That could be too late."

"Can you initiate contact?" I ask.

De Luca is silent at first. "We have procedures in place, of course, but it's usually Young who initiates contact."

"So what's the procedure for you initiating?" I ask, feeling like a bit of a peacekeeper.

"I send him a text. But with a new, untraceable SIM card to be on the safe side."

"Okay…so let's do that."

De Luca drums his fingers on the table. "What to put in the message? Young's mother has been sick recently, so if her condition changes I'm supposed to send a message that says 'Call Mom.' And if I think his cover's blown, it's 'Haven't seen you in ages.'"

"This is a little different." Brady leans back.

"Yes." De Luca is still hostile.

"How about 'It feels like I haven't seen you in ages,'" Petrov suggests.

De Luca nods. "I've got a couple of spare SIM cards at my task force desk."

Brady stands up. "Good luck. Let me know how it goes." He leaves, his half-full coffee cup still steaming on the table.

"What an ass," De Luca says as soon as Brady's out the door.

Petrov shrugs. "He's not that bad. People skills just aren't his forte."

"I'll say."

Petrov stands. "Come on, let's drop into the office."

The three of us walk the couple of blocks to L.A.'s FBI field office, sign in and ride the elevator to the fifteenth floor. Except for Petrov and me making a few reassuring comments to De Luca, we're silent.

At his desk, De Luca hunts around for a locked money box and opens it up. Inside is about a hundred dollars in smaller notes, a couple of keys, a phone and a few SIM cards.

"Okay." He takes the SIM card out of his phone and puts in one of the new ones. While he works the keypad, Petrov and I wait.

"Done."

Petrov nods. "Now we wait." He leans against the desk behind him.

"What if Young doesn't have his phone switched on? Or doesn't hear it?" I am worried about Young, but part of me agrees with Brady—he's deep undercover and there'll be times he can't check in.

"Young always has his cell on, and handy." Sure enough, as if on cue, De Luca's phone gives a double beep.

"That's promising." Petrov pushes himself fully upright.

"What does it say?" I ask, peering over De Luca's shoulder.

De Luca reads out the message. *"Yes. Feels like ages to me, too...too long. The info came through."*

"Is that code?" I ask.

"No. It's not code." De Luca hunches over.

"So he can't get away and he's worried his cover's been blown?" Petrov confirms.

"Yes."

"What about the info part?" I ask. "It must mean the information about Park Ling and Quon Liao."

"Uh-huh." De Luca takes a deep breath. "I wonder how easy it is for him to receive and send messages. Phone calls, even."

"Well, obviously he's still got his phone on him. That's a good sign," I say.

"But for how long?" De Luca starts pacing. "If I send another text right away, it might arouse even more suspicion. But if I wait, he might not be able to get the message or text me back."

We're silent for a few beats.

"You have to text him, now." I bite my lip. "Like you said, it might be the last chance."

De Luca stops pacing and lets out another quick, sharp breath. "Okay. I'll say, 'Maybe it's time to go home. Name the time and place.' That way if he wants out, we can extract him tonight, now."

Petrov and I both nod, and then De Luca presses the send button.

Agent Dan Young never responds.

The next morning it's business as usual at the office, with most people oblivious to our predicament. Only De Luca, Petrov, Brady and I know that our agent in the Yakuza is in danger…maybe already dead. Although if Young's cover has been blown, then the leak probably knows all about his predicament.

"The fact that the names of our two suspects filtered through to the Yakuza indicates the leak must be Agent Williams or Hana." Petrov's comment is met with silence. It's no revelation, but it still stops us in our tracks.

"But how would that put Young in danger? How would it blow his cover?"

We're silent at first. Brady leans in, resting his arms on the table.

"Maybe something else blew his cover," I suggest.

"Like what?" Petrov drums his fingers on the table.

"Is it possible someone's been eavesdropping on our conversations?" I move us on to another option. "Either physically or electronically?"

Brady stands up. "Let's organize a bug sweep. See what we get." He pauses. "But it will have to be done out of hours, when our mole isn't around."

"We should also check the diner, sir," Petrov says.

"Given that's where most of our sensitive conversations took place."

Brady gives a short nod. "I'll authorize the paperwork. Get it rolling." He walks to the door and turns back with his hand on the knob. "We need to keep working this case. Find out who contracted our killer. If Young is in trouble, it might be related. Especially if the hit wasn't sanctioned by Moto."

Petrov nods, slowly. "It's possible they don't know Young's DEA. Someone might be trying to clean up their own mess, and Young found out who the contract killer was or discovered who betrayed Moto in the organization."

"And so this third person needs to get to Young before he talks." I stand up, too, going with Petrov's theory. "Needs to cut him off from all communication, like his cell phone. Whoever put a contract on Saito would also need to make sure the news of his identity doesn't move up the hierarchy, to Moto." I'm eager to get back to my desk and in contact with Interpol. Hopefully the information from Japan has come through overnight.

Petrov nods. "That's what I'm thinking." He sighs. "That brings us back to Agents Williams or Kim. For the leak."

We all pause, processing the implication.

"Yes." Brady lingers at the door. "Let's get confirmation before we go to the regional bosses of the ATF or DEA, though." With that, he exits.

De Luca rubs his eyes. "What a mess. And how are we going to confirm whether it's Williams or Hana if we can't reach Young?"

"I'll put a tail on both of them." Petrov taps his pen on the paper. "See if either of them leads us to someone in Yakuza."

After a moment of silence I make a move for the door. "De Luca, I'm going to contact Interpol. See if they've got anything yet."

"I'm with you." De Luca stands up. "I'll get us set up with the paperwork we already have in one of the meeting rooms."

Back at my desk I check my e-mail, but when there's nothing new in my in-box I ring Latoya Burges at Interpol.

"Hey, Latoya. It's Sophie."

"Hey. You're chasing your Japan info?"

"Yup."

"I'm still sorting through my e-mails. Hold on a second."

I wait while she scans her in-box. "Okay, I've got something from our Japan office. I'll forward it now."

"Thanks, Latoya. You're the best."

"Yo." She hangs up and within less than a minute the e-mail arrives. It's a big file and I scan through all the different attachments. It includes full police and autopsy reports on all three murder victims, plus some historical reports on the Yakuza's activities in Tokyo. One's dated May 1990 and the other one June 1995. All useful information. I print everything out and look for De Luca. I find him in meeting room two.

We start with the crime-scene photos, even though some of them were in Saito's file already. When nothing hits us there, we move on to the surveillance shots. And that's when I see it.

"This guy looks familiar." I point to a man standing with the person who would eventually become Saito's third Tokyo victim.

De Luca takes a closer look at the pic, which hasn't scanned well. Eventually he says, "It looks a bit like Jo Hoshi, Tomi Moto's bodyguard, but the age is all wrong."

I study it once more, comparing it to our most recent pic of Jo Hoshi. "It really does look like him."

There's a knock at the door and Hana enters. "You guys aren't going to believe this—we got a hit on the facial recognition software."

"What? Our hit man's here?"

"Looks that way. The software came up with an eighty percent match, and our analyst reckons it's a definite match, bar bonier eyebrow structures and a bigger nose."

"Facial disguises," I say.

Hana nods. "That or recent plastic surgery."

"What about the fingerprints and iris scans? And the name?"

"All different. Although the first name's the same as one of our marked guys."

"So a totally new identity."

"Yup."

"When?"

"Flew in early this morning. His digital entry pic was sent to us with a lunchtime batch from State."

"This morning…" I wonder where he's staying. I feel a slight hint of dizziness, accompanied by a rush of nausea.

I'm on a plane, reading. I glance at my watch, and then pull my personal screen out in front of me. Using the touch screen, I bring up the flight's progress. Hawaii. Eight hours to go. Enough time for a good sleep. I recline my seat fully, taking up the extra space of first class to get horizontal. I drift to sleep, an image of my target in my mind. He's committed to memory now and I'll recognize him anywhere.

It's a replay of the dream I had on Monday night with one key difference. This time I remembered the target's image…it's Dan Young.

Thirty-Three

We hover around Damien Rider's computer screen on the sixteenth floor as he takes us through the photos.

"So, we've got a facial match here, here and here." Rider points to the eye shape, the cheekbones and mouth of one Lok Hung who entered the US at Los Angeles International Airport exactly five hours and six minutes ago. "And if we overlay the photos of An Kwan, Lok Ng and Park Ling, we can see the similarities," Rider continues, as his computer screen merges all four photos together. "We're talking about a ninety-two percent match." The jawline is different in one, the brow line different in another, the cheekbones slightly more pronounced, and even the hairline is farther back for Park Ling…but there are more similarities than differences.

"We need to find him. Now." I try to keep my voice as calm as possible, despite my panic. Agent Dan Young's days are numbered.

"He listed the Kyoto Grand Hotel and Gardens in Little Tokyo as his address," Hana says.

"The chances of that being legit are zero." I shake my head. "Our guy's smarter than that."

"So how can we find him?"

Silence.

"We have to find who put the hit on Saito. He or she will know how to contact our hit man."

De Luca is right—especially given the source of the hit on Saito is probably the same person pulling Park Ling's strings now. Find him, and hopefully we find Ling before the next contract is fulfilled.

"I'll still check out the hotel, just in case."

"Good idea," De Luca says to Hana before turning on his heel and heading for the meeting room. De Luca is keyed up enough as it is; if he knew Young was next on our hit man's list… Although I'm still not sure *why.* If his cover was blown and the Yakuza wanted him dead, wouldn't they just kill him themselves? I can only assume that whoever's contracted the hit on Dan Young wants it to look like an accident, maybe even a heart attack. And Ling can deliver that.

"Where were we?" I say, looking at the photos on the table. "Yes, the surveillance shots and this one that looks like Jo Hoshi, standing with Saito's third suspected victim, Hiroki Kawa."

De Luca and I both look at the photo again.

"It's not Hoshi, but I guess it could be a relative. Older brother, uncle maybe," De Luca says.

"Let's check out everything we've got on Hoshi and see if we can link him back to the Tokyo victim," I suggest.

De Luca shuffles files and brings Jo Hoshi to the top. "Here we go." He flips it open to a recent photo of Hoshi, blown up as an eight-by-ten color picture.

"Was he born in the US?" I ask.

De Luca flicks through the papers. "No. Came here in eighty-five at the age of fifteen."

"And this man, Hiroki Kawa, was murdered in Tokyo in 1993." I pause. "So Hoshi wasn't even in Tokyo during the murder."

De Luca looks up Hoshi's immigration paperwork. "No. Hoshi immigrated here with his mother. The father is listed as deceased, one Naoko Hoshi."

"The man in this picture isn't old enough to be Hoshi's father."

"No."

"What about brothers or sisters?"

De Luca shakes his head. "He doesn't have any, according to the immigration paperwork they filled out."

That rules Hoshi out.

"What if one of Saito's victims was a good friend or a cousin of someone in the L.A. Yakuza?"

"I doubt those records will be here." He points to the pile of paperwork in front of us. "We'd probably have to make a special request to Japan. Ask them."

I shrug. "Well, let's do that then."

"It might not even be someone in the L.A. Yakuza," De Luca says.

"You know how you've got a hunch that Agent Young's in trouble?"

"Uh-huh."

"Well, I've got a hunch that someone in the Yakuza has a connection with one of Saito's victims."

De Luca isn't entirely convinced, but he gives me the benefit of the doubt. "I guess it can't do any harm."

"Leave it with me."

I go back to my desk and prepare all the photos and names we've got on the L.A. Yakuza to send through to Japan. If we can get someone who worked organized crime back in the nineties to look at the file, we might have a shot. I e-mail Burges and explain the urgency of the case—that we think an undercover operative has been compromised and might be in danger, but that it's extremely confidential. I hope to give her and a Japanese cop enough incentive to make them work fast, but not so much that I'm blowing the confidential nature of the case and potentially Dan's cover— if it isn't already blown. I follow up the e-mail with a call.

"Hey, Latoya. Me again."

"What's up?"

"I've got another request…this one's urgent. Really urgent. I've just e-mailed the details through."

A slight pause before she says, "Yup, got it. Give me a sec."

I wait while she reads through the e-mail.

"Undercover operative?"

"It's a long story. And I can't go into details."

"Damn, girl. How'd you get someone into the Yakuza?"

"Like I said, I can't talk about it. We're very worried about him but you have to keep this one hundred percent confidential. Just you and your Japanese contact."

"Sure." She pauses. "It's three in the morning there at the moment. Hopefully our guy will understand the 3:00 a.m. call when I tell him what's at stake."

"Thanks, Latoya. Appreciate it."

"No problemo. I'll get him to call you directly."

I go back to De Luca and update him.

After a few moments of silence he says, "Let's get back to the surveillance shots while we're waiting."

We flip through the next set of surveillance photos from Japan. They're classic organized-crime surveillance shots— men coming out of buildings, two men talking, guys at coffee shops and on street corners. Not many shots feature women, although by flicking through the images I discover that most of the major players had wives…and mistresses.

"This woman was reported missing," I say, tapping my finger at a shot that shows her kissing Jun Saito's victim number three, Hiroki Kawa. I hand De Luca the police report.

"The date…" He scans the document, looking for a date. "Seventeenth of October, 1993."

"That's two days after the man she was having an affair with was shot dead outside her apartment building."

De Luca skims through the report. "The police thought she may have seen something or known something about the murder, and that she took off."

"But according to this—" I motion at the paperwork "—she was never found, either."

"Dead?"

"Could be. What's her name?"

De Luca checks the document. "Ima Yamada."

"Ring a bell?"

He shakes his head.

My BlackBerry rings and I answer it eagerly.

"Is that Agent Sophie Anderson of the FBI?" There's a delay in the phone line and the male speaker has a thick Japanese accent.

"Yes, speaking."

"Agent Anderson, my name's Akio Endo. I used to work for the Tokyo police."

"Ah, Mr. Endo. Thank you for calling."

"You're welcome. I understand Jun Saito is dead. That you're investigating his death."

"That's right. He was killed by a Chinese hit man and we're trying to find out who ordered the hit. We're looking at the Yakuza here in L.A."

"Yes. I understand," he says formally, briefly.

"You're not surprised we're looking at the Yakuza?"

"You must understand, Agent Anderson, we thought he was already dead. At the hands of the Yakuza."

"Of course."

"I worked on a Yakuza-dedicated team in the nineties and was in charge of all three murder investigations in which Saito was a suspect. And that of his girlfriend."

"You believe he was the killer?" I ask.

He pauses. "I was not so sure about his girlfriend. He was a young man in love and his father had trained him too well to leave a bloodied knife with his fingerprints at the crime scene."

My thoughts exactly. "One of the angles we're working over here is revenge. Perhaps Saito's girlfriend was killed as an act of revenge."

"It's possible."

De Luca weighs in to the conversation. "Mr. Endo, we sent you the names of our active Yakuza members here in L.A."

"Yes. I have the information."

For us it's like finding a needle in a haystack, but Endo still probably knows this stuff backward.

De Luca reads out the names. "Tomi Moto…Jo Hoshi—"

"I saw one name—Takeshi Suzuki."

"You know him? We have nothing on him from the Tokyo files."

"We don't think he was part of the Tokyo Yakuza, but he operated on the periphery. However, that's not why his name concerns me."

"Go on."

"Takeshi Suzuki is the brother of Ima Yamada, the mistress of Hiroki Kawa. She went missing two days after he was murdered."

De Luca stands up forcefully. "That's it. Suzuki must be behind the hit on Saito."

I'm as excited as De Luca, but I want to confirm a few facts first. "So she was never found? Dead or alive?"

"No. Although legally she has been declared dead."

"And why the different last name to Takeshi Suzuki?"

"She was divorced. Her maiden name was Suzuki."

"What if she witnessed Saito killing her lover? Saito goes after her and kills her but someone finds out and Suzuki takes revenge on Saito's woman." I voice the theory.

"An eye for an eye." De Luca paces.

"Saito must have disposed of the body very carefully," Endo says. "All these years later and she still hasn't been found."

"Perhaps he knew what would happen if Takeshi Suzuki ever found out that his little sister was dead," I say.

"Suzuki must have known," Endo says. "We thought perhaps the family had hidden her, to protect her. But if she wasn't with them, Suzuki would have known the fate that had befallen his sister."

De Luca nods. "All the more reason to kill Saito's girl-friend."

There's momentary silence.

"Thanks for your help, Mr. Endo. And for calling us back so quickly."

"You're welcome, agents. Good luck with the case."

"Thanks. Okay if we call you if we have any more questions?" I ask.

"Certainly."

We say goodbye and I've barely hit the disconnect button on my BlackBerry when De Luca is off. He leads the way through the open-plan office, beckoning Williams and Hana excitedly on the way to Petrov's office.

Petrov looks up. "What's up?"

"It looks like we know who put the hit out on Jun Saito," De Luca says.

"Really?" Petrov stands up. "Who?"

"Our *fuku-honbucho,* Takeshi Suzuki. Turns out his sister was the mistress of Hiroki Kawa, Saito's 1993 victim. The mistress was reported missing a couple of days after the murder, but maybe Saito killed her the night he killed Kawa."

"Maybe?" Petrov's initial enthusiasm is waning.

"We just spoke to one of the cops in Tokyo. The woman's still missing, been declared dead." De Luca starts pacing again.

"It all fits," I say. "Suzuki finds out Saito's alive and has a daughter living in L.A.—"

"How?" Williams interrupts me.

I shrug. "That's a question for Suzuki." I pause, before continuing. "Then he decides to exact revenge for his sister's murder. He lures Saito here, gives Park Ling a couple of weeks to plan the hit, and voilà. His sister's death is finally avenged. The only thing that doesn't fit with personal revenge is that Suzuki didn't pull the trigger himself. But I imagine he was there on the night Saito met his end—he would have had to watch to satisfy his anger."

"Well, let's prove this hypothesis one way or the other." Petrov rubs his chin. "It also means Suzuki might want Mee dead, as the final act of his revenge. Although why he'd fly Ling in just for that—"

"I was thinking about that, sir. Ling has a unique gift in his ability to kill someone and make it look like they had a heart attack. And that's something Suzuki desperately needs if he's doing all this behind his boss's back." I know Ling's here for Young, but the logic applies to Mee, too.

Petrov nods. "Joe and Anderson, can you stick around and take me through Suzuki's past life in Tokyo? Williams and Kim, I want you shaking down your contacts for information on Suzuki's current whereabouts."

"Yes, sir," Hana says, and Williams gives a nod.

Once they're out of sight, Petrov nods at the door and I close it.

"Mee's not as safe as I thought," Petrov admits.

"No." De Luca manages to sit down. "She may have been while Agent Young was looking out for her, but now...."

"We still can't confirm that Young's cover has been blown." Petrov clasps his hands together. "And without word from Young we can't confirm if Mce's alive or dead."

We sit in silence.

"Maybe Young found out Suzuki was behind the contract, and Suzuki intercepted him before he got to Tomi Moto."

De Luca adds his voice to the theory. "Suzuki might not realize Young's an undercover agent. He might just think he's someone who can jeopardize his standing with Moto."

"Either way," I say, "Young's in trouble."

Quiet again.

The conversation's path is such that I feel I can add in the next part without it sounding too left field. "What if Park Ling's in town to kill Agent Young?"

Petrov slowly nods his head. "It's possible that Suzuki would bring Ling in again to tie off all the loose ends...including Mee Kim. It'd give him distance from the hits and like you said, Anderson, he's probably hoping that if they look like natural deaths Moto will never suspect his involvement."

De Luca stands up again. "We've got to get Young and Mee Kim out now. They're both in danger."

"Agreed," I say.

Petrov is silent on the matter, and both De Luca and I look at him expectantly.

He puts his hands in the air. "It's just that we don't know for sure that this mistress, Ima, isn't alive and well in Tokyo or somewhere else. Jun Saito disappeared for fifteen years, why can't she? Her brother may have been the one who organized for her to disappear." He sighs. "We'll put Takeshi Suzuki under surveillance for the next twenty-four hours."

"But what about Park Ling?" I ask. "He might take the hit on Young in the next few hours."

"Anderson, you think that's likely?" Petrov says with some disbelief. "You profiled the guy."

Petrov's right. I'm letting my emotions run away without thinking about our hit man's behavior. Each hit is planned, and well planned, and he's only been in the country for six hours. Our hit man isn't going to be rushed by anyone. And if Suzuki needs it to look like Young died of natural causes, they'll need to find a location for the attack to occur.

"No, you're right. He normally plans the hit for days or weeks. I don't think he'll wait that long this time, but we've probably got twelve to twenty-four hours."

Petrov nods. "Good." He looks at De Luca. "What was the latest report from Young on Mee's location?"

"An address in Carson. But she'd been moved once already."

"Okay, let's check out the Carson address and the earlier one, too. Put them on twenty-four hour watch and see if anyone's coming or going. If Park Ling enters either premises, or if anything else looks potentially threatening, we go in."

"I'll take first watch on the last address Young gave me," De Luca says, "the house in Carson."

"Okay. I presume you'll take Agent Kim?"

"Uh-huh." He looks down. "I'd like to keep her close at the moment."

Hana can't report in to the Yakuza if she's with De Luca.

"And I'll take the other location, with Williams."

"No way, Anderson. You're desk-bound."

"Come on, sir. It's only surveillance. What's the difference between sitting in a chair here or in a car seat?"

"You know the difference, Anderson. Here you won't have to draw down on a suspect, you won't have to watch Williams's back."

"But, sir, Suzuki's probably moved Mee and Young to a new location. One that Moto doesn't know about."

"Where is the other address, Joe?"

"California Heights. Another private house."

Petrov's silent for some time. "You can ride out there with Williams, but I'll be sending someone to relieve you."

"But, sir—"

"No buts, Anderson." He looks down at his computer, not even returning my stare…or should I say glare. "I'll organize people from the Gang Impact Team to work on shifts with you guys."

"But what about the leak?" I ask. "What if it's not Hana or Williams? If it's someone in the wider Gang Impact Team, we'll be letting them know we're on to Mee's past locations. Then Agent Young's cover will definitely be blown."

"It has to be Kim or Williams, Anderson. It's the only thing that adds up." Despite his words, after a few seconds Petrov lets out a sigh. "Okay. I'll talk to Brady, get a few of our regular field agents assigned to this for twenty-four to forty-eight hours. But I might only be able to get four, which would mean twelve-hour surveillance shifts."

"Fine by me." De Luca is quick to respond. He's got an agent inside.

"Me, too."

Petrov catches me out. "You'll be on about a one hour shift, Anderson."

I keep silent, resisting the temptation to argue—it's futile.

"Okay, Joe, you give the assignments to Agents Kim and Williams and e-mail me through the addresses. At least this way we can keep them close to us." Petrov looks at his watch. "Someone will relieve you guys at 11:00 p.m. and you'll be on again at eleven tomorrow morning."

Petrov's made it nearly nine hours from now, which will make for an extremely long day for De Luca, Hana and Williams. I wish I could say the same for me—it wouldn't be the first time I'd have to work around the clock.

I follow De Luca back to his desk and write down the California Heights address. Then we pull Williams and Hana off their task of trying to find Takeshi Suzuki's current whereabouts and split up to start our surveillance work.

On the way to Cerritos Avenue in California Heights, Williams calls his wife to let her know he won't be home until late.

"Petrov must be real worried about Mee Kim," he says, "to order round-the-clock surveillance on two locations. Especially given they're only addresses of interest."

Williams still doesn't have the benefit of our extra knowledge—that *two* lives are in the mix and that these locations are confirmed Yakuza hiding spots for Mee. I'd like to tell him all this so he's not operating in the dark, but I could be sitting next to the very person who's been feeding the Yakuza information.

"Yeah," I say, "well, I guess with Park Ling back in town it's possible he's here to take out Mee Kim this visit. Any lead is better than nothing."

Williams shrugs. "I guess so."

The house on Cerritos Avenue is two stories, bagged and painted white on the outside with dark blue window frames and door frames. It looks well kept, not something I was expecting of a gangster hideout. But maybe the Yakuza has high standards. We drive by, U-turn and park six doors down so we have a good line of sight of the house and its front door.

We'd stopped for some food and drinks and take-out coffees on the drive over. We both finish our coffees before Williams says, "So, what do you want first? Your cashew nuts or fruit?" Williams motions to the stash in the backseat.

I smile. "I'll hold off for a little while, thanks."

"I'm going to start with my donut."

Our food choices at 7-Eleven were quite different. I went for a bag of unsalted cashews, a sandwich and my treat food of a chocolate bar. I also got a couple of Diet Pepsis for extra caffeine. Williams, on the other hand, went for pure refined carbs and sugar, and lots of it—donuts, bags of chips, several chocolate bars and lots of Coke, the nondiet variety. And that's what will be his body's fuel until 11:00 p.m.

As he munches into his donut I try to think of a way to convince Petrov that I'm okay for surveillance. Yes, it's

active duty, but we all know that nine times out of ten surveillance is anything but active. We don't even know if this
house has any occupants at all, let alone Mee and Agent
Young.

An hour later I'm still trying to think of a work-around
when another car pulls up. I recognize the occupant as FBI
agent Rob Black who works under Rosen in our Criminal
Division.

I sigh. "This must be my replacement."

Williams gives me a sideways glance. "Don't look so
down, Anderson. You're going to be sitting on your sofa
tonight."

"Yeah, but I'd rather stay here. Just in case something
happens." I couldn't bear it if I missed the action.

"Well, I'd love to trade places with you."

"Why don't you?" I say. "You can take my car and I'll
stay here with Black."

Williams gives me a look. "It's a tight race between
facing my wife's wrath at midnight or Petrov's later today,
but I'm going to stick with the rules this time."

"Chicken."

He laughs. "You're right about that one, Anderson."
Williams gathers his stakeout goodies. "So, what's this Rob
Black like?"

"A complete ass," I lie. "You'll hate him."

Williams laughs again. "I'll tell him you said that."

A few seconds later Williams is in Agent Black's car and
I'm driving off alone.

Thirty-Four

Driving by either location—the Carson house or the California Heights house—is probably not a good idea, at least until after 11:00 p.m., when there's a chance the agents on duty won't know my car. Of course, depending on who Petrov assigns, the relief agents may well know both me and my Bureau-issue car. So for the meantime, I head to the office—it's only 1:00 p.m. At the moment we've got most of our case invested in Ima Yamada being dead, not missing, and Takeshi Suzuki as our contractor on Jun Saito. But I need some sort of verification that Suzuki is our man.

I go through the files De Luca and I were reviewing this morning, paying particular attention to the information we have on three people—Takeshi Suzuki, Hiroki Kawa and Ima Yamada. After I've gone through Suzuki's file, I spread the photos of him out in front of me, pushing the other materials away. I pick up a photo, hold it in my hand and study his face closely. I slow my breathing, taking longer, deeper breaths in and out. I focus on relaxing my toes, then my feet, then my torso, my shoulders, and lastly I let the tension in my face drop away. I close my eyes, enveloped in a bubble of relaxation.

But nothing comes. No vision, not even a flash of Suzuki. I open my eyes again and look at the photo for another twenty minutes or so. Still nothing.

Frustrated, I move on to Saito and repeat the process. This time I am rewarded with a vision, but it's a replay of Saito discovering his girlfriend's body—Saito's tense, trying to get home to his girlfriend, but when he arrives she's dead.

Next I move on to Ima Yamada. Is she the reason Saito's dead? The reason Saito's girlfriend was murdered, too? The file we've put together on her is small. A couple of surveillance shots taken with Hiroki Kawa, a couple of interior shots of her apartment after she'd gone missing, and a two-page missing-persons report filed by her mother. I wonder if Takeshi helped with the report, or if he already knew the likelihood of his sister's fate. I close my eyes, controlling my breathing once more.

I'm naked, rocking backward and forward on top of him. He looks up at me in awe.

I lie on the bed, watching him get dressed, and take a drag of the cigarette he holds out for me. I get up and pull on his favorite silk negligee. Maybe he will stay a little longer? Draping my arms around him from behind, I kiss his neck. He leans into me, but shakes his head.

I stand at the window, like I always do, sad to see him go. But instead of watching the retreating figure of my lover, I see a flash from a doorway. Gunfire. I lean harder into the window, my open palms smudging the glass. I can't see his body, but I know the shots must have been meant for Hiroki. I'm frozen, immobile. And then I see him. A man comes out of the doorway. He moves closer and now I can see his face under the streetlight. I take a deep breath in, and just at that moment he looks up at me.

I hold my breath, knowing what I must do but unable to move. He's seen me, I know him. I must run. It only takes a few seconds for my body to answer my mind's pleas. Run! I bolt out the door, and up the stairs. He's only one person. If I can get out of his sight, I could lose him. I must outrun him.

I keep hurtling myself up the stairs, faster and faster. But then I hear footsteps behind me, heavy and fast. They get closer, and I open my mouth to yell for help but I'm too late. One hand grabs my arm, the other quickly cups my mouth, silencing my scream before I could get any sound out.

Our breathing is fast, and in sync, just as it was with Hiroki only fifteen minutes ago. But this is different…so different. Hiroki. A small tear runs down my cheek.

Seconds pass and nothing happens. He's still, silent behind me. Maybe he won't kill me. I cling to the glimmer of hope. I can tell him I'll never reveal his identity. I try to speak, but his hand forces down harder on my mouth, and starts to block my nose as well. I'm gasping for air, and the panic returns. I try to move my head, get my airways clear, but his grip is so strong…too strong. His hands move from my mouth to my head and in that moment I know death is imminent. My eyes widen and two small tears form, but I don't feel them trickle down my face. Instead, I hear a loud crack that reverberates inside my head and then darkness.

I pace on the landing between floors, glancing every now and again at Ima Yamada's lifeless form. I take a deep breath in. I need to come up with a plan, fast. But first I need to get her somewhere private. I pick her up and carry her down the stairs and back into her apartment, locking the door behind me.

This wasn't meant to happen. This wasn't part of the deal. I never wanted to kill her, not a woman. And now, what will I do with the body? I have to make the call. I have to trust him.

We lower her body into the grave, placing it on top of a coffin, and then replace all the soil. She's been erased.

I find myself slumped over the meeting-room table, waves of nausea riding me. The nausea is more severe than usual, and I can't help but wonder if it's because it was such a long vision. Usually I get much smaller snippets.

Eventually the feeling subsides and I'm able to straighten up without worrying I'll be sick all over the files. The first part of the vision was from Ima's point of view, and then once she was dead I jumped into Jun Saito's shoes. And there's no doubt, it was Jun Saito. Ima Yamada's dead all right, and no wonder her body was never found—she was buried soon after her death, atop who knows whose grave. Without the name on the tombstone she lies under, her body will never be found.

I start to replay the vision, hoping to find something else useful in there. One of the men lowering her body into the grave must have been Saito, but who was the other man? Whoever it was, I'm guessing he told Takeshi Suzuki what really happened to his sister that night. And once Suzuki knew, Saito had to run. We'll never know the exact sequence of events—maybe Saito just sensed something was wrong, was worried he was being followed and decided to run with his girlfriend. Or maybe he knew of his friend's betrayal, knew that his days were numbered if he stayed in Tokyo. Either way, Saito was ready to pack up with his girlfriend and leave the Yakuza and Japan for good.

I think back to the start of the dream…Hiroki and Ima in her apartment making love. There's something familiar about her bedroom. Something that I've seen before. I take out all the photos we have relating to Takeshi Suzuki, including shots Agent Young has taken. We have surveillance shots of several Yakuza buildings: the two "safe houses" where Mee was held, a restaurant in Little Tokyo out of which Tomi Moto runs an office, a karaoke bar and night-club that Suzuki runs; and, through Agent Young, we know where some of the key players live. Moto lives in a large security-gated house in Rancho Palos Verdes, and Suzuki lives in a smaller but still glamorous house in Newport Beach. Both houses have swimming pools and tennis courts and both have high levels of security. Young has been to their homes, and was able to take a few snaps on his cell phone during visits about six months ago. It's in these grainy photos that I see the familiar item—a painting of a cherry blossom that hung above Ima Yamada's bed. Obviously Suzuki brought it with him to the States.

Looking at the photos gets me thinking…could Suzuki be stupid enough to hold Mee and Agent Young at his home?

I dial Petrov's number. "Hi, it's Anderson. Are Moto's and Suzuki's houses under surveillance at the moment?"

"Hold on, I'll just check for you."

I hear papers shuffling and the sound of a keyboard as Petrov looks up the current surveillance operations.

"Not from the Gang Impact Team. Why?"

"Just wondering." I bite my lip, trying to work out how much I can tell Petrov without him asking questions. I can certainly present the hypothesis. "You think Suzuki might be holding Mee Kim and Agent Young at his house?"

Petrov's silent for a few beats, thinking. "He's married with three kids. How's he going to keep two prisoners in his own home without major questions?"

Women who are involved with members of organized crime syndicates rarely have more than a superficial under-standing of what their partners do. Sure, she may know he's involved in the Yakuza, but she probably prefers not to think about it. It's a strange arrangement, and the women defi-nitely subscribe to the old saying: See no evil, hear no evil, speak no evil. So Petrov's right—Suzuki isn't going to hold Kim and Young in the house while his wife and children go about their normal day-to-day lives. That would be way too close for comfort. But he might have somewhere else he can take them.

"Have you tracked him down yet? For the tail?"

Another moment of silence from Petrov. "Not yet. I'm still trying to get some people."

"Okay." Resources are tight, particularly when we don't want to use anyone from the Gang Impact Team or anyone Petrov doesn't feel he can trust one hundred percent. And I imagine after spending over twelve months trying to find the bad apple, Petrov's trust levels have plummeted.

"Leave it with me," Petrov says.

We say goodbye and hang up. I'm sure Petrov will assign someone to Suzuki in the next twenty-four hours, but in the meantime, what harm is there in a drive-by? Or maybe even sitting out front for half an hour or so. Plus I've still got a few snacks in the backseat, so at least I'll be set up if I decide to stick it out at Suzuki's home.

I pull into Seascape Drive just before 6:00 p.m. and try to get a fix on numbers. Eventually I see a number on my right, and I cruise slowly down the street until I come to Suzuki's home. I recognize it from the surveillance shots, although now the trees are bare instead of laden with crisp green leaves. Most of the fence line is marked by a high cream wall, but a large wrought-iron security gate at the driveway gives me a visual on the house.

I park opposite and at an angle that allows me to see up the driveway and to the double-story redbrick home. The house itself is modern, but the grounds have been land-scaped with touches of Japan—cherry blossoms, Japanese maples and a large Japanese-style water feature. Taking out my binoculars, I focus on the front room and catch a glimpse of movement. I move my binoculars until I find the source, a woman and two children sitting up at the table. I keep my eyes peeled, but it looks like Takeshi Suzuki is out. I reach for my cashews and a Diet Pepsi. Surveillance is definitely not good for the waistline. Although at least I'm doing a little better than Williams.

Two hours later a silver Mercedes pulls up at the house. I can't see the driver, but I have to assume it's Suzuki. I check the license plates—it's a match for his car. The wife greets him at the door, but I know the kids went to bed nearly an hour ago. Within a few minutes, Mr. and Mrs. Suzuki are sitting down to dinner. There's still no sign of any of Petrov's agents.

At 9:45 p.m. Suzuki goes into the front room to take a call. He paces while he talks and within five seconds of putting the phone down the front door opens. I keep the binoculars trained on him as he gets into his car. The headlights go on, and soon he's rolling down the drive, heading to me. I sink down in my seat, conflicted by my need to get a visual confirmation that the man is Suzuki and my desire to stay hidden. In the end, self-preservation wins out and I sink low—too low for him to see me, and too low for me to see him.

I wait about five seconds before I start my car, swing a U-turn and follow the man that I have to presume is Takeshi Suzuki. Who else would be in his house and driving his car?

We cruise through the streets of Newport Beach, making our way north and toward downtown L.A. It's easier to tail someone in the dark, because all they can see in their rearview mirror is lights and general shapes. Soon we're cruising into Little Tokyo and turning into a laneway that runs alongside Takeshi Suzuki's karaoke bar.

I idle out the front, taking a little bit of risk for a big return. The man parks the car in a space at the end of the laneway and gets out. He makes his way to a small door, presumably a back entrance to the bar, and once he's under the light that hangs on the door I can see him properly. Bingo…it's Takeshi Suzuki, all right. With the visual ID confirmed, I roll the car forward, looking for a spot and considering my options. I want to go into the bar; problem is, Suzuki was in the warehouse the night I got shot. He knows what I look like. I pull into a parking space a little less than a block from the bar.

My options are limited, so limited that I decide to take an even bigger risk. I sweep my hair up into a French roll and hunt around the car for one of my baseball caps. I tend to have hats lying around the place—in the car, in the house, in my bedroom, in bags—ready for the time I need sun protection. I'm not disappointed this time, as my hands clasp around a black Nike baseball cap. I take a look at my reflection in the rearview mirror. I still look like me, of course, but the cap hides my hair and hopefully changes my appearance enough to fool someone who's only seen me once. I'm also expecting the karaoke bar to be appropriately dark.

I walk the block back to the bar's entrance, which is simply a door with flashing neon above it, and make my way up a narrow staircase to the bar's internal door. Once I'm inside I quickly scope the place and the patrons, as if I'm looking for someone. To my disappointment, about three-quarters of them are Asian, which will make it much harder for me to blend in. The fact that I'm a single woman in a bar won't help matters, either. I look for the most likely target, someone I can approach. Two men sit on a table by themselves and I can imagine it would be easy for me to join them, although it may lead to complications later. Instead, I go for a group of three women.

I focus on the nearest one and make a beeline for her. "Hi, Jane, isn't it?" I put on my best American accent and place my hand on her shoulder.

The girl turns around. "No, sorry." She smiles. "I'm Emily."

"Emily. That's right."

The smile stays, but becomes more uncertain. "I'm sorry, I can't…"

"I'm Tiffany. Don't tell me you don't remember me?" I say it with what I hope is enough indignation that Emily will feel too embarrassed to admit that she doesn't remember me…she doesn't even know me.

"Tiffany," she repeats. "Yeah, hi, Tiffany."

She introduces me to her friends, Beth and Mary.

"Do you mind if I have a drink with you guys while I'm waiting for my friend?" I ask. "Don't you just hate drinking alone?"

The girls all agree and soon I'm firmly entrenched in Emily's girls' night out, sipping a gin and tonic. I edge myself around in the booth slightly so I can see more of the bar.

Suzuki is nowhere to be found, but I presume he's out the back somewhere, perhaps in an office. Maybe the front-of-house wasn't the best place to stake out. How will I see him if he leaves via the back door? I decide to give it another twenty minutes before going back to my car and waiting for Suzuki to make a move—assuming I haven't already lost him.

I only just manage to keep my head above water with Emily, Beth and Mary, but my attention isn't really on them, it's on the other patrons. I study each Asian male carefully, wondering if perhaps one of them is our hit man in one of his many disguises. It's the height I concentrate on, and there are only five men I'd judge to be around six feet. One man sits by himself, but I can only make out a partial profile, not enough to be sure one way or the other.

I glance at my watch. "Gee, my friend's running real late. Hope you don't mind me sitting here a bit longer?"

The girls all agree it's fine, and I continue to superficially contribute to the conversation. It's hard going when they mostly seem to be talking about fashion and the latest TV shows, but every now and again I'm able to add something or move the conversation to a celebrity or movie I have seen.

The solitary man stays by himself, still nursing the same beer. I'm about to excuse myself and go back to my car when Suzuki comes out of a side door near the stage, marked Employees Only. I wait for him to make a beeline for the man's table, but he doesn't. Instead, he looks around the bar. I manage to be engrossed in conversation as his eyes pass quickly over our table, a group of four women not holding his attention. He's looking for someone specific. He looks around once more, before taking a seat by himself in a corner table with a Reserved sign on it. Again, I keep myself half in the conversation and half on the lookout.

It's a full five minutes before the man moves from his table to Suzuki's. The man gives Suzuki a little bow, and at first Suzuki's face is blank, but soon he smiles. From this angle I get a closer look at the man's face and I'm sure it's our guy, our hit man. Time to call in backup.

I'm about to excuse myself and find a quiet corner—if that's possible in a karaoke bar—when both Suzuki and Ling stand up. They make their way to the Employees Only door. My mind races with possibilities. Are Mee Kim and Dan Young out the back now, and Ling's about to execute them? Or are they just going out the back to talk privately? I can either make a run for the door and hope to sneak in before it latches, or I can wait it out. In the split second I have to make the decision, I decide following Suzuki and Ling is too risky. But it's also time for a move.

I sigh. "Looks like my friend stood me up." I stand up. "Great to see you again, Emily. And nice to meet you, Mary and Beth."

We say our goodbyes and I head out the front door. But instead of going back to my car, I slip around to the laneway that runs alongside the double-story building. I move past Suzuki's Mercedes and farther into the laneway until I find a spot behind a charmingly smelly Dumpster. From here I can see his car, and if I step out a bit farther I can see the back door to the bar. I lean on the Dumpster, despite the smell, with my head peering out for a clear line of sight of the door. I've spotted Park Ling and I should ring Petrov, but I know he'll kill me for being out from behind my desk when I'm still recovering; so I try De Luca first.

"De Luca."

"Hey, De Luca," I whisper, "it's Anderson."

"What's up?"

"I've spotted Park Ling. He's with Takeshi Suzuki at his karaoke bar."

"Really!"

"You guys wanna come back me up or what?"

"You're there by yourself? Injured?"

I sigh. Maybe De Luca is going to be as bad as Petrov. "Long story. Just get your ass down here."

"What about Petrov? You called him?"

"No, thought I'd leave that to you." I disconnect. Just as I hang up, the door creaks open. I lean harder into the

Dumpster, ready to crouch down or move farther behind it, but also wanting to make sure I get a good visual.

Suzuki and Ling walk out the door, both smoking. Suzuki says something, Ling nods, and then Suzuki makes a call before getting in his car. The men don't formally say goodbye, only the slightest nod before Suzuki drives off.

I stand in the shadows, gun ready, safety off. Ling's only a few feet away. I can smell his cigarette smoke, getting closer. I pin myself against the Dumpster and edge backward. Fear takes a tight grip on me. I know what the man is capable of, and even though I'm armed, if I let him get much closer, it'll be too close for me to draw before he disarms me. His kung fu skills are too good.

I try to steady my breath, but now I can even hear the faint tread of his footsteps. I'm not sure what shoes he's wearing, but he's able to walk extremely softly in them. I kneel down slowly, desperate not to make a sound. Even a crack of my ankle or knee would alert him to the fact that someone's here, only steps away from him. Thankfully my joints are good to me. My right knee is on the ground; my left leg steadies my weight, planted out in front. My gun is aimed high, at where I estimate his chest will be. I take deep, but hopefully silent, breaths.

The footsteps get closer so I take a breath and hold it, ready to take the shot. I can't let him get too close, can't give him even a split second. But just as I see his shadow on the pavement before me, he stops. A cigarette butt lands on my side of the Dumpster and Ling extinguishes it with his shoe, a black, rubber-soled shoe with a soft leather upper. The shoes of a hired killer. Next his hand reaches down. My heart beats faster—will he see me? He picks up the cigarette butt but his head doesn't come into view, which means I'm still out of sight, too. He takes the butt with him; he wouldn't want to leave his DNA lying around, especially near the business of his employer. The footsteps move away and, keeping low, I peek around the corner. On the street he flags down a taxi and I sprint down the laneway, catching up to him just as the taxi takes off. The traffic is slow, so I decide to make a run for my car. I force myself to jog the hundred yards, but the pounding motion takes a toll on my body.

I ring De Luca from the car. "He's on the move. Traveling south on Central. I'll call you again soon." I disconnect and concentrate on keeping Ling's cab in my sights. I can't afford to lose him.

Just over five minutes later, the cab pulls over. I pass the taxi and keep Ling in my rearview mirror, before parking in an illegal space a few yards in front of him. I take out a map of L.A. that I keep in my car in case my navigation system ever goes down—today it serves as good cover. If Ling looks in the car as he passes, all he'll see is a lost tourist. But Ling doesn't come my way. Instead, he crosses the road and disappears into another small alleyway.

I call De Luca with our new location.

"We're about five to ten minutes away. I'll see if I can get an LAPD patrol car to you sooner, but in the meantime keep your distance."

"Will do," I say, but immediately get out of the car. There's no way I'm letting Ling disappear for good. As I'm crossing the road a car turns into the alley, so I hang back, pressing myself against the corner building. The car comes to a screeching halt and someone is shoved out of the backseat before the car spins around and makes a hasty exit from the lane. What the—?

I can't make out who the figure is from this distance, so I quickly reach for my pocket binoculars. It's Dan Young…beaten up. This is the drop, this is the plan. And it's happened fast, much sooner than we were expecting. Suzuki is in a hurry and has forced Park Ling to change his usual routine.

Then it hits me. This is the alley from the dream I had before I was shot—I was fighting someone extremely well-trained in kung fu. I must have seen it from Young's perspective. Hopefully my presence will alter the outcome.

Ling runs toward Young, as he's still trying to get to his feet. But our hit man actually allows Young to stand fully before he starts his attack, a Double Back-fist aimed at Young's eyes. Ling's diving into the fight, into his next kill with his calling card—a Killing Hand move. Young, still obviously disorientated, moves just in time while also holding his hands up in a cross block to catch the punches. If Ling's using *dim mak* strikes, any contact could be deadly for Young.

I move in quickly, gun drawn. I know my physical fitness is below par…way below par…but Ling's fifty yards away and no match for a gun. He can't reach me now. "FBI, freeze."

Both men stop, midstrikes. Young staggers backward, out of Ling's reach, and Ling spins around.

"Let me guess…Agent Anderson." Although his accent is strong, each word is enunciated perfectly. He's well practiced in English, not surprisingly.

"Hold it right there, Ling."

But Ling doesn't hold it there. Instead he moves closer to me. "I'm going to enjoy this, Sophie." The way he says my name, with an almost tenderness, is disturbing.

"Stop right there, Ling. I will fire."

He smiles, hesitates, but keeps moving forward, holding his arms up. "You wouldn't shoot an unarmed man who's surrendering to you, would you?"

The answer would be no under normal circumstances, but I can't let this man get within striking distance of me. I give him a final warning, but he doesn't stop. I take a breath, hold it, and fire.

Two shots, direct hits into his chest.

Ling's body jumps backward from the force and he falls onto the ground.

"You all right?" I yell out to Young.

He nods, but he's still bent over, nursing his ribs. Just like my vision, Ling struck and broke Young's ribs. Plus whatever else Suzuki's thugs did to him before they dumped him in the lane.

"Where's Mee?" I ask.

Young shakes his head, straightening slightly but wincing from the pain. "I don't know. We were being held together but then they beat on me, blindfolded me and dragged me here. They would have taken her somewhere else by now."

We both move toward Ling's body. Young's still closest, at only a couple of feet away, but I'm closing the distance, fast.

"Is he dead?" I ask, still not able to see Ling's face and any rise and fall in his chest, in this light.

Young bends down over him and presses his finger to Ling's neck. "He's alive. Pulse is very slow, though."

I nod, reholster my gun and bring out my BlackBerry to call for an ambulance. It may even get here before our backup. I bend down and notice it.

"Dan, there's—"

But my sentence is cut short as Ling puts a foot on either side of my ankle and brings his legs toward his butt, up-ending me.

I hear Dan wheeze out, "no blood."

I'm on the ground and Ling's instantly on top of me, grabbing my gun out of its holster. But instead of shooting me he tosses it to the other side of the laneway and then rolls over onto his back. I guess shooting me wouldn't be any fun.

Dan straightens up as Ling rocks his weight back onto his shoulders and then pushes his legs skyward, pushing off the ground with his hands behind his head at the same time. In one fluid movement he's standing. Yes, he's probably got two almighty bruises from my bullets hitting his bulletproof vest, but that's it. And slowing your heart rate is part of traditional kung fu training in China. Damn it, why didn't I think of that?

My shoulders aren't up to Ling's maneuver, so I move my legs over my body and head in a circular scissor movement before using their momentum to come to a standing position. My gun's twenty yards away, and while I'm interested in it, Ling isn't. He prefers to use his bare hands.

Ling smiles. "I'm going to enjoy this. I understand from my research that you both study kung fu."

I don't wait for the formalities normally observed in traditional kung fu fighting. I strike. I keep it simple and sharp, going for a low side kick to Ling's knee. He checks the kick by effortlessly picking up the target leg so my strike lands on his shin, which is rock hard, even harder than Sifu Lee's shins. Luckily I used the hard, side part of the sole of my foot and there's no serious pain, but I certainly don't want to make contact with Ling's shins again if I can avoid it.

"It's not really fair, I know," he says, repositioning himself backward slightly so he can target both Young and me, "given you're both injured."

"It's two against one, Ling, don't be so cocky." Young does a fast side step toward Ling and delivers a side kick like mine, but his is aimed higher, at Ling's ribs.

Ling uses a lower gate block to deflect the kick. "Time to get down to business." He targets Dan first, delivering a powerful and super-fast combination of strikes and kicks. As Dan's on the defense, I'm on the offence, but Ling's superior skill is able to keep me at bay with a few well-timed strikes while he keeps the pressure on Young. At least Ling hasn't gone for any *dim mak* strikes…yet.

My adrenaline kicks in, and the searing pain in my left shoulder from all the movement begins to subside. That, and the sight of Dan wavering, sends my senses into overdrive. But instead of lunging at Ling, I accept the inevitable and go for the gun. No sense fooling myself—Ling's better than me by a long shot, even if I was uninjured. My gun's only twenty yards away, but that's a long way against an opponent like this. Ling's better than me and Young put together and in top form.

I hear Ling's footsteps behind me, at least giving Dan a break. I only make it just over half the distance before I feel the weight of Ling as he launches himself at me. I come to the ground with a thud, Ling on top of me. I brace the fall by putting my arms out, with my fists clenched and arms bent so I'm taking the impact on my forearms, not on my hands, which would snap my wrists clean. Even so, our combined weight overshadows my adrenaline surge and I scream in pain as my wounded shoulder jolts from the impact. I try to scramble forward when Ling gets off me. I can see the gun, it's only a few yards away. But he starts to hit me and I have to abandon the gun to defend myself. I curl into a ball, fetal position, fists clenched and arms protecting my head so any kicks or strikes will hit the bony part of my forearm. At the same time, I peer around my arms and look for any openings in Ling's defenses. He comes to standing and is close enough for me to bring him toppling down. I quickly anchor his ankle with my left foot and kick at his knee with all my might with my right leg. He was on the move backward to escape the leg lock, but I did make contact and I can tell from an ever-so-slight wince on his face that it wasn't exactly pain-free. A small victory, I suppose.

Dan's moving toward us, but he's in no condition to fight—not for much longer anyway. Even so, he brings his guard up and delivers a roundhouse kick. It comes quickly enough after my own kick that it catches Ling off guard. While Ling regroups, I commando-crawl toward the gun. It's at my fingertips when I hear the unmistakable crunch of bone breaking and a yelp of pain. I hope it's Ling. I know it's more likely Dan.

I don't look back, instead I grasp the gun, rolling as my fingers close around its butt. I wind up on my back, gun pointing toward the incoming figure of Ling.

As he leaps onto me, I fire four shots.

My aim's off, affected by the pain in my shoulder and the fact that I didn't have enough time to properly prepare. But even so, one shot hits Ling in the neck. He lands on top of me, his eyes wide. I quickly roll him off me and scramble to my feet.

Young's on the ground, not moving, and Ling's rolling around in agony and bleeding, but still alive. I doubt even he would be able to slow his pulse now. Keeping my eyes and gun trained on Ling, I back up to Dan and kneel down beside him.

"Dan?" I say, glancing at him for a second.

He manages a grunt. I take a second quick look at him.

His face is bloodied and bruised, and even from this angle I can tell his elbow's badly broken.

I grab my BlackBerry and call 911, just as I hear the sirens and then see the flashing blue of an LAPD patrol car.

Thirty-Five

I check Dan's pulse. It's extremely slow, especially given he's just been fighting for his life. Ling must have attacked at least one of the *dim mak* points. I think back to my *dim mak* reading and how to reverse an attack on the parasympathetic nervous system…I need to apply pressure to one of the points that stimulates the sympathetic nervous system. That'll get his heart rate and blood pressure back up. It's also possible Young suffered a *dim mak* knockout. But first, I go for a carotid massage in case Ling used the pressure points that will induce a fatal heart arrhythmia. I rub the side of Young's neck, hard, hoping I've caught him in time.

An LAPD officer rushes out of the car and toward me, gun out and pointed at me, his partner quickly coming to his side.

"I'm FBI," I shout as I place my gun slowly on the pavement next to Young. "Let me get my ID." I slowly reach my right hand inside my jacket and pull out my ID. The cop comes closer to examine it and his trigger finger relaxes.

"We've got a DEA agent down here. I've just called 911."

"Okay." They take the information in quickly.

"That's our suspect." I motion my head toward Park Ling. "Be careful, he's dangerous even in that condition."

One officer trains his gun on Ling, but keeps his distance, while the other bends down to me. "Is he going to be okay?"

I don't bother explaining *dim mak*—it'd take too long and be met with too much skepticism. Instead, I just say, "I think so."

"I'll radio for a second ambulance."

I nod, and move from Young's carotid artery to gall bladder 20, a pressure point on the back of his head, near the base of his skull.

I look up at Ling—he's losing a lot of blood. "You better apply pressure," I say to the officers.

One of them applies pressure to the throat wound, while the other keeps his gun on Ling. After a minute, I check Dan's pulse and notice it does seem to have increased somewhat.

He moans, coming around. "Pressure-point knockout?" he manages. He's definitely with it now.

"I think so." Many of the *dim mak* points cause an instant faint or knockout, and according to the medical explanation it's a vasovagal faint, caused by a sudden drop in blood pressure.

"Where is he?"

"Down. Shot."

Young nods. "Good." He pushes himself to sitting and looks around, clutching his elbow in pain. He winces. "Man, this hurts."

"An ambulance is on its way."

He nods, but the wince doesn't go away. It will hurt even more when his adrenaline wears off.

"I also did a quick carotid massage, in case he targeted other heart points."

Young gives me a weak smile. "Thanks. I think I'll go to a Chinese doctor in the next few days, just to be on the safe side."

The first ambulance arrives and as much as I want the paramedics to check out Young first, now that he's conscious he has to be their second priority. Ling's bleeding, profusely, and if they don't control it quickly he'll die. So even though the paramedics are directed to us first, Young sends them over to Ling.

"Was Mee okay the last time you saw her?"

"Yes." Young's face crumples. "But I've got no idea where she is now—or if she's all right." He pauses. "I know what this is about now."

"Suzuki's sister," I state.

Young furrows his brow. "I don't know anything about Suzuki's sister, but I know Suzuki's running drugs on the side, skimming a large chunk off of Moto's business."

"So he doesn't know you're DEA?"

Young shakes his head. "No. But I overheard him talking to his driver about how the Feds were getting close, had names of hit men, and that they needed to secure their source and isolate her from Moto."

"Her?" I notice that this time the gender of the mole has been revealed. "Hana?"

Young shrugs. "I still don't know."

It has to be Hana. If Suzuki knew we had the hit man's name, it can only be Hana or Williams, and with the gender confirmed...

"Damn," I drop my head, "Why'd it have to be Hana?" I like...liked Hana. Even though the evidence implicated her, I couldn't bring myself to believe that Hana was capable of betraying us and the law. Obviously she's a better actor than I thought.

"Sorry," Young says.

I blow out a heavy sigh and the deep breath sends a sharp pain across my shoulder. By fighting Ling I've undone some of the past two and a half weeks of healing and I can feel it.

"How is he?" I ask the paramedics lifting Ling into the ambulance.

"He's lost a ton of blood, but he should make it."

I give the paramedic a nod.

The second ambulance arrives just as the first drives away. When Agent Dan Young is safe and sound on his way to hospital, I take stock. Mee Kim is still being held in an unknown location and Suzuki is still at large. And I know

Ling's not going to be the most cooperative suspect, either. Of the few hit men in his league that have been apprehended, all have maintained their code of silence. Some have admitted to crimes, talked about their life even, but none have given up their end employers. Park Ling will be no different. It's up to us to find Mee Kim and Suzuki.

Ling had thirty thousand dollars in cash on him, in a yellow envelope inside his jacket pocket. The cash will be examined by forensics and hopefully Suzuki handed it to Ling personally. At least then we'll have another round of evidence for charging and convicting Suzuki of contracting the murder of a federal agent. At the moment, Suzuki's at home, oblivious to the fact that Ling's attempt to kill Marcus/Agent Dan Young has failed…oblivious to the fact that I was in the alleyway with a gun and able to even up the odds.

A couple of minutes after the second ambulance heads off, De Luca and Hana arrive.

"Are you okay?" Hana asks.

"Fine." I can't look at her. "I shot Ling. He's on the way to hospital now."

De Luca eyes me carefully. "Did the paramedics take a look at you?"

"Yeah. I'm okay." Well, sort of. They said I need to take it easy, maybe come in to get an X-ray to check my ribs, but I know what a cracked rib feels like and mine are just bruised, not broken.

De Luca shakes his head. "I know it's sexist but a woman with a black eye just never looks right to me."

"And a man does?" Hana asks.

He shrugs. "Guess you're right."

I bend down into the nearest car's side mirror. It's a beauty, all right. Man, that's going to take a lot of foundation in the morning. Thank goodness my parents are back in Australia and never need to hear about this. Guess I'll tell them I shot Ling, but I don't have to tell them I got a shiner and bruised ribs in the process. Not to mention the dozen or so other bruises I know I'll have all over my arms and legs in the morning and the renewed pain in my shoulder blade. But first things first.

"De Luca. Mind if I have a word? It's about Petrov." I lead him away from Hana and make sure my back's to her. "Agent Young was here. Ling tried to kill him."

"What? Is he okay?"

"Yeah, he's fine. Couple of broken bones but the paramedics have taken him to hospital, too."

De Luca nods, the relief evident on his face.

"There's one other thing."

"Yes?" He runs his hand over his head.

"Young wasn't able to confirm who the leak is, but it is a woman."

De Luca glances at Hana. "Damn it." His jaw tenses.

It's going to be hard on De Luca—Hana's his ex-partner.

"I know." I look at my shoes. "And Suzuki knew that we had names of possible hit men."

"Okay, thanks, Anderson." He stares into the distance. "I rang Petrov."

"And?"

"He's pissed with you…though I imagine he'll be less pissed when he finds out you saved Agent Young's life."

"Guess I evened the score."

De Luca smiles. "Yeah." He starts walking toward Hana but keeps his voice low. "Petrov's organizing simultaneous raids on both properties known to have housed Mee in the past, as well as the Long Beach house the Asian Boyz have been using to produce meth, and Suzuki's home address."

"But we don't think Mee's at any of those places, do we?"

"Probably not, no."

I sigh. At least Dan's been able to confirm that Mee was alive and well only hours ago.

"Everything okay?" Hana asks once we're back within earshot.

I force a half grimace, half smile. "Apparently I'm in trouble. For coming here when I'm not supposed to be on active duty."

"But you got Park Ling. Surely Petrov can't be that pissed."

I shrug. "We'll see." My phone rings, unknown caller ID. "Agent Anderson."

"Agent Anderson, this is Mee Kim."

"Mee? Where are you, Mee? Are you okay?" I ask.

De Luca and Hana both look at me, eyes wide. I nod and mouth the word "Mee."

"I'm okay. I'm calling from a payphone in…" She trails off. "I don't know where I am." Her voice breaks.

"That's okay, Mee. What's the payphone number?"

"Um…5-6-2-4-5-1-6-8-9-8."

"Okay, got it." I scribble down the number and repeat it back to Mee, just to make sure. "Stay near the phone, Mee, but out of sight if you can. I'll be there soon."

"Okay."

Once Mee's off the line, I ring the FBI switch and get routed through to the tech area. "It's Agent Anderson here. Can you please give me an address for this payphone number?" I repeat the number and wait on the line until I get the answer.

"She's in Lakewood. On South Street near Bellflower Boulevard," I say.

De Luca looks me up and down. "I'll drive. You come with us."

No need to take two cars, and he's right—driving isn't exactly going to be easy or pain-free for me, at least for another couple of days.

Half an hour later we see the payphone on South, just before Bellflower. De Luca waits in the car while Hana and I linger by the payphone. We're only there for a few seconds when I see Mee crossing the road toward us.

I draw my gun, just in case she's not alone, and Hana follows suit. When Mee's this close, the last thing we want is for her to be snatched or shot right in front of us and I have to keep my eye on Hana as well as my surroundings.

Once Mee's in the car, I put my gun back in its holster and climb in next to her. "You okay?" I ask.

She nods, but I can see the fear in her eyes. She's a different woman from the Mee Kim I met a couple of weeks ago. Her hands rest in her lap and she looks down at them.

"I'm sorry. I shouldn't have run. It's just…when you told me about Jun Saito…"

"You realized he must have been your father?"

She nods. "Yes."

"Why didn't you call us?"

"I thought maybe *Omma* had done something wrong. Something illegal. I was scared…of you and the Yakuza." She shakes her head. "I needed time to think, time to find out exactly what my mom's role was in all of this. But then they found me. At first it was okay. A man called Tomi Moto told me that they were concerned for my safety and that Jun Saito was my father and had been his friend. He seemed…honorable. And Marcus checked in on me…he seemed nice and I trusted him. But then yesterday everything changed. Another man, someone I hadn't met before, came and told Marcus there'd been a change of plans. That Mr. Moto wanted to move me again. We went with him, but when Marcus was getting in the car the man's bodyguard hit Marcus over the head and blindfolded and drugged me. When I woke up I was locked in a caged room in a basement. Marcus was gagged and bound, tied to a chair, and I was chained to the wall by a foot iron. Then they took Marcus away…." She looks down at her hands.

"Marcus is alive." At this stage I presume Young won't be trying to resume his cover in the Yakuza as "Marcus Miki," but I still use his false name—for both Mee and Hana.

"Really? I know—I know he's Yakuza, but he was nice."

"He's in hospital with a few broken bones, but he's going to be okay."

She nods. "He was different from the others. Like he was really looking out for me."

Maybe Young wasn't doing such a good acting job, or maybe just not around Mee Kim.

After a few moments of silence I say, "Then what happened?"

"They left me with a woman." She hangs her head. "I saw the opening and took it. I hit her…hard."

A woman? Could this woman be the leak and not Hana?

Someone else from the Gang Impact Team? Mee obviously doesn't recognize Hana, but it's possible the Yakuza kept Mee away from the mole.

Mee wrings her hands. "Please let her be okay." Despite her situation, Mee's worried about the physical well-being of this woman—she feels guilty.

"Can you take us back to the house from here?" I ask. She nods.

De Luca starts the car and Mee Kim directs him, only motioning a couple of lefts and rights.

A bit later, we pull up at the house, and just then a woman staggers out the front door and onto the lawn.

"No! No!" screams Hana.

"Oh, shit." De Luca slams on the brakes and reaches for his gun, while Hana leaps from the car, even though it's still rolling.

"Jae!" Hana runs forward and I suddenly realize what's going on. The woman is Jae, Hana's sister. Jae's the mole. And just like Hana and the woman from my vision, she has long, dark hair. It was her on that park bench.

Jae holds a gun, which she brings up.

Hana stops dead. "Jae, it's *me*."

Jae's badly beaten, and seems out of it. Still, there's recognition on her face and the gun wavers, ever so slightly.

Hana moves closer. "Jae, put the gun down."

De Luca jumps out of the car. "Put the gun down now, Jae."

I hold my ground in the car. The situation is heated enough without me adding to it.

Hana holds her hand in a stop sign behind her to De Luca. "I've got her, Joe. Get back in the car."

But De Luca stands his ground.

I think Hana's right, the situation is much more likely to defuse if it's just her and her sister, but De Luca's protective streak is showing.

Jae brings her gun up again, and her swollen eyes dart from Hana to De Luca.

"It's all right, Jae. It's my old partner, Joe. You remember Joe. He's not going to hurt you. Just put the gun down, Jae."

Jae looks confused, but she keeps the gun up.

Hana puts her own gun down on the front lawn. "It's okay… I know you didn't mean it."

A tortured sob erupts from Jae's lips. After a few seconds she says, "You really thought I wanted to follow in your footsteps?"

"Jae, no." Hana's voice is full of pain.

Jae staggers a few steps closer to Hana.

"Don't take another step," De Luca warns.

Shit, shit, shit, shit, shit. I can see the situation escalating and someone getting shot. "Get down, Mee."

Mee does as she's told, bobbing down in her seat. The last thing we need now is for Jae to see her attacker. If she wasn't so badly beaten up she'd probably already have realized that Mee is sitting in the backseat. Besides, I want to make sure Mee isn't on the receiving end of a stray bullet.

I undo my holster and take my gun out. Jae can't see it, and I keep it under the line of the car's windows and out of sight.

"Everything will be okay, Jae. Just put the gun down." Hana tries again and Jae wavers. "Please, Jae," Hana begs.

Jae shakes her head. "Takeshi's right about you."

"Takeshi?"

"My lover. He's right about all of you." She waves the gun at De Luca and toward me in the car. "You're sheep. You follow The Man. Do what you're told. Right and wrong, it's not that black-and-white."

The behavioral analyst part of me is dying to step in. I know what to say to calm Jae down, but does Hana? Does De Luca?

"It's never black-and-white, Jae. We both know that."

I find myself nodding my head at Hana's response.

"This was justice." Jae's trying to defend her actions, defend Suzuki's actions.

"Justice? You mean because Jun Saito killed Takeshi's sister fifteen years ago. That's revenge, Jae. Not justice."

Jae shakes her head. "Sometimes the justice system doesn't work. You tell me that all the time, Hana."

"Yes. But no one should take the law into their own hands. And Takeshi? He's using you."

Another bitter sob. "To get to you, I suppose?"

"Jae, look at what he's made you do! This isn't you. You're holding a gun, for Christ's sake! You used to hate guns."

She looks at the gun in her hand, her resolve wavering again.

"It's all right, Jae. Put the gun down and it ends here."

We all know that strictly speaking, that's not true. Jae's an accessory to kidnapping and an accessory to a murder-for-hire plot.

She looks at the gun in her hand again, and it shakes more.

Even though Hana's back is to me, I can tell she's crying. She walks forward, leaving her gun on the ground and out of reach. I think perhaps she's being a little too trusting of her sister. Or maybe it's De Luca she trusts.

"Jae, put the gun down." This time Hana's voice is soft, but also firm. A big sister asserting her authority. It has the desired effect and Jae lowers the gun ever so slightly. "It's okay, Jae. I'll look after you." Hana keeps moving closer to her sister, both arms reaching out to her. "Just put the gun down."

And in that instant, Jae drops the gun and falls to her knees. "What have I done?"

Hana closes the distance and throws herself down next to her sister. She cradles her in her arms and strokes her hair as Jae sobs uncontrollably.

Thirty-Six

Jae's face has been patched up and she sits in a hospital bed. Mee managed to crack two ribs, break Jae's arm and her nose, and split her cheek so Jae needed a few stitches. One eye is swollen and bruised and she's got a concussion—enough that they wanted to keep her in overnight for observation. Still, Jae's come out of this lightly...for a second there I thought De Luca was going to take her out.

"Jae, I'm going to leave you with Sophie and Agent Petrov now. It's best for both of us if I'm not involved in your questioning." Hana looks down.

A few tears trickle down Jae's face.

"It's all right, baby sister." Hana leans over and gives Jae a kiss on the forehead. "I'll just be outside."

Petrov gets straight down to business when Hana has left the room. "Ms. Kim, are you sure you don't want to have a lawyer present?"

She shakes her head. "I just want this over with."

Petrov nods. "When did you meet Takeshi Suzuki?"

"A year and a half ago."

"Where?"

Jae hesitates. "He approached me in a bar. Bought me a drink." She shakes her head. "I've been thinking about this a lot for the past few hours, but I'm sure he had no idea that my sister was a DEA agent. I know it sounds bad, but—" she sniffles "—I love him."

She won't be the first woman fooled into a life of crime by the promise of love. She won't be the last.

"I didn't realize he was involved in anything…untoward until we'd been seeing each other for a few months. And by then it was too late. I was in love with him."

Again, I've heard that story before. "What was the first thing he asked you to do?" I ask.

She sighs. "He was worried that maybe he was being watched. That Hana would find out about us and she'd get in trouble. So he suggested I ask her if she was investigating anything on the Yakuza."

"And you did."

"I didn't want my relationship to get Hana into trouble."

Takeshi concealed the manipulation, pretending to be concerned for the relationship and Hana's career. And it worked.

"Hana loves her job, loves talking about it, but at first she was very careful not to mention specific cases. So I made it a game. I'd say, 'I know you can't tell me, but it won't do any harm to just nod or shake your head. Is it Asian Boyz? Mafia?' And that's how it started. As a guessing game. At first she just shook her head to everything, but after a week or two, when I told her I wanted to join the DEA but didn't feel I had a real understanding of the kinds of cases I'd work on…" She sighs again. "Then she started giving me little snippets of information. She liked the idea that one day we'd work together."

"And you relayed anything she told you to Takeshi."

"Yes." She pauses. "And he'd pass them on to his boss."

Suzuki was in the driver's seat—as far as Jae knew, Suzuki was passing information on to Moto, but he was probably being very selective about what his boss did and didn't know. Especially given Agent Young's discovery that Suzuki's been running drugs on the side.

"But then…it just spiraled out of control." She rubs her hands over her face gently. "I don't know how it happened.

How I let it go that far. At first I thought I was doing it to help us. You know, to make sure Takeshi and I could be together and to keep Hana out of trouble. But now, now that I look back on it…I don't know what I was thinking." She shakes her head. "About six months ago, I started going through her BlackBerry." Tears of shame form in her eyes. "I'd check e-mails, phone calls, everything, and pass it on to Takeshi. And each time I gave him something useful, he'd buy me presents. Jewelry, clothes, payments on my student loan."

"Did you guys ever go out in public together?" Petrov asks.

She hangs her head. "Not exactly. Takeshi was paranoid. Paranoid that he was being tailed by the Feds, and worried that I'd get in trouble. So we used to meet in a little apartment he owns in Santa Monica. It's a beautiful place." Tears start to roll down her face. "I imagined we'd live there together one day."

I know Jae's only twenty-two, but part of me can't help but wonder if she really believed that lie. Men like Suzuki don't leave their wife and kids. But they do sleep around.

"Do you know if Takeshi took anyone else to the apartment?" I ask. Dan Young has already filled us in on the apartment's existence, and the existence of another mistress.

"What do you mean?"

I don't push it for the moment. Instead I ask her how often she saw him.

"Once or twice a week. We always met at the apartment on a Wednesday night, for dinner. I told Hana I was taking salsa classes. She was usually still at work when I left and in bed when I got home."

"Jae, we have something to tell you." I sigh, wanting to spare her feelings but knowing that there's no way I can. "Something you won't like."

"Yes?"

"We believe Takeshi Suzuki did seek you out. He's been running drugs on the side, without his boss's knowledge, and he was worried we knew…or would discover it. You were his insurance."

"No." She shakes her head. "You're wrong. We're in love. If it wasn't for Hana, I wouldn't be telling you any of this. But I can't hurt my sister. Not even for him. Not anymore."

I take a deep breath. "Suzuki has another mistress. There's his wife, you and another woman."

She keeps shaking her head. "No. That can't be right. He's married, but he never loved his wife. They got married because their families wanted them to."

I shrug. "I don't know about his wife, but I do know he's seeing another woman."

"You're wrong. And how do you know that? Whenever I accessed Hana's files, there was never anything about surveillance on Takeshi."

"We had an undercover agent in the Yakuza." Petrov says it quietly, almost gently.

"No. There was nothing like that. I checked. Takeshi made me check!"

Petrov leans forward. "Your sister didn't know, Ms. Kim. Only a handful of us did." Petrov takes a breath. "And our agent will look you in the face and tell you all about Takeshi's other mistress and the drug running."

Her hands come up to her face and she gently rubs them up and down her bruised cheeks. "This can't be right. He loves me. And only me." She falters. "No, I won't believe you."

"I'm sorry, Ms. Kim." Petrov leaves and returns a few minutes later with Agent Young. Like Jae, he sports many bruises and also wears a plaster cast on his arm, from his wrist to his bicep.

"Do you recognize her, Dan?"

Young looks closely at Jae. "No. He kept everyone in the dark about her. Not surprising, given who her sister is. I'd say only his personal chauffeur knows."

Jae scrunches her face a little. "Takeshi did have someone in the car with him. Always the same man. And sometimes I would meet the driver at a park if I had information and Takeshi couldn't get away from his wife."

Young gives her a single nod. "Ms. Kim, I'm Special Agent Dan Young and I've been undercover in the Yakuza for twelve months. Trying to find you, actually."

"I…I don't understand."

"I was brought in from New York to find the Gang Impact Team's mole."

"Takeshi did mention one man from New York. A Miki."

Young smiles. "That's my alias. That's me."

"You're…you're DEA?"

"Uh-huh."

"You work with my sister?"

"Not exactly. I haven't met Special Agent Kim yet." He smiles, a gentle smile. "But I have been close to Takeshi Suzuki and I can tell you that he loves his wife and he has a mistress in Long Beach."

Jae looks intently into Young's eyes. "You're telling the truth? This isn't some trick to get me to make a statement against Takeshi?"

"I'm telling you the truth. Swear to God." He looks around at us before continuing. "But we do need you to make an official statement and we'd like you to testify down the track, too. Trust me, I've seen what Takeshi Suzuki is capable of—the man needs to be in prison, and with both of our testimonies, and Mee Kim's, we can ensure maximum charges and penalties. My testimony will only be half the story."

It'd be nice to get Suzuki for Jun Saito's murder. He may not have pulled the trigger, or in this case delivered the fatal blow, but he did contract Park Ling to do just that. And the fact that Jac knows who Jun Saito is, knows about the history between the two…that's gonna put him away.

She hesitates. "I don't know. Are you sure about Takeshi and this other woman?"

I was hoping it wouldn't come to this. "We have photos, Jae. Photos of him with her."

Her lip quivers. "I need to see them."

Petrov gets a file out of his briefcase. "Are you sure?"

"I have to see for myself."

He hands Jae two photos. One shows Takeshi kissing the other woman, and another one shows them holding hands.

Jae looks away. "I'll tell you whatever you need to know."

"Jae, I think we need to get you a lawyer." I can't hold my tongue on the subject any longer. "I assume you realize that you're an accessory to much of what Takeshi has done. A lawyer will cut you a deal."

She shakes her head. "No lawyers. You tell me what you need and what my charges will be."

Petrov leans back. "Do you know for sure that Takeshi contracted someone to kill Saito?"

"Yes."

"And you'd testify to that?"

"Yes."

Getting the second-in-charge of the L.A. Yakuza for murder-for-hire is a huge catch. One that I think Petrov, or anyone, would deal for aggressively. And like Young said, his testimony will only tell one side of the story.

"We'll only charge you with accessory to kidnapping Mee Kim."

She nods. "Okay."

A lawyer may well have been able to get her off scot-free, but I keep my mouth shut. Maybe down the track Jae's deal will get better.

"So," Petrov says, "let's start with Jun Saito. Do you know how Takeshi Suzuki found him? Got him to come to L.A.?"

"Yes. Takeshi got a phone call from a friend who was on vacation in Singapore. He saw Saito, recognized him, and realized what the information would mean to Takeshi, what it was worth. So he followed Saito and contacted Takeshi. One day, when Saito was out, this guy broke into Saito's home and found out about Mee."

"And Suzuki wanted Saito dead?"

"Yes. But he wanted to see him for himself first, so he lured him to L.A."

"And do you know the name of the hit man?"

She shakes her head. "No. He told me that Saito was a bad

man, a murderer, and that the justice system had failed to make him pay. It's Saito's fault that Takeshi's even in the Yakuza."

"What do you mean?" I ask.

"Takeshi knew his sister was seeing someone in the Yakuza, so when she went missing he immediately suspected their involvement. Takeshi offered his services in exchange for information. He got the information—found out his sister was dead, killed by Jun Saito. Then Takeshi had to come to L.A. to pay off his debt to the Yakuza. Like I said, if it wasn't for Jun Saito, Takeshi would never have gotten mixed up in the Yakuza or anything illegal."

Even after finding out Takeshi's got another mistress, Jae's still defending him. It's hard to know how much of what Takeshi Suzuki told Jae is true. While it does gel with the Japanese cop's belief that Takeshi Suzuki wasn't involved with the Yakuza in Tokyo, Suzuki always had choices. And then there's Saito's girlfriend.

"Did you know Saito's girlfriend was killed?" I ask. "Presumably by Suzuki."

Jae furrows her brow. "Takeshi never said anything about a girlfriend." She shakes her head. "He wouldn't… couldn't…"

"Maybe he didn't want you to know that part of the story," Petrov says. "Didn't want you to know that he organized the murder of Saito's girlfriend, a pregnant woman."

Jae winces.

"So, you knew Suzuki hired someone to kill Saito?" Petrov brings Jae back to the here and now.

"Yes." She hangs her head.

"And you'd definitely be willing to swear to that in court?" Petrov confirms.

"Yes." Jae tears up. Her world is crumbling around her. She believed Suzuki, she loved him.

Our search warrant is exhaustive, covering Suzuki's entire property and his computers, so hopefully we'll find some damning evidence. Given my lack of field fitness, I'm not officially part of the raid team, but Petrov has allowed me to "bring up the rear." I wear my bulletproof vest just in case.

The house is quiet and dark, with only a single light on in the kitchen. However, the curtains are drawn and we can't see inside. We file into the property's garden and make our way toward the house. Once everyone's in position, the team leader gives the order. It's 7:00 p.m., so we'll probably catch Suzuki and his family by surprise, sitting around the dinner table. Who knows if he's worried about the hit or is even aware that things didn't go as planned last night.

The front door gives and the team files in. There are eight of us taking the front door, six at the back door and another eight are stationed around the building's perimeter, ready to catch anyone who tries to make a run for it.

The front foyer is opulent, an ornate staircase leading upstairs, marble everywhere and tall ceilings. The SWAT leader puts his finger to his lips and, sure enough, we hear it.

A woman crying.

He mouths "Go" and leads us around the corner, toward the kitchen. I'm the last one into the kitchen, but instead of walking in on dinner, a woman sobs over Takeshi Suzuki's body.

"Who did this?" I demand.

His wife, now widow, looks up and notices the room full of law enforcement for the first time. Her eyes focus on me and she shakes her head.

"Where are the children, Mrs. Suzuki?"

"Not here. My husband—" she strokes his head "—he told me to take the kids to my mom's house for the night. He must have known. But I knew something was wrong so I came back, alone."

"And he was already dead?"

She nods and covers her face with her hands.

"Who did this?" I repeat my original question, even though I've got a feeling I know the answer.

She looks up at me, tears streaming down her face. "He's untouchable."

Moto. He said he'd keep his affairs in-house, and this is

how an organized crime boss cleans up. Maybe he knows about Suzuki's skimming, maybe not. Either way, in his mind he's righted a wrong, meted out his version of justice. But where does it end? Jun Saito was no saint, that's for sure. He was made to pay for taking Ima Yamada's life with the death of his girlfriend and unborn child. But that wasn't enough for Takeshi. He needed to kill Saito, too.

Takeshi got his revenge, but what about Mee? She may not have known her father, but I was hoping she'd see Suzuki behind bars.

Where's Mee's justice?

Thirty-Seven

Darren's breathing evens off. "I guess we can give tender a go next time."

I laugh. "Guess so." I look around my apartment at the clothes scattered through the room and Darren's overnight bag still at the door. At least we closed the front door. "It has been two weeks."

"Two weeks and one day."

"It was that one day that tipped us over."

He smiles and brings me in for a kiss. "So, you're better?"

"Almost one hundred percent. Still not jogging, but I have started brisk walks and pilates. Jogging's next week."

He strokes the scar on my left shoulder. "It's pretty small."

"The doctor was a whiz." My fingers go to the small bubble of tissue. "She said I could have plastic surgery to make it virtually invisible."

"You going to?"

"Nah. It adds character…doesn't it?"

Darren manages a small snort. "Well, it's a war wound. You've had your fair share of trouble."

I shrug. "Maybe. But that's all in the past."

Darren turns away suddenly and sits up.

"What's wrong?"

"AmericanPsycho's not in the past." He turns back to me.

"No. But next time I come up against that beast, I'm taking him down."

Darren's mouth only upturns slightly. "I hate the fact that he's out there. Doing goodness knows what. Maybe watching you."

"His prints and name have been flagged. No way he's getting into the US again."

"It's not impossible."

I don't say anything, knowing that Park Ling managed to fool the biometric tests, and I know AmericanPsycho has an almost unlimited supply of money to throw at new identities—documents, plastic surgery, the works.

Darren looks at me. "What?"

"I probably shouldn't tell you this, but the hit man from my last case got into the States again. It was only facial recognition software that picked him up in the end."

"This is what I'm talking about." Darren stands up and paces, but it doesn't have the usual conviction because he's naked.

I can't hide my amusement.

"What?"

"Sorry, it's just that pacing doesn't have the same sense of purpose with your clothes off."

He looks down. "True." He sits next to me. "So you got your man, the hit man?"

"Uh-huh. No confession, of course. But he had money on him with Takeshi Suzuki's prints, plus we've got him on attempted murder of our undercover agent and assault on me. I don't know if we'll be able to bring him to trial for all the other murders—the prosecutors are still sorting through what we've got and working out the best way to maximize the charges. But given the circumstances, I'm sure he'll get the maximum sentence for the attempt on Special Agent Dan Young's life and that's life imprisonment. I can deal with that."

"And what about the person who put the contract out?"

"He's dead."

"Dead?"

"Murdered by his boss, the L.A. head of the Yakuza, Tomi Moto."

"Wow, so you've got the head of the Yakuza for murder. That's amazing."

"Got?" I sigh. "Not exactly. We know he did it, and he now knows that his organization was infiltrated by a DEA agent. But we haven't got him by any stretch of the imagination. First off, one of his foot soldiers would have actually pulled the trigger. No way he'd get directly involved. And secondly, it's a clean, professional crime scene. No fingerprints, no DNA, no match on the bullet, no witnesses. For the moment, and maybe forever, no one will be brought to justice for Takeshi Suzuki's murder."

"And how is the victim's daughter doing?"

"She's okay…given what she's been through. I think this whole thing's changed Mee Kim. A month ago she would have been outraged at Suzuki's murder, outraged that Moto had him killed. Now…well, you should have seen her face. I think she was actually happy that the man who ordered her father's murder is dead, too." I lay my head in Darren's lap. "Vengeance was served this time, but I don't know about justice."

Darren strokes my head. "At least no one walked free."

"Except Moto." I look up at the ceiling.

"Except Moto."

We lie on the floor, silent for some time, until Darren says, "Time for another shot at tender?"

I smile and lean into him. "We should at least try."

A thriller from the author of *Body Count*

P.D. MARTIN

Increasingly haunted by her ability to experience the minds of killers in the throes of heinous crimes, FBI Profiler Sophie Anderson's talent is uncontrollable and unpredictable. When bodies start showing up on a university campus, she and Tucson police detective Darren Carter are pulled into the case. However, Sophie's puzzled by the fact that certain signature elements are different in each killing. The FBI database has a record of many of the signatures—but they have been used by different serial killers.

As the bodies continue to appear, Sophie must hone her terrifying skills to try and track down the killer—or killers.

THE MURDERERS' CLUB

MIRA®

*Available now
wherever books are sold!*

www.MIRABooks.com

MPDM2604R

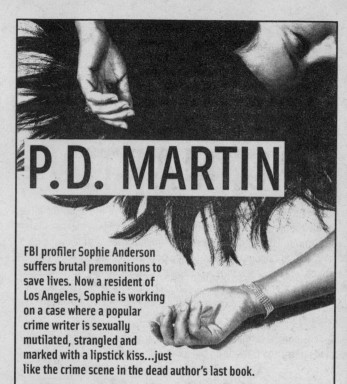

NEW YORK TIMES AND *USA TODAY* BESTSELLING AUTHOR

ERICA SPINDLER

Nearly killed as a teenager by a hit-and-run boater, Jane Killian has everything to live for—especially now, as she and her husband, Ian, are expecting their first child.

Then a woman with ties to Ian is found brutally slain and Ian is the prime suspect. Determined to prove her husband's innocence, Jane starts to have doubts. When she begins receiving anonymous messages, she's convinced they're from the boater she always believed deliberately hit her and got away with it.

Now Jane must face the tormentor who knows everything about her—including her deepest fears, which he will use mercilessly until he sees Jane dead.

SEE JANE DIE

Available now wherever books are sold.

MIRA®

www.MIRABooks.com

MES2833

MICHELLE GAGNON

When sixteen-year-old Madison Grant is abducted, a terrorist plot is set in motion—pitting special agent Kelly Jones against her most powerful adversary yet. The kidnapper's ransom demands come at a cost that no American can pay.

As Kelly's fiancé, Jake Riley, races to find Madison, Kelly is assigned to another case: a senator's murder. The two cases don't appear to be related until Kelly navigates her way through the darkest communities of America—from skinheads to border militias—and discovers a shadowy figure called the Gatekeeper, who's uniting hate groups and opening the door to the worst homegrown attack in American history.

> "Utterly gripping...an addictively readable thriller."
> —*Chicago Tribune* on *Boneyard*

THE GATEKEEPER

REQUEST YOUR FREE BOOKS!

2 FREE NOVELS
FROM THE ROMANCE/SUSPENSE
COLLECTION PLUS 2 FREE GIFTS!

YES! Please send me 2 FREE novels from the Romance/Suspense Collection and my 2 FREE gifts (gifts are worth about $10). After receiving them, if I don't wish to receive any more books, I can return the shipping statement marked "cancel." If I don't cancel, I will receive 4 brand-new novels every month and be billed just $5.74 per book in the U.S. or $6.24 per book in Canada. That's a savings of at least 28% off the cover price. It's quite a bargain! Shipping and handling is just 50¢ per book.* I understand that accepting the 2 free books and gifts places me under no obligation to buy anything. I can always return a shipment and cancel at any time. Even if I never buy another book from the Reader Service, the two free books and gifts are mine to keep forever.

185 MDN EYNQ   385 MDN EYN2

Name _____
(PLEASE PRINT)

Address _____ Apt. #

City _____ State/Prov. _____ Zip/Postal Code

Signature (if under 18, a parent or guardian must sign)

Mail to **The Reader Service:**
IN U.S.A.: P.O. Box 1867, Buffalo, NY 14240-1867
IN CANADA: P.O. Box 609, Fort Erie, Ontario L2A 5X3

Not valid to current subscribers of the Romance Collection,
the Suspense Collection or the Romance/Suspense Collection.

Want to try two free books from another line?
Call 1-800-873-8635 or visit www.morefreebooks.com.

* Terms and prices subject to change without notice. Prices do not include applicable taxes. Sales tax applicable in N.Y. Canadian residents will be charged applicable provincial taxes and GST. Offer not valid in Quebec. This offer is limited to one order per household. All orders subject to approval. Credit or debit balances in a customer's account(s) may be offset by any other outstanding balance owed by or to the customer. Please allow 4 to 6 weeks for delivery. Offer available while quantities last.

Your Privacy: Harlequin is committed to protecting your privacy. Our Privacy Policy is available online at www.eHarlequin.com or upon request from the Reader Service. From time to time we make our lists of customers available to reputable third parties who may have a product or service of interest to you. If you would prefer we not share your name and address, please check here. ☐

P.D. MARTIN

32613 FAN MAIL	___ $7.99 U.S.	___ $8.99 CAN.
32604 THE MURDERERS' CLUB	___ $6.99 U.S.	___ $6.99 CAN.

(limited quantities available)

TOTAL AMOUNT	$ _____
POSTAGE & HANDLING	$ _____
($1.00 for 1 book, 50¢ for each additional)	
APPLICABLE TAXES*	$ _____
TOTAL PAYABLE	$ _____

(check or money order—please do not send cash)

To order, complete this form and send it, along with a check or money order for the total above, payable to MIRA Books, to: **In the U.S.:** 3010 Walden Avenue, P.O. Box 9077, Buffalo, NY 14269-9077; **In Canada:** P.O. Box 636, Fort Erie, Ontario, L2A 5X3.

Name: _____

Address: _____ City: _____

State/Prov.: _____ Zip/Postal Code: _____

Account Number (if applicable): _____

075 CSAS

*New York residents remit applicable sales taxes.
*Canadian residents remit applicable GST and provincial taxes.

MIRA®

www.MIRABooks.com

MPDM1109BL